NightLock

SOPHIE EDWARDS

LILLABE BOOKS

First published in Great Britian in 2024 by
Lillabe Books

Text © Sophie Edwards, 2024

The moral rights of the author have been asserted.

ISBN 978-1-7385689-0-1

For Cally,
who loved Sally and Co. long before anyone else
(except me)

And for Dad,
who made life as adventurous as Sally's
(without the murders and obviously questionable choices)

1

It burned, the fresh-off-the-hob milk and the streak of sunlight through the window. It stifled. Filled my office with the smell of sweat and made my armpits itch.

Stupid milk.

Stupid job.

I mean, I got it. I had tenure. Benefits. A successful career. With all the jobless people out there, who wouldn't be grateful? I had a guaranteed cage for the rest of my life.

I sighed – one of those big ones that was supposed to blow away all my frustration. It didn't work. It rarely did. And when I reached out for the door handle, the smudged metal warped my reflection, bending my fingers like some contortionist.

Something fluttered in my chest. "It's not hard," I muttered. "Just do it." I'd open the door, march into Lia's office, and all my thoughts would spill out. Finally, I'd take control. My life. My choice.

My hand balled.

My life.

In theory.

I sighed again and trudged back to my desk. This was stupid. What kind of wuss couldn't take a stand? I was nineteen, for goodness sake!

Voices flitted through the window from The Four – three girls, one boy. They passed by every day at the same time, all

5

happy and unconsciously rubbing their lives in my face.

"And I told them, orange juice," the boy said, and the girls laughed – more of a chortle really. And one cackled like she always did before they passed on to the college. It sat over there, the college, towering and glittering in the morning light like some kind of trophy I could never reach.

How hard was it? *I hate selling estates. I quit. No, I mean it. I'm going to college.* It was easy.

In theory. Lia would fight me. The same fight she always won. What would you study? she'd say. You don't know what you want.

Well, I might if she'd let me find out.

Lia opened the door, tucking her shirt into her trousers. She'd rolled her sleeves carelessly above her elbows – a sign she meant business. "I'm squeezing another client in."

My shoulders dropped. "I'm full."

"No, you're not. You've ten minutes between Spencer and Phillips."

That was hardly time for another client. "Assign them someone else."

She shook her head, fringe flapping against her eyelashes. She batted it away. "This client wants to meet you. Specifically."

"Why?"

She shrugged. "You impressed him at auction. That's all I know." She turned to leave, but grabbed the door mid-close. "Oh, and he mentioned the Haroldson property."

Great. One of them. Those rich benefactors made me feel like common muck.

She came in and leaned over my desk, pressing her hands on the wooden surface. Her necklace dangled above the surface: a silver tree encrusted with a single ruby. That crease marked her forehead – the one she wore when she meant to press her opinion on me. Like it would change how I felt. "I needn't remind you sales are down. We need this, Sally. This could be good for us. For the company."

"Yeah." I balled my fists beneath the desk. "I'd *hate* to let the company down."

"Atta girl." She beamed and flounced away, leaving cloudy handprints on the desk. "I'll see him in."

I sat in bitter silence, glaring after her. "Oh, and Lia?" I said. "I quit."

I jerked the printed catalogue in front of me and straightened my pen. Horizontally. No, vertically. That was better. It'd make an organised impression. I tucked a loose piece of hair behind my ear as an afterthought and braced for the benefactor.

A black-gloved hand pushed open the door. From his rounded cheeks and thin lips, I guessed he was around sixty. His shoulders wore his jacket like a cape from one of the old musketeer films, and a crooked tie reached his middle where his buttons gaped.

Lia stood beside him. "Sally, this is Mr Blake." She flashed a toothy smile and gestured to me. "And this is Sally, but you know that, don't you? I hope you find what you're looking for."

The benefactor gave a little nod. "As do I."

Lia flitted away.

Mr Blake removed a glove. "Ms Rivers. A pleasure." He approached the desk in long strides and held out his hand.

I reached out instinctively, hissed, and jerked back. A thin cut oozed blood from a scratch on my inner wrist.

He clamped a handkerchief over the cut, drawing my gasp with the sudden pressure. "I am so sorry," he said. "My ring." He nodded at a thick, golden signet on his middle finger. "Has a sharp edge – a tendency to … you know." He withdrew the handkerchief, folded it twice, and slipped it in his pocket. "You might want to treat that," he said and left.

A drop of blood trailed to my elbow and dripped onto the catalogue. What just happened?

Lia peeked in. "That was quick. What—" She gaped at my wrist. "What happened?" She rushed forwards, yanked tissues from a box on the filing cabinet and pressed them to my cut.

I nudged her hand away and pushed against the tissues. Blood seeped through, so she grabbed some more.

"Did he invest?" she asked.

Typical. I'm standing there bleeding, and all she can think about is business! "I barely said hello. He scratched me with his ring and left."

"That's it?"

I stared at the door, half-expecting him to return. Why'd he ask for me and leave before we spoke? Embarrassment? He'd hardly made a good impression.

Lia's voice turned hard. "What happened?"

"I told you—"

"He scratched you, yes." She grabbed my forearm. "Did he do anything?" She shook me a little. "Anything before he left?"

"No, he—I mean, he dabbed my blood with his hankie but—"

Her grip tightened, and a vein stood out in her neck, pulsing with increased rhythm.

"What?" I asked.

She looked at my wrist, up to me, and swallowed, and though I couldn't explain why, my stomach grew heavy.

"Lia—"

"I'll get the first aid kit." She ran from the room.

2

Lia never got the kit. Five minutes later, I grabbed it myself, muttering at the kitchen cupboards. "Stupid, workaholic numpty. If you say you'll get the kit, you get the kit. How hard is that?" I flipped open the lid. The tissues had done little to stop the spread of blood. I half-expected to start feeling dizzy with all the loss, but perhaps that was a little dramatic. Even so, the cut was deeper than I'd realised. A couple of millimetres, at least.

I was just sticking a dressing over the wound when Jessica opened the door, her braid hanging over her shoulder in the usual, neat manner. "Hey, Sal?"

I cringed. What was wrong with using my actual name? Like I hadn't asked her to a thousand times.

"The Bensons are here," she said, "but I can't find Lia." She nodded at my wrist. "You okay?"

I waved her off. "What do you mean, you can't find her?"

"She went to talk to you and never came back." Jessica pushed the door open fully, showing me the couple waiting at reception. Suited and booted, Lia would say. The air's jingling like their wallets.

Whatever. I threw the spare dressing in the kit. "She's not in her office?"

Jessica shrugged. "Or the bathroom. She already missed the

morning briefing."

My shoulders stiffened. Lia never missed the briefing. Ever. This job was her life. "You tried her work phone?"

"Obviously." Jessica huffed. "It rang out."

I slammed the lid on the kit. "Stall the Bensons. I'll find Lia."

She nodded at my wrist. "What did you do?"

"Stall them." I shoved the kit away and pushed past her to my office. What was going on? First Mr Blake's weird visit, now Lia's disappearance. Something was up. My phone lay where I'd left it in my drawer. One advantage of being sister to the boss was I had Lia's personal number. I pushed her name and stuck it on loudspeaker. It rang twice.

Hi, you've reached Lia.

I hung up and rang again. This time, it didn't ring.

Hi, you've reached—

My phone clattered to the desk. Lia was gone. She'd missed the briefing. Now her phone was jumping to voice mail. It *never* went to voice mail. And my wrist stung. The whole situation made me want to punch something.

And the Bensons were still waiting. Lia would be furious if that sale fell through. She'd claimed them as her own clients just so it wouldn't fail. Of course, it was her own fault if it did. She shouldn't have wandered off.

A niggling worry churned my gut. This was not like her.

I picked up my phone and hurried from the room, past the Bensons and Jessica, to the stairwell. Lia wouldn't have left. She wouldn't.

Still, my feet padded down the steps to the underground car park where Lia's space lay empty.

Empty.

I just stood there, staring at it. What was she doing? Was this because of my wrist? Because of the crazy Blake client? I ran my thumb over the dressing. It was just a scratch. Just a weirdo tucking a hankie in his pocket. Stealing my blood.

I lifted my phone again and found Mum's name with

trembling fingers. Adrenaline shook my limbs.

"Hello?"

"Mum? You heard from Lia?"

The traffic whirred on the road above me, almost blocking out her answer.

"...no ... day ... why? Isn't she at work?"

"She left." And I hardly believed she'd gone to get hot chocolate, even if we had run out.

"Have you tried ringing her?"

I pressed the phone to my ear, straining to hear. Someone beeped a horn. "She's not answering."

Mum said something else, but someone else beeped, and I all-but gave up.

"Mum, if you hear from her, let me know, okay?"

"Sure, sweetie."

I hung up and climbed the path to the road. Traffic filled it – everyone rushing to get to work or school or wherever else. Red cars. Black cars. The odd Ferrari. A hundred different licence plates. But none of them Lia's.

A black car pulled into the roadside parking spot. Another one pulled up beside it. And another. And another.

I hesitated with my hand on the railing, half-turned back towards the car park.

A black van pulled up behind them, and all at once, the doors to each vehicle opened and suited men climbed out. Not just men. Two wore their hair in buns, and when rain started to sprinkle, their buns glistened.

From the back of the van, they produced cones and police line. No, not police line. Yellow tape with arrows on them.

A sixth van stopped in the road, and the traffic drew to a standstill until the driver got out to direct them around him.

I jolted at my phone vibrating in my hand. Jessica. "Hey, Jess. I'm on my way."

"Where are you? I can't stall much longer."

Of course, rolling my eyes didn't help, but since she couldn't see me ... "I'll be right there."

I shook the rain from my hair and jogged back up the stairs to the reception. The Bensons had rounded on Jessica.

"…outrageous," Mr Benson said. "I was assured all would be in order—"

Jessica raised calming hands, her ears reddening. "Mr Benson, I can assure you—"

I popped a hand on her shoulder and extended my other to Mr Benson – the wrist with the dressing. The one Mr Blake had stolen blood from. "Sir, I'm sorry for the delay. There's been an unfortunate turn of events, and Ms Rivers can't complete your sale today. If you prefer, I can take you through the paperwork."

I couldn't take them through the paperwork. That would burn half an hour, and I had two clients of my own to meet with.

Mr Benson looked to his wife, who shook her head. "No," he said, and lifted his finger. "This is unacceptable. I'll submit a complaint."

"I understand," I said, and forced my calmest expression, even if I did squeeze my thumb to make it happen. "Shall I remove your name from the offer?"

Mrs Benson nudged her husband, and his chin creased. "Now let's not jump to conclusions. We arranged to meet with Ms Rivers, not stand here for ten minutes while she doesn't show up."

"Unfortunately, it couldn't be avoided," I said. Except it could. Heat spread through my chest. "But I'm happy to rearrange, if it suits you, with our greatest apologies."

He lifted his head and frowned at me over his nose. "Well. I hardly think you're qualified to offer that."

And there it was. The common muck treatment. I simply smiled – with gritted teeth, mind – and reached for the appointment book.

3

By the time evening came, my teeth hurt from gritting them so much. Lia hadn't returned. Every client, every meeting, every bit of essential paperwork that had to be filled in or signed that day had been left to me. I'd covered all of it. All day. And still had no explanation.

Lia's parking spot still lay empty.

I didn't know whether to be afraid or furious. Her phone kept going to answerphone. I'd called Mum again in the two minutes of lunch break I managed to squeeze in – still nothing. And I'd stayed four hours late to complete all the work *Lia* was supposed to have done.

A breeze cut through the car park, carrying with it the scent of rain. It pounded against the path and spat over me when I climbed the slope to the exit.

The line of vehicles, cones and yellow tape blocked half the road, including the entrance to the car park, and a couple of the suited, now-coated people stood there, stopping cars on the way out. They held umbrellas – a luxury I didn't have since my own was tucked in Lia's car boot.

I'd arranged to have Mum pick me up since I'd lost my lift, and with the road blocked off, I'd have to walk around the corner to meet her. Rain pummelled the ground so hard that even here, in the shelter of the building, it splashed me.

The suited women stood by the entrance to my left, speaking to people on their way out.

A figure emerged from the side of the van and waved me on. He had an umbrella, too. Black, to match the rest of him. But hey, maybe he'd walk me to the corner.

I checked the road. It was nine at night. The orange of streetlights highlighted rainfall that made the ground writhe and hiss.

He waved me on again, so I ran to him, cringed when water soaked through my blouse, and ducked under his umbrella. "Thanks."

He raised an eyebrow.

"You mind walking me to the corner?" I asked. "It's kind of wet." I'd be dry if Lia hadn't gone off. Why hadn't she called? She must know we'd worry about her, Mum and I. But she'd left without a thought. Taken her car. Gone by choice. Right? She hadn't been abducted or anything.

My throat tightened.

I glanced back at the building for signs of struggle.

Right. Because that's something I'd see.

The man shoved the umbrella in my hand. "Take it, and get on your way."

One last car pulled out of the car park, only to be stopped by the people. I pointed at them. "Don't you want to question me?"

Creases in his forehead deepened. "Go home."

"What's happening?" I asked. "Why've you blocked the road?"

He steered my elbow towards the corner. "Goodnight," he said, and walked away through the pelting rain.

This day was getting weirder and weirder.

Just when I rounded the corner, Mum pulled up in her little Ford Fiesta, its paint almost as black as the vans behind me. I clambered inside, soaking half my seat in the process. The folded umbrella wet my trousers.

"Lia rang," Mum said.

All at once, the weight on my chest lifted, and I sank into my chair. She was okay. Thank goodness. But then heat burned through me, and I tensed. "Where was she? I had to cover for her all day! I didn't eat. Couldn't even pee. She'd better have a really good reason for disappearing like that." Just wait till I saw her. I'd give her a good piece of my mind.

Mum pushed the car into gear and rolled off down the road. The rain picked up, streamed down the windscreen like a river, and the wipers beat furiously, making little difference. I edged my feet closer to the radiator to soak in the dry heat.

Mum squinted at the road. "She said she had business to take care of."

"Business?" Was she kidding? "Her business was at the office." I shook my head, ran my thumb over the dressing.

"I'm sure she had good reason." Mum leaned forward. She hated London roads at night. Always said driving them made her shoulders ache. She shouldn't have been here. Shouldn't be carting me around.

I cleared my throat. "About those driving lessons."

"We've talked about this."

"I'm nineteen, Mother. You can't keep telling me no." Nineteen! I'd begged, planned, dreamed of driving. "Why keep giving me lifts? I'm capable—"

"There are times you simply need to trust us," Mum said. "Now is one of them."

Us. Her and Lia. Mum and sister. They were stifling. They refused to let me live any life of my own choosing. What was I still doing here? If I had anywhere else to go, I'd have left by now. Sure, I was working. A few thousand pounds more and I'd have enough to rent a house. Enough to buy a car. I could live on the road. Travel. Find a job and settle down somewhere else. I could do something I actually wanted to do.

I could break their hearts.

I pushed my head against my seat. How could two people make a decision so difficult?

Mum had her heart broken before, back when Dad died. A

mugging attempt. I'd been too young to remember it. Too young to remember him, as well. I had a few fuzzy images, but they might've been more imagination than memory.

Mum remembered, though. It'd made her paranoid. Overprotective.

I balanced my phone on my knee and removed the dressing to study the inch-long scratch on my wrist. Why had Blake taken my blood? Was that what he'd actually done? Maybe he'd neglected to put the hankie in the bin. Perhaps he'd wanted to wash it. It'd been silky. One of those washable ones. Probably had his initials sewn into it or something.

And how did that link to Lia's strange behaviour? I mean, did it link at all? Maybe I was the one being paranoid.

Ahead, a streetlamp flickered and went out.

I bit my lip. Nothing. That was nothing. "Is Lia at home?"

"She was heading there when I left."

Another streetlamp went out. And the next. And the next, cloaking the road in darkness. The tyres sloshed.

Mum stopped at a junction. The engine's rumble broke the beat of wipers, and the headlights stretched into endless darkness. How could she see? I could barely make out the dead lamp beside us.

"Power cut?" I asked.

Mum hesitated. "Maybe."

"It's quiet," I said. Too quiet. Nine at night or not, there should've been traffic. This was London. I searched the empty road behind us.

So did Mum. "Did I miss a sign?"

"For what?"

"Saying the road is closed."

"They'd have blocked it off." Wouldn't they? With all the rain, maybe people were just staying home. Speaking of which … I fidgeted on my seat. "We should go."

Mum nodded. She rubbed the wheel with her fingertips, shifted into first and edged onwards.

"I almost quit today," I said.

She cast me a sharp look. "Again?"

"Yes, well. Lia disappeared. I hardly had the chance."

"Sally, we've talked about this."

"I don't care that you want me to work for her," I said. "I'm miserable there. Is that really what you want? Don't you want me to do what I really love? Something that'll make me happy?" I was going to tell her. *Mum, I'm leaving. Going travelling. It'll be good for me, and I'd really like your support.*

But she flinched, and I found myself scrambling back into my shell. Wuss! I was nothing but a great big, cowardly softie, too chicken to do what was right.

She sighed. "Sally—"

Light flared ahead. A horn shrieked.

I gasped. "Look out!"

Mum yanked the steering wheel. Tyres screeched, and our car rocked and veered into the wrong lane, narrowly missing the vehicle.

I clutched my seatbelt with clammy hands, and my pulse practically raced through them, throbbing my fingers where they grasped the leather.

"Are you okay?" Mum asked.

"Fine." I twisted to look behind us, breathing heavily. The car, or truck, or whatever it'd been had melted into the night. Was he crazy? Stupid driver, driving on our side of the road. I bit my tongue to hold back a rising insult.

"He's gone now," Mum said.

Thankfully. People really shouldn't drink and dr—

Light pulsed through her window. An engine roared, and a truck slammed into her door. The force lurched me to the side. Pain stabbed my shoulder. Glass shattered, and shards bit my skin. The roof crumpled, a little at first, and then again, the sound grinding at my ears.

4

My eyes snapped open.

The rain shushed somewhere far away, eerie and distant, and something crackled. My head and cheeks ached like something heavy pushed against them, and my shoulder pulsed. My arms touched the wrinkled roof of the car where glass fragments lay scattered across the fabric.

Mum sat beside me, arms dangling above her, eyes closed.

My stomach cramped. "Mum?" I felt for my belt and unclipped it. It reeled back, and I thumped to the roof. A sharp ache spread through my neck, and it took me a moment to raise my head.

The sight of Mum's white skin drew my hands to my mouth. Blood covered her torso, spreading quickly through her shirt. "Oh, you're bleeding." I struggled to my knees in the small space. Her chest rose and fell.

"Mum? Wake up." I shook her. "Please, wake up."

A crimson bead dripped from her collar and merged with the glass shards beneath me, a surreal mosaic feeding the liquid through the cracks.

I fumbled with her belt clip, but it wouldn't release, and when my wrist brushed her top, blood painted my hand. I reeled back with a whimper. My phone. I scrambled in search of it. I'd had it when we crashed. Where was it?

Vibrating crackled through the hiss of rain, and when I squinted through the gaping windscreen, there it was, lying on the road beyond a maze of shattered glass. Droplets bounced off the screen.

Lia probably. The numpty likely got home and *finally* decided to find out where we were.

I wished she were here.

It stopped ringing.

Sliding on my belly, I shuffled into the rain. Fragments clinked and stung my hands, but I pushed on and snatched the phone, a chill setting in my bones. Cracks covered the touch screen like spider webs, and the light spasmed in distorted colours. I pressed the screen, the once-smooth surface rough against my fingers.

The phone beeped once, and the screen turned black.

"No." I stabbed the screen again. Pressed the buttons. Shook the thing.

Not so much as a flicker.

This couldn't be happening. I needed my phone! Mum needed help!

Our car lay upside down, surrounded by glass and dented metal. The bumper rocked near a kerb, and glistened under the headlights of the van that hit us. They flickered like strobes at the funfair, and steam hissed from the van's crumpled bonnet. No sign of the windscreen remained.

A deflated airbag protruded behind the wheel where the driver's head lolled.

I stood on shaking legs, and the ground seemed to tilt beneath me. My shoulder ached when I steadied myself, and I staggered over to the van.

The driver barely focused on me. He just sat there, blinking back tears.

At least he was conscious. "Can you help me?" I asked. "Mum, she's stuck."

"I canna." He grimaced. "Me leg."

I tugged open his door, almost falling in the effort. The

ground wouldn't stay still. It turned and tipped like the Earth was trying to knock me off, and I grasped the handle, determined to stay grounded.

The stench of tobacco and beer triggered nausea, and I sucked in a breath, turning my head to the outside before taking in his situation.

The dashboard had dropped, trapping his leg.

I cringed at the blood. "Do you have anything?" I asked. "A phone? A crowbar? I could try to lever you free."

"I ain't got nothing to give you. 'Ere. Help me lift this." He grasped the dashboard.

I took hold and pushed hard, but his strangled cry stung my ears, and I lurched away.

The board dropped deeper.

"I'm sorry!" I said, and my knees buckled.

5

I don't know how long it took me to scramble back to Mum where she still hung in the upside-down car. A blackening, bloody pool beneath her filled the air with a sharp, coppery odour and a bitter taste.

"Mum?" I pressed her belt button. Yanked the belt. It would *not* move. "Get off her!" I screamed, and pulled with everything I had – but considering I was twisted awkwardly, and I'd all-but crawled back to the wreckage, that didn't count for much.

I'd have cried if tears would come. Fatigue swept over me, and my mind lifted, almost floated, like it disconnected from my body. It called me to sleep. Darkness cradled me, soft on my arms, coaxing me deeper. "Mum."

Something caught my leg.

I jolted, broke from the depths, and kicked at the hand holding me. A whimper slipped my lips.

"It's okay." The hand retreated, and a face emerged at the opening – a man's, mid-thirties, glistening with rain and surrounded with blue, flashing light. "Don't panic," he said. "We're here to help." The paramedic studied me. Water dripped from his fringe. "Are you hurt?"

My throat strangled my breaths. Paramedic? He couldn't be. My phone …

"Can you come outside?" he asked.

I did, wincing when glass cut into my palms. They stung. Bled, too, though I couldn't care right then.

He crouched. The ambulance flashed behind him, sitting in an area of road not littered with glass.

A second medic tried the handle of Mum's door. A woman. Young. Barely older than me. The door didn't open.

"Come on." The man took my hand. "Let's stand up."

"She's bleeding." I pushed his hand away and turned back to the car. My trousers clung to my legs, cold with rain.

"Look at me. Miss. Look at me." He twisted me to him. "I'm Mark. We can help her if you focus on me. Let's work together, okay?"

The woman cupped her hands to the window, taking in the damage.

"Do you know her?" Mark asked me, nodding at the car.

"She's my mother."

The woman crawled through the windscreen. "Hello? Can you hear me?"

Mark squeezed my arm. "What's her name?"

"Elizabeth."

"Elizabeth?" the woman called. "I'm Helen. Can you open your eyes?"

A third paramedic ran to us, an emergency kit in hand.

Helen took it from him and flipped the lid. "She's unconscious," she said. "Bleeding heavy. Vitals are weak. She needs fluids. Mark, she's trapped."

"I'm on it."

Helen crawled back through the window, a clear tube trailing behind her. The third medic held a bag of fluid.

Mark sat me in the ambulance and disappeared around the door, muttering something about coming back.

A second ambulance arrived, blue lights flashing, and two medics raced to the truck. Police blocked the road with yellow tape.

I shivered and my hand trembled. Mum's blood marked my

blouse and smeared the back of my hands, and grains of dirt lay black beneath my nails. I picked them out, only spreading Mum's blood under them.

Mark climbed up beside me. "Fire department's on the way. How you feeling?"

My nails were red. Red with Mum's blood.

Mark's gloved hands took mine. "She has oxygen and fluids. They'll help to stabilise her." He plucked a tiny piece of glass from the skin of my palm and pressed gauze against the cut. His thumb touched the scratch on my wrist, and for the briefest moment, I thought he smiled.

Flames spat from the rear of Mum's car, billowing smoke into the night.

"Mum!" I dashed into the rain, full-on sprinting towards the car. I'd tear out the seat if I had to. She was not going to die by fire.

Shouts filled the road, and Mark snatched my arms. "You mustn't."

"Let go of me!" I pulled against him, but his strength exceeded mine, and he dragged me backwards.

"It's too dangerous," he said.

Sirens cut through the noise. The flames leapt higher.

"No! Mum!" That darkness soaked in again, squeezed past the cold, and tilted the ground from under me.

6

"Easy." Bright light filled my vision, drawing my wince. When the light clicked off, a nurse scowled in its place. "Good to have you back."

I lay on a gurney, covered in a blanket that did nothing to the soaked clothes sticking to my skin. I struggled to sit.

"Stay still, dear." The nurse sighed when I ignored her. Paper curtains hung beside me, not quite hiding the sink on the wall, the posters on the whiteboard. The hospital. This was the hospital.

"What happened?" I asked.

"You were in an accident," she said. "You have concussion. Nothing to worry about, but we're going to keep you in for a few days."

"An accident? But I was at work." I'd just met with that Blake man. He'd scratched me, sure, but that was hardly grounds for an accident. No, hang on. Lia disappeared. For the whole day. I'd covered for her and …

Memories flooded back: the suited guys outside the office, the power cut, the lurch of the car. I stiffened. "Where's Mum?"

"They got her free." The nurse fastened a blood pressure monitor to my arm. The strap tightened, and a faint pulse ebbed in my hand.

"Is she badly hurt?" I asked.

She took back the strap and grabbed a clipboard. "Let's concentrate on you for now."

A hot feeling spread through my gut. Why wouldn't she look at me? "I want to see her. I want to see Mum."

"I need to observe you."

"No." I threw off the blanket. "I want to see her *now*."

The nurse grabbed my elbow, finally meeting my eyes. Dark circles ringed hers. Or maybe it was smudged mascara. Flakes of it stuck to her cheeks. "You've been in an accident. My job is to make sure you're okay, not cart you around the hospital like a chauffeur."

I pulled my arm away. "I'm fine."

She sighed again, and I got the feeling that was part of her daily routine. "I finish here. We get you changed. Then you see her. Yes?"

I nodded.

The door opened, and Lia rushed in. She snatched my hand. "Thank goodness, you're all right. When you didn't come home, I thought—where's Mum?" She turned around.

The nurse plonked a gown on my knee. "You family?" she asked Lia.

"Her sister," she said.

"Where were you?" I asked. "I called you and called you."

The nurse's lips tightened. "I'll give you two a minute," she said, and left the room.

Lia rubbed her neck. "Sally, I—"

"All day," I said. "You've been gone all day. Have you any idea what I went through? What I had to do to protect your precious sales?"

Her shoulders dropped.

"I hate that job," I said. "Hate it!"

"I know it was difficult," she said.

"No, I'm done." And just like that, the truth was out. It was relieving. A huge weight off my head, like a headache that'd finally gone away. I let the freedom carry me on. "I quit. I'm

25

not coming back. You want your sales, deal with them yourself."

Lia's stance widened. "That's not an option."

"I don't care what you say. This is my life. My choice. I'm done working for you, you hear? Done!" I slid off the bed, gown-in-hand, and the room tilted.

Lia grabbed me. "You okay?"

It took a moment, but the room stopped moving. "I'm fine." My head ached. So much for relief.

"Why don't we talk about this later?" she said, and all the stubbornness I'd expected from her washed away with her tone.

I shook my head – there was nothing to talk about – and went into the ensuite to change. By the time I emerged, the light hurt my eyes, and my temples throbbed. I sported a good cut on my forehead, too, stitched together with tape. How had I not noticed it after the crash?

The nurse took my clothes and gestured to the door. "A quick visit," she said. "Then we admit you to the ward."

It wasn't necessary. But the longer I stayed there arguing, the longer it'd take to see Mum. Arguing could wait.

The nurse took us through wide, bleach-scented hallways that turned my head pain into sharp pangs. She'd gone back to no eye contact and made no conversation. Her people skills really sucked.

I'd have exchanged a look with Lia once. We'd have silently laughed. Not now. I could barely look at her. Hot anger welled inside me, filled every inch of my chest that I wanted to scream and put my fist through the wall.

The nurse stopped at a set of double doors. "You'll find you mother through there." She pointed at Lia. "And you bring her straight back to the ward, you hear?"

Lia nodded. "Yes, ma'am."

Ma'am. So used to sucking up. I pushed into the ward and stopped at a desk. A nurse smiled, though it didn't reach her eyes. "Can I help?"

"I'm looking for Elizabeth Rivers," I said, and Lia stepped up beside me.

The nurse tapped on a keyboard. "Right-o. Elizabeth. She's in room …"

"Eight," I said.

Lia and the nurse stared at me.

My cheeks warmed. Where had that come from? I should've just waited. "Just guessing."

"Room eight," the nurse said. "Good guess."

The rhythmic beeping of a heart monitor flitted through the door of room eight before we got there. Mum lay on a gurney, hair mangled with blood. Wires surrounded her, stuck to her hand and wrist and head. An oxygen tube rested by her nose. Her pale skin sent goosebumps prickling down my arms.

"I couldn't help her." My words scratched my throat. "She was stuck in that seatbelt and bleeding, and I couldn't …"

Lia pulled me in a hug. "There's nothing you could've done."

The door clicked open, and a blue-clad doctor sauntered in. A stethoscope hung around his neck, though I didn't see what difference it'd make with the heart monitor beeping away. "You must be the daughters," he said. "Doctor Brown." He stretched out a hand.

I ignored it. "What's wrong with her?"

He sighed, a long, drawn out, almost dramatic one, and his forehead creased. "I have no good news. Your mother's kidney was damaged. We removed it."

"But that'll leave her with none," I said. Mum had kidney surgery already, three years ago.

"That, I'm afraid, is what makes her situation so dire," he said. "Without her kidneys, she's exposed to renal failure."

"What does that mean?"

He tucked a clipboard under his arm, showing a black shirt collar beneath his overcoat. "It means she has less than forty-eight hours to live."

I sank onto a chair.

"There has to be something you can do," I said. "A transplant. Or a machine that can keep her alive?"

He shook his head. "We need a kidney compatible with her blood type: AB-. She'll never survive the waiting list, and since her blood type is rare, you're unlikely to find a suitable donor."

"I'll give her one of mine," I said.

He frowned. "You're incompatible. Her body would reject it."

"Lia?" I asked.

Lia stared at the doctor, fists clenched. "Wouldn't work."

"I'm sorry," the doctor said, his tone strangely cold. "There are no alternatives. We can make her comfortable. If she can hear you, she'd appreciate knowing you're with her."

7

I peeled the skin off my chip until potato stuck out like dandelion fluff – and I dropped it. How was I supposed to eat considering everything? Mum still lay unconscious. Kidneyless. Dying.

The hard, industrial lights outlined streaks of spray on the table and cast ripples from my water. The whole place smelled musty, of fat and chips and damp mop, but at least I had the cafeteria to myself. Well, aside from the canteen woman wiping crumbs off the counter, her face gaunt in the two a.m. down-time.

Lia had brought me an overnight bag. She'd wanted to stay, too. Insisted on it. I'd waved her off. A few cuts were nothing compared to Mum. Besides, I still wanted to thump her after her disappearing stunt.

Dialysis, she'd said. They could use dialysis to save Mum. It was some kind of temporary kidney machine or something – I don't know. Either way, it'd made no difference. The doctor refused, launching into technical explanations I didn't understand.

I understood none of this. Lia's leaving, the accident, the power cut right before. It'd been rainy, not stormy. Something had gone wrong. I could feel it my gut. Being there, out in the darkness, those lamps flashing off …

I buried my head in my hands. My sneak-out to the café was supposed to calm me. But all I had was fear and Lia's ripped jeans. A piece of home, she'd said.

Home wasn't jeans. Home was Mum. Family.

Lia had shaken her head. "There's nothing you can do."

Nothing I could do. How could I be so helpless? So weak? Weren't there doctors here? Why couldn't they call for a kidney? Announce it on the news. Put it on social media. Surely, someone would help. *Anyone.* I squished a chip between my fingers. The salt stung the scratches on my palms like papercuts.

Someone pulled the chair across from me and sat down. I stiffened at the sight of him: the sharp slant of his nose, his tailored suit that bulged at his middle. My thumb traced the cut on my wrist.

"Evening." He rested his briefcase on the floor and took off his glove. There was his signet ring, showing no signs of sharpness.

I leaned back. "I won't shake your hand this time."

"I'm not offering." He rested his hands on his knees and just … sat there … watching me.

What was this? Another shot at our meeting? "No offense, Mr Blake, but now isn't the best time to talk business."

"Actually, now is the perfect time."

The café woman plopped a cup in front of him. A bead of coffee slid down the porcelain side.

He smiled at her, and something about it made me cringe. "Much appreciated, dear," he said, and she headed back to the counter.

I dusted my hands, bit my tongue at the salty sting, and stood up. I'd had enough weirdness for one day.

"How's your mother?" he asked.

I paused, heart suddenly thudding.

He sipped his coffee and wrinkled his nose. His thick brows dipped to his eyes.

"How'd you know about that?"

For a moment, I thought he hadn't heard. He drank again, pulled his face, and used one of my napkins to wipe the cup's side.

"Are you a doctor?" I asked.

"We were acquainted once, your mother and I." He inclined his head. "My condolences for your loss."

I shivered. "She's not dead."

"Not yet."

And just like that, I hated him. It didn't matter how he knew about Mum. Didn't matter who he was or why he'd taken my blood or why he was here in the middle of the night. Nausea rose at the sight of him, and it took all my strength not to punch him.

"Have you found her a donor?" he asked.

My fists shook, and my head pulsed. Painkillers. I needed painkillers. "Look, I'm sure you're perfectly charming when you're not being a jerk, but I'm not in the mood. Do us both a favour, and leave me alone."

He stood up suddenly, snatched my forearm, and stepped in until his shadow covered me. The smell of coffee and musky aftershave stifled me, and the heat from his body burned against my cheeks.

"Let go of me." I tried to pull away.

He yanked me closer. "Do you want your mother to live?"

The woman restocking the counter had her back to us. I could call out, get help. But then what? What would Blake do?

His fingers dug into my arm, hurting me, and his oily nose glistened where blackheads dotted it. Threads of grey weaved through his eyebrows. "Take a seat." His breath touched my ear, and he released me.

Blood tingled through my arm in a cold ache. I sat down, breathing erratic and peeled my dry lips apart. My hands trembled too much to reach for water.

Blake sat, too, and took another sip. So relaxed. So calm. Like he hadn't practically attacked me. "I have a donor."

My chest lurched. "You do?"

31

His clasped fingers tucked under his chin, and he perched his elbows either side of his drink. The steam curled upwards, collecting in the cup of his hands. Why all the aggression? Why hadn't he just said he had one to start with?

"Who are you?" I asked. For him to just appear out of nowhere, to know about Mum's accident, to just *happen* to have a willing donor – it made no sense. And then there was his taking my blood. "Why'd you meet with me yesterday?"

"That's irrelevant to our current conversation. Our topic is whether I'll let you use my donor."

"Whether you'll let me?" Clammy. That's what the air was. Clammy and humid and growing hotter by the minute.

Blake raised his chin. "I'm still undecided."

Seriously? He'd dangle Mum's salvation and snatch it away? He was lying. He had to be.

"Come now, dear," he said. "There's no need to get upset. This is all good business."

Business. "What do you want?" I asked. "You want money?"

He waved a hand. "Nothing so trivial."

"Then, what?" Lunatic or not, he could have anything if it meant saving Mum.

"Work for me."

My scalp prickled. "You're kidding, right?"

"I don't make a habit of kidding." His eyes narrowed. "You accept the job, I'll make sure you get your donor. Yes?"

No. He was clearly mad. Aggressive. Dangerous. Why on earth would I work for him? "What's the job?"

"It varies." He folded my napkin and slipped it under my plate.

"That's it?" I said. "You can't just dismiss it as that." Thoughts of being sold to the highest bidder crowded my thoughts. But so did Mum, dying on that hospital bed. I shuddered.

Blake straightened his sleeves. "I'm a private contractor. Of sorts. Which is what you'll become. Each assignment will differ, dependent on our clients' needs."

"That's not good enough." I shifted to stand – and didn't. My arm hurt where he'd grabbed me. And the woman had gone from the counter. I dug my fingers into my legs. "I won't accept unless you give me specifics."

He nodded. "Generally, I'd say that's wise. But under the circumstances …" He pushed his cup away. "Besides, I think you'll find my client very … interesting."

"I already have clients."

"None like mine." He slipped into silence again – a riddleman, awaiting the answer.

What else could I do? The doctors had given up. So had Lia. I couldn't just sit back and let Mum die. "You really have a donor?"

"I do."

A donor. One kidney for a rare blood type who just happens to need it urgently. It wasn't one of those black market types, was it? Some poor abducted girl they were going to cut open for 'business'? "How'd you know about Mum?" I asked. "Where'd you find a donor?"

His jaw tensed. "I'm not a patient man, Miss Rivers. Make your choice."

What choice? I had none. I squeezed the bridge of my nose, aggravating my headache. I'd wanted a new job. Wanted out of Lia's company. Just not like this. When I met Blake's gaze, smugness filled his smirk.

"Why me?" I asked.

"Your abilities are invaluable."

"What abilities?" I only sold estates. That hardly amounted to much.

"That's not important." He collected his briefcase and stood, buttons gaping on his front. "I'll send the donor in. Get some rest, Sally. You're going to need it."

8

True to his word, Blake's donor arrived in the nick of time. Mum had been wheeled straight into theatre.

I was stuck in the ward again. The nurse had been furious I'd snuck off. Like it mattered. I was wasting a bed anyway. Who needed hospital for a headache? I fidgeted on my pillow – more plastic than pillow. It crinkled when I moved.

Lia plucked a playing card from the pile between us just when a nurse passed by the curtain. I straightened a little. It'd been almost three hours. Mum should've been finished by now.

"Try to relax," Lia said. "She'll be fine."

I'd believe it when I saw it. I touched the cut on my forehead. It still hurt, my head – the joys of concussion – but painkillers only took the edge off. Still, the cuts on my hands didn't sting anymore. It was progress.

"Where were you yesterday?" I asked.

Her pendant had slipped between the buttons of her blouse, the branches of the tree peeking out. She always wore it and never spoke of it, except for the one time she told me of its significance in a moment in the dead of night. No one else knew, and as far as I could tell, no one ever would. Lia's shoulders dropped. "I'm sorry for what happened."

"That's not an answer." I was so tired of the secrets. Of

people keeping me in confusion. "You missed the briefing. You never miss …" I swallowed back rising heat. "Tell me where you were."

"I had a meeting."

"A meeting?"

"A really important meeting." She sighed and put down her cards. "I know it's hard, but I need you to trust me on this."

Well, trust had to be earned.

"And I need you not to quit," she said. Her lips pinched at the sides, and she rolled up her sleeves.

Quitting. I drew my elbows in to my core. It was hard not to quit when I'd already agreed to work for some madman. Pressure fluttered in my chest. How could I tell her about the job? I didn't even know what it was. A private contractor. That could be anything. Besides, she'd go mad.

Agreeing to the offer was foolish, I knew that. But I couldn't let Mum die.

Assuming the surgery worked. What if her body rejected the kidney? What if she didn't survive? I wouldn't work for Blake after that. Not ever.

But then what? He'd grabbed my arm – bruised it – all because I'd tried to leave. If I refused to hold my part, who knew what he would do?

"Don't quit," Lia said.

I tugged a loose thread on the blanket. No way was I going back now. I'd finally said the words. Finally quit. Blake or not, job or not, I was out. I'd be mad to go back. "I get that Mum and you want to help me."

"It's not that," she said.

"Yes, it is. It's been that way since Dad died." Not that I could remember it. Or any time before that. Her and Mum, they'd been this way as long as I could remember. But I liked to think they weren't so stifling once. That they'd been laid back before his death. I wrapped the thread around my finger. "I appreciate you looking out for me. Really, I do. But I'm not a child anymore. You can't protect me forever."

Lia tilted her head. "You don't know how wrong you are."

I rolled my eyes and slid off the bed. "Whatever."

"Where're you going?" she asked.

"To the toilet." Not like I needed permission for that, too.

Lia got up and drew back the curtain, waiting until I got to the door. Occupied. Great. I headed to the corridor instead. I'd use the guest one.

Lia hopped up.

"You don't need to follow me," I said.

"Just keeping you company." She nudged me, though her smile strained.

What could I do? This deal with Blake was coming out sooner or later. It'd be better to come from me than him, but even then, Lia would do her nut. What kind of idiot agreed to work for a man without knowing what the job was?

We passed the desk where three men in suits stood guard. One touched his watch, muttered something to the guy beside him.

"What's with the suits?" I asked.

Lia only shrugged.

There were others by the bathroom, too. Two of them, just standing outside the women's door. They sidestepped when I got there.

"What do you reckon?" I asked Lia when I returned. "There's someone rich or famous in the ward?" I nodded at the suits to make my point. They still stood by the desk, oblivious, it seemed, to the glares of the nurses.

"Yeah, maybe," Lia said.

"Weird, though. There wasn't anyone in the bathroom." Only me. So why were they guarding the door?

As though they read my thoughts, the two moved away, wandering towards the exit.

Weird, indeed.

A nurse stood by my bed when we got back, a blood pressure monitor beside her. "How you feeling?" she asked, and picked up the strap.

I rolled my sleeve. "Fine." Mostly fine. My head ached more than earlier. Walking hadn't helped. "You heard anything?"

"Just now." She nodded. "She's in recovery."

"So, it worked?" My chest thudded. Mum was safe? Suddenly the job seemed worth it. Mum was alive. She'd live. No job could be worse than if I'd done nothing.

The nurse took my blood pressure silently, pausing to study her watch. Only once she removed the strap did I stand up.

"I want to see her."

She popped her hands on her hips. "Yeah. I figured that." She put down the strap and turned to Lia. "You bring her straight back, you hear?"

I didn't wait for Lia's response. Mum was all right. The accident, the lost kidney, none of it mattered anymore. She would live.

The corridors stretched on forever, wider and longer than I remembered. Lia caught up quick enough. "Slow down," she said.

"I can't." I had to know Mum was okay. Had to see it for myself.

"Sally." She took my shoulder.

"It was my fault." For the first time, my eyes stung. "I asked her to pick me up. If I hadn't, she'd never have been out there. We'd never have been in …" I batted a tear away.

"You can't blame yourself," Lia said. "It was an accident."

"Was it?"

Her brow furrowed.

"Too much is off," I said. "The guys at the office, the power cut, that Blake guy—"

"What about him?" Her tone sliced through the passage.

"I just …" I ran my thumb over the thin scab left from Blake's ring. Not that it stood out anymore. It blended in with my other cuts. "Where did you go yesterday?"

She swallowed.

"Did you know him?" I asked.

"Course not."

"Well, he seems to know Mum."

She grabbed my arm, stopping me in an instant. "You said he left before you spoke."

I tensed. "He did."

"Then, why would you think he knows her?" The fuzzy hairs on the side of her face stuck out from her foundation that flaked a little on her jaw.

It was now or never. I couldn't keep it quiet anymore anyway. He'd turn up soon enough, and I didn't know what to do when he did. I licked my dry lips. "Lia, you should know—"

"Ah, the daughters." Doctor Brown marched down the hallway, his black collar protruding above his overcoat. "I'll take you to her, shall I?"

Behind him, one of the suited guys from the ward shifted into the passage. Was he following us?

Lia shot me a scowl. "What were you saying?"

"We'll talk later."

9

Doctor Brown led us to a private room where Mum lay sleeping on the bed, a heart monitor beeping beside her. She no longer breathed through a tube, and her cheeks held more colour. Warmth spread through me, and I stepped closer to her.

"We're keeping her under," the doc said. "Just to monitor things. We'll wake her in an hour or so."

I frowned at him. "Is that normal?" I thought they woke patients quickly after surgery. Wanted them to eat, drink, use the toilet.

"It's procedure," he said. "She's doing well. Should be on her feet in two or three days."

That was something.

"Before you go, I have some forms for signing," the doc said. "If you can give me a minute." He gestured to the door.

"I'll go," Lia said to me. "You wait here."

"You sure?"

"I'll not be a minute." She followed the doctor, leaving the door to click closed behind her.

I took Mum's hand. It almost felt silly. I hadn't held her hand in years. And she didn't grab mine back like she used to. "Hi, Mum." The heart monitor beeped. "Can you hear me?" Beeped. Steadily. Wouldn't it have sped up if she could?

Wouldn't her pulse have shown a reaction? "I guess I don't know if you can." Which could've been good. I could get my thoughts off my chest. Not have to deal with her lecture. And she'd be awake soon. "I wish you were awake now."

Nothing changed with the beeping. She didn't move. Didn't stir.

I tightened my grip. "Something happened." And even here, with Mum unconscious, I couldn't find the courage to tell her. "I couldn't let you die. I don't know what's going to happen. But whatever does, it's worth it. Because it saved you."

I swallowed the ache in my throat – it'd be so much harder to tell the truth if I cried. When the door clicked open, I braced. "Lia, I—" I turned around, and my chest tingled, the same way it did when I stepped off a kerb without seeing it.

Blake stood in the doorway. His red-and-blue striped tie reminded me of an overgrown schoolboy. Wrinkles marked the space beneath his eyes, and stubble darkened his face. Hadn't he slept at all? He carried the same briefcase. Still wore the same suit. "I see the surgery went well."

"So the doctor says." My fists clenched and unclenched behind my back. Would he give me details now? Finally explain the job role? "Thank you. For helping her."

"Well, it wasn't without price." His gaze lingered on Mum for a moment. "Time to go."

I stiffened. "Go?"

"You recall our agreement."

"I agreed to work for you. Not leave before she wakes up." Surely, he wasn't that cruel? I'd expected the weekend at least. Start on Monday, all that jazz.

"You start now."

"You can't be serious." I hadn't even been discharged. Hadn't even told Lia.

Blake shifted his weight. "I've allowed you more time than I should." He reached for the door.

"No." I stood straighter. Cleared my throat. He'd bruised me. But no more. I'd lived under others' control long enough.

He raised his eyebrows. "No?"

My fingers tightened on the bed. "I'm not leaving. Give me details, I'll start on Monday."

"Miss Rivers." He took a step closer. "It takes a brave person to trifle with me."

I pressed my legs together to stop their trembling. Sweat stuck to my back, and the faint scent of body odour reached me. "That's my final offer."

He narrowed his eyes. "Need I remind you that I've been true to my word?"

"Need I remind you I'm a patient here?"

"That's been dealt with." Something changed in his voice. It almost growled, projected something deeper, darker. He opened the door. Expectant.

"What do you mean it's been dealt with?"

"I mean it's time to go. Now." He stepped into the corridor. Was he delusional? Did he really think I'd pick up and leave on his order? I should never have made the deal. If he was like this now, what would he become over time?

But Mum was alive. I squeezed her arm. Living. Breathing. Because of this. Because of Blake.

The whole situation was messed up.

"Where we going?" I asked.

"Brazil."

"Brazil?" My voice hitched. "Hang on a minute, I didn't agree to that."

He scowled at his watch. "The terms were clear. Your mother lives." His shoulders dropped, his jaw relaxed, and his stance widened. "Amelia, on the other hand …"

My stomach flipped so hard it hurt. "What about her?"

He nodded pointedly down the corridor and waited while I approached him.

Lia stood at the desk, head bent over a clipboard, a pen in her hand. Behind her, a man dressed in leather drew aside his jacket. A gun rested in the waistline of his jeans.

I gasped.

Blake's fingers dug into my shoulder. "Imagine what might happen if you were to go back on our deal."

He wouldn't shoot her here. Not in a crowded hospital.

"You're doubtful," Blake said, and his grip shifted. "How's this for proof?" He nodded at the leather guy who wandered a little way up the passage and opened a cupboard.

Someone toppled out and thudded on the floor. The suited man I'd seen following us.

Sweat burst over my head, and my breath caught in my throat.

The leather guy hopped backwards to make room for three nurses who rushed to the suit. Lia looked over, too.

Unconscious. He was just unconscious.

One of the nurses looked up. "He's dead."

Blake grabbed my arm and hauled me out of the room, away from the chaos. The bruises hurt. So did my chest. And every muscle shook.

Lia turned to me. "Sally!"

Too late. Blake yanked me into a lift, and the doors closed seconds before Lia could stick her hand through the gap.

"Please," I said, and the gravity twisted, beginning our descent. "I'll come with you. Just, please, don't hurt her."

Blake sniffed. "That really depends on you."

On me. On my obeying this killer. This so-called private contractor who meant nothing to me. "Who are you?"

"Blake. And you belong to me now."

10

A Legacy 500 sat on the airstrip of Heathrow airport, filling the air with exhaust fumes and a thick, heavy heat. Blake stood over me, hand back on my arm after the car ride. There'd been one driver. He never spoke. Never even looked at me. Now, he drove away across the concrete, either not knowing or caring about the man he'd left me with.

I could run. The airport wasn't far. But one man had died already. What if Lia was next? I pressed my fingers against my temples. The painkillers had worn off, exposing me to the full brunt of my headache. How had I got into this?

"Come," Blake said. "There's medication onboard."

I stared at him. "I didn't know you cared."

He huffed and urged me to the plane.

An air hostess stood by the open door at the top of the stairs. "Benvenuto a bordo, Signore."

Blake ignored her and marched me past a three-seater sofa and several leather seats to the far side of the cabin where he bid me sit by a table. A screen in the wall showed the plane's position on the ground. He snapped something at the woman, and she rushed behind a curtain.

There was the exit, clear and unguarded, taunting me with a breeze that brushed my skin.

"Get comfortable," Blake said. "She'll be online shortly."

"Who will?"

The stewardess came back and sealed the door.

My insides felt hollow. I should've struggled more. Should've hit Blake, screamed out a warning to Lia.

Blake sat across the aisle, popping his briefcase between him and the wall. It wasn't too late. If I attacked him, hit him with … what? There was nothing here but seats and a table and … and my fists. He had a bruising hold, but I had surprise. Right? If I ran, got to the door on time—

"I wouldn't recommend it," Blake said. "It'd only end with you getting hurt."

I blinked. How did he—

"It doesn't take a mind-reader to know your thoughts." He crossed a leg over his other and tapped his nose. "Body language. It gives you away."

A phone lay beside him, connected to the plane by a single wire.

My heart thumped. One phone call. That's all I needed. If he'd just go to the toilet, I could call for help.

The stewardess handed me a glass of water and a small pot. I took it, frowning at the two tablets inside.

"Paracetamol." Blake leaned back, perfectly relaxed. And perfectly ready to grab me, no doubt.

I shrunk away. "Prove it."

"I've no reason to lie."

"But you have," I said.

He cocked his head. "How so?"

"You won't answer my questions."

He sniffed. "Refusal to answer is not a lie."

The stewardess opened a door to the cockpit. She didn't wear a name tag like other stewards back when Mum, Lia, and I went to Spain. But this was a private jet. Blake probably knew her name. I silently called her Maria and put the water and pot down. "Please don't do this." I grasped my chair with a clammy hand.

The engines whirred, increasing in pitch. Through the

window, the airport moved away. No, *we* moved away. The concrete passed below us in a blur.

I whirled to Blake. "Please. I can't offer you anything. You've got the wrong person."

The airport slipped away, disappearing around the back of the aircraft. I strained to see it.

"Please." I took the arm of my chair. "Please let me go."

Blake straightened up his tie, though it wasn't wonky. "I'd put your seatbelt on if I were you."

The plane turned some more and drew to a stop. The building, now visible through Blake's window, glimmered in the morning sun, setting spots in my eyes.

Blake clipped on his belt.

My whole body pounded. Lia would've called for help. Police would come swarming onto the runway, sirens blazing. Any minute now.

The aircraft slid forwards. The engine whined. Weight pressed me against the seat and stuck my skin to the leather. My water tilted in the glass.

It was too late. Too late to stop the plane.

My chest ached. My head stung with every thud of my pulse.

The ground outside blurred. Tilted. Fell away. And in a minute, it seemed, clouds covered the windows.

My face tingled. How had this—this couldn't—what had I done?

Blake snapped something at Maria.

I was his captive. I'd saved Mum. And now I might never see her again. My head thumped. My stomach churned.

Blake shoved a cardboard bowl in my hands, and I threw up violently, gasping for breath just when I thought I'd pass out. Hot tears stung. I squeezed my eyes shut, and someone took the bowl, leaving me to bury my head in my hands.

"That'll be your concussion," Blake said. "Take those painkillers now."

I had to credit his timing. I'd have thrown up everywhere without the bowl. I should have thrown up on him.

45

Maria crouched beside me and pressed the cool glass into my hands. The pot came next, and she muttered something foreign.

"You got any juice?" I croaked. Anything to get rid of the taste.

Blake maybe relayed it in her language, because she rushed away and came back with a glass of apple juice. Concentrated, judging by the smell. I swallowed down the tablets with a burning throat.

Blake nodded his approval.

The screen on the wall flickered, and a woman appeared, glaring out from shadows that turned her irises black. "So, you're Sally Rivers." The softness in her voice barely concealed a layer of ice. She smiled, showing perfectly white teeth – unnaturally white, like the kind I'd seen on film stars. A gleaming, ruby pendant hung round her neck. "You look positively pale, dear."

"Really?" I said. "I can't imagine why." I put the glass down, hiccupping lightly, and shielded myself from the lights. They hurt. Ached my eyelids.

"I'm told your mother is safe and well," she said.

I closed my eyes, leaning into the darkness. "She's well. I don't know about safe."

The aircraft's engine rumbled through my seat. Lightly, but noticeably. And it whined in the distance, like the walls muffled the sound.

"Look at me," she said.

"Stuff off." They'd already blackmailed me. Besides, the light hurt my head.

"Blake, for goodness sake, turn the lights down," she said.

The brightness dimmed.

"Now, look at me, child."

I did. The screen reflected off the cabin walls, still bright, but not as painful.

She frowned. "You're afraid."

No kidding.

"You needn't be," she said. "Do your job right, and you'll be just fine."

"Easier said than done when I don't know what the job is," I said.

Her nostrils flared, and she brushed her hair aside, flashing a diamond earring. "We're a criminal organisation, Sally. What do you think the job is?"

The air grew cold. I should've known. The bruises. The murder. "I'm not a criminal," I said. "Never could be."

She smiled. "You're young. There's room to reach your potential."

"No, you've made a mistake." Whatever Blake had picked me for, he was wrong. I had no skills. No interest in any of this. Unless this was one of those suicide bomber situations. But why all the effort to recruit me? Why not pick someone else or simply blackmail me straight into it? Despite the apple juice, my mouth turned dry.

"We don't make mistakes," she said, ice in her words. "Now, get some sleep. And Blake." She paused. "Get her under control." The screen turned black.

Blake glared at the screen, fingers drumming. The same fingers he'd bruised me with.

I touched my arm. "You've got the wrong person."

"I assure you, I haven't." He turned his glare to me. "You're in more danger than you know. You'd be wise to keep your head down and do as you're told."

"You want blind obedience," I said. "I can't give you that."

"I want you to survive. You're no good to me dead."

Any response got lost on my tongue. What was so important to him that he wanted me so badly?

He exhaled slowly and leaned back to smooth out his tie.

"I don't understand," I said. "What do you want from me?"

"You don't need to know." He rubbed his nose. "Just stay alive. You hear?"

11

At half past three, pressure built in my ears, signalling our descent. Through the window, buildings filled the landscape like toy blocks.

"Why are we landing?" I asked. "We're nowhere near Brazil."

Blake raised his eyebrows. "How could you know that?"

I … had no idea. "Just a guess."

He rubbed his chin. "Interesting. As it happens, you're quite right. This is a stop-off before the long haul to Rio." A pile of paper rested on his table. He lifted the top piece and studied the page beneath it.

An early landing. If I could somehow get off the plane, get someone's attention – I didn't have a passport. This could work.

"You're not getting out." Blake scribbled something, gathered the pile into his briefcase, and clicked the locks shut.

The phone lay beside him, tucked into an alcove. Blake hadn't gone to the toilet. Hadn't left his seat at all. But if he got off the plane, if he got up for anything, I could make a call. One minute was all I needed.

Blake popped the briefcase beside his chair, and the screen flicked on to show our journey back to the ground.

"How's your mother coped?" he asked.

I blinked. "What do you mean?"

"Without a husband. He died, didn't he? She raised you alone."

How did he know that? He said he'd known Mum once. Were they friends? Hard to believe.

"It couldn't have been easy," he said.

"No harder than having some psycho try to turn me into a criminal." I dug my nail into my thumb. What was I doing? He'd already threatened Lia's life. Already had one man killed.

His jaw tightened. "You should control your snark. It won't do you any favours in Venom."

"Venom?"

"The organisation." He turned to his window. "Quite fitting, too, I'd say."

"Why's that?"

"You'll see." The light outside bounced off his oily nose.

"Venom's a bit obvious," I said.

His arm twitched. "How so?"

"Shouldn't it be more subtle?" I asked. "You hear Venom, you think terrorists."

He chuckled. "We are what we are. We don't hide that."

The plane touched the runway. I jolted in my seat and swallowed back the fullness in my ears. Wheels on concrete roared. I closed my eyes, only exhaling when we drew to a juddery stop.

"There are boiled sweets in the pocket beside you." Blake nodded at a panel by my hand. "Have one of those in the next descent."

Maria tugged open the exit, and warm, spring air blew in. I wrinkled my nose at my body odour. I'd been sweating too much. A foul taste coated my tongue, like a layer of hair lay over it, and my hair matted against my face, hardened with tears – and, I'll admit, a little snot.

Blake got up, and I sucked in a breath. I studied the carpet, the lighter patches where people had worn it down. I wouldn't look at the phone. Couldn't give myself away. Especially if he was reading my body language.

He padded down the steps outside towards a balding man whose blazer flapped at his arms. He greeted Blake with a handshake.

I bit my lip and peeked at the cockpit. Maria followed Blake out. Through the cockpit door, the pilot watched the controls.

It was too easy. Hadn't Blake thought of the phone? Hadn't he known I'd try something?

But then, he was only human. Maybe, just maybe, he'd made a mistake.

I dove across the aisle and grabbed the phone. My fingers fumbled over the numbers, twice pressing the wrong ones. I stabbed the disconnect button and dialled again.

Blake still stood outside, speaking with the man. The stranger handed Blake an envelope, and Blake passed it to Maria.

I held the phone to my ear.

It rang once.

"Hello?" I said.

Silence.

Dead battery? No. The phone was wired up. It'd rang.

Blake climbed the steps, hair whipping flat.

With a jolt of panic, I replaced the phone and leapt back to my seat.

The pilot met Blake at the door, and after a quiet exchange, went back to the front of the plane.

I should've run outside. Should've jumped the steps and run to the airport instead of trying to call Lia. But with Blake's threat to her—

I stifled a gasp. The phone hung crooked on its holder. If Blake didn't know what I'd done, he would soon.

Blake stood with his back to me.

It was now or never.

I stretched over, clicked the phone into place, and sat back just as Blake turned. My cheeks flamed. He'd hear it, my heart beat. Hear it banging in my ears.

He lifted the arm of his chair. Perched on the seat. His gaze burned into the back of my head. "Do you know much about aircraft?"

I forced my eyes to meet his. He'd see the guilt in my cheeks. He'd know what I'd done. "They fly."

He lifted an acknowledging finger. "That, and they give a remarkable amount of control to the pilot." His rested his fist on his table. "Very little happens onboard without him knowing. So, if someone was to attempt an unauthorised call, for instance …"

Funny, how the air could get so thick, so hard to breathe, and hot enough to soak every inch of my back.

Blake's features showed nothing. He almost looked bored. Except for the fist. "Of course, I'm not surprised you tried. The pilot disconnected you. It's not an issue. But you see, if I don't follow through on my threats, you'll never take me seriously."

So thick. Like something sucked out the oxygen. Dried my mouth. "You're not—"

He lifted a hand.

The screen in front of me flashed to life. There was my living room: the scratched-up sofas from the neighbour's cat when we cat-sat, the Egyptian vase Dad had loved, the lacy curtains fluttering in a light breeze.

And Lia.

She paced past the window, mobile to her ear, tree pendant gleaming in the light.

They'd been in our house. I pushed my feet on the floor until my legs ached. *In* our house.

Blake crossed his leg. "Interesting that she doesn't know the house is bugged."

"Why would she?" I asked, my words barely slipping out.

Blake's smile distorted his face, creasing his cheeks with wrinkles. "She's looking for you. Using her resources."

"What resources?"

Lia kept talking, free hand gesturing through the air. Talking in silence. Maybe the bug let sound through to someone, but not us.

Blake drew out his mobile, pressed a button, and said something in a language similar to Maria's.

I swallowed – well, tried to. My tongue stuck to the roof of my mouth. "She's not involved in this."

He lowered his phone. "You got her involved."

Lia spoke. Listened. Spoke some more.

Through the window behind her, the apartment block across the street stood cloaked in shadows. Something glinted in one of the flats.

"Don't." I grabbed Blake's table, sinking to my knees. "Please, don't. I get it. I shouldn't have tried."

"Sally, dear." He laid his hand on mine, drawing a cringe. "I am Venom. And Venom never break their word."

Lia paused by the window.

My body trembled. Vibrated so much the table shook. Or maybe that was the engine starting up again.

"That vase," Blake said. "It's a replica of the unguent vase, isn't it? From the Tutankhamun tomb, if I'm not mistaken."

Dad's vase. He'd loved Egypt. Loved collecting replicas.

"I'm sorry," I said. "Really."

He pursed his lips. "See, I don't think you are. What's to say when I turn my back, you won't try again?"

"I won't." Not knowing the pilot would cut me off. "Please. Let her go."

He tilted his head and spoke into his phone. A single word.

The vase exploded, showering Lia in clay.

I snatched my hand from under his, and cold shot through my limbs.

Lia dropped and rolled behind the sofa, out of view.

"Stop it!" I said. "Please! Leave her alone."

Blake nodded. "That was your final warning. Next time, he won't miss." He pointed at the screen. "And just to be sure my point fully sinks in …" He spoke into the phone again.

The door to the living room burst open. It bounced off the

wall, and three hooded figures rushed in. They grabbed Lia. One hit her, and they dragged her, kicking and squirming from the house.

"Lia!" I pushed my hands on the edges of the image. "Stop it! Lia!"

The video feed cut out.

They shot at Lia. They took her. And it was my fault. All my fault. I sank onto my seat.

"Venom expect complete loyalty," Blake said. "We don't tolerate disobedience. Step out of place again, and she'll die."

12

The plane dipping threw my stomach and pulled me from dreams of bearded hunters chasing me with knives. The food Maria had given me lay on the table, cold, congealed and untouched.

Blake sat opposite, holding a steaming mug. "Sleep well?"

"Would you?"

"I rarely sleep." He sipped his drink, a sharp scent of coffee wafting through the cabin. The light reflected on his watch face. Six a.m.

"We travelled all night," I said.

"And most of the morning." Blake pulled the dial of his watch. "It'd be ten o'clock in London."

It'd been hours since they'd taken Lia. Since they'd dragged her from her own home. "Is Lia okay?"

Blake shrugged. "Fine, I'd wager. A little shaken up, perhaps."

"Perhaps?"

He took another sip.

Didn't he care what happened? What was I thinking—of course, he didn't. I rubbed my heel against the carpet. What must Mum be thinking? She'd have woken by now. Woken to find her daughters gone, kidnapped by murderers.

Pain stabbed in my gut, so I bit into a carrot. Rubbery.

"Leave that." Blake gestured to Maria who whisked the plate away. "You can eat when we arrive."

It'd been hours. Between throwing up and restless sleep, my dry mouth and pulsing headache screamed of dehydration, and my whole core tightened with hunger. I grabbed a sweet from the compartment just as the engine grew faint and the pressure increased. The minty flavour set my tongue tingling and cleared my sinuses but did little to curb the hunger.

Blake ran his finger around the rim of his cup. "Not long now. Just one more flight."

"We're not in Brazil?" But we were landing.

"Oh, we are, but we've a way to go yet."

Weakness dropped through my limbs, and when I shifted on the seat, my odour tainted the air. "Where exactly are we going?"

"You'll see." He clipped on his belt. "There's an outfit behind your seat. You'll find its your size."

And how would he know that? Sure, he could've looked at the clothes from the hospital. He could've guessed, too. It probably wasn't hard. But still. "How long were you planning to take me?"

He cocked his head.

"You bugged my home. You have clothes for me. It clearly wasn't a spur of the moment decision."

"You'd be surprised what we can do on short notice."

"We being Venom?"

"Mm." He tapped the handle of his mug. "A word of advice. You're entering a new world. More dangerous than anything you've known. One mistake can be fatal. Not just for you." He paused to tug his cuff. "Don't rebel. Don't try to escape. It's not just your life on the line."

I flexed my fingers. After everything he'd done – threatened my family, taken my freedom – what could be worse?

The plane touched the runway, lurching me against the leather. Wheels screeched on tarmac, and the plane slid to a stop.

"Use the bathroom to change," Blake said. "And clean up."

My cheeks burned. Course, he'd noticed the smell. Who wouldn't? My legs shook when I stood. I reached for the outfit: an olive-green dress and pair of black stilettos, and held up the skimpy fabric. "I can't wear this."

Blake huffed. "Your attire is inappropriate. We're not a cheap organisation. We certainly don't wander around in ripped jeans."

Lia's jeans.

A dry, musty scent wafted in through the open door, mixing with my own. Lia's jeans were far better than the dress, even with the rips.

Blake pointed at me. "Don't show your fear. If others know your weaknesses, they'll use them against you."

Shocker.

He collected his briefcase and sauntered to the exit. "Change, and come outside," he said over his shoulder. "I'll give you five minutes."

Funny how leaving the plane suddenly made my insides go hollow. Brazil. How'd I end up like this? I'd been smuggled out the country! I'd heard about that on the news, but for it to actually happen … the whole thing fuzzed like a dream. Surreal.

The silky, thin fabric slid over my fingers. It made my throat ache. I'd never have touched something like this. Never imagined I'd be forced to wear it. What if I didn't? What if I just cleaned up and kept my own clothes on?

The memory of Dad's vase shattering cut into my mind.

I batted away the tickle on my cheek and shuffled to the bathroom.

13

It was stupid, standing crying in the little cubicle of the WC, squeezing into the dress that was clearly my size but way too tight for comfort. And for what? For the satisfaction of a sadistic, messed-up old man who thought himself better than anyone else? Clearly, he was used to getting his own way. I mean, look at the private jet and his suit and his chauffeur driver who'd brought us here from the hospital. He was all money and power and control. A pompous windbag if I ever saw one.

I glared at my reflection in the mirror, all pale and tear-streaked and scratched and cut. This wasn't me. This would never be me.

Whatever he wanted, I wouldn't quietly give it to him.

He'd regret taking me, if it was the last thing I did.

14

Maria collected my bunched-up clothes from me when I emerged at the exit – though it took me a moment to let go. Maybe it'd been five minutes. I didn't know. Crying tended to whisk time away. I'd tried to hide it, washed my face with cold water, but my reflection only betrayed me like every other bit of luck recently.

Blake waited on the concrete, silhouetted by soft, morning light. The sunrise reflected off the sleek sides of a helicopter on my right. The pilot flicked a switch, and the blades rotated, gradually picking up speed.

I accepted a glass of orange juice from Maria, downed it in seconds, and headed towards my captor. Every step towards Blake wobbled on the horrid stilettos. They clipped like some wannabe supermodel, taunting me, threatening to break my ankles. The breeze slid over my legs, way too high for comfort.

Blake raked his gaze over me, and he nodded. "Better."

My face burned. "It's disgusting."

"It's classy." He steered me towards the helicopter and helped me climb inside – hand on my elbow since I refused to take his hand.

I tugged the hem of the dress towards my knees, nowhere close to hiding my leg stubble. The hairs stuck out, dark and coarse. Because the helicopter was just that: luxury, with leather seats and champagne glasses in cup holders against the far window.

Blake passed me headphones and secured his own before adjusting the microphone by his mouth. He slid the door closed, and the helicopter took off, leaving the plane and Maria far below. At least she could go home.

In minutes, a city stretched to the horizon like glinting silver, bouncing the sunlight until it left spots in my vision. I kept watching though. Sunspots were better than a view of the bulging Blake, probably eyeing up my legs and thinking how un-classy they were.

"You've never been to São Paulo before," Blake's voice said in my headphones.

I clenched my fists. "What's your point?"

"No point. Just making a statement."

Let me guess. Another one of those 'you'd be surprised what we can find on short notice' excuses. What'd he really done? Researched me, clearly. Bugged the house. Figured out my clothes size. And now my travel history. What did he want from me? "Are you going to kill me?" My voice barely rose above a whisper, got lost in the chopping blades.

"That would defeat the object."

Almost got lost then. The headphones picked up more than I thought. I forced my focus to where Blake adjusted his briefcase.

"I won't make a good criminal."

He sniffed. "Criminals get caught. We don't."

"Then, what are you?"

"Investors in a more powerful future."

People believed that rubbish? I rested my head in my palm, running my finger over the raised cut from the accident. It hurt. "Then why am I here? I didn't ask for this."

"Didn't you?" He inclined his head. "Your mother—"

"Has nothing to do with this. I wanted her saved, but I haven't ever asked to be taken for … whatever this is."

He shrugged. "Yet here you are."

The city line changed to ocean that glistened like a thousand diamonds, and the land fell away behind us.

"We're not staying in Brazil?" I asked.

Blake pointed at a familiar stretch of land some way ahead of us: an island covered in trees and shrubs, rimmed by rock and white-crested waves. "That is the Ilha da Queimada Grande," Blake said, "otherwise known as—"

"Snake Island," I breathed.

"You know it?"

"It's infested with snakes." Approximately one per square foot, if I remembered correctly. Bit excessive, but it wasn't the world's most deadly island for nothing.

Blake's lips twitched. "That's our destination."

"No, it's not."

He raised his eyebrows.

He couldn't be serious. No one survived on Snake Island. It was forbidden. Illegal just to land on it. What could he possibly want there? I gripped my knees with slippery hands.

"Conceal your fear." Blake nodded at them. "You're too easy to read."

"Either you're joking, or you're crazy," I said, "because there's no way to safely pass those snakes."

"Things are never as they seem."

As though in confirmation, the pilot veered off to the right towards a second, much smaller island – empty, apart from some foliage.

I tucked my trembling hands under my legs and closed my eyes against my growing headache. He'd been frightening me. Nothing more. Jerk.

15

I shivered in the heat, watching the helicopter abandoning me on the tiny island. I wobbled in the stilettos, careful to keep my weight on my toes since a miniature lean in the wrong direction meant losing the heel in the soil.

Any hope I held deflated with the dropping wind, and when I licked my lips, my tongue stuck to them. If I'd had any chance of escape, of getting help in any form, it was gone now. The mainland lay on the horizon on one side – way too far to swim to – and deadly Snake Island lay on the other. It was just me and Blake, alone on this abandoned slab of land.

"Are you ready?" Blake asked.

"For what?" What could he possibly hope to accomplish on this scrap of weeds? A wash of nausea shivered through me. If I didn't eat soon, I'd throw up again.

Blake's thumb stroked the handle of his case. "Remember all I told you. It might just save your life. And from here I won't be able to help you."

I clutched my stomach. "You think you've been helpful?"

He took a long breath, setting his focus on the sky. Eventually, he exhaled. "I'm trying to protect you."

"Why? Why do you care at all?"

He chuckled then, a dark, twisted sound that set my teeth on edge. "I care very little about you. See, you have it in your mind that you're of any importance at all." He leaned in closer until his eyes lay level with mine, until his coffee-stained breath and made my gut ache something rotten. "What I care about is infinitely more important. Infinitely more powerful. A force you can barely imagine. And thanks to you, it'll soon be mine."

16

I should've expected a hidden staircase leading below the island.

Blake stepped aside and gestured to the rough-cut steps. "After you."

Each step differed in height. Every surface bumped and dipped in random places. If I fell, I'd break a leg. Or my neck. I leaned against the wall to steady myself and bent to remove my heels.

"Heels are the shoes of a lady." Blake said. "If you can descend with grace, you're one step closer to field work."

Field work. Another phrase he'd refuse to explain, no doubt. I hesitated, fingers on the strap. "I'll fall."

"You'll be fine."

A salty breeze caught my legs, stung them like grains of sand bashed against them. Stuff this. I took off the shoes and climbed down, keeping a steadying palm on the wall. Cold seeped into my feet. I shivered. Still, better cold feet than broken ankles.

Blake hadn't spoken, either, so that was a plus.

My foot slipped.

His hand clamped on my shoulder, so instead of falling forward, I thunked to my bottom. Pain spread through the section of back that scraped the edge of a step – that'd bruise later – and the heels clattered on the rock. I bit back a rising insult and got up.

Down below, light seeped in through a cave-like opening, and the swoosh of waves reached us. Where was he taking me? The deeper we descended, the more underground caves seemed likely. I flinched at the thought of being buried in darkness and unnatural light.

I slipped again on the bottom step, earning another one of Blake's cringey touches, and stepped on to a curved ledge of rock. Water sprayed over the shining platform with each pulse of a wave, and my toes grew purple with chill.

Blake glanced at his watch. "It's time."

Time for what? There were no ledges. No walkways. No doors leading back into the island.

Metal burst from the sea like a dark whale. Water streamed and foamed down its curved sides, sizzling back into the ocean.

I gasped at the submarine. Its engine reverberated against the rocks. Sea spray caught my hair and cheeks, and lined my mouth with salt. A hatch opened, and a grim-faced man appeared. He extended a long, narrow board between us and the vessel.

Blake nudged me on. The sea bubbled and churned, probably hiding some propellor that'd cut me to shreds if I fell. One wobble in the wrong direction, and I'd be seafood. A sick feeling filled my throat. Would it bother them if I drowned?

The wind dropped a little, so I staggered across the board, stumbling just before I reached the hatch. Grim caught my arm. "Watch it, newbie." He shoved me toward a vertical ladder leading into the sub. With every rung, my heels clunked against them. I should've dropped them in the sea.

Blake climbed down next and marched me along a narrow passage into a long room with windows for walls, leaving Grim to secure the hatch. The sea bubbled against the glass, hiding any coral reefs or whatever there might've been under the water's surface. Blake directed me to one of the tables that lined the windows and sat down opposite.

Great. The hospital café all over again.

"Put those on," he growled, nodding at my heels.

I obeyed, teeth gritting. Definitely should've dropped them.

He drummed his fingers on the table, only speaking again once I finished. "The training grounds are on Snake Island, accessed by an underwater chamber."

"Training grounds?"

"You can't do the job without training."

Right. The mystery job he wouldn't explain. "So, you want me to hide underground." Some plan. Keep me in the dark, cut off from civilisation until I broke.

17

The submarine surfaced in a chamber full of salt-scented air that wafted through the open hatch – along with a sweeter smell, orange and jasmine. I clenched my stomach, swaying slightly where I stood by the bottom rung.

Grim jerked his chin towards the hatch. "Go."

I balled my fists, fighting a rush of hanger. If they didn't give me food soon, I might just punch someone. "You first."

He snorted a chortle and climbed up, leaving me alone with Blake.

The floor tilted, and the first hints of seasickness built a lump in my throat. "Where are we?"

"The training grounds."

"That's not what I meant."

Blake clasped his briefcase with both hands, half-hiding his bulging gut. Was that why he carried the case around? Maybe under all the bravado, he was secretly self-conscious. "Go on. We haven't got all day."

What else could I do? I could hardly steal the submarine and go back to the mainland. I didn't have the first clue how to use one of these things. Besides, Lia needed me to be strong. To be obedient. For now, at least.

The sub bobbed in a wide, underground chamber cut smoothly from the rock. The water practically glowed where the submarine floated, maybe affected by underwater lights. Or lights from the vessel. It was hard to tell. Round lights set into the walls lit the cave and lined a gloomy passage where two guards waited.

Grim kept a foot on one side of a metal walkway connecting the sub to the land, and I staggered over it, glad when the floor stopped moving.

Blake marched me past the guards without so much as a glance, barely keeping a comfortable pace. My heels clipped against the stone, and with his grip on my elbow, slowing wasn't an option.

Someone murmured behind me, and I tugged the hem of my dress down. It only sprang back up. My face burned.

The walkway turned right, and a short, glass staircase led up to a group of trees outside. Sunlight streamed between the leaves, and dust glided through the beams. The scent of baking bread, orange, jasmine, and soil filled the air, and my stomach growled, earning a glance from Blake.

We emerged in a sun-flooded clearing. Flowers lined paths covered in gravel that crunched underfoot. There were pointed leaves in vibrant greens painted with crimson streaks, yellow buds mid-bloom, and orange flowers pecking through patches of bark. How was this possible? I could see the sky. Which meant the sky could see us. *Satellites* could see us. How could something like this exist without someone knowing or doing anything about it? Unless Venom had paid people off.

Beyond the clearing, the space opened to an expanse of walkways that criss-crossed between fields and buildings, stretching all the way to a thick line of trees. Was that where the snakes were? The telltale glint of light on glass marked some kind of barrier. Protection from the vipers?

"That's the boundary," Blake said. "It's completely reinforced, so you needn't worry." He let go of my arm. "Welcome to Snake Island."

Snake Island. The deadly, *forbidden* island. I searched the sky, the treelines for something familiar, something to prove we really were there. It was ingenious: to land on the smaller island and take a submarine into the illegal one. No one would see. No one would know. If we weren't outside.

Criminals get caught. We don't.

Blake smiled that twisted smirk. "It's fitting. Trespassers are killed by snake venom. Where better to keep the Venom training grounds?"

I leaned away from him, absently touching my arm. What kind of maniac found that appealing?

"This way," he said.

My ankles tilted and twisted and ached with the effort to keep me upright on the shifting gravel. The only thing classy about stilettos was the satisfaction I'd get in snapping them.

We passed an open field dotted with wooden blocks. Beyond that, a cluster of stone constructs with coloured handholds towered. Rock climbing? How did that relate to criminal training?

"There's the range," Blake said, "where you'll learn to shoot. And there's the climbing wall."

"Yes, I know what rock climbing looks like." I bit my lip to hide the tremble. Shooting? I didn't want to learn that.

A few paths in, a stone building with glass balconies became visible. Each one held a table, wicker chairs, and sheer curtains that flapped in the breeze. Someone stepped on to one: a man, thirty-years-old. He was well-built: slim, muscular, with close-cropped hair and keen eyes that clamped on us briefly. He sat on a chair, a book in his grasp.

"What kind of training do you do here?" I asked. Everything was so light. So open and beautiful.

"You expected everything to be rough?" Blake said.

"Well …" Yes. Rundown shelters. Dirt and grime. Tattoos and smoking. Piercings. The typical criminal stereotypes.

Blake pointed to the rock-climbing constructs, and panned his hand across. "There are stages. The nursery. The schoolers. The teens – that's where it gets more militaristic. And those of age." He paused at the balcony where the man sat, head buried in his novel. His tanned fingers covered the title, the image on the cover, and the flash of sunlight on his watch face put more spots in my vision.

"We're not common thieves," Blake said. "We cross paths with the rarest population – the richest. We have to blend in, live like they live. If we're raised like soldiers, they'll see us coming."

"Who will?"

Blake veered away from the building and crunched on to an area of villas made of white stone. "These are the office blocks. You'll have one-to-one sessions here with Dakota, amongst others. Field practice takes place at the range." He jabbed a thumb over his shoulder before opening one of the doors and going inside.

An ornate desk with a high-backed chair stood before two patio doors that overlooked a small garden and pond. Petals curled backwards, and a sweet scent overpowered the air. Nothing like the bread. Was there a canteen here? Anywhere I could eat? I perched on the desk, legs trembling.

"I need food."

"Niagra will deal with that." Blake tapped his briefcase. "This is where I leave you. I recommend resting when you can. Things won't get easier." And he strolled away, as calm and collected as though he hadn't just delivered a captive girl to a deadly island.

18

If there was ever a perfect time to escape, now was it. Here I was, alone in this office, unguarded – and weak with hunger. And lost. And surrounded by lethal snakes on an island too far from land to ever swim.

Right. The perfect time.

Time ticked by, swinging from the pendulum of a grandfather clock near the desk. I'd never seen one before – not in real life. The clock must've been as tall as me and smelled earthy, woody.

"You're the new girl." The man from the balcony emerged, skin glistening in sweat, and even though he wore a top – black, which was crazy considering the heat – every muscle showed through. He leaned against the doorframe, smirking.

I gripped the edge of the desk. "You're Niagra?"

He laughed, a pleasant sort of sound. "Goodness, no. I'm Niall."

"Oh." I tugged my dress towards my knees – a mistake. It pulled his attention to my legs. "You're training?" I asked.

"You could say that." When he finally looked up, there was something in his eyes, in the tilt of his head and the pinch of his lips that set my skin crawling.

A golden name plate rested on the otherwise empty desk, the name 'Niagra B. Storm' engraved into it. The room amplified the passing seconds on the clock, and Niall's gaze prickled my cheeks.

I clamped my hands in front of me. Tugged the hem again. "Do you have to stare at me?"

He smiled.

The clock ticked on.

"What's the B stand for?" I pointed at the name plate. Anything to shift his attention off me.

Niall shrugged. "Bloodthirsty."

I shivered. "What?"

"Well, no one knows for sure, but it fits."

"How do you figure?"

"'Cause of what he did." Niall approached the desk. Strands of grey threaded his hair despite his young appearance. "See, clientele were in the market for organs, and Niagra collected them. Not the musical kind, if you catch my drift." He leaned on the desk, an arm either side of me. The scent of sweat mingled with deodorant overwhelmed the earthy tone of the clock.

I leaned away from him, straining not to fall onto the desk.

"He was good at that," Niall said. "Good at finding the right victims. The ones no one would miss."

I pushed a hand on his chest, and thankfully, he pulled away and propped his hands on his hips.

"He was an interesting one, was Niagra," he said. "Thought the surgical tools got in the way. Preferred to use his hands." And he smiled so wide that his teeth seemed to leach the colour from his irises.

And any strength in my face. "You can't be serious."

"They were dying anyway. What difference does it make?"

My chest constricted. Who were these people? Was I really supposed to train with them? Become one of them? I couldn't. Not ever. Which meant I couldn't save Lia. What could I do?

"See for yourself." Niall nodded to a photo on the wall showing an elderly, greying man. Wrinkles framed cold eyes. Laughter lines, Mum would call them. Niagra didn't look like he'd laughed in his life. He glared out from the image, his hands tainted red. "See his hands?" Niall asked.

"The stains?"

"How do you think he got them?"

I swallowed. "Chemicals?"

"Blood. Dip your hands in enough, it'll never come off."

I backed around the desk, hiding my legs behind it, putting as much distance between him and me as possible. "You're crazy."

He shrugged. "Look, I'm just saying, don't get on the wrong side of Niagra." He lifted eyebrow. "Not standing on his side of the desk would be a good start."

He'd noticed. Of course, he'd noticed. I'd hardly been subtle.

Footsteps crunched, and Niagra came in – same suit, same red hands, same laughterless eyes as in the photo. He carried a folder with 'NightLock' scrawled in black ink on the top corner, and he limped somewhat, shoulders hunched. "Niall," he said. "There a problem?"

German. That was my first thought. It was trace, but his accent held the sleek tones of a German speaking English. But there was something else. Something sharper. Something I couldn't quite place.

"No problem, Professor. Just passing by."

"Better get back to work, then."

Niall winked at me and jogged away, and once again I was left alone with a stranger – a murderer – and truth or not, my chest pounded like my heart might burst through it.

19

Niagra limped around the desk, pointing with the file at the chairless side. "That's where you stand."

I sidestepped to where he pointed, clenching my fists at another wave of stabbing hunger.

Niagra sat down. He reminded me of an old photo, the colours faded with time. Especially his eyes. They held a pale shade of grey and a harsh demeanour that could only belong to a killer. I swallowed. I never should've listened to Niall.

"I trust you had a safe journey," he said.

I shrugged. It'd been safe enough. Not for Lia, though. I pinched my knucklebone. Where was she now? Was she okay? Her attacker had hit her hard. Had he made her bleed? Given her a black eye?

Niagra pursed his lips. "You're worried about Amelia."

"Blake took her."

"So I heard." He clasped his hands on the desk. "You bear the choice of how to act, but not the choice of consequences. Your mother's abduction ensures your co-operation."

"Mother?" He meant sister, surely?

Niagra reached into a drawer and produced an iPad. On it, was the image of a hospital room. Or a cell. Bars covered the windows. A single bed held a sleeping woman with wires connecting her to a monitor. He zoomed in.

Mum. That was Mum.

My knees locked. "What is this?"

"Potential retribution, should you step out of line. It's unfortunate your sister escaped. But not for long, I think."

Lia escaped? How? There were three against her. Had a neighbour helped? Police? It didn't matter. Lia was free. They couldn't hurt her.

Niagra snapped the drawer shut, and my excitement deflated.

No, they couldn't hurt Lia anymore. But they'd taken Mum. After everything I'd done to save her, she'd ended up in more danger.

"Let Mum go," I said. "The agreement was that she'd be safe."

"The agreement," he said, "was for a kidney. She got that." He lowered his head, and shadow fell on his nose, highlighting its crookedness. He must've broken it once. Or twice. Hopefully from one of his victims fighting back.

"Down to business." Niagra adjusted his nameplate – only a millimetre. "Blake explained the dangers of the island?"

"Most of them."

He blinked. "Most?"

"He didn't tell me about you." The alleged cold-blooded killer who'd stained his hands with blood. The same killer who'd have Mum killed if I wasn't careful.

Niagra barked a chuckle. "Every soul here is dangerous. Aside from you." His amusement sobered as fast as it'd come, and his eyes flashed. Or maybe that was the sun suddenly streaking through the door. "Not to worry, though. We'll soon fix that."

Fix what? My innocence? That wasn't a weakness.

"Now," he said, "you'll be shown to your quarters and the dining room. Feel free to rest and explore this morning. Your schedule begins after lunch. Any questions?"

Plenty. Not that Blake answered any. Why would Niagra be any different? "Do you expect me to kill?"

"Why wouldn't we?"

"I'm not a killer."

"Labels." He tutted. "You're a member of Venom now. You'll meet all the requirements."

"What requirements?"

He tucked his hands beneath his chin, studying me.

"It doesn't make sense," I said. "Why take me? I have nothing you want."

"Nothing, you say?" He rubbed his nose, aggravating his wrinkles. "Tell me, how did you know the first plane-landing wasn't in Brazil? Or that your mother was in room eight?"

"How do you … They were guesses." He couldn't know about that. We'd been alone, Lia and I. And the nurse had been at the desk, but that was it. And sure, Blake could've told Niagra about my guess on the plane. Or maybe the aircraft was bugged. Maybe the woman from the screen had been watching the whole time.

"Interesting guesses," Niagra said. "You seemed quite confident at the time."

"So, what? You picked me for a few guesses?" I'd already met Blake by then. Already made the deal. There was more to this.

"We brought you here because you have a habit of knowing things you aren't supposed to know."

What kind of answer was that? "I don't understand."

"I don't expect you do, but that's all I'll tell you for now. I suggest you go outside. Breakfast won't be served all day."

20

Sunlight flooded the path outside Niagra's villa, swimming in the scent of cooking sausages, bacon and bread. My stomach cramped.

Puzzling over Niagra's statement did nothing. *Knowing things I shouldn't.* Like what? Before I'd met Blake, the only details I knew were the daily office schedules, but Lia was predictable. Everyone knew what she'd plan.

Well, they would've done if they'd known her as well as I.

"Sally, right?" The speaker must've been a couple years older than me, and wasn't half as tanned as Niall. He pushed off the wall of the villa and strolled over, moving like a model on the catwalk. He looked like one, too: strong jaw, hair styled to the side with just the right amount of height, and a build as chiselled as Niall's. It wasn't hard to imagine the chest beneath his t-shirt, snug as it was.

But his eyes stood out the most. They were silver-blue, ringed by a line so dark and thick that they could've been plucked from the richest depths of space. "I'm Yakov," he said. "I'll show you around, okay?" I caught a whiff of sweat and a woody aftershave. Like the Silverstone Forest Park I'd visited once.

"You're Russian," I said.

"Accent gave it away?"

I nodded. "And the name."

Yakov's slightly crooked smile brought out a dimple on his left side. "No point hiding the accent here. Shall we?"

I fell into step beside him – and almost fell in the stupid stilettos. "You can hide your accent?"

"Naturally. I speak twelve languages and can pass off their accents and dialects."

Twelve? At his age? That was either a huge exaggeration or a downright lie. "How long have you been with Venom?"

"A while. I was young when they took me in."

Weird. He said it like they'd done him a favour. Took him in. Like I'd ever believe Venom was the caring type. "What happened? Why'd they choose you?"

He pointed ahead at the field with the wooden blocks. "You'll have seen the range when you arrived."

Three children stood beneath the metal shelves lining the far end. They couldn't have been older than eleven, but each wore a set of earmuffs, and each held a gun. One fired his, and a crack pierced the air.

"Aren't they being supervised?" I asked. "They're just children." Three children. That was it. *Children.* Alone with guns.

"The earlier they learn, the better they become," Yakov said.

"But they're using guns. Real guns. With real ammunition. What if someone gets shot?"

Another fired her weapon, and the paper hooked opposite her rattled.

"They're sensible enough," Yakov said.

Sensible, yes. And training to kill.

Yakov fixed me with interest. "They've been trained since age four. They know what they're doing."

That's what worried me.

A few more paths took us to the building with the balconies. A courtyard lay before it spilling water from a marble fountain – the kind you'd find in the historic cities of Italy. The scent of bacon was strong here, and I clutched my stomach again. "Any chance of some food?"

Yakov stepped between the pillars guarding the entrance into a foyer with polished tiles. Mirrors cast rectangles of light on the floor, and vases rested on single podiums. Nothing like Dad's vase though. These were still intact. "Your quarters are here," Yakov said. "The canteen is there." He headed to a room on our right. "You're expected, so they'll have your meal ready."

"What do you mean?" Wouldn't I get to choose my own breakfast?

Tableclothed tables filled the dining room, and the place was dotted with pillars, like the architect decided without them the building would collapse. Floor-to-ceiling windows overlooked the courtyard, where a few people walked past the fountain.

About quarter of the canteen was occupied with people aged between eighteen and thirty. A few sat together in groups of two or three. The rest sat alone, and quiet filtered through the room until the urge to whisper dominated.

Yakov headed straight for a counter. Any plates or platters there held nothing but crumbs or grease. Were we too late? I dug my nail into my thumb and struggled not to slip in the heels. I couldn't go without breakfast. I just couldn't.

I needn't have worried. Beyond the counter lay a kitchen brimming with buns, sausages, bacon and ham. There were eggs, too, and fruit of every kind. Melons, bananas, apples, papaya, mango, the works. By the wall stood jugs of milk, water, and fruit juice. No cereal, but so what? I'd have eaten a rack of ribs and cheesecake for breakfast with how much my gut cramped.

A burly chef in kitchen whites and hat waddled out and lay two plates in front of us. He pushed one to me: two fried eggs on seeded toast with avocado. Yakov had the same as mine but with three sausages.

"Any chance of some sausage?" I flipped the avocado off the eggs. I hated avocado like I hated the stilettos. I could take the heels off again. The tiles would be lovely and cool on my sore feet. Relieving. Blake wasn't here to stop me.

The chef shuffled back to the kitchen and returned a moment later with several slices of avocado. He dropped them on the eggs.

"Oh." Not an English speaker? "I meant sausages." I pointed at Yakov's.

The chef just grinned, flashing yellowed teeth and a faint scent of smoke.

Yakov collected our food and nudged me to a nearby table. "Marcel's been here longer than I. He's the best chef in the seven quarters."

Seven quarters? What was that? I wrinkled my nose at the avocado and pressed my toes against the tiles when I sat down. Cool. Just as I'd guessed. "Doesn't he speak English?"

"Oh, he does," Yakov said. "What he lacks in kindness, he makes up for with the finest food."

"I hate avocado."

"He knows." He plucked a knife and fork from a pot on the table and dug into his meal.

What didn't Venom know about me?

"Marcel plans everyone's meals," Yakov said. "Each is different depending on the BMI and circumstances of the student. It's designed to give just what we need to gain the greatest energy and growth."

"I want sausage."

"You don't need it." He popped a piece in his mouth. Three. He had three sausages. He could easily give one to me.

Right. Because that would happen. Me and the training criminal, sharing meat. I sighed.

Another man pulled out the chair beside me and sat down with a plate full of fruit. "Yakov. Who's the newbie?" He sat tall, blond-haired, clean-shaven, and with the poise of a ballerina. He stabbed a fork into some melon.

"Sally, this is Nick," Yakov said. "Nick, Sally."

Nick nodded. "Welcome."

"And that's Joe," Yakov said, nodding at a third, far larger man who popped his plate beside mine – plate being an understatement. It was more like a platter, brimming with croissants, scrambled eggs, bacon, beans, and at least four sausages.

How was that fair?

He dragged a chair from the next table, screeching the legs across the tiles, and grabbed my hand in a shake. His freckled fingers swallowed mine, each one as chubby as his sausages, and he smelled remarkably like the meat crammed into his meal. "Joe," he said. "Always good to meet a newbie." He slid a piece of toast from under his bacon and took a bite.

I took a bite of my own – my much thinner, not even buttered slice. The slimy taste of avocado touched my tongue, and I scowled at the smushed piece on the crust before devouring the thing anyway. "What do I have to do to get a meal like that?" I jabbed my thumb at Joe's plate.

The men laughed and dug into their food. I finished mine too quickly – and didn't enjoy any of it. The few pieces of avocado that'd mixed with the egg ruined the taste and slimed the meal up like I'd eaten frogspawn. Maybe Joe wouldn't finish his.

"How long you here?" Joe asked Yakov.

"A while." He'd cleared most of his food, and nodded at the horrid chef who handed him a glass of orange. Nick got orange, too. Milk for Joe.

Water for me.

"I'd love some milk," I said.

Marcel grimaced and walked away. He never brought the milk out.

Nick sat a good head taller than Yakov. Long limbs, Lia would say. The perfect ballet body. "You having a break?"

The Russian sliced into his egg, coating his plate with yolk. "Not exactly. I'm on assignment."

"Wait," I said, "you're not training?"

Nick smiled. "We graduated years ago."

"The island is sometimes used as a rest place between

assignments," Joe said. His freckled cheeks bulged like a chipmunk's. It was a wonder he could get any words through the food. "It's fun to meet the newbies."

"Do you get new people a lot?" I asked.

"Babies, mostly," Nick said. "Adults are rare. It takes someone real skilled to join Venom outside of childhood."

21

"This is mine?" I asked.

Yakov had shown me to an apartment bigger than the entire level of home, complete with a queen-size bed, huge wardrobe, sofa and wicker chair, and a glass table with vase and flowers. A floor-length mirror and dressing table stood beside a bathroom with a curved bath, two sinks, multiple cupboards and gleaming floor tiles. And don't get me started on the balcony.

"No barracks?" I asked. Blake had said something about militaristic training. Why hadn't he put me there? Not that I was complaining.

"You won't be living harshly," Yakov said. "Venom want you fitting in with royalty."

Did they? "Why? What do they want with me?"

Yakov nodded at the table. "Your schedule's there. I'll teach your first lesson. It's at one."

I didn't want a lesson. Didn't want to be here at all. I just wanted to go home. Memories of Mum in that cell cut through my awe of the apartment. How could I stay here in all this luxury when she was a prisoner in … who knew what? Air conditioning whirred from a ceiling vent, chilling my arms. I rubbed them.

Yakov turned a dial on the wall, and the cold air faded. "You should rest. Clean up. Change."

I flinched. Did I still smell?

"You'll find all you need in the wardrobe," he said. "I'll be sparring with Nick. If you'd like, come find us."

Not likely.

The door swung shut behind him, and every moment of the day rammed on me like a thunderstorm. I sank to my knees and let it all out. Ugly crying. That's what Lia would've called it. The kind that drips off my chin and summons enough snot to fill a third world country.

I'd wanted a new job. Wanted to leave Mum and Lia. I was going to travel. See the world. Do things I'd never imagined.

I'd got all of that. Even a suite for a millionaire.

And I wanted none of it. Ironic, wasn't it? Was that why Blake picked me? Had I accidently made him think this was right for me? I sniffed. Dark steaks marked the dress from my outburst. I tugged it over my head and kicked off the heels. Horrid things. What purpose did clothes like that have other than to humiliate? There were my hairy legs, cold on the tiles, having been shown to every person I'd passed.

My house had been bugged. Maybe the plane. Was the room?

I grabbed the bedsheet and wrapped myself in it, searching the place for cameras. Without clothes, my body odour wafted out again, stronger than on the plane. The grime and sweat of the journey practically crawled over my skin. The scratches from the accident marked my arms, my shoulder, but the cut on my wrist extended longer than them all.

I used the sheet to wipe my face dry. Crying would do nothing. It only made my head hurt, and no doubt gave Venom the satisfaction. Criminals or not, professionals or not, I wouldn't let them win. Mum may have kept me sheltered all my life, but I was clever. Smart. I'd find a way out of this, one way or another.

22

13:00. Shooting.

Was that what Lia faced? A manhunt with guns? Maybe she'd been put in witness protection or whatever the equivalent was for being wanted by criminals. If I was out there, I could fight the people hunting her. Stop them with my own guns.

Water dripped from my hair on to the schedule. I smeared the droplets across the page and squeezed my hair with the towel draped over my shoulders.

14:00. Stamina.

If it was anything like descending a stone staircase in stilettos, I didn't want to know. Not that I had a choice.

Or rather, I did. I had a plan.

This place had everything. A wardrobe full of clothes – all my size, go figure. Between tops, leggings, workout pants and vests, I had the pick of the lot. Not to mention nightgowns, shoes, and drawers full of undergarments, most of which I'd never touch.

A fully stocked bathroom with every product ever needed – cleaning and sanitary – now had me smelling fresh and citrusy, but I'd neglected the electricals. Who needed a hairdryer in this heat? The morning temperature slipped in through the open balcony doors, dry and tasting of florals. I had grabbed a band, though, and took the chance to tie my hair back.

It didn't matter what Venom thought appropriate for a shooting session. I'd gone with white t-shirt and black bottoms – what I wouldn't do for a pair of shorts – and trainers. They'd do.

A box on the dressing table lay propped open and ignored. From the top peeked mascara, foundation, eyeliner, and other make-up in pink and neutral shades. No doubt Venom would expect me to use them eventually, if it was anything like Blake.

I took a long breath. What had I learned?

Escape wasn't happening. Not stuck here on the island.

And Venom thought they had me.

What harm would it do if I let them think that? The reluctant teenage criminal-in-training. I'd finish their training. Get off the island. And I'd free Mum, save Lia, and take down anyone who stood in my way.

My core fluttered. The plan was simple. Except these were professionals. Ruthless killers-to-be. I wouldn't be that. Whatever they wanted, I wouldn't let them have it, and they'd have wasted their time bugging the house. Wasted their time checking my travel history and my clothes size and finding a donor for Mum. How'd they even know to find a donor? They couldn't have predicted the accident.

Unless they'd caused it.

What a stupid thought. It wasn't possible to plan something like that, to have damaged Mum's kidney without accidently killing her. Or me.

Like it mattered. I'd been stuck in my thoughts long enough. Time to act. I dropped the towel on the bed, dumped the dress and stilettos in the bin, and returned to the courtyard.

So this was Snake Island. How'd Venom build a base like this without someone seeing? Weren't there satellites watching the place? Wouldn't a government somewhere have discovered their secret? Sunlight flooded the courtyard, so clearly nothing was hiding us. A few branches at night, a quick SOS sign by the fountain – someone would see it. Wouldn't they?

"Sally, right?" Joe crunched over the gravel. Muscles bulged beneath his top, almost bursting through his sleeves. He frowned, looked me up and down. "How'd you end up here?"

"Oh. That's a long story." And not one I wanted to get into with a fully-fledged assassin or whatever he was.

"You don't seem the Venom sort," he said.

No kidding. I shrugged. "When life gives you lemons …" Make a plan and figure out how to take your enemies down. It was weird. Enemies. I'd barely had a friend before, let alone an enemy. Let alone a whole island of them!

Joe nodded – one of those that said *I'm utterly unconvinced.* "So, where you going?"

I didn't know. What was I doing? Complete my training, find Mum, save Lia. That was the plan. How was wandering the place going to help with that?

Joe shifted his stance, awaiting my answer.

"Yakov said something about sparring with Nick." The ballet man. If he moved anything like a dancer, Yakov wouldn't stand a chance.

"I'm heading that way." Joe beckoned and started down one of the paths. "Come on."

I fell into step beside him. Water dripped from my ponytail onto my back – strangely cool on my top. Not that I'd complain. The air had grown hotter since Yakov brought me in. My hair would dry in no time.

The path led to a low, rock wall that ringed a space covered in mats. Nick knelt on them, holding Yakov in a headlock. The Russian twisted, flipped Nick over his head, and pinned him to the ground. Yakov chuckled and let him go.

"All good?" Nick asked, shifting his attention to us.

Joe shrugged and sat on one of the three benches that looked in on the mats. "Can't complain."

Yakov grasped Nick, pulled him to his feet, and struck out.

Nick blocked and returned with a strike of his own, forcing Yakov to twist away, and when Yakov spoke in an unfamiliar tongue, Nick answered in kind.

I sat next to Joe. "They're speaking Russian, right?"

"Sure are." He rested his arm on the bench behind me, wafting the smell of those sausages.

My stomach grumbled. "Can you understand them?"

"Sure can."

Nick jumped and kicked at Yakov, only to have him block it with ease. They were sparring a dance, one movement leading smoothly into the next. Neither hit the other. Neither gained ground. Nick spoke again, and they both looked at me. So did Joe.

"What're they saying?"

"They're talking about you," Joe said.

I tugged my damp hair. It wasn't dripping anymore, but it frizzed slightly in the heat. "What about me?"

"If they wanted you to know, they'd speak English." Joe rubbed his nose, eyes fixed on the men.

My insides cringed. "Maybe I'll learn Russian while I'm here."

"They'll just switch to Italian."

I stared at him. I should've expected the coldness. After Blake and the woman on the screen, these people weren't going to be—

He smiled.

"You're teasing me."

He laughed. "You need to lighten up."

Under the circumstances? How was I supposed to do that? "I didn't think Venom had a sense of humour."

"True." He inclined his head. "This is a focused organisation, but it's important to have fun. Take me and Nick. We're a good team. We have some laughs."

"You work together?"

The men continued to spar, their movements perfectly in synch.

"For the most part of a decade," Joe said. "Most get partners. Another set of eyes and ears as it were. Not that we're friends, so much." He leaned back a little, crossed his foot over his knee. "If they ordered us to separate, we would."

"And that wouldn't bother you?"

"Not in the slightest. There are no attachments in Venom."

I studied him for signs of joking, struggling to read his thoughts. No attachments. How could he be okay with that? Wasn't he lonely? Frightened? Anyone could turn on him at any moment. That was no way to live.

Yakov blocked a strike and caught Nick in an armlock. Nick twisted out of it and rolled across the mat.

"Who's Yakov's partner?"

"Doesn't have one," Joe said.

"Why not?"

Joe's brow furrowed, and something in his eyes darkened and brought a chill to the air. "Because he's the most dangerous. Partners slow him down, and Venom like their recruits … effective."

Was that jealously? Or contempt?

Nick grabbed Yakov, pulling him off balance. Yakov countered and knocked him to the mat. They laughed.

He didn't look all that dangerous. If anything, he looked normal. A couple years older than me. How deadly could he be?

23

As unsettling as Niall's story about Niagra's stained hands had been, it was nothing compared to him handing a child a knife. Not a butter knife, no. A serrated blade that must've extended from my wrist to elbow, hilt included. The girl must've been seven-years-old. Seven!

She pursed her lips. Adjusted her grip on the blade. And threw it at a target.

"This is the armoury." Yakov opened a door at the back of the range and nudged me inside.

I shivered and tugged my arms to my chest, rubbing away the chill.

Guns covered the walls: hand guns, pistols, rifles, you name it. And was that a rocket launcher?

Yakov picked a gun off a table, reassembled it, and popped it on an empty shelf. The entire length of one wall was covered with shelves and cabinets, cluttered with knives, boxes of ammunition, and a couple of swords. Three barrels stood against the far side, leaking a sharp scent of … I wasn't sure what. Gunpowder?

I wrinkled my nose and stepped closer to a silver-bodied pistol with a wooden slab down its handle.

"You like that?" Yakov picked it up. "This is a Kimber 1911 9mm pistol. Easy to use. Compact. They come in three frames:

steel – this one – stainless steel, and aluminium." He assembled the pieces. "I prefer the steel, but it's heavier than aluminium. This weighs thirty-eight ounces. The aluminium weighs twenty-eight. Here." He handed the gun to me.

My hand dropped a little. "Oh, it's heavy."

His lips twitched, and he rubbed his nose like he was holding back a smile.

I put the gun down. "Have you used all these?"

"We're trained with everything. The more we know, the better prepared we are. After training, we choose our own weapon. Our signature, if you like."

Signature? Like a serial killer's card? I took a step back.

He reached behind him and pulled a white gun from his waistband. "This is my choice: an improved model of a Beretta 90-TWO pistol. It's lighter than the Kimber. Shots can be taken one after the other rather than reloading first. It holds fifteen rounds, more than necessary for our requirements, but there you are. There are more Berettas over there." He pointed to a section where black guns hung, almost identical to his.

"Yours is white."

"I had mine personalised." He tucked his gun away and plucked a Beretta from the wall. "This is an easy weapon to start with." He took a box of bullets, some earplugs and a piece of card with black rings from a cabinet.

I rubbed my head, mind buzzing. "There're so many weapons." It'd take years to master them all. Years Mum and Lia didn't have.

"I know it's overwhelming now," Yakov said. "But it'll become second nature eventually." He picked up two disks about the size of a two-pence-piece. "Take these, for instance. Put enough around a building, and they'll trigger a chain reaction big enough to take the whole place down." He replaced them with a smile. "Not these ones, though. These are blanks. Don't want any accidents."

Accidents. Right. More like don't want me trying anything. Not that I would. Not while they had Mum. "What're those?" I pointed at a different set of disks, a little smaller than my thumbnail.

"Bugs. The surveillance team use them. Venom have two groups. The prep people – surveillance, weapons, equipment, transport – and the action people. They're the ones who carry out assignments."

Prep sounded preferable. I wouldn't have to kill. "Which are you?"

"Action, definitely. I hate the prep. Painfully boring."

Not killing people was boring? *Of all of us, he's the most dangerous. Partners slow him down.*

I touched the table to steady myself.

"Prep is important, though," Yakov said. "Understand a place's security, and half the work is done for you. Ready for your first session?"

Not a bit. "I guess."

Back outside, I flexed my fingers in the heat. Bees buzzed around a flowering bush that smelled of jasmine.

Yakov walked past the few shooters practising on the range to an empty section of metal shelving about halfway down. "These are the benches." He put the gun, earplugs, and ammunition on the shelf. Across the field stood blocks – some rectangular, others shaped like people. Yakov nodded at the other shooters who waited while he attached the target sheet to the block opposite us.

"Right," he said when he got back and picked up the Beretta. "This button releases the magazine. Load the bullets like this. Pop the mag in. Release the safety catch. Easy." He pulled out the magazine and emptied the bullets. "Your turn."

Slowly, I copied him while he explained again, but I hesitated to press the catch. No safety meant I could shoot someone. *Kill* someone.

Yakov placed his hands over mine, and pushed my finger against the button. His breath brushed my ear. "Release the safety."

I shivered.

"Adjust your grip." He moved my hand. "Now, aim."

My target stood a good twenty metres away. How was I supposed to hit that?

Yakov stepped back, leaving me suddenly cold. "Fire."

I pulled the trigger. The gun cracked and kicked up, and I let out an involuntary scream.

Yakov laughed – one of those contagious laughs where you couldn't help but join in – and took the gun. "When you shoot, prepare for the kick. Hold the barrel straight, or you'll miss your mark again."

"I missed?" I'd had the little black bullseye in front of the barrel when I shot.

"You did this time." He pointed above to where my target showed on a screen. I hadn't even hit the edge of the card.

My cheeks burned. Shooting was hard.

Niall dropped a rifle two spaces down from us. "You're starting her too difficult, Yakov. Put her on the schooler's blocks." He nodded to where the girl had thrown that knife. Her block stood far closer than mine – maybe twenty feet from where she'd been.

"Ignore him," Yakov said.

Niall loaded his rifle and fired three consecutive shots at his own target. It stood so far across the field, it almost touched the bricks on the other side.

I shifted to see his screen. He'd pierced his target in three places, millimetres from the centre. Great. I had a long way to go before they'd let me out of here.

Yakov tugged me back to him and lay the gun on the bench. "Protect your ears." He pointed at the ear plugs. "And try again."

24

My breaths came quick and sharp, inhaling the sweet scent of soil and leaves. Gravel crunched beneath me. I leapt over a fallen trunk and plunged deeper into the woodland. A stitch stabbed at my side, but I couldn't stop. Not here. Not now.

The glass barrier glinted beside me.

"Come on," Yakov said. "Faster." He ran a little way ahead – more a jog than a run. He barely sweated, the jerk. Stamina was an essential part of training, he'd said. It followed a four-mile track spanning the safe zone's perimeter. The majority had proved to be gravel or dirt, but a section of mud had splattered my legs until I looked like the bottom half of the yeti's cousin. In the growing darkness, the muck looked almost black, and I tugged on the top now sticking to my skin, desperate for a shower.

I stamped over loose branches, caught my ankle on one, and hit the ground hard. A sharp piece of stick scratched my cheek. My breath caught in my throat, and I coughed on dirt.

I couldn't do it. I couldn't run four miles. It was too long. Too hard.

Something moved at the barrier, and my whole body prickled. A snake with golden scales pressed on the glass, testing for weaknesses like it could smell my sweat.

I stared at it.

It stared back, eyes unblinking.

Poison inside. Poison out. How'd I get in to this? What could people like these possibly want with me?

Yakov hauled me up by the arm. "Shake it off." He wasn't even out of breath.

Blood oozed from a stinging graze on my ankle.

The serpent rose higher, pushing the glass.

Yakov shook me. "Never mind the snake. Keep on."

"I need a break."

"No breaks. Go." He pushed me – not enough to make me fall but enough to make me move. "Faster."

"I can't."

"Yes, you can." He pushed me again. "Faster."

We passed behind the building with the balconies. My shower was in there. My bed. Heaviness ached my eyes. The path turned, delivering us to the courtyard. Water spilled from the tip of the fountain, urging me to jump right in.

Yakov stopped. "We'll finish here today."

Oh, thank goodness. I collapsed beside the fountain, chest heaving. My face burned, and my hand inched towards the water.

"You ran two miles," Yakov said.

"That's it?" That couldn't have been it. I'd been running for hours.

Yakov frowned at a stopwatch. "Forty minutes."

No way. It'd been longer than that. An eternity, at least. I squinted at him. "Is that bad?"

"Most have done the whole track by now."

"The whole track? In *forty* minutes?" I straightened up to a wave of backache. "That's not possible."

"Anything is possible." He tucked the watch in his pocket. "Go shower. Sleep. I want you back at five o'clock."

I jolted. "In the morning?"

"That's a sleep in."

I half-laughed. "You're kidding." Didn't anyone sleep here? Even now, my head pounded and tremors flooded my muscles.

Dirt darkened the scratches from the accident. I'd barely climbed out of the wreckage, and here I was training to run four miles. The whole situation was messed up. I pinched the bridge of my nose, willing my headache to ease.

Yakov pulled me up. "We rise early to be productive. You'll adjust to it. But for now, go see Chef Marcel. He'll get you some meds."

25

The run two days later was worse. Much worse. My muscles seized with every step. Yakov jogged beside me, but I kept falling behind. My breath rasped. My sides stung. The early dawn tinged the sky pink and cast streaks of golden light through the leaves, and I couldn't enjoy any of it.

When we finally reached the courtyard, he pulled out the stopwatch while I sprawled on the edge of the fountain and let my hands dip into the pool. Every breath hurt.

"Fifty-three minutes," Yakov said. "Longer than last time."

I bent over, resting my elbows on my knees. "My muscles are killing."

"Stretch through it." He stepped into a lunge. "The pain will fade."

"Easy for you to say. You don't even look tired."

He brushed a dusty patch from his shoulder. "That was a leisurely walk."

"Yes, well, we can't all be marathon runners." Their expectations would have me winning a medal at the Olympics – you know, if they weren't trying to make me as dangerous as Yakov. It was a strange truth. Here I was training with the deadliest man I'd ever met. Apparently. So, why did I feel safe with him?

"Come on." He bent over to stretch the back of his legs.

"Get up."

I scowled and copied him. My legs shook, struggling to hold me, and I flinched with a flash of cramp.

"Give it time," Yakov said. "You'll get there."

I didn't want to give it time. I wanted out. I finished the stretch and stood up with a groan. "I've got cramp."

Yakov knelt and rubbed the back of my legs, pressing hot fingers against my muscles.

I bit my tongue. How many people had he killed with those hands? The hands he used to ease my pain.

"Rest day tomorrow," he said. "Your muscles need time to adjust. We'll build distance over time. For now, go clean up. You've got Dakota next."

I nodded once and tromped to my room. Dakota. I'd had a friend with the same name once. It meant ally. Would the Dakota here live up to the meaning? I highly doubted it.

When I returned to the foyer fifteen minutes later, Yakov stood by the entrance with Nick and Joe. Joe waved a bread bun at me. "Morning. Sleep well?"

No. I stifled a yawn. "Well enough."

Nick stood a good head taller than Joe, his pale arms framed by a sleeveless top. "I hear you've started stamina," he said to me. "How you finding it?"

"Sucky." My legs stung. I'd hoped a hot shower would help, but my muscles had only seized up, and I'd had to stretch some more before I could walk down here.

Joe nodded. "I hated stamina at first. Took ages to get fast."

That was something.

He crammed the bun in his mouth, freckled cheeks bulging.

"How long does it take you to run the track?" I asked.

"Thirty-four."

"*Minutes?*" That wasn't possible. No way at all. Two miles had taken me forty. To do four miles in less than that, you'd have to be an Olympian. "How?"

"Oh, I see." Joe folded his arms, and something rustled in his pocket. Crisps? I could eat crisps. I could eat anything right now. A five a.m. run had hardly given time for breakfast. "You think I'm too fat to be fast," he said.

My cheeks burned. "No, I didn't mean—"

Joe knocked me on the back, and the men laughed. "Control your breathing. That helps with the sprint."

Yeah, because I can control breathing when my heart's trying to burst through my chest.

"Come on," Yakov said. "Time to meet Dakota."

All at once, Nick and Joe exchanged the sort of look that made my gut tighten and my throat constrict. The kind of look that was difficult to pin down. What was it? Wariness? Fear?

"What?" I asked. "Is Dakota that bad?"

Joe scratched his stubble. "He can be—shall we say—intense."

Yakov clamped a hand on my shoulder. "You're only having a chat."

Right. Except the last time I had a 'chat' with someone, Blake had started the reaction that landed me here. Yakov nudged me outside on aching feet.

He led me around the range to the white brick villas Blake had shown me. Yakov opened a door to a spacious office two doors down from Niagra's. That sweet scent dominated the air, drifting from Niagra's way. Jasmine. And something else. A floral scent I'd never quite smelled before.

Yakov pointed at two sunlit sofas. "Better wait there. Dakota will be along soon." The sofas sat opposite one another, directly in front of a large window. A desk filled the other half of the room, three times the size of the one from my office. It was thick, too. Thick and carved and varnished to a shine. And empty, except for a phone: the old kind that plugged in to the wall. My throat tightened. Did I dare? Certainly not with Yakov here, but if he left ...

Dad's shattered vase flashed in my memory.

Yakov rested his hand on the door frame, revealing a tuft of underarm hair and a whiff of woodiness. "You'll be next door after this. And then can you find your way back to the dining room?"

I nodded. Should be easy enough.

Shadow filled the doorway, and a man in his forties entered holding a clipboard. He wore a black suit and shirt – wasn't he sweltering? – and carried an air of confidence in his stance. Like everyone else I'd seen here, there wasn't an ounce of flab to him. He gestured to the sofas. "Take a seat." His accent was … middle-eastern? I couldn't tell. It held traces of I didn't know what. Something sharp and lilting and nothing like I'd ever heard before.

Yakov nodded at me and left us alone.

I dropped on a sofa – my legs had all but given up – and risked a glance at the phone.

Dakota sat opposite me, facing the window. "How are you?"

I swallowed. Exhausted. Homesick. Worried about Mum and Lia. "Fine."

"Liar."

I stiffened. Had I heard that right? I hadn't been called a liar since childhood.

He scribbled something on his clipboard. "Enjoying training?"

Not a bit. "It's been interesting."

"Liar."

My mouth turned dry. What was this? An interrogation? I could hardly open up like he was some therapist. He was one of them. One of Venom.

He watched me without emotion, studying me beneath dark eyelashes. Sunlight streamed through the window, casting spotlights in his eyes, washing out their colour. He licked his lips, and shadow fell on a pinch in his chin.

I fidgeted. "I don't—"

"You're not progressing," he said. "Why is that?"

This was only my third day. "I'm doing my best."

"Liar."

"I'm not lying." The tremble in my voice betrayed me.

He leaned forward, his words growing sharp. "Tell me the

truth."

I clasped my hands, squeezing my fingers. Behind him, a clock ticked on the wall, a blood-red needle flicking between roman numerals. What was wrong with him?

"What's holding you back?" he asked.

Seriously? Didn't he know they'd taken a shot at Lia? If I fought back now, they'd kill Mum. What was I supposed to say? "Nothing."

"Liar."

My cheeks burned. "It's a hard adjustment."

He slapped my hand.

I jolted back, rubbing my stinging skin.

"Stop fidgeting," he said. "It's a classic sign of deception."

My hand reddened, showing his finger marks.

He dropped the clipboard beside him and leaned back on the sofa, surveying me silently for a moment. "You're worried about your mother."

"You're holding her hostage."

He tilted his head.

"You have cameras in her cell." My voice cracked.

"That bothers you?" he asked.

Obviously. "Should it not?"

He tapped his forefinger against his knee, almost deliberating. The seconds ticked on, and he held my gaze, almost challenging me to look away.

I did.

"Do you know the problem with attachments, Sally?"

I blinked furiously. I wouldn't cry. Not here. Not in front of him.

"They cloud judgement," he said. "They prevent one's focusing on the job. You have attachments."

"She's my *mother*."

He pointed at me. "Attachments are dangerous. Attachments lead to mistakes." The silky tone of his voice rose the hairs on my arms. He traced a curling flourish on the arm of his sofa, trailing his thumb over the criss-cross pattern. "Do you know what Venom does to attachments, Sally?" His finger paused on the point of a thin line. "They eradicate them."

"No." They couldn't. I'd—

"Do your attachments need to be eradicated?"

The air grew thick. So thick. And hot. How was I supposed to breathe? Like the walls were closing in. Those fans in the ceiling – the slow revolving ones that did nothing to cool the air – they weren't even on. I needed air. Needed out.

Don't show your fear.

What difference would it make when they knew my weaknesses already? "I don't have attachments."

"Liar."

I fought to be still, to relax my fingers on my legs. "I'll work harder."

"Liar."

"I didn't even move!"

"It's not just body language that gives you away. It's the tone of your voice." He leaned closer. "The sweat on your brow." He pressed my forehead.

I balled my fists to avoid batting his hand away. My eyes stung. He knew the truth. And he wouldn't stop until I admitted it. But why? What was the point? "I never wanted to be here. I just want to go home."

He smiled, finally lowering his hand. "Now *that* is the first truth you've uttered. Tell me, have you considered calling your mother?" He nodded at the phone on the desk.

I swallowed. "No."

"Liar."

"I need to know she's okay. Let me call her. Just once. Then I'll really try." Because if I was going to get off this island, I had to try. I'd escape from Venom and protect my family. Somehow.

"Another truth," he said. "But what of your sister? Wouldn't you rather call her?"

And risk exposing her whereabouts? If Venom hadn't found her, I wasn't about to help them. It was safer this way. "I don't have her number. She only used the office phone." Another lie – one he was bound to notice. But I wouldn't give in.

His shoulders dropped. "I see."

Good. If he was disappointed, they mustn't have found her.

He studied me again, hands steepled at his pursed lips, his pen hanging between his palms. "Okay. Go ahead and call."

My pulse pounded in my ears. He would let me? Really? Blake never had. And these people could hardly be trusted. "Promise me Mum won't be harmed."

Dakota inclined his head. "Your mother will not be harmed because of this phone call."

I hesitated. Wasn't he a master of deception? If I did this and Mum was killed, I'd never forgive myself. I'd never forgive Venom.

"I'm a man of my word," he said.

"I don't believe you."

He nodded. "Good. You're learning. But in this instance, I speak the truth. You may call your mother without repercussions."

I didn't move. He was convincing, I'd give him that. But if he was lying, if they hurt Mum—

"Make your decision quickly," he said. "I will not offer again."

Too good to be true. But the only chance I'd get. I dashed to the phone and dialled Mum's number with trembling fingers.

"On loudspeaker," Dakota ordered.

I obeyed. What did loudspeaker matter when I could speak to Mum, when I could tell her I was safe? Ish.

He approached the desk, setting my teeth on edge.

Ringing buzzed, once, twice, three times. "Sally?" Mum's voice. Weak, yes, but undoubtedly hers.

Dakota jabbed the disconnect button.

My core jolted, and my fingers tightened on the receiver. The clock's ticking clashed with my pounding pulse. "Why did you—"

"I said you could *call* her," Dakota said. "I never said you could converse."

Why, the lying—

"You heard her voice," he said. "She's fine. Time to work."

26

I entered the next villa an hour later with a numb weight in my gut. Dakota had called me a liar so many times, the word bounced around my head and echoed in my ears.

Several dressing tables with cushioned stools covered the area around the edge of this office. Boxes of makeup covered several of them. Wardrobes lined part of the wall, and mirrors bounced my pale, fuzzy-haired reflection back at me.

Niall, the creep who'd told me about Niagra's stained hands, stood beside one of the desks, his tanned skin even darker in the shadows. He gathered papers into a pile and smirked at me. "All right?"

No. "Fine."

"Liar."

Heat travelled down my arms. "Don't start. I've had enough of that with Dakota."

On the wall behind him hung a photo of the devil woman from the plane.

Niall followed my gaze. "Met her yet?"

"Not in person." And I never wanted to. I sidestepped, putting a stool between us.

His gaze flitted to it, and his eyebrows lifted. "What do you think of her?"

"She's as likeable as the rest of you."

He chuckled, scooping paper into his hands. Was he training, too? Yakov wasn't. Neither were Joe and Nick. How many others were on break between assignments? How many were actually training?

"She's Backer," Niall said. "The standing Head of Venom."

So, she would know why Blake took me – *me*, a useless, unwilling recruit to their madness. All because I knew … what? I'd guessed a few things right. That didn't make me superhuman. I surveyed the photo, wondering if her heart was as black as her eyes. "I didn't know Venom had a leader." Although it made sense. Someone had to be calling the shots.

Niall propped his free fist on his hip. "Every organisation has one. Her grandfather led Venom before she left golden lanceheads in his bed."

I shivered, picturing the snakes surrounding the training grounds. "You're saying she killed her grandfather?"

He shrugged. "No one leaves Venom. Unless they die."

Funny how the stool didn't feel safe anymore. All these killers, all these monsters, no one here cared about life. Didn't it bother them? If Backer had killed her grandfather, didn't it plague her dreams? Didn't it haunt every waking moment?

No, this had to be another of Niall's stories. "Aren't lanceheads the snakes on this island?"

Niall nodded.

"Then, how did she—"

"Not get bitten?" Niall leaned on his pile, eyes glinting. "There's a rumour she can tame them. That she's immune to their venom. Did you know Backer can draw her weapon so quickly, you don't know she's shot you till you're dead?"

She sounded like the devil. Or his wife. "Do you have a story for everyone?"

"Absolutely." He flashed brilliant teeth. "Though not all of them are as fascinating as hers."

27

"Again." Mayra tossed me another wipe and snatched the eyeliner from my hand. "A *straight* line. You keep wobbling like that, and you'll end up with the hookers."

"I'm trying," I said. There was nothing wrong with my application. At least, not to me. But Mayra wanted perfection.

"A sloppy lady is no lady at all," she said. "Now, again."

I wiped the liner away, gritting my teeth. I'd redone it so many times, my eye stung. "I don't see why this is relevant."

Mayra threw her hands in the air and muttered something in French. "You are a lady." She pinched her forefinger and thumb together in the 'okay' sign. "A lady does not splonge about in baggy clothes and pale faces."

Splonge? Was that even a word?

"A lady," she said, "is the epitome of grace and beauty. She carries herself with class whether at a ball, in her bedroom or when taking a life." And as though to prove her point, she glided in a wide circle, never teetering despite her ugly stilettos. But when she laid eyes on me again, not even her long lashes could hide the venom in her gaze. "Now, wipe off. Go again."

28

The moon washed my balcony with silver light, turning my hands deathly white. Appropriate. I was surrounded by killers, after all.

I'd have thought two weeks of training would've made a difference. Nope. Not a scratch of it. I failed at almost everything: shooting, stamina, languages, convention, rock climbing. I mean, who can fail at rock climbing? I'd made it to the top, but not quick enough, apparently. The longer I spent here, the more their expectations seemed impossible to meet.

The only thing I did have was perfectly curled hair and make-up that would make me fit in with a catwalk of models. Minus my height. It was a miracle I had any skin left with the times Mayra had made me 'clean my canvas' and start again. Now when I looked in the mirror, any hints of tiredness lay hidden beneath subtle shades of foundation and blusher, eyeliner and mascara. No product could hide it from my eyes, though.

Horrid woman. Mayra strutted around the training grounds, quick to interrupt my sessions if my hair lay out of place.

In two weeks, I'd seen my fair share of girls around here, and I had to admit, Mayra's work paid off. They were stunning. Ranging in ethnics and race, each one could win a beauty contest hands-down. They'd be the envy of anyone off the island.

Including me to an extent. If they weren't so cold and unaccommodating, I might've tried to befriend them. You know, sit with them at breakfast, chat to them when they stopped to watch others spar. As it was, they smiled and gave direction when my mascara smudged or whatever, and at the same time left me feeling utterly judged.

I sighed. At this rate, I'd never get off this island.

"You're up late." Yakov leaned on the balcony beside mine, his face cloaked in shadow. Moonlight glinted off his watch. "Everything all right?"

"Peachy." I couldn't help the sarcasm. Ask an obvious question, you're going to get a snippy answer.

Yakov climbed over his balcony railing.

I stiffened. "What you doing?"

He leaped, catching my railing with surprising soundlessness. He hopped over to stand beside me, and the silver in the night light reflected in his irises. "Talk to me."

Was he crazy? Those railings were at least five feet apart. He could've chatted from the safety of his own ledge.

He stepped closer, engulfing me in his soapy scent. Sea salt and lemongrass. The same bottle sat in my shower. "You're irritated."

"Course I am. Nothing's working. You've had years to train, and I've …" I turned to face the courtyard, gripping the cool handrail. I'd never get out of here.

He squeezed my shoulders with hot hands. "It's only been two weeks."

Two weeks too long. They still had Mum. Still hunted Lia. Dakota had assured me as much that morning.

Yakov tilted his head. "Is this about training or your family?"

I tensed. "What do you know about them?"

"Enough. You're worried for them." So gently spoken. So empathetic. Dakota had trained him well. If I didn't know better, I'd believe he cared.

"I can't shoot straight, I've been knocked on my backside more times than I can count, Dakota's broken the world record for calling me a liar, and don't get me started on languages." I could barely string two words together.

He lowered his hands and nodded like he got it. "I can help with that."

"Yeah? You'll translate to English?"

"Not that." He batted away the comment. "You can study languages from the database."

"There's a database?" Would it have killed someone to tell me that? The foreign master – I still didn't know his name – spent an hour a day shouting at me in who knew what language, and hit me each time I answered wrong. My only reprieve was Mayra sticking her head in long enough to order him not to bruise me.

Bruises or not, he knew how to sting.

A heavy ache weighed on my eyes, on the bridge of my nose. I rarely slept anymore. When I did, the master chased me with sticks, determined to break my bones unless I could tell him the federal subjects of Russia – in Russian.

I blinked back tears.

"The database is between Dakota and Niagra's office. Come on." Yakov pulled me into the corridor. A wall of glass overlooked the woodland beyond the barrier, now nothing more than a mess of shadow and gloom. Something moved. A snake? Could they sense us in here? Smell the sweat? Were they actively searching for a way to get in, to feast on the meal inside? I swallowed the ache in my throat and went with Yakov to the courtyard.

"Where we going?" I asked.

"To the mats. I want to see how you fight."

Combat, one of the few practical sessions Yakov didn't teach me, involved a burly instructor, Victor, and a lot of barked Russian comments, probably all insults. Niall often laughed when Victor hit me. I hated those hours the most. A fist-sized bruise still marked my thigh from three days ago, much to Mayra's disdain. Only that afternoon, Victor made my nose bleed. I touched it at the memory. "That's not a good idea."

"What's the matter?" Yakov said. "Afraid I'll best you?"

"No doubts there."

Yakov sauntered on to the mats, slipping off his jacket. A form-fitting, sleeveless vest outlined every curve of his torso. He plucked two staffs from a stand, threw one to me, and beckoned. "Show me what you've got."

I sighed and traipsed closer with the staff dragging beside me, only lifting it into position once I reached him.

"Widen your stance." He pointed his weapon at my legs.

I obeyed and braced for his attack.

He struck out, his staff cracking against mine.

My arms jolted at the impact, and I staggered.

"Don't panic," he said. "The moment you do, the fight is lost."

Tell that to my pounding heart. "You have more experience."

"And it shows. Strike with confidence." He raised his staff.

I stabbed forwards.

He blocked effortlessly.

I jabbed again.

He knocked my attack aside, twisted behind me, and pressed the edge of his staff against my throat. His body heat flush with my back made my skin burn, and the sweet scent of his sweat mingled with blooming lilies just south of the mats. "Step into the blow," he said, breath on my cheek. "You'll increase its strength." He released me.

I spun to face him, face flushed, grateful for the darkness.

For a moment, we circled each other, weapons up. He lunged, caught my attempt to block and snatched my staff. He jerked me forwards and paused with the end of his weapon inches from my neck. My skin itched beneath it.

"Be smart," he said. "Don't wait. There are no second chances." He let me go and circled again. "Always attack first.

Kill or be killed. First rule of survival."

What kind of survival was that? Didn't you lose a piece of your soul when you killed someone? There had to be a better way.

He raised his weapon.

I crouched, spun and swiped his feet from under him.

He dropped to his back with a thud.

A surprised laugh burst from me, and I stared at my staff. I did it. I knocked him down. That was the better way. Knock them out and run. No killing required.

Yakov sprang, grabbed my waist, and yanked me to the mat. His knee dug into my thigh, and the edge of his staff pressed against my throat.

I cringed at the ache of Victor's bruise.

Yakov stared down at me, almost a silhouette in the moonlight. "*Never* let an opponent out of your sight." He removed his weapon. "Never turn your back. Never look away." He pulled me back to my feet.

"I'll never remember all this," I said.

"You will." He spun his staff around his torso, blurring the points into a circle. "One day, you'll be able to hold your own against Victor, and when you do, you'll be ready."

"For what?"

"The field." He tilted his staff towards me with a whoosh. "Assuming you can shoot straight by then." He laughed.

I didn't join in. Getting out of here would be a victory, but then what? I was no killer. "Can you beat Victor?"

"I can defeat him," Yakov said. "You could, too, if you focus."

"I'd have better chances against a bull with a mane of horns."

"Size doesn't matter," he said. "With any opponent, find their weakness. Take Victor, for example. He has a weak knee. A swift tap to that, he'll go straight down."

Weak knee. I'd remember that. "What about you? What's your weakness?"

He lifted his staff. "Enough talking. Again."

29

The database villa had at least a dozen computers. Each desktop had double screens with identical screensavers: a curved V with the point embedded in a silver circle.

Why hadn't they told me about the database? There was no internet. Just files and files of languages. My constant struggle and lack of help made my throat burn. It was like they didn't want me to progress. Like they wanted me stuck here forever. Why? What was the point? Did they consider two weeks too short a time to tell me about things like this?

A clock hung on the far wall, so I sat facing it. My language session started in eight minutes. Eight minutes to try to make some difference that would stop the master hitting me. My eyes stung. It'd never happen. Not today. But I'd study all night if I had to. Anything to get out of here quicker.

I scanned the folders on the computer. There were hundreds, each labelled with a new language, and each opened to hundreds more: locations. Dialects, probably.

I didn't have to learn all of them. Yakov only knew a handful. How many had he said? Twelve?

Okay, more than a handful. What did Venom expect from me? One? Three?

I opened the top file: Portuguese. That opened to a document with thousands of pages with listed words. A dictionary? Thesaurus? Encyclopaedia? I couldn't tell. Everything looked so foreign.

I scanned a few pages, none of it English. How was reading this going to help me?

Someone clamped a hand on my shoulder.

I jolted away from the Russian. "Yakov. You startled me."

"What happened to you?" Blood flushed his cheeks, and the sun streaks though the door emphasised his figure. Odd. The sun should've been shining on the other side of the villa. "When you didn't turn up for shooting, I thought—"

"That's not till this afternoon." I peered at the clock, and my stomach lurched. Over three hours had passed. No. The clock must be wrong. I'd only been here a couple of minutes.

"You didn't come for lunch," he said.

As though in response, my gut rumbled, and heaviness weighed my head. That wasn't possible. I studied his expression for signs of humour – a slight smile, a twinkle in his eyes. Nothing. Only … concern? "I haven't been …" The screen showed a time identical to the clock. "It's only been a few minutes." I can't have lost track that much. Sure, I was tired, but not delusional.

Yakov frowned until his forehead creased.

If I'd lost three hours, I'd have missed my language session. And the one with Dakota. They still had Mum. What would stop Niagra from hurting her?

But they'd have come to find me. Wouldn't they? They wouldn't just leave me out here.

I stood up to go look at the sun, and my knees buckled in a crash of dizziness.

Yakov caught me and leaned in while I steadied myself. "Take it easy."

What was going on? I couldn't have lost time. I couldn't—I closed my eyes. The room swayed. Tilted like a boat. Like the island was trying to throw me off.

"You're overworked," he said. "Go back to your room. Get some sleep before combat."

"I don't understand," I breathed. "It's only been a few minutes."

He walked me to the door, and there was the sun, beaming down above us, nowhere near where it'd been when I came in a few minutes ago.

A few hours ago.

It wasn't possible. It couldn't be. Venom could mess with the clocks. Trickery. That's what it was.

But Venom couldn't mess with the sun.

My gut sank. "What about shooting? And the other sessions?"

"Never mind them."

"But Niagra—"

"Will understand. You need to rest."

I stared at Yakov. His hair product released a scent of coconut that mingled with his woody aftershave. Niagra would never understand. I didn't understand.

Yakov studied me with gentle eyes. Gentleness. Reassurance. What was this? A friendly cold-blooded killer? I hardly believed it.

"You know Niagra has my mother," I said. There was no point pretending. Why Yakov knew remained a mystery, but he knew. He'd made that clear last night.

Yakov brushed my hair behind my ear. "She'll be fine. Rest. You need it."

"But—"

"You'll be useless fighting if you're exhausted." He straightened up, and just like that, his compassion was gone.

30

I trudged to the mats, groggy and fuzzy-headed. After Yakov walked me to my room, I'd collapsed into sleep and woke four hours later with gut-wrenching hunger. Five o'clock. The day had passed in a blink. I'd stopped long enough to not enjoy a chicken salad before heading off for combat.

Salad. After the day I'd had, how was salad supposed to strengthen me? The more rabbit food Chef Marcel fed me, the weaker I grew. It was ridiculous.

Victor, the combat specialist, spoke with Niagra by the mats. My body prickled in sweat. What would he do? Niagra must've heard about my truancy by now. Yakov said Mum would be fine, but how much of that could I trust?

I took a shaky breath and shuffled towards them.

Yakov, Nick and Joe stood by the surrounding wall. Had they come to watch? After Yakov's hint about Victor's knee, maybe he wanted to see me go for it.

Niagra nodded at me. "I'll leave you to it."

"Probably best." Victor looked like a bulbous butternut squash in his loose robe, a black belt stretched around his middle. "I don't know why you chose her. She wouldn't last two minutes in combat."

"I'm trying," I said. I knew how to block a punch now, and how to punch without breaking my thumb. That was something. Making it effective was a whole other skill, though. Victor moved so fast I couldn't get anywhere near him, as the bruise on my thigh proved.

Victor stared at me. "You understood that?" Stubble covered his chin and upper lip, barely hiding the blackheads beneath.

Well, duh. "Yeah. I am English." Was he so self-absorbed that he'd trained me for two weeks and still didn't know? I'd spoken to him often enough.

He crossed his arms over his chest. "I'm not speaking English." Flecks of spit flew from his mouth on the word *speaking*, not quite reaching me, but I stepped back all the same. His words sounded strange. Off. Victor turned on Niagra. "You didn't tell me she speaks Russian."

I blinked. "Russian? I don't." I knew the word *no*. That was it.

"What is this?" Victor growled.

Niagra's lips twitched. "How about that. You are learning. I was beginning to wonder." He raised his eyebrows, flicked his attention to the mat beneath us. "Now let's see how you fight. Yes?"

"I guess."

Victor gawped. "Dutch, too?"

"Dutch?" What kind of joke was this? I couldn't speak Dutch. Or Russian. Only English. "Is this a tactical thing?" I asked. "To get in my head?" Distract me? It was hardly needed. I couldn't stand against anyone here and win.

Niagra beamed, crinkling the corners of his eyes. He turned to face me fully and clamped his stained hands on my shoulders. "How much of what I'm saying can you understand?"

Seriously? "Everything."

"And now?"

"Still the same." I balled a fist against my leg, longing to pull away from him. This was punishment, wasn't it? Some kind of twisted lead-up to a threat to Mum. I hadn't meant to lose time. I couldn't explain it.

Niagra stepped closer. A scent of washing powder touched my nose. Shadows deepened the wrinkles on his cheeks and around his mouth, and sunlight highlighted furry hairs above his lip. "And now? Can you understand this?"

"Understand what?"

Niagra bellowed a laugh and clapped me on the back, nearly knocking me over with the force. His crooked nose distorted his glee. "She's so fluent, she doesn't notice the change!" He clapped his hands together, celebrating something only he could understand.

Fluent? Change? "I don't understand." I couldn't be speaking different languages. There was no possible explanation.

"Please." He gestured to the weapons. "Don't let me keep you." And he wandered off to join Yakov, passing Joe and Nick on their way to me.

"Grab a weapon," Victor snarled and marched to the rack.

It took a second for his command to sink in. What just happened?

"What's your secret?" Nick asked.

"To what?"

"Speaking Russian," Joe said. "And Dutch. And Italian, Spanish, French, and Mandarin. Niagra spoke them all."

"No, he didn't. He spoke …" Not English. I sensed the strangeness of the syllables, the difference each time Niagra switched. Had I somehow absorbed the computer's database? Is that what my blackout had been?

"Move it!" Victor barked.

"Remember what I told you," Yakov called. His Russian accent sounded different this time, like it wasn't an accent. Like he was actually speaking *Russian.*

I nodded. Weak knee. Right. I could think about this language weirdness later. Right now, I had Victor's beating to take. Unless I could beat him first.

31

I glowered at the target, knife in my hand. Concentrating was difficult in light of my new Victor-inflicted injuries. I hadn't lasted two minutes before he'd knocked me unconscious. He'd protected his knees well.

In my knife's reflection, a bruise peeked beneath my hairline. And it ached.

The child I'd seen the day I arrived – Meilin – stood a few feet away, frowning at an iPad. She was the only child I ever saw out here. Yakov had walked me past the nursery a few days ago: a long line of white brick and sun-sparkled windows, pristine lawns and walkways. Meilin was more advanced, Yakov said. She'd earned a place on the range.

She threw a knife, piercing the outer ring of her target, and pouted.

Advanced or not, she struggled. So, good. One less killer in the world. "That wasn't bad," I said to her.

"He'll make me run again." She nodded at Niall across the field. "He makes me do a lap when I get it wrong."

"Of the track?"

She nodded.

"But that's four miles long."

"Yeah, I know." She rolled her eyes and reached for a second knife.

Four miles. I could barely make that without passing out. Yakov refused half-laps now. It was the full thing, no excuses. The last time I'd done it, dark spots flashed in my eyes. Yakov wouldn't let me walk, though. I could jog or run. Nothing more.

How could four miles not bother Meilin? She was so young. I got the sense she could beat me if we raced. I picked up her iPad to study the image of her knife. It was wrong letting her use one. If it slipped—

"Hey! Hello?" Meilin waved a hand in front of my face. "What are you *doing*? You're all staring and weird, like." Her eyes narrowed, and she sidestepped away, her weapon held loosely in her hand. Her gaze flicked between the iPad and me. Wary.

I handed the iPad over. "I was just looking."

She snatched it back. "Well, don't do it like that. It's freaking me out."

Why? I'd barely glanced at the screen. Seemed an odd overreaction, but not one worth arguing about.

"Focus on your work, Meilin." Niall stood behind her, hands propped on his waist.

I frowned. Hadn't he been standing across the field?

Meilin raised her knife.

"Adjust your grip." I shifted hold on my own weapon. "Like this." Although, what difference would it make? I hadn't even hit my target yet. I could hardly help her.

She obeyed, then paused, squinting at the knives scattered around my target. "Didn't work for you."

"I wasn't throwing like this before." Which was weird. This felt right somehow.

"You do it, then," she said.

I flung my knife. It whistled through the air and pierced my target, dead-centre. I stared.

Meilin raised her eyebrows, then threw her blade. It hit the outer rim of the bullseye. "Huh." She shrugged. "Yeah, that's better."

Niall straightened. "Why'd you switch position?"

I rubbed my neck. "Don't know. Felt right, I guess."

The light reflected off his watch face.

I gasped. An hour had passed. But I'd only thrown six knives. I raced to get them. My next session began in five minutes.

"Hold up, Meilin," Niall said. "We don't want her stabbed in the back. Better hurry," he called after me. "You've got a problem with time keeping."

A concerning problem. What was going on? At this rate, I'd end up losing a whole week. I sprinted towards the armoury to return the knives. I only hoped I'd beat Dakota to his office.

32

The sight of Victor standing by the armoury made my lips tingle. It'd been seven weeks since the time loss. Seven weeks of bruises and beatings and abuse. But shooting was a reprieve. Shooting with Yakov didn't involve pain. It was almost fun.

Something told me today wouldn't be.

Victor scowled. "You're late."

I glanced at my watch. "I'm right on time."

"You were due thirty-five seconds ago."

"Thirty-five seconds?" I said. "You're judging me on that?"

Victor slapped the wall, sending my heart into a sprint. "I'm judging you on your lack of skill, common sense and knowledge, your blatant signs of emotion, your weakness. From now on, I expect perfect punctuality. Not one second late." He jabbed his finger at my chest. "Venom pride themselves on time-keeping. Understood?"

I nodded.

He pushed open the armoury door. "Get the Glock, ammo, plugs and target sheet. Quickly."

I distinguished his Russian better now. It'd grown easier to recognise the languages over the weeks, and since it started, three more popped into my head, bringing the total to nine. I'd have been impressed if I wasn't so confused. How on earth had I absorbed the database? That must've been what I'd done, but why? And how?

Was that the reason Blake took me? What had Niagra said? I knew things I wasn't supposed to know. Like learning nine languages in three hours? I'd never done the likes before.

I picked up the Glock, recognising it from previous sessions. I was learning. "Where's Yakov?"

Victor's nose creased at the question. "On business."

My shoulders dropped. "For how long?"

"Ammo," he snapped.

I grabbed a box of ammunition and a target sheet and headed outside to a bench.

"No." He shoved me on. "That one."

An empty, wooden block-target stood at the far end of the field. The farthest one there. "I've never shot that far."

He pushed the target against my chest. "Attach this."

Why did I bother arguing? Yakov would've listened. Victor wouldn't. I hurried down the field and slipped the paper on the hook. The black ring in the centre seemed tiny. How would I hit it? The closest I'd come to a bullseye was the outer ring, and that was on a block only halfway across the green.

Victor's impatience burned into my back, so I jogged to the shelf.

"Load up," he ordered.

I released the magazine on the Glock.

"Not like that," he said. "One bullet."

"One?"

"One."

Why? I'd probably miss. Wouldn't it make sense to have the next one loaded and ready to try again? I clicked the magazine back into place and loaded a single bullet into the top of the gun.

Victor nodded at the target.

I cocked the weapon, aimed, and fired. A glance at the screen above confirmed I'd caught the very rim of the paper. Not bad, considering.

"Again," he ordered.

I reloaded, cocked, aimed, and fired once more. It wasn't much better.

He scowled. "Again."

I obeyed, pulling my aim a little to the left. This time, a hole appeared in the outer rim of the largest ring. Still not close enough.

My cheeks burned, and my back muscles tensed. Yakov would've been patient, but Victor's irritation made my skin itch. His fingers drummed on the shelf. Any second he'd lash out.

"Again."

"I'd still have hit the guy," I said.

"Again!"

For the next two hours, he made me repeat the same pattern over and over: load, cock, aim, fire, load, cock, aim, fire, until my arms ached and my dented thumb stung. He never allowed more than one bullet.

"Why can't I load the magazine?" I asked.

Victor's lip curled. "Discipline. You'll never be successful in Venom without it."

"I never asked to be in Venom." No point hiding it. It wasn't a secret.

"But you are." He leaned in until his face hung inches from mine. Until the garlic from his lunch was almost tastable. Tiny beads of sweat clung to huge pores over his nose. "No more questions. Again."

"But—"

"Again!"

When he finally announced we stop, I let the gun clatter to the wood. My fingers shone red. Several holes marked the centre of the target. I'd become a perfect shot.

Even so, Victor didn't compliment me. He growled at the screen. "Get changed, and meet me in the courtyard for stamina."

"Stamina? Aren't we stopping for dinner?"

He plucked out my ear plugs and scooped up the gun. He

wasn't going to make me starve. Was he? Hunger tugged at my stomach. "You eat after training. Go."

33

I stood in the courtyard, rubbing my aching arms. A week into Victor's torture brought a level of exhaustion I hadn't known possible. Each day, he'd expected me on the mats at dawn and worked me until dusk through combat, weapons, and stamina.

My waist had gained new curves, and my arms and legs had thinned and firmed as Victor's regime cut away any fat I'd carried. Even my face had slimmed, though it appeared gaunter and paler than bright and beautiful like supermodels', much to Mayra's distress.

"More blush," she'd say. "You're a noble now, not a porcelain doll. I expect my ladies to *exude* beauty." And she'd tug an out-of-place hair from my head.

Her ladies. Like I'd ever be one of hers.

Once a day, Dakota pried into my mind, calling me liar. His desk phone taunted me.

My only breaks came when I ate and slept, though with cold, left-out food for meals, and my shrinking stomach, eating was hardly a joy.

Aquamarine tinged the sky, signalling the onset of dusk. Right on cue, Victor marched into the courtyard from the open doors of the dining room, dabbing his mouth with a napkin. I stared at the room, desperate to rush past him and snatch up a bun. Or a sausage. It'd been months – *months* – since I'd had a sausage.

He slid into a jeep and turned the key. The engine roared. "Two laps."

I straightened. "Two?" I'd already done one today. Sure, my legs weren't cramping like they had in my first couple of weeks, but *two*? Eight miles before food. Before sleep. Eight impossible miles.

"Two." He glared, almost daring me to challenge him.

I bit my tongue – if I spoke, he'd make it three – and plunged into the foliage. I met the track beside the barrier with bitter familiarity and leaped over the first log. My legs screamed in protest, but I pushed through the pain, flinching at the grate of wheels beside me and the flick of grit against my bare legs.

"Faster," Victor barked. "Move it, move it, move it!"

I pushed harder. Light reflected off the barrier, but I ignored the thought of snakes. The dangerous one was Victor. If a snake bit him, it'd spit his poisonous blood back in his face.

By the end of the third mile, a stitch cut into my side. I gasped, stumbled and scraped along the stone-ridden muck.

Victor's jeep ground to a halt. "On your feet."

The sting burned. Blood oozed from grazes where stones had peeled the flesh off my knees. I gritted and pushed on, followed by the roar of the jeep. Air seared my lungs.

"Faster!"

I tripped and fell again. Dirt curled up to my face.

"Move it!"

I pressed my hands into the dirt. "I can't." It was too much. The dusk highlighted my knuckles, the barely concealed bones in my fingers.

The jeep stopped again. "Drop and give me thirty."

"Please—"

"Now it's thirty-five. Move, move, move!"

I couldn't do it. I couldn't. I forced my shaking legs into push-up position. The scent of sweat and dirt and leaves lay heavy in the air, strengthening with each dip. My arms and torso trembled. Beads of sweat slid down my nose, itching it.

Victor crunched closer, his heavy boots marked with dust. "Listen, maggot. Venom is strong. Venom is powerful. Venom never fails." On my last three, he pressed a foot against my back, increasing the weight, speaking with every rise. "Strong. Powerful. Invincible."

I scrambled back to my feet and stumbled on another half-mile to the mats where I doubled over, clutching my burning side.

"Keep going," Victor said.

"I can't do it," I gasped, barely getting the words past my tongue. Cracking thirst cut my lips and scratched my mouth.

He stepped off the jeep, almost a blur in my periphery.

"Don't." I held up a hand. "No more. Please."

He slapped my hand away, but I backed off and hunched over, fighting a wave of nausea. I wanted to swallow, to ease the sting in my throat. My body wouldn't obey. Tears pricked my eyes. Or dust. I couldn't tell.

"Keep moving," he said through gritted teeth.

"I can't." My voice cracked.

He advanced on me.

Behind him, Niall leaned against the wall, along with others. None I knew. None I cared about.

"You're pushing me too hard." Tears streaked my cheeks, dripped from my chin. I didn't care. How long was I supposed to hold it in? I was dying. Slowly being killed by his abuse. "You beat me, bruise me. I hardly eat. Hardly sleep. And now twelve miles—it's impossible. I can't do it!"

Victor's hand cracked across my face, knocking me to the ground. Spots flashed, and I tasted blood. He towered over me with a look of disgust. "Pathetic." And he spat at the ground.

Niall smirked. Of course, he did. Victor could kill me, and Niall wouldn't care. He'd use it as another story. Another pointless, exaggerated story.

Victor advanced, fists balled.

I crawled backwards. Coward. Too weak to beat the beater.

"Your emotions weaken you," he said. "They hold you back.

And for what? Your mother? Your runaway sister? They are nothing."

Fear spiked, blazing in hot sweat. I was doing this for them. I'd grown stronger because of them. Strong. Not weak.

I staggered to my feet. Every muscle trembled. My legs cramped. Even my breaths stung in my chest.

"I'll visit them," Victor said, nose wrinkling. "Put you out of your misery."

I ran at him.

He simply twisted and flipped me to the ground.

My breath whooshed out of me, and a deep ache spread through my back to my torso. But I didn't care. Rage burned through my veins, flared in my cheeks. I kicked out, aiming at the very place I should've caught the first time: his knee. My heel struck it head-on with a satisfying crack.

He thudded to the ground, let slip a strangled cry, and reached for his belt. Maybe he had a gun. It didn't matter.

I lurched at him, getting in two punches before he jabbed my stomach and swung me over his head. My back hit the stones. Hard.

I stood up, clutching my middle, and caught the thing Niall threw at me.

A staff.

Victor stood, murder in his eyes. He leaned to the left, keeping weight off his knee. But he grimaced, exposing his pain. His weakness.

I had him.

I swung the weapon, blocked Victor's attack, and advanced, beating him with viper's speed.

He defended, but the pain in his limp and twist of his mouth betrayed him.

Now who's weak? I spun and slashed down with the weapon, whacking it over his head.

He dropped, finally unconscious.

I glared at Victor's unmoving form, the staff crossed over my body in preparation for another attack, and waited for horror to wash over me.

It didn't come.

But why? I'd knocked him out. Or killed him. No, his back rose and fell steadily.

Niall nodded his approval. Not that I needed it.

I thrust the staff at him. "You sort that out." My voice sounded hard and unyielding. Frighteningly so. Just like Backer, the woman from the plane. But I didn't care. Victor deserved it, and given the chance, I'd do it again. I turned towards the courtyard without a shred of guilt. "I'm done for today."

34

Dakota rested his chin on his interlinked fingers. "How are you this morning?"

"Fine." *Liar.* The thought came so easily now after two months of hearing it. I couldn't remember the last time I felt fine. Scared. Exhausted. But fine? No.

Raging. Raging at Venom. Raging with Victor. Raging with Niall and everyone else who'd done nothing after Victor struck me. A cut on my inner cheek stung from the previous day, but it was easy to ignore. My insides burned. The urge to punch Dakota in his perfect nose bubbled its way to the surface. I pressed my feet against the tiles. Kill or be killed. That's what Yakov had said. Well, I hadn't killed Victor – something I'd probably regret once he got to me.

Dakota watched me silently, scrutinising my expression. His foot bounced mid-air where he'd crossed his legs. Probably thinking about his newest punishment. What would it be this time? Another cut-off phone call? An hour beyond the boundary? A special one-on-one session with Victor to work out our differences? My neck prickled.

Dakota cocked his head. "I heard about your ordeal with Victor last night. It must have been hard, being pushed like that. Trained until you broke."

"I didn't break."

"Victor did," he said. "You fractured his knee."

"Good." A strange satisfaction flooded me. It felt wrong. Maybe Victor had broken me. Maybe he'd crushed part of my humanity. My fingers wanted to twitch. I kept them still. "He deserved it." What kind of statement was that? If I'd witnessed this scene when I first arrived, I'd have been horrified. But now? The memory of me kicking Victor's knee flashed to mind. I wasn't sorry.

Dakota leaned forwards. "You seem different today. Surer of yourself." He pointed at me with the butt of his pen. "What's changed?"

My patience. "Nothing."

"It doesn't bother you, what you did to Victor?"

It should have done. Maybe it'd hit me later. I hoped so. I didn't like this new me. This potential assassin. "That's the point, isn't it? To train killers? Soulless monsters?"

Dakota touched his pursed lips. "Is that what you think we are?"

"Absolutely." None of them cared. They were all monsters-in-training.

He uncrossed his legs, and when he leaned back, he gave a little smile. "You've come a long way. And despite lying to me again, you hid it well."

"I haven't lied."

"You said you were fine."

Ah. That one. "I am."

"And anyone would believe you. Except me."

That didn't surprise me. No one could deceive Dakota.

"I think we're done here." He scribbled something down, folded the paper and handed it to me. "Please give this to Niagra."

My punishment, no doubt. A lump filled my throat. Whatever it was, I wouldn't let them hurt my family. One way or another, I'd stop them.

35

Niagra's office was empty when I got there. He sat in the garden beyond glass doors, an open file beside him on the bench. Blake stood with him, dressed in a suit and jacket despite the morning heat, his briefcase clasped in his hand.

I bit back a scowl – I'd hoped I'd seen the last of him – and rubbed my thumb over Dakota's note. Curiosity inched my fingers to its edge. I peeled it open. Scrawled in rough letters was a single word.

NightLock.

Typical. Had I really thought it would give me answers? I closed the note and knocked on the door frame.

Niagra closed the file. "Come on out."

I bit my tongue to avoid glaring at Blake. What was he doing here? My attacking Victor couldn't be the cause. Sunlight on the pond filled my vision. I sidestepped out of range, catching a stronger whiff of the sweet flowers.

"You've seen Dakota?" Niagra asked.

I held out the paper.

Niagra took it and glanced at the word before crumpling the note and looking to Blake.

Blake pulled his briefcase in front of him. "You're done with training."

Already? But I'd only just started. The little over two

months had changed me, sure, but enough to be done? Especially when others spent their whole childhood training. Still, I wasn't about to contest it. The sooner I got out of here, the better.

"Your first assignment will be on the mainland," Blake said. "Have you eaten?"

"Not yet."

"You can on the journey. Go and change. I trust you remember what you wore here?"

I pressed my palms against my trousers. "I'd rather wear this."

"I didn't ask what you'd rather do," he said. "Change. Be back here in twenty minutes."

I left without further argument. His twisted ideas of propriety would leave me with a broken ankle one of these days. But thanks to Mayra, I could semi-walk in the stilettos without falling.

The too-tight, olive dress hung at the far end of my wardrobe with the stilettos tucked against the back. I had to get on hands and knees to reach them. I'd put them in the bin that first day. The bin. And someone had washed the dress and added both to the wardrobe. I'd have burned them if I'd known Blake would make me wear them again. The heels, thin as a knife, looked like they'd snap off. Maybe they were supposed to. Maybe Venom used them as weapons, too.

With aching muscles, I slipped on the dress. It fit better than when I first arrived. My reflection, with its toned appearance and subtle shades of makeup, stared out the floor-length mirror. The dress held appeal. Like I suddenly fit in this world of luxury and violence.

I tugged the hem to my knees. It sprang back up, showing the scratches from my fall the day before. Typical. Even the dress resisted me. Well, Victor couldn't. Not anymore. I gritted my teeth and strapped on the heels with trembling hands. I was leaving. I'd be free of Victor and his cruelty. But what now?

Could I speak to the police? Language wasn't a barrier any

more. *Strong. Powerful. Invincible.* Victor said nothing about all-knowing. I could get away with it, get Lia and Mum the help they needed. Except I didn't know where they were. Where did I start?

I dropped my keys on the dresser and returned to the foyer, mind buzzing through the possibilities. It all came down to one thing: escape Venom.

Victor sat at the far end of the cafeteria, a wooden walking stick propped beside him. He glared at me, and I got the sense if he had a gun, he'd shoot me.

"You were wrong," I muttered. "You're not invincible, after all." The urge to smile ached my lips – right up until Chef Marcel caught my eye. He leaned into the counter, grabbed a plate, and weaved between the tables towards me.

"For you," he said – the first English words he'd spoken. They were heavily accented, and I guessed he originated from Egypt or somewhere nearby. He pressed a plate in my hands.

Sausages. Sausages with eggs, bacon, mushrooms and bread and butter and hash browns, and he gestured to an empty table by the door. Empty except for a glass of milk.

I stared at him, resisting the urge to grab a sausage. It had to be a trick. He'd poisoned it. Right? "Why?"

He shrugged. "You work hard. You need …" He waved a hand, fishing for the word? "Good job. Need energy. Sit. Eat." He wiggled his gesture at the courtyard. "Leave." So rusty. Hadn't he been made to learn English like the rest of the recruits? Or was he just a chef?

I glanced at my watch – I'd been ten minutes. Blake had given me twenty – and sat down. Of everything I'd eaten, I hadn't enjoyed a meal this much in … well, at all. Yakov hadn't lied when he said Marcel was a fine cook, and by the time I headed back out to Blake – with three minutes to spare – my hunger had settled for the first time in months, even if I had wolfed the food down.

36

Salt air caught my face when I climbed out the submarine. I'd missed the cold, the sea scent, the taste of freedom. I inhaled deeply, soaking in a few seconds before Blake pushed me up the stone steps. A helicopter hovered up top, its wind rippling the grass. Two people sat in the aircraft: the pilot and a shadowy figure in the back.

Something welled in my chest at the sight of Yakov. As weird as it was, I'd missed him. He, at least, had been a decent teacher. I risked a smile, but he met it with a frown, and the something dissolved. Course he didn't care. Wasn't he a killer, too? Just another agent of Venom.

Blake sat beside him, leaving the opposite seats unoccupied. I slid onto one, tugging down my dress.

"You ready for this?" Blake asked.

My throat tightened. With all the excitement of getting off the island, I hadn't given any thought to what they expected. They'd hardly been training me to raise children. Did they want me to kill? Sure, I'd attacked Victor, but that didn't make me a murderer. "Ready for what?"

"A test," Blake said, "before your first assignment."

I swallowed. Except for my skill with shooting and the languages I'd mysteriously learned, I'd barely progressed – unless I counted the near-constant ache in my muscles and obvious loss of any fat. I pressed a finger to my wrist bone.

"Yakov will accompany you," Blake said, "to make sure all goes smoothly."

"You mean to make sure I don't escape." I dug my nails into my legs. I should have expected this. They wouldn't let me so much as glimpse a policeman, let alone escape. I'd been a fool to think I could run.

Blake inclined his head. "You have your part to play."

Yakov stared through the window. He'd been different at the training grounds. Relaxed. Almost fun. But out here and on the job who was he going to be? No one I'd like, no doubt.

"What's the assignment?" I asked.

"You'll find out soon." Blake crossed his leg. "First, Backer would like to meet you."

Backer. The devil woman who killed her own grandfather and shot people so quickly they didn't know until they were dead. I shivered. Fiction or not, Niall's stories had a way of staying with you.

The pilot flew us across the mainland and over a sun-glamoured city until the helicopter descended on a silver skyscraper. Blake climbed out ahead of Yakov. The Russian offered his hand to me, expression revealing nothing.

Nope. No one I liked. I ignored him and stepped out, semi-glad of Mayra's lessons on walking in stilettos. I managed the decent with a fair amount of grace considering my hands were trembling like earthquake-starters.

Blake led the way to a lift, the doors opened right on cue, and we filed in. He swiped a card over a scanner before turning to me. "Remember what I told you. Emotions are no good here. Hide them. You understand?"

I hardly needed reminding. Dakota had carved it into my memory in such a way that I'd never forget.

The lift opened on to a corridor with plush carpets, stands with vases, and golden frames hanging on the walls. The place smelled of bleach. Blake headed for the farthest door and strode into a long conference room.

Backer sat at the head of a table, a ruby half the size of my fist resting on a grey suit. Light streaked in through floor-to-ceiling windows that overlooked a forest of skyscrapers and clear, white sky. Backer flashed a smile and clasped her fingers. "I've been waiting." Her voice carried the same silky tone as it had on the plane, with an air of coldness that even her smile failed to hide.

I pressed my toes against the floor.

"I've heard good things about your training," Backer said.

She obviously hadn't heard about Victor, then.

She chuckled. "You gave Victor quite the beating."

Or she had.

"I wonder," she said, "how did you know about his weak knee? I presume it wasn't an accident you fractured it." Her gaze strayed to Yakov. "It'll be a while before Victor forgives you."

Yeah. Because that would happen. I may have got the upper hand yesterday, but if he got close to me again, he wouldn't hesitate to stab me in the back. Or the front. Whichever was closer.

Backer slid a file to me.

I flipped open the cover. It contained a single page: a monochrome photo of a security guard with broad chest and shoulders. Gel plastered his hair to the side. His name tag was blotted out.

My target, no doubt. The focus of my 'test'.

My gaze finally fell on Backer, and I flexed cold fingers. "Who is he?" I asked.

"That's not important."

"What's he done?"

She narrowed her eyes. "That's not important."

I bit the inside of my cheek, sensing her irritation, daring me to question again. "What is important?"

She blinked. "Him."

I studied the photo again and turned the page. It was blank. "What am I to do?"

"Kill him."

My gut turned as cold as her voice.

She popped her elbows on the table. "Will this be a problem?"

"No." The word scraped at my throat. My lack of hesitation pleased me, but my eyes stung. I snapped the folder shut, fighting the need to swallow. If she was anything like Dakota, she'd notice the action. She'd know what it meant. "When do I leave?"

"The helicopter's outside." She kept staring. Kept watching me like Dakota would. Like she was trying to read me. Trying to see my weakness.

Not today.

I swept from the room ahead of Yakov and into the lift. A killer. They wanted me to kill. Numbness spread through my arms and chest. I had to run.

Yakov jabbed the button for the roof and led me to a helicopter – smaller than the previous one. His hand stayed on my back. Dry heat whipped my hair until it obscured my vision. He paused by the open aircraft door, fingers steadied on the handle. The white grip of his Beretta peeked beneath his jacket. If I tried to take it, could I? Would he expect such a move?

I climbed in the empty rear: no seats. Just a duffel bag. And sat as comfortably as I could in the tight dress and heels. Tugging the hem did nothing. It only sprang back up.

Yakov sat beside me, and the helicopter lurched and took off. Yakov's reflection in my window focused ahead, but every now and then his gaze fell on me, his jaw set straight, expression unreadable. A completely different man to the one I'd trained with on the island. Could he sense my fear? Maybe his lack of emotion was a gift – any doubt in my ability would be masked from Venom.

Until I failed.

Warmth tickled my cheek. I swiped the tear away.

Yakov edged closer, glancing at the pilots. "You can talk

freely. They don't speak Russian."

I blinked. That was the first he'd spoken since the training grounds. But what did he expect me to say? I was hardly going to pour my heart out to him.

"Choose a weapon," he said.

"What?"

"You remember I told you when you completed your training, you could choose one?"

"Oh." That I remembered. I drew my arms to my chest. "Doesn't matter. I didn't get one." I didn't want one.

He pulled his knee up and rested his wrist on it. "Choose. It's better to hold a weapon you're comfortable with."

I wasn't comfortable with any of them, but I forced lightness into my tone. "I don't know. A Beretta, I guess."

He reached into his jacket and produced a Beretta in a holster.

I stared at it. "What if I'd said a torpedo?"

His shoulders gave a silent giggle. "You always chose the Beretta in training. I figured you might now." He put it in my palm.

I gestured to the dress. "I don't exactly have anywhere to put it."

He unzipped the duffel and passed it to me. Inside lay a black pant-suit, white blouse and belt. All my size, no doubt. "No shoes?"

"You've got some."

"I can't do anything in these." The balls of my feet already hurt.

He shrugged. "Helps you blend in."

More like stops me running. I shook my head. "Flats would have worked, too." I stood up. "Do you mind?"

His lips twitched, but he turned around.

With my attention flicking between him and the pilots, I took off the heels and scrambled to change. The clothes fit perfectly. Go figure. After attaching the belt, holster and gun, I sat down again.

Yakov waited while I did up my heels. The Beretta pressed against my side like a bowling ball. How could I use that? How could I take a life? If I didn't they'd kill Mum, but if I did, I'd be the killer. There had to be another way.

"Here." He produced two bullets from his pocket.

My hand tightened on my strap. They really expected me to do this. To put a bullet in someone's head. "Two bullets?" I only needed one to hit my target.

"Standard protocol," he said. "In case of nerves."

"I'm supposed to be in control," I said. It was the biggest irony Yakov taught me. "If I miss, I fail, right?"

His silence confirmed my statement.

I took the bullets and loaded my weapon, thoughts on Mum. Thank goodness she couldn't see me now, her mess of a daughter, a nearly-assassin.

Yakov leaned in. His body heat reached my face, warming it. "Are you sure you're ready for this?"

"I don't have a choice."

The engine's judder grated on my nerves. Yakov unholstered his Beretta and set about dismantling, cleaning, and reassembling the pieces. Each click put my teeth on edge.

The aircraft slowed.

Yakov yanked open the door, letting in a wave of warm wind, and pointed. "That's our drop." The chop of blades distorted his words. "Get ready."

I staggered to the edge and clutched the rim of the door, shivering at the sight of a reddish, flat rooftop ahead of us. Red like blood. Dusty blood. Could I refuse to go through with this? Knock out the co-pilot? Force the pilot to fly away at gunpoint?

The pilot would shoot me before I got close. Actually, Yakov would beat him to it. Friendly or not, he was still an assassin.

The helicopter hovered a few feet above the rooftop.

"Ladies first," Yakov said.

I was out of options. Mum's life. My life. They were gone if

I didn't jump. My shoulders tensed, and I stepped out.

37

My knees buckled on the roof, and I rolled until my back slammed against a wall.

Yakov landed on his feet close by, hair ruffled. "All right?"

I stood, wincing at the grind in my ankles from the wretched heels. I should've taken them off. "I'm fine."

Liar.

Yakov pried open a door and padded down a flight of stairs.

Wide, empty corridors wound through the upper floors of the building. Windows overlooked offices filled with filing cabinets and suited businesspeople, their expressions twisted in boredom. A passionate place indeed. They had no clue what was about to go down. But then again, neither did I. There had to be another way. There had to be.

Yakov paused by a large vent, and after a brief glance in both directions, removed the cover with a firm tug. He crouched by the opening, waiting for me.

My nerves grew until my teeth tingled. This wouldn't work. Someone would see us and sound an alarm. Anyone. I caught glimpse of a logo and name of a bank frosted into a window.

Yakov tapped the grate impatiently.

I crawled inside, biting back rising nausea. Maybe my target wouldn't be here. Maybe he'd called in sick. He did work here, didn't he?

The shaft led to another grate overlooking a hall where people crowded a reflective floor and lined the counters. Security guards stood out from the clusters in their sapphire uniforms. Clammy. That's what the bank was. Clammy and humid and so full of people that 'crowd' felt an understatement.

I lay stomach-down, separated from the chaos. Thank goodness. I didn't do people, despite being made to in Lia's office. I hoped she was okay, wherever she was.

I ran a shaky thumb over my gun – a Beretta TWO-90. Of all the weapons I'd trained with, this was the easiest. It didn't feel that way now, though.

Yakov shuffled up beside me.

I scanned the crowd, sweating beside Yakov's body heat, and spotted my target standing by the counter, hair slicked back, badge glinting. He scanned the room, too, but with tired eyes.

Maybe he'd killed someone. The guilty should die, right? It wouldn't matter that I killed him. One less criminal to worry about.

The walls of the vent pressed in, thickening the air. I had to kill him. It didn't matter why. I was to follow orders. Nothing more. It'd be easier if I'd asked for this. If I actually wanted to be here. But it didn't work like that. Not with Venom.

The Russian passed me a silencer that I screwed onto my gun. Mum's image filled my mind. I could still see the footage of her, lying unconscious in Venom's personal prison. Her life in their hands.

In my hands.

I steadied the barrel on the grate. Aimed at the target. Because that's all he was. A target. Another cardboard cutout.

For Mum.

A child skipped through the crowd, his mess of brown hair bobbing between the people, and leapt into the man's arms.

The target's arms.

The smiling, still tired, happy *father*.

My gun might as well have jammed. My finger certainly had.

A woman stopped beside them. She stood out from the others with her patterned bandana and gentle touch on the father's arm. His wife. She had to be. She pecked him on the cheek, took the child, and they weaved away through the crowds.

I opened my mouth, peeling my lips apart.

"Don't hesitate," Yakov said.

I could shoot Yakov. He'd never see it coming. I glanced at him.

His Beretta sat in his hand, white silencer pointed at me.

The guard. He was a target. Nothing more. Take a life to save a life. Right?

My gun shook. It sent vibrations through my arm.

For Mum.

My finger wouldn't move.

"Shoot him," Yakov hissed.

They'd kill Mum if I didn't. It wouldn't save the man. Venom would make sure of that.

The guard shuffled to the exit. Another few moments, he'd be gone, and I'd have lost my chance.

But what about next time? Or the time after? How many people had to die for Mum to live? Five? Fifty?

It was one trigger. One press of a button.

A button so stiff, my finger cramped.

I could do it.

I had to.

For Mum.

Crack! The sound cut through the vent.

The guard jerked and collapsed. His head hit the tiles, and blood splattered the ground. His leg stuck out at an odd angle. His mouth hung open in an expression of shock.

Someone screamed.

I stared at the gun in my hand, my numb finger still poised on the trigger, my bullet unfired.

Yakov lay beside me, Beretta parallel to mine. He slid out

the shaft, hauled me after him, and dragged me along the passage. His grip hurt. But Mum's death would hurt more. I had to help her.

I struck at Yakov.

He blocked easily, like he knew I'd try, and slammed me against the wall. My breath whooshed from me in a gust, and my knees wobbled. Yakov's grasp kept me upright. "We don't have time for this."

Voices sounded down the corridor. Workers? Police? Who knew?

"Trust me," Yakov said. "You won't survive Brazilian prison."

"I didn't do anything." I lifted my weapon, but he snatched it from me and twisted my arm. Pain shot through it.

"You're an accomplice. Now, move." He ran me up to the roof where the helicopter hovered, blades whipping dust in a rippling cloud. I couldn't go back. I had to find Mum, had to save her.

I struggled against Yakov's grip, tried to slip out of it.

He only dug his barrel into my side and forced me on board, proving once and for all just how powerless I really was.

Fear shook my body. I'd failed, and my family would suffer for it. If Venom had bluffed about searching for Lia before, they wouldn't now. They wouldn't stop with Mum. I shivered violently. I had to do *something*. Yakov had my gun, but the thought of touching it again made me cringe. I could attack the pilot. If the helicopter went down, they might leave Mum alone. Or they might kill her to tie up loose ends.

I tensed when Yakov sat next to me and leaned in close. "Everything went according to plan," he said, his tone hard. "That's what we tell them. You felt nothing. No remorse. No regret. Understood?" His silver eyes bore into mine, the colour broken in places by tiny flecks of blue.

I stared. Had I heard him right? Had he just—"Why would you lie to them?"

"I have my reasons." He shoved my gun in my hand. "Don't

try anything stupid. I've taken the bullets."

38

"Well?" Backer sat at the head of the table in that conference room. Same position. Like she hadn't moved at all.

"It went according to plan," Yakov said, his Russian smooth on his tongue.

"Any problems?" she asked, effortlessly matching his language.

"None."

A clock behind me ticked lightly. I counted the seconds, determined to hide the unease filling my throat. Why would he lie for me? If Backer found out, she'd kill him. And then Mum.

"Your gun." Backer turned her steely eyes on me.

I drew out my Beretta and slid it across the table. My heart thumped.

She unclipped the magazine where a single bullet rested. I resisted the urge to glance at Yakov. So much for taking the bullets. Liar. But he'd taken one. The one I should've used to shoot the banker.

"How did you find it?" Backer asked.

I forced myself to meet her black eyes. *Don't fidget. Straight face. Eye contact.* All things Dakota had taught me. But he could still see my lies. Could she? She was the head of Venom, after all. "It was fine."

Her eyes narrowed. "Just fine?"

"I felt nothing." My breath caught. She'd sense my fear. She'd see my heart pounding. I'd never get away—

"Good." She smiled, flashing a row of pearly whites. "Seems we didn't underestimate you." She dipped into a briefcase with golden clasps and slid me a blue folder and the Beretta. "Your first assignment."

39

Orange streaks of sunset reflected on the windows of a multistorey hotel. Yakov guided me through a pillared entrance and spacious reception to a gold-edged desk.

A dangerous sense of hope welled. Yakov's lie paid off. It'd saved Mum. For now. But for what cause? What did Yakov want? He'd taken my gun right after we left the conference room. A pointless move. We both knew I couldn't stand up against him.

A pang stabbed my stomach. I hadn't eaten since the submarine journey that morning. My dry tongue stuck to the roof of my mouth, and I yearned to use a bathroom.

An elderly woman behind the desk saw us and scampered to the wall where she plucked off a key. She handed it to Yakov with a wrinkle-rimmed smile. "Enjoy your stay, sir."

He took it wordlessly and steered me towards a staircase. I turned to the lift, but his hand on my back firmed. "Always choose stairs," he said. "It's harder to be ambushed."

I frowned. Did he always think like that? How awful, to live without trust, constantly on edge. But always choosing stairs made him predictable. It was a weakness. If I was his enemy – or an enemy capable of beating him – that's exactly where I'd attack.

One floor later, Yakov unlocked a door to a suite with two

sofas and a glass table. Double doors opened to a curved balcony. A silver platter on the table held fruit, bread, and cheese, and a large lid-covered dish stood beside bowls, glasses, and a jug of water.

I filled a glass and downed it before grabbing a bread bun. The crust had staled slightly, but I ate it anyway. What did stale food matter when you were hungry?

Yakov locked the door, sweeping his focus over the room. Looking for what? Bugs? Cameras? What reason would Venom have to spy on their members? Unless they were watching me.

"She knew we were coming," I said between mouthfuls, remembering the receptionist and her instant reaching for our key.

"Venom always plan ahead." Yakov's stance relaxed. He slipped off his jacket and dropped it on a sofa.

Relaxing. No cameras then. Or bugs. Which meant it was safe to talk. "Why'd you lie?"

He lifted the lid off the dish. Steam billowed out, misting the polished surface. Seasoned meat surrounded by potatoes, carrots, and broccoli filled the platter. My tongue tingled at the scent.

"I told you," he said. "I have my reasons."

"I have a right to know them."

"No, you don't." He filled a glass with water. "Your mother's safe. Isn't that what you want?"

"I *want* to go home."

"Not an option." He filled a plate and sat on the sofa, sinking into the cushion. He was so relaxed considering he'd just killed a man. Didn't it bother him? Had it ever bothered him?

My next assignment – another target, this time in Rio – was scheduled for tomorrow. A man with curly hair and who knew what family was destined to die. His colourless photograph didn't hide the glimmer in his eyes. Had a child caused the sparkle? Would that child be crying in the arms of his widowed mother, like the one from bank probably was?

151

I shivered.

Yakov's brow furrowed. "Are you cold?"

"No." But I should've been – cold to the bone. Because that man would die tomorrow, and there was nothing I could do to stop it.

40

I stood on the balcony alone, wearing black trousers and a white blouse. Not exactly pyjamas but a better option than my sweaty, dirt-coated outfit from earlier. The new clothes fitted perfectly, no surprise.

The patter of shower water reached me from the bathroom. Yakov had been in there five minutes. He probably wouldn't be much longer.

I leaned on the wide, stone rail rimming the balcony to better see the tree. Its thick trunk stretched up to my level, leaves branching out beneath the starlit sky. It wouldn't take much. A short leap. I'd catch a branch, shimmy down the trunk, and be running free.

Until Yakov noticed my absence.

If I could borrow a phone, find police, I could get help in place before Yakov found me. He'd lied to Venom for a reason. It couldn't have been to keep Mum safe. There was more to it. Which meant he'd lie again. He'd hide the truth and search for me himself.

I'd tried the door already. Yakov had locked it well – which made no sense. In theory, the lock should've released when I twisted it.

Which left the tree.

I climbed onto the railing, and the ground seemed to tilt

away. A numb weight shook my legs, tempting me back to the balcony.

I could do this. The nearest branch was a few feet from me. An easy jump. Adrenaline would help me hold on. Assuming the branch didn't break.

The shower fell silent.

My heart jolted. It was now or never. I could do this. I had to.

My breath stuttered, and I jumped.

Strong hands grasped my middle and hauled me back, lurching my heart against my chest. My breath escaped me in a gasp, and I struggled, failing to break Yakov's hold.

"Let me go!"

He carried me inside, not releasing me until we got to the table.

I twisted to him, ready to fight.

"Are you mad?" Yakov demanded. A towel around his waist hung to his bare feet. His hair dripped water down his shoulders and over his chest. "Do you want to die?"

"If you think I'll sit around and—"

"You can't run from Venom," he said. "They'll kill your mother long before you find help."

"Because you'll tell them?" He wouldn't call them now. Right?

He raised his chin. "No."

"Exactly. So, Venom wouldn't know—"

"They'll know."

Someone rapped at the door.

I froze. Venom? Had they been watching us after all? Had they seen me on the balcony?

"Room service," a voice called.

Room service. Yakov wouldn't tell Venom, which meant I'd have time. Time to shout for help.

Yakov leapt forwards, grabbed my arm, and twisted it behind my back. Pain struck my shoulder. His other hand clasped my mouth, smothering my shout.

"We're busy," Yakov snapped, his Portuguese as fluent as a native. "Come back tomorrow."

I struggled. Pointlessly. His strength far exceeded mine.

Yakov spun me around and pushed me backwards onto the sofa, pinning my arms above me. "Stop," he hissed, switching to English. "I'm not the only one watching you."

"What do you mean?" Were the staff in on this?

His lips tightened into a frown. "You want out. You want your family safe. I get it. But this goes deeper than that. There's more at stake than your life. Than theirs."

His breath, hot on my skin, rose the hairs on my arms. I tugged against him. "What aren't you telling me?"

He let me go, leaving a burning heat in place of his fingers. "Just settle down." He walked to the bathroom. A risky move. What was stopping me from trying again? From running straight for the balcony? I sat up. Steam misted the bathroom mirror through the open door. Yakov slipped a black t-shirt over his head, covering his muscled torso.

"Who else is watching?" I asked. It was the only way Venom could know if I escaped. The only way if Yakov wasn't the one to tell them.

He scowled. "Venom."

"The hotel staff?"

He stepped out of view, returning in black trousers and towel-scrubbed hair. "Not the staff."

"Then, who?"

"That's not important."

I huffed. "You sound like Backer." Of course, he wouldn't tell me. Knowing my enemies would give away their advantage. Or his bluff.

He stepped out of the bathroom. "You should get some sleep. It's late."

I pushed off the sofa, standing on a wet patch where he'd dripped on the floor. "You can't expect me to accept that."

"That's exactly what I expect." He ran his fingers through his hair, smoothing it down.

I balled my fists. That wasn't good enough. He could try to hide the truth, but I'd get my answers – his true motivation, the reason for my blackout – all of them. Sooner or later, I'd understand. And when I did, I'd be the one with the advantage.

41

Sunlight beamed through the window, warming the sheet over my legs, and chatter filtered in from outside.

Chatter from Brazil. I was in Brazil.

Where Yakov had killed a man.

I sat up. How had I slept? The horror of the security guard's death should've kept me up all night. I'd witnessed it, an actual murder. And for a moment, could've pulled the trigger myself. Not that I could, though. Not really. I wasn't a killer. If yesterday had proved anything, it was that.

I slid off the mattress, put on a hotel robe, and went into the main room. Fuzziness clung to my head – the kind that came with sleeping too long.

Yakov looked up from the sofa, holding a glass of orange juice. "Good morning."

"Is it?" I rubbed my forehead, willing the heaviness away. Months of sleep deprivation had partly been made up last night. I should've felt better.

Yakov smiled. "Sleep well?"

"Well enough." Too well. A clock on the wall read 10:05. That late? "You didn't wake me."

"I think you needed rest." He sipped his drink, completely relaxed – like the man at the training grounds. The impossible man. One minute he was gentle and calm, the next, hard and cold. Which was the real Yakov: the killer or friend?

I sat on the opposite sofa in the glare of sun. Leaves rustled by the balcony. I should've jumped sooner. I could've got help instead of being stuck here, knowing someone else was about to die. "What now?"

Yakov threw a croissant to me. "You saw the file."

"Yeah." Another day, another murder.

"You won't be the killer this time."

"This time?" I frowned at the croissant. "I wasn't the killer last time."

He jabbed a finger at me. "Keep that to yourself." He stood up, refilled his cup with orange juice, and sat beside me, pressing the glass into my palm.

I shivered at the cold.

"This time, you'll be my guide," he said. "You'll watch the cameras, guide me to my destination. I must not be seen."

Okay, so I let him get caught. I escape and get help, and he gets apprehended and maybe imprisoned. What was stopping me? The thought must have crossed his mind. "What makes you think you can trust me?"

"The same reason you trust me," he said.

"I don't."

He lifted an eyebrow. "Don't you?"

"No." Why would I? He was Venom. He'd covered for me, sure, but for his own agenda. He was still a killer. A killer I sat inches from. I shifted back a smidge. "You speak twelve languages, right?" Three more than me.

"What's your point?" he asked.

"Did you ever blackout on the island? Lose hours of time? Is that how you learned to speak them?" I ran my thumb through the condensation on my glass, setting a waterdrop avalanching a line down the side. Maybe that's how it worked. One timelapse led to another, and another, until a cascade of assassins were expert linguists.

"No," Yakov said. "I never lost time."

Which meant it was unique to me. But for what purpose?

How had it happened? It seemed pointless, speaking nine languages when I couldn't communicate with anyone outside Venom. My gaze strayed to the door.

"I told you," Yakov said, "I'm not the only one watching you."

"And I think you're bluffing."

"Then, take the risk." He gestured to the door. "I promise you'll regret it."

Another bluff, no doubt. But it made little difference. He'd never let me leave. "If you're anything like Dakota, your promises mean nothing."

He shrugged. "I'm like him only where I can lie. I take no pleasure in it." He tugged the collar of my robe closer to my neck, his warm fingers scraping my throat. "With you, I will always be truthful. Trust me."

I swallowed. It'd be easier to believe him if his fingers weren't inches from my neck. But he could bet his buck I'd challenge his statement. "Truthful, huh? Well, I have questions."

He dropped his hand. "None I'll answer unless it's about our assignment today."

"Yeah, didn't think so."

"Keeping secrets isn't lying," he said. "I would choose silence over lying to you every time."

"An assassin with a conscience. How refreshing."

He chuckled, flashing his crooked smile. "We're not all inhuman, you know." He leaned closer, filling the heat with the scent of last night's shampoo. Aloe vera. His hand brushed my shoulder, and heat warmed my cheeks.

I stood up before he could speak again, forcing down a mouthful of juice. My heart pulsed against my throat. What was that all about? He was a killer. As confusing as he was, I wasn't going to let blushing start now.

He reached behind a sofa cushion and pulled out a long, blue roll that he spread over the floor: a blueprint of some sort. "This is our setting. You'll be here, in the security room." He pointed at a rectangle at the bottom of the paper. "And you'll wear that." He pointed to the jug of juice where a tiny, peach-coloured earpiece lay.

I pressed my glass to my cheek, cooling the skin while he looked down.

"You'll direct me here." He tapped a tiny square at the centre of the sheet.

"Isn't that an air vent?"

He nodded. "Most don't catch on that quick, especially on a blueprint this scale."

"It's pretty obvious." Although, was it? The shapes looked kaleidoscopic. Nothing like a map. But each hallway, storage compartment, room, and vent shaft read clearly to me, like they were labelled. But they weren't, so how could I know it was a vent? I glanced at the clock. No lost time.

"What do you want with an air vent?" I asked. Silly question. Hadn't we just used a similar one in the bank?

"It's the stealthiest way to access the centre room," Yakov said.

I put down my glass with cold fingers.

Yakov pointed to the bottom right of the paper. "In the security room—"

"What about the guards?"

He met my gaze, finger hovering over the rectangle. "What about them?"

"They're not going to let me in to the security room, are they?" Although, I could speak their language now. I could pass on a message.

Yakov waved his hand dismissively. "A minor nuisance. They'll be dealt with."

I shifted on the spot. "And by dealt with, you mean …"

His eyes bore into mine, locking my muscles like a stasis pod. He didn't need to answer. He must've known as much because he pushed the sheet towards me. "Memorise it. I must not be seen."

Well, he would be. I wouldn't help him. Venom was full of

killers. Yakov was a killer. But I wasn't. It was my right – my *responsibility* – to betray him. To stop him killing again.

42

Yakov led me to a BMW outside the hotel, a warm hand against my back. He'd given me a pair of thick, black boots in place of the heels – a welcome reprieve. The soft soles cushioned my feet, but heat boiled inside them, coating my toes in sweat, unaffected by the air-conditioning inside the vehicle.

Tourists crowded the path outside the car – a multicoloured mosaic of palm-patterned shirts, sun-creamed noses, and flapping sandals. Was Lia somewhere in a crowd? Was she still hiding, or had Venom found her? She wouldn't have a clue who she was hiding from. She'd have gone to a police station, been stuck in protection, been given an alternate identity. At least, I hoped so. The farther away from Venom she was, the better.

"Why am I coming?" I stuck to speaking Russian. "You're wearing a suit, you speak Portuguese. Can't you blend in? Walk in through the door? I thought that was Venom's thing." It wouldn't be hard for Yakov to memorise his route to the vent.

"Your instructions are to guide me," Yakov said. "We don't question. We just do."

"Even if the instructions don't make sense?" It almost seemed like Venom wanted Yakov to get caught. 'Let's put the girl we blackmailed and abused in charge of guiding the assassin to kill someone'. Where was the sense in that?

"Especially if they don't make sense," Yakov said. "Everything happens for a reason."

"How very philosophical."

Time passed in relative silence, broken only by the purring engine and the occasional burst of Portuguese on the radio. After an hour, the car turned on to a narrow stretch of drive leading to a security kiosk with a striped barrier. A guard stood by the door.

Yakov put down his window and unholstered his Beretta.

I stiffened. "What are you—"

A low shot flashed. The guard jerked backwards, thudded against a button, and slumped to the ground.

I covered my gasp. Yakov killed him. Killed him in broad daylight. The guard had been innocent. A simple bystander doing his job. There'd been no need for that.

The barrier juddered and swivelled skywards, and the car set off again.

"Was that really necessary?" I asked, failing to hide the tremor in my voice.

Yakov tucked his gun away. "Collateral. Part of the job."

"It didn't have to be. We could've got through another way."

He shook his head.

A multi-storey building towered at the top of a slope. Low-cut grass lined the road, and sun glinted off the windows. Dirt steaked the walls between the windows like it had rained mud. A few people wandered around the edge. No guards. No security.

Yakov stared ahead with a blank expression. No hint of concern. Surely, someone had seen the murder? Surely, someone would come to stop us. Yakov pressed something small in my palm. An earpiece. "Put it in."

I obeyed with trembling fingers. It fit perfectly. In fact, I couldn't feel it at all, and I jolted when Yakov spoke.

"Can you hear me?"

"Yeah." Clearly. Too clearly. He could've had his lips right by my ear.

The car veered off the road, wheels crunching on loose gravel, and stopped beside a propped-open fire exit. Yakov nudged me and got out.

Heat thickened the air. It burned my head. Yakov marched ahead of me. Inside, shadows plunged the corridor into a yellow haze while my eyes adjusted.

I turned to the exit, debating escape. What was the point? Yakov would catch me. Besides, where would I go? Until I found Mum – even some clue about where she was – running would be a waste of time. Besides, the exit hadn't been left open by coincidence. Someone was expecting us. And where Yakov had allies, I had enemies.

Three muted shots rang out from the room Yakov had gone into, and something thudded.

I pressed a hand to my mouth.

Someone. Three someones. The guards? Had Yakov killed so many times that he didn't hesitate anymore? I trudged forwards on numb legs, pulse thudding in my throat, and rounded the corner.

Two guards lay sprawled on the carpet. A third slumped on a revolving chair, still turning. If it wasn't for the spreading red patch on his chest, I'd think he was sleeping.

Just sleeping. That's all they were.

My throat tightened. My eyes stung. Joe hadn't been joking. Yakov really was dangerous. Deadly. The friendly man at the island didn't exist. How could he in this monster?

Yakov tilted my chin towards a screen-covered wall with the same hand he'd used to murder the guards. I forced myself to focus on the images, the rooms and hallways of the building. Familiar rooms. The one at the top, the one with the vase turned right at the end. That was the section across the bottom of the blueprint I'd seen at the hotel.

"You understand where we are?" Yakov asked.

I swallowed.

"Start here." He tapped the nearest screen to him and left me with the corpses, appearing a moment later in the screen. He moved with the grace of a figure skater, his movements so smooth, he could have crept up on a bird. No trembling. No troubles at what he'd done.

"How could you kill them?" I whispered. What Venom had turned him into was horrific. Beyond horrific. It was—

"Easy as breathing," Yakov said in my ear.

I jumped. I'd forgotten about the earpiece.

An analogue clock above me marked ten to one. Ten minutes until he killed again. I stepped away from the guards. I couldn't help him do this. It was no better than pulling the trigger myself. But to save Mum, was it worth it? The bank guard, these ones, whoever Yakov was after now – that would be five. Five lives taken.

But to do nothing and let Venom kill Mum … how was I supposed to make a decision like that?

Yakov paused at the corner. "This is the point where you start talking."

My fists balled. For Mum? Or selfishness? "Go right."

Yakov disappeared from the bottom screen and entered the second from the left.

"Second door," I said. "Cut through to the hallway."

He didn't hesitate and shifted to the screen in front of me.

Some images flashed and changed, showing previously hidden corridors. Two women walked along one. A lone man travelled another. All three would cross Yakov in seconds. But apparently blending in wasn't an option. I had to keep him hidden.

"Stop."

Yakov's image paused with his hand on a door handle, hair almost black in the shadows. It made no sense. Why couldn't he wear a suit instead of black clothes? Why couldn't he have done this himself?

"There are people coming," I said.

He ducked back, his gun raised, a white silencer attached to the barrel.

My chest constricted. "You don't need to kill them. Just hide."

The man and women stepped between screens and crossed by Yakov's door unaware of the man they passed. Unaware of the danger.

I exhaled. "It's clear. Go through. Turn right."

Yakov put his Beretta away and left the room.

I stepped closer to the screens. He was close now. Too close. Another minute and I'd have helped him—

Yakov disappeared.

43

I blinked. What happened? Where'd Yakov go? Weakness swept over me, and my knees buckled, dropping me to the floor. I turned instinctively for the chair, but the guard still slumped there, his chest black, blood sliding down his hand. My breaths came thick and fast like I'd run a lap of the track.

What was going on? I frantically searched for Yakov. If someone saw him, if he decided I hadn't done my job … what? What would happen? I ran a hand over my arm – healed now from Blake's bruises. The Russian hadn't hurt me before, but that didn't mean he wouldn't.

There he was, top left screen, several floors above where he'd been moments before and only around the corner from the vent. How'd he get there?

A suited man walked towards him down the passage.

"Go back," I said. "There's an empty room on your right."

"Where have you been?" Yakov hissed. He backtracked.

"No, your other right," I said. "That's the one."

He slipped into the room but didn't close the door.

The worker turned the corner.

"Explain," Yakov said.

"The cameras glitched." That explained his disappearance, but not his sudden transportation to another floor. And the weakness – my body trembled. Every limb urged me to lie down, to sleep. Sweat coated my back.

"You've been silent several minutes," he whispered. "If you tried to—"

"I haven't! I've been here the whole time." My stomach lurched at the time on the clock. Ten forty-nine. I'd lost almost ten minutes. "That's not possible." The blackout at the island had been something to do with Venom. Something about their technology. Hadn't it? It couldn't have happened out here. It shouldn't have.

"Keep it together," Yakov said. "How many people are in the passage?"

People. Innocent people. Like the one he planned to kill in less than a minute. Maybe he wasn't innocent. It didn't matter. I wouldn't help Yakov kill anyone else. I couldn't.

"Sally?"

"I won't help you," I said. "I'm done helping you kill."

He huffed. "You're done when I say you're done." He stepped out and shot once, the sound zipping in my ear.

The worker jerked backwards and collapsed, the hole in his head a bluish tinge in the screen.

Shock cut through me like I'd been shot instead. "You—he didn't—you murderer!" I pulled the piece from my ear and staggered to my feet. No more. I'd get out of here no matter what it took.

A taser hung on the guard's belt. I grabbed it and raced from the room, stumbling against the wall. Nausea welled, the kind that strikes when you haven't slept. I pushed on down the corridor and shoved open the exit.

Sunlight spilled around a muscled figure. Joe clamped his hand over my mouth, shoved me against the wall, and in one swift motion, snatched my taser and crushed it beneath his foot. "Come with me." He grabbed my wrist and dragged me past the security room.

I struggled to get free. "Let me go!"

He whirled on me and yanked me closer. "There's no time for this. We need to go. Now."

"No. I'm not—" I struck out, but like Yakov, Joe blocked it easily and twisted my arm in a lock.

"Keep moving."

So, he was the ally. The one Yakov kept referring to. He was the one waiting to make sure I didn't escape. I strained against him, earning a pinch of pain along my shoulder.

"Do you want to get arrested?" he growled.

Arrested? Were the police—

"You're a known Venom assassin," he said. "Do I need to explain what they do to people like us?"

How was I known? I hadn't killed anyone. But I'd seen Yakov kill. Did police stand a chance against Venom's assassins? Against people like Yakov and Joe?

He marched me down a staircase into an underground car park, thick with the scent of rubber and sweat. Tires screeched on concrete.

Joe pulled me into a crouch behind an ebony BMW, his stance poised, watchful. "Where's your gun?"

"I don't have it."

He cast me a sharp look. "Why not?"

Because Yakov took it. "I didn't need it."

"You always need it."

A door burst open, and Yakov barrelled through, Beretta ready. The white surface caught the reflection of the lights.

Joe cursed and tugged me lower with a freckled hand, forcing a hiss of pain. He pulled out his gun. What was he looking at? I saw no police. No one at all except Yakov.

Joe stood up and shot once at the Russian.

I gasped. "What are you doing?" Since when did Venom shoot at their own members?

Yakov dove behind a vehicle and fired back blindly – a waste of a bullet – urging me against the car door. All it took was him lying down, seeing our feet between the tyres. Joe's sweaty odour filled my nose, marred my tastebuds with its musty flavour. I tried to slip free, but he banged me up against the car. "Stay still."

"You shot him."

He cocked his gun. "Yakov should have stayed out of it."

"Out of *what?*"

A car squealed around the corner and screeched to a halt beside us. Joe forced me in at gunpoint and slipped in after me. The driver hit the accelerator and we burst forwards, pummelled with Yakov's gunfire. A patch of red spread over his side where he crouched by his vehicle.

I gripped the seat with clammy hands. "What is going on? Since when do Venom turn on their own?" Yakov had followed their orders. Was this about my silence? About my blackout? I pulled on the handle, but the door didn't budge.

Joe flipped open the lid of a small box, releasing a strange, sweet smell and pulled out a handkerchief.

My neck tingled. "What—"

He clamped one hand around the back of my head and shoved the hankie against my nose. Dizziness flooded my senses. I struggled, pushed and kicked, but his vice-like grip didn't soften. My limbs weakened. His body tilted. My breath caught.

His eyes met mine. "I'm not Venom."

44

Someone breathed nearby. Joe? Or someone else? Metal bit into my wrist, and something hard pressed against my back. Images of dank basements with leaky pipes and trays full of blades and skewers filled my thoughts, and I shuddered.

"I know you're awake." A woman's voice. A gentle voice. Weird. Venom didn't know how to be gentle. Had Joe really meant what he said, that he wasn't Venom?

I opened my eyes. Sunlight flooded through a large, open window. I squinted against the groggy pain in my head while my eyes adjusted, only then noticing distant birdsong.

A woman sat opposite me. I guessed early sixties, though judging by the wrinkles on her bare feet, potentially older. Her low-heeled shoes rested beneath her chair – one of them on their side – and a flowery dress hung to her knees. The epitome of a doting grandmother. A grandmother with a gun beside her.

She smiled at me. "Welcome back. Joe certainly went all out to bring you in. I was beginning to wonder how long the chloroform would hold you. I apologise for that."

"What do you want?"

She blinked. "Not 'who are you'? That tends to be the first question."

"I've learned questions are pointless," I said.

171

"And yet, you still asked one."

Good point. I wriggled my wrist in the handcuff, testing for weak spots. The chair dug against my back, so I leaned forwards a little. I shouldn't have asked anything. Victor would've sent me around the track for it. Heat welled at the thought of him. "Are you going to answer me or not?"

Her expression hardened. "Venom certainly changed you, didn't it?"

I didn't answer. Didn't do anything. I just … looked at her. Expressionless. Hiding everything. My thirst. My pain. My insane worry about Mum. Was I near her? In the same building? Is that why they'd brought me here? I swallowed back the nausea, and the woman gave a little smile.

"I understand your distrust. Living with Venom must have been hard."

Understatement of the century.

"You can relax," she said. "I am not Venom."

The second claim. What was this? Another test? Another one of Dakota's ways of reading me under pressure? If they were looking for loyalty, they weren't going to get it. I'd never been loyal to Venom, and they knew it. I'd tried to run, too. I closed my eyes against the dread. That's what this was. Punishment.

"You don't believe me," the woman said, drawing my gaze.

"I've been surrounded by secrets and lies since Venom took me. Why should I?"

"Because it's the truth." She brushed a hand down her knee. "And I think you know that somewhere deep down."

"Uh huh. Instinct, right?"

She shrugged. "Something like that." She crossed her legs, foot hanging mid-air. "My name is Spencer. I'm the Head of the SIO – Special Intelligence Operations. It's an undercover unit of UK intelligence."

"Never heard of you."

"We've been watching you," she said. "Ever since you were taken to the Ilha da Queimada Grande."

"You know about that?"

"Of course. We keep a close watch on Venom's training. Satellites."

I knew it. Out in broad daylight with no cover from the trees, the training on the island couldn't possibly be a secret.

"Infiltrating it though," she said, "well, that's a whole other game."

"Wouldn't be hard," I said, "with the right team, the right equipment."

When she shook her head, the creases on her neck deepened. "They have more safeguards than you know." She leaned closer, and I caught a snatch of floral perfume. "And Venom's recruits tend to be unwaveringly loyal."

Not all of them.

"Loyal to their own agendas, I mean." She popped her foot on her shoe. "To their own desire for money or power."

Sounded about right. Yakov had his own agenda. Why else would he lie for me? "What are you loyal to?" I asked.

Spencer cocked her head. "Would you believe me if I said justice? I want what's right."

Yes, well, right was an iffy subject. Venom brainwashed children into thinking killing was right. So, her answer meant little to me.

She wandered to a table on my right, hair bouncing with each step, and filled a glass with water. The sound of trickling liquid awakened an aching thirst and made my tongue feel like sandpaper. She brought the cup to me. "You're different, aren't you?" she said. "You didn't want to be recruited."

There it was. The loyalty test. If she was Venom, if I made a wrong move—what? They'd threaten Mum again? Her danger was clear enough. I didn't need a reminder.

Spencer stood over me with the water in one hand, a key in the other.

I tried to swallow, but my throat wouldn't obey. "I won't help you get on the island. I have enough at stake."

"Your mother," she said. "Yes, I'm aware. Would you like to

speak with her? Or Lia, perhaps?"

My muscles locked. They'd found Lia? Sweat broke out over my neck. That's what this was. Another threat to another family member. More control for them, more helplessness for me.

Spencer unlocked my handcuffs and handed me the cup. "The phone is over there."

I downed the water, but the effort to swallow felt like gulping tar. Dakota had offered a call, too, but that hadn't ended well.

"You're fearful," Spencer said. "I understand. Venom pushed you. Abused you. But we are not them." She walked over to the phone and dialled a number, switching it to loudspeaker. It rang three times.

"Hello?" Lia.

My pulse hammered in my ears. They'd found her. Where was she? Had they captured her yet? Were they waiting for orders to?

Spencer gestured to the phone and stepped away.

I approached it warily, half-expecting her to hang up. Seventy-three days. That's how long it'd been since I heard Lia's voice. Since I'd seen her.

"Hello? Anyone there?"

I paused by the phone.

Spencer didn't move.

"Lia?" I said.

"Sally? Is that you?" Urgency flooded her voice. Urgency— and relief. She must've been as worried about me as she was for herself.

Spencer simply smiled – a gesture of confirmation.

I stepped closer to the phone. "Are you okay? Where are you? Are you hurt?"

"I'm fine. I'm with the SIO. You're with Spencer, yes?"

I hesitated. Spencer had sat down again. She ran her toes along the tiles, picking at something on her dress. "Yeah," I said. "I am."

"*Good.*" She breathed a sigh. "*I knew she'd find you. Trust her, okay? She helped me. She can help you.*"

I bit my lip. How much of this was real? There was technology that could replicate voices. Wasn't there? It wouldn't be hard for Venom to get it. All their money, all their power. Or maybe they did have Lia. Maybe they were forcing her to say this. "Lia, tell me something – something only we would know."

A pause. "*Do you doubt it's me?*"

Yes. "No. I doubt what you're saying."

Spencer raised her eyebrows.

"Something only we would know," I said.

Another pause. When she spoke next, her tone brimmed with reluctance. "*My necklace. The tree with the ruby. It belonged to my mother.*"

My throat tightened. Her secret.

"*You were upset once,*" she said, "*in the dead of night, so I told you about it. Like you don't have your Dad anymore, I don't have my mother.*"

I didn't want her to share this. It was her secret. Her pain. "Lia, you don't—"

"*The necklace is proof that our loved ones are never truly gone. We can keep a piece of them with us. Forever in their memory.*"

I exhaled a stuttering breath.

Spencer stared at the phone, eyes glistening. Was she holding back tears?

"*You believe me now?*" Lia asked.

How could I not? "Yeah. I believe you."

A third pause. Lia collecting herself? "*Trust Spencer. She's one of the good guys.*"

Spencer tucked her feet beneath her chair, propped hands on her knees, and cast me a little smile. The good guy? Really? Lia must've believed it or she wouldn't have shared her secret. Was this how she'd been protected from Venom, how they hadn't managed to find her? Because of the SIO?

"Okay, Lia. I'll hear her out." If Lia was right, if Spencer really was an ally, she could help. We could save Mum. She could protect me from Venom.

We could be free.

"I'll see you soon, all right?"

Could I? Would they really take me to Lia? "Yeah," I said, more in hope than anything. "See you soon."

The line went dead.

45

"How did you know?" I asked. "Venom took me, they took Lia, how did you know to save her?"

Spencer gestured to the chair opposite her, the handcuffs dangling from the arms. "We keep a close eye on Venom's comings and goings."

"They have my mum."

"I'm aware. We know her location." She ran a hand along her skirt. "As it happens, I have agents in place poised for her extraction."

I sank on to the seat. "You mean it?" First Lia, then me, now Mum. She was really going to help us escape? After all those weeks of worry and hopelessness, it looked like luck was finally in our favour.

She flipped her shoe over with her bare feet. What was the deal with that? I'd feel too exposed. Vulnerable. Maybe that was the point. She wanted me to trust her. "My agents are ready to extract her," she said, but her gaze lingered on me a little too long and the corners of her mouth bore a tightness that shouldn't have accompanied good news.

Unease made my fingers tingle. "I sense a but."

"I'd like to make a deal."

My hope deflated. I should've known. No one gave something for nothing. Freedom didn't come without price.

Sure, Lia wanted me to trust her, but Lia was a civilian. What would she know about the SIO? She hadn't seen the other side, the side of Venom, the side of greed. "What do you want?"

Spencer squared her shoulders. "You."

"Me?"

"You must see it," she said. "Why would Venom recruit you, an ordinary girl with no particular aspirations or skills?"

Thanks for that. "Venom is mad. Who knows why they do what they do?"

"They're anything but," she said. "They're genius, intelligent, and cunning as snakes. They could whistle the wind into a frenzy and convince even the sun to sweat."

She sounded like a crazed fan. "A little much, don't you think?"

"Venom are many things," she said. "But they are not mad. Only a fool would dismiss them, and if we're to truly defeat the terrorists, we have to know them for what they are."

It made sense. Like Yakov said, know a place's security and half the job is done for you. So, if I know my enemy, I'd stand a chance of winning. "You know why they recruited me," I said.

"That's the thing about Venom," she said. "They never do anything without a reason. And you are undoubtedly the greatest weapon they've ever had."

What a load of rubbish. I was just me. Normal, boring me. That hardly constituted 'greatest weapon' material. "What do I have that Venom could possibly want?" Something related to my blackouts and impossible new skills?

Spencer tapped her forefinger against her leg, and her lips pursed. "What do you know about NightLock?"

"Never heard of it."

"No?"

"No." Actually, yes. NightLock. That's what Dakota wrote in his note to Niagra. Another riddle in all of Venom's riddles. "What is it?"

She clasped her hands. "We're interested in a document – or

series of documents – under the codename NightLock. We believe it's located in Niagra's office on the island."

My breath caught, and the whole room seemed to spin. "You want to send me back there."

"For a time."

"No." I grabbed the arms of the chair, not trusting myself to stand up. After all this, I couldn't go back. I just couldn't.

"Look at it this way," Spencer said. "We'll have your mother. She'll be safe with us. Protected, just like Lia."

"Mum's life isn't the only one at risk," I said. "If Venom catches me snooping around, stealing a file—"

"They won't kill you."

"You don't know that."

"Yes, I do." Such confidence. How could she have that? She sat there, utterly relaxed, like the world was hers to command. But I'd seen Venom kill. I'd seen how ruthless they were. Had she?

"What do they want with me?" I asked. "Why'd they recruit me?"

"That's a story for when you return. And believe me, Sally, I want you to return." She reached forward to pop her hand on mine.

I pulled away. "Why can't Joe do it? He's one of yours, isn't he?"

"We can't expose him. It was risky enough extracting you without the Russian seeing him."

Yakov. He'd been shot. Not killed, though. Right? The blood had been on his side, not his chest. Something tugged within me – something that hoped he was okay. That couldn't be right. Me caring about the Russian killer? No way. I wouldn't accept that.

"Joe's the spy," I said. "It's his job to take risks, not mine."

"You have skills Joe doesn't."

I huffed. "Like what?"

"Like learning seven languages overnight." Sheer curtains beside the window fluttered in a slight breeze. Spencer shuffled her chair closer to me, expression lighting up in sudden awe. "Maybe more. Our best agent couldn't achieve such a feat."

Of course, Joe would've told her. No doubt he'd reported back on everything he saw.

"I don't know how it happened," I said.

"But you don't deny it did."

I drove my fist against the chair and stood up. "Speaking languages won't do what you're asking. Even if I get in the office, I can't access Niagra's computer. It'll be protected. And watched, no doubt. The place is probably crawling with cameras." I backed to the door. If I tried to leave, would she let me? Would there be guards outside? Was I even free, or was I simply another prisoner? "I won't do it. I won't go back to Venom."

She eyed the handcuffs, almost thoughtful. But she wouldn't put me back in them. Not if she was really an ally. "That's your final answer?"

"You have agents. Not so you can risk civilians' lives."

She narrowed her eyes. "You're hardly a civilian anymore."

"I'm not a criminal." I'd done nothing wrong. Done nothing Venom wanted me to do.

"No." She inclined her head. "You're not a criminal."

"Then, I'd like to go home."

She stood up, lips tight, and resolve set in her features. "I understand. I'll honour your decision, of course." She padded to the phone. "I'll call my agents, tell them to abort."

A hot shiver carried down my spine. "Abort?" She wouldn't leave Mum with Venom. She wouldn't abandon someone in need. Would she? I knew nothing about her.

"Sally, dear, we have limited resources. I can only extend them to my own agents." She began to dial. "You understand, of course. If we stopped to help every civilian, where would the country be?"

I rushed across and stabbed my finger on the disconnect button.

She peered at me innocently. "Something wrong?"

It took a moment to answer, a moment to break through the sting in my throat. "You're no different to Venom. You know that?"

She shifted her hand to the edge of the table. Probably had a gun under there. Or a silent alarm. "We both want the same thing: to stop Venom. If project NightLock goes ahead, the world as we know it will change forever. There'll be no coming back from that."

"And then what?" I asked. "If I do it," – assuming I could without getting caught or tortured – "how do I get the file to you? I can hardly come and go from the island as I please."

She lowered the phone, mouth twitching in satisfaction. "We'll equip you with a drive. When you have the file, one of my agents will find you."

"Joe?"

"Not necessarily. And I'd appreciate it if you didn't mention his true allegiance."

Well, duh. "And how would I get back?" I asked. "You can hardly drop me on their doorstep."

"We won't need to. Venom went to great lengths to recruit you. They won't give you up now."

I sniffed. "All they did was find a donor."

She folded her arms. "You really believe that? That they just *happened* to have a donor, that they just *knew* the situation? Just like that? I suppose you were lucky they were in the right place at the right time."

"You're implying they caused the accident." I'd been over this thought. It was impossible. Venom couldn't have worked it so they killed no one, so that Mum could be saved with a simple surgery. The crash could've killed me – too big a risk if they were so determined to recruit me.

"No, dear," Spencer said. "I'm not implying anything." When she put the phone down, her features brimmed with nothing but sombre truth. "I'm stating it outright. You do this job for us, and I'll show you the proof."

46

There was something about the sweat-smelling air that triggered the kind of travel sickness that made me want to curl up and block out the whole situation. Three heavily-armoured agents surrounded me in the back of the van, rifles on laps, foreheads glistening despite the air-conditioning blasting from the vents: more warm air than anything. Helmets obscured most of their heads so only their faces showed: high cheekbones on one agent, forest-green eyes in another, and gravelly stubble on the chin of the third.

The sky looked deep sapphire through the bulletproof windscreen. A perfect day in Rio. Two cars travelled in the distance – the only vehicles I'd seen in several minutes. According to Spencer, the escort would 'transport me' to a safehouse located within Corcovado – a mountain lying west of the city centre.

"It used to be named Pinaculo da Tentacao," she'd told me. "I presume you know the translation."

"Pinnacle of Temptation," I said.

She'd nodded. "It's fitting. The journey will tempt Venom after you."

So far, there'd been no sign.

The SIO had taken one of my boots and tweaked it to conceal a tiny pen drive in the sole. "Plug this in Niagra's desktop," she'd said. "It'll copy the files."

"The NightLock ones? Or all of them?" I asked.

"Does it matter?"

If she was anything like Venom, very much so. The last thing the world needed was another set of terrorists. Not that anything would make a difference if Dakota spoke with me. He could read my lies in his sleep, and since I'd been missing for twenty-four hours, he was probably the first person they'd send me to.

The previous night included me standing with Spencer by a wall of screens, watching the headcams of her agents while they infiltrated the building holding Mum. Gunfire and shouted commands had my heart in my mouth until they gave the announcement. They had her. Mum was safe and on her way to Lia even while I was heading back to Venom.

That travel sickness welled, and I touched a handcuffed hand to my lips.

Stubbles and Cheekbones glanced at each other.

I knew the lie. I'd repeated it over again through the night, answered Spencer's questions, responded without hesitation. "Nothing to worry about," she'd said. "They'll buy it easily." Clearly, she hadn't met Dakota.

"Any chance of some water?" I asked in perfect Portuguese. Anything to settle my stomach.

Green's eyes met mine, and Stubbles adjusted his grip on his rifle.

"What?" I asked.

"You make them nervous," said Green.

"Really?" I asked. "Why?"

"You're Venom."

I huffed. "Hardly." Coldness touched my tone, and for a brief second, I sounded just like Backer. I forced softness to my voice. "I despise Venom."

The three exchanged looks. Wary looks.

"You don't trust me," I said.

"You can't blame them," Green said. "You have a

reputation."

"Do I?"

"Venom does," Green said. "And you were one of them." Were. So they kind of knew the truth. Except I'd never been Venom. I hadn't even killed – but only Yakov and I knew that. Would that come back to bite me when this was over? I could hardly prove my innocence. Even with Yakov's word – which they'd unlikely get – why would they believe him?

I shrugged. "I get it. Who wouldn't be nervous of a ruthless murderer?"

Cheekbones adjusted his weapon.

I lurched forward, and all three men jolted where they sat, leaving me giggling. "Relax," I said. There were three of them and one of me. I was handcuffed, unarmed, exhausted from a near-sleepless night and anxious as ever. What did they expect me to do? Sprout horns and eat them alive? "I don't suppose you'd believe me if I told you I've never killed?"

Green raised his eyebrows.

"No," I said. "Course not." No one believed anyone anymore.

The engine vibrated through my seat. "I spy with my little eye," I said, "something beginning with R." Rio.

Stubbles stared at me.

"R," I said. "You know the game? I pick something, say what—"

"I know how to play." Stubbles curled a finger on his trigger.

I swallowed down my fear. "So, R."

"Rocket," Green muttered.

"What? Where can you—"

"Get down!" He dove over me.

The van lurched. Glass shattered and rained over our heads. Green's crushing weight pinned me to the seat. Metal screeched. The world tilted in a sickeningly familiar sensation.

47

A low ringing buzzed in my ears, and my wrists stung. Flames crackled somewhere outside the van, flickering orange light over the seats. The exposed light in the roof hung jagged and broken.

I saw a flash of Mum. Her pale face. Blood dripping from her collar. No. I couldn't do this again. I struggled against my seatbelt, trying to tug it from the clip. My breathing hitched.

Green grabbed me. "Take it easy."

I pushed him off, let slip a sob.

"Hey. Stop." He pressed me against the seat. "Come back. Focus on me."

Focus on the agent. That's what he was. An agent. Not Mum. This wasn't *that* accident. Not that accident.

Green grasped my chin. His eyes grazed my face, studying me, and he nodded. "You're not hurt. Breathe."

Tell that to my wrists. I jerked my chin from his grasp. Mum was okay. Spencer had her. She was safe.

Stubbles stirred, head lolling. A trail of blood ran down his cheek.

"A rocket." Cheekbones cursed. "No one said they'd shoot us off the road." He pressed his fingers to Stubbles' pulse.

"Is he okay?" I asked, voice shaking.

Cheekbones waved a hand. "Get her out of here."

Green undid my belt and hauled me outside.

Gunfire sounded around us. Smoke billowed from the crumpled bonnet. Leaves and branches lay scattered over the road, several pieces on fire.

Green shoved me against the van with a gloved hand, his rifle in the other. "Stay close to me. We're not far from the safehouse."

The safehouse? I gritted my teeth. The point was to get me back to Venom. "Spencer didn't tell you?"

"Tell me what?"

A man burst through the smoke, clothed in black. He raised a knife.

Green blocked it and twisted aside to miss a strike to his head.

Cheekbones grabbed my shoulder and tugged me around the van. Behind him, the city of Rio gleamed like marble structures beneath the sun.

What was Spencer thinking? They needed to know to back off. They had to let Venom take me, not fight against them. The thought made my stomach hitch, and I dry heaved over the road.

A gun fired, and Green's attacker slumped to the ground, a hole in his head.

People were dying. Venom, SIO: it didn't matter at this point. This had to stop. I gasped for breath and twisted out of Cheekbones' grip. "You need to let me go."

He coughed a huff. "Not going to happen."

"But—"

Green grabbed me. "Bob?"

"He's taken the front." Cheekbones pushed me at Green who grasped my arm. "Try anything, I'll shoot you. Understand?"

I shook my head. "You need to listen."

A Venom agent rounded the van and slashed a knife at Green. He jerked aside and lost his grip long enough for me to slip between them and sprint to the roadside. A bullet hit the ground, spraying stones through the air.

I yelped and plunged into the trees. Weed-ridden grass sloped downwards. My feet skidded on dirt, and a branch scratched my leg.

I was out. Free from the watch of the SIO and the hold of Venom. What if I kept running? What if I escaped into Rio and disappeared? I spoke the language. Could I survive there? Somehow find my way out of Brazil?

Venom would hunt me at every turn. So would the SIO. And Mum, Lia: what would happen to them?

A rock caught my foot, my chin bumped the dust, and a sharp ache spread through my jaw. The handcuffs dug into my skin, hindering my attempts to stand.

Someone grabbed my arm and hoisted me up, his broad nose and freckles hidden behind black streaks.

"Joe." I cringed away from him, remembering the scent of chloroform, the crippling dizziness, the strength of his hands on my head.

He pressed the barrel of his pistol to his lips, shushing me, and shot twice at Green when he burst into view. The bullets collided with his vest, and Green jerked backwards, disappearing amongst the grass. Joe shoved me to the left. "That way."

What choice did I have? Joe was the one part I hadn't counted on. The one agent who knew exactly what I was doing. He wouldn't let me run. Wouldn't let me deviate. But perhaps he would try to save some lives like he had with Green. Sure, Green would get a bruise or two from the bullets in his vest, but at least he'd survive.

The trees thickened. Sunlight streaked between the leaves, and flies buzzed in the shadows. The scent of grass and dirt filled the air. My wrists stung, irritated by growing sweat.

The bushes ended suddenly, plunging me into a clearing. The chop of helicopter blades rippled the grass and whipped my hair against my face. I squinted at the silhouetted aircraft above me, blinded by rays of sun. Someone jumped from the cabin in a blackened blur of rope and muscle before landing lightly in front of me.

Yakov. A vest covered his shirt, and a streak of browned blood marked the collar. The Russian held out a gloved hand. "Come with me."

Stubbles ran into the clearing, rifle pointed skyward. He'd lost his helmet somewhere, showing wavy, black hair, a receding hairline, tiny ears, and a streak of blood curving around his eye. He fired repeatedly, his bullets sparking off the side of the helicopter, oblivious to the agent who emerged from the treeline behind him.

Nick raised his gun with ballet-poise. But he wasn't Joe. He wouldn't aim for the vest.

I lurched towards them. "Don't—"

Yakov grabbed my waist, hauled me back, and Nick's gun flared.

Stubbles' head whipped forward, and he collapsed in a bundle of bullets and red spray, leaving my gut hollow and my muscles weak with shock.

Yakov's grip on me tightened, the world lurched, and we lifted into the air, veering slightly when the helicopter flew over the hillside, away from the killings.

48

The heat inside the helicopter was stifling compared to the whip of wind, but all I could do was sit there, staring through the door, limbs tensed and aching. So many people had come for me. Joe. Nick. Yakov. Others on the road. Some in the air. Why? What was so important about my blackouts that they'd send an army to retrieve me?

Now Stubbles was dead. I didn't even know his name.

Yakov pushed me against the back wall of the aircraft – more a cargo hold than anything – pulled a thin, metal hook from his pocket and used it to pick the lock on the handcuffs. They clattered to the floor. Redness burned my wrists, and a sudden stinging spread up my arms. Yakov scowled at the marks. "Here." He passed me a water bottle and brushed my hair back from my forehead before reaching for a first-aid kit. "It's not too deep."

Had I hit my head?

He tore open a packet and pulled out a wipe.

"Leave it," I said. "I'm fine." People had died. What was a cut to me?

He touched it to my head.

"I said, I'm fine." I went to push him away, but he snatched my wrist, just below the mark and dabbed my head, coating the wipe with blood.

"I wasn't asking."

No one asked anymore. Between murder, abduction and forced assignments, it was a wonder anyone had any loyalty. Or life. They'd shot a rocket at us! How stupid could they be? It was a miracle no one was killed. In the car crash anyway.

"Sally." Yakov pulled my chin to face him.

"What?"

He frowned. "What did they do to you?"

"I'm fine." The image of Stubbles jerking forwards flashed through my mind. My nails dug into my palms.

Yakov's hand closed around my fist. "Did they hurt you?"

They helped me. And coerced me into working for them. They were no better than Venom, stopping at nothing to get what they wanted.

Something stabbed my forearm. I gasped and tried to jerk away, but Yakov held me still. His thumb pressed on a syringe, pumping its contents into me before pulling out the needle. "Anaesthetic. It won't do much for your injuries, but it'll help with the pain."

Would it? Was I supposed to trust that's what he'd given me? As though in answer, the pain in my wrists began to ease.

"Little warning next time."

Before long, the ocean glistened below us, stretching beyond the horizon. A boat with a meagre flag bobbed over the waves. And there was Snake Island, as green and deadly as ever. My gut clenched. What was I doing? I had a way out, and here I was, willingly going back to the people who abducted me in the first place.

Victor would be there.

I pitched forward, heaving again. He'd kill me. Given the slightest opportunity, he wouldn't hesitate to hurt me.

Yakov pulled me back to him and shoved the bottle in my hand. He'd opened it. "Drink," he said. "Sips."

It'd take more than sips to deal with this madness.

Yakov's gaze burned into me. "What did they do to you?"

Interesting that he thought the SIO were to blame. Didn't it occur to him that Venom was what I feared? The reality of stealing from them was so utterly insane that the most psychotic wacko on Earth wouldn't try it, but here I was. Even my boot blazed against my sole. They'd catch me. They'd find the drive, and because I'd be stuck on the island, there'd be no extraction.

49

I'd hoped I'd seen the last of the submarine room with the big windows looking out over the open ocean. I couldn't deny the bubbles darting past were pretty, but I could hardly enjoy it under duress.

Yakov touched my shoulder – a gentle touch, but it still made me jolt. "Sit down," he said. "We need to talk."

I did. My legs hardly held me anyway. Clusters of fish billowed past the glass like miniature, underwater clouds. Glittering clouds. Like bullets. Hundreds of gleaming bullets. I blinked rapidly and turned to the assassin sitting opposite.

"You can start with the op," Yakov said, his hands below the table. Was he holding his gun, training the barrel on me? Waiting for me to slip up? "What happened?"

"I don't know." My voice shook. "The screens glitched. I lost track of you."

"For ten minutes?" His expression showed no irritation. No anything. Just calmness. Like we were discussing the weather over hot chocolate.

What was the point in lying? I needed all the strength I could get for Dakota. Even then, I'd never be able to trick him. He was the lie master for a reason. "I blacked out."

Yakov nodded, and his gaze fell on my shaking hands. "You're blaming your disappearance on the comms?"

"No." Hadn't he listened to a word I said?

His eyes matched the shade of the sea, deep blue and flecked with silver like the shoals of fish through the windows. He shook his head. "You're blaming the comms."

I frowned at him. "You want me to lie." Why? Venom knew about the blackouts. They had to. They never asked me how I learned the languages. Never questioned me about the lost three hours. Which meant guiding Yakov had been pointless. He could've done the job himself. Which meant Venom wanted me to blackout. They wanted something to happen. But what? Why choose that building, that person to die? I'd learned nothing from it. No new skills had mysteriously popped up.

"The comms malfunctioned," Yakov said. "A loose wire. When you got them back up, you guided me as before."

"They'll never buy it," I said. "Dakota can read me. I can't lie to him." Hiding the whole NightLock issue would be hard enough.

"You must," Yakov said. "Trust me."

"Trust you?" How could I? He'd done nothing trustworthy since I'd met him. "I don't know you. Can't read you. How could I trust someone who just killed a man out of spite?"

"Six, actually. Though the first was, admittedly, an unfortunate casualty."

"An unfortunate casualty?" My tone hitched. "He was innocent! It wasn't my fault I black—"

He clamped his hand sharply over my own, startling me into silence. "Keep your voice down." He pulled back, leaving a cold patch where his hand had been. "You are not in position to speak freely." He glanced at the closed, double doors. The engine thrummed somewhere in the distance.

I lowered my voice and dropped my hand to my knee. "You could've let that worker pass you. He could've had family."

Yakov's voice turned cold. "You care too much."

"I disagree."

His eyes bore into mine, staring me down.

I glared back. I was done being intimidated. Done looking away first.

"What happened with the SIO?" he asked, and just like that, my resolve cracked.

I looked down at the table, tracing the light's reflection. I had to test the story sooner or later. Why not now? "They stuck me in a room. Wanted information."

"What did you tell them?"

"Nothing. I'm just a prisoner here. What could I share?" My speech flowed smoothly, just as I'd practised, but I clenched my trembling hands beneath the table. "They've got me tied to a banker's murder in Rio, and the ones from yesterday: the security guards, the workers, the guard at the kiosk." All people Yakov killed. I could count them on the freckles of his knuckles. Recent cuts marked one of them.

"You've practised that speech," he said.

"What?" My cheeks flushed. "Course I haven't." But my burning cheeks must've been a dead giveaway.

"You don't think I can spot deception?" Yakov asked. "Dakota's not the only one who can read a lie."

Tingling sweat broke over my back. Coming back here was a mistake. A huge one.

"Now you're pale," he said. "Take a long breath. Slow your heart rate."

"You think you've got me pinned, but you're wrong," I said.

"Oh, I'm not. But luckily, Dakota won't debrief you." Yakov pointed to his eyes. "Look here. If you look down, Niagra will know you're lying."

Eye contact. It was one of the first things Dakota taught me. How could I let that slip? For that matter, what was Yakov doing? He had enough on me now to get whatever he wanted. Why delay the inevitable? "Why are you helping me?"

He cocked his head, ran his thumb over his knuckle. "I have my reasons. Now remember what I've said. You won't get a second chance."

50

Yakov marched me to Niagra's office, his words stuck in my mind. *You don't think I can spot deception? If you look down, Niagra will know.*

Would he? In my last session with Dakota he said anyone would believe my lies. Except him, but he wasn't here. I took a shaky breath and uncurled my fists.

Yakov cast me a warning look, knocked twice, and opened the door.

Niagra sat behind his desk, reading a file. Sunlight on the pond gleamed through the open patio doors, putting spots in my eyes and reflecting ripples on the wall and over the grandfather clock where a golden pendulum swung. Niagra put the file in a drawer. "Take a seat." He gestured with red hands at the chair across from him, and gave Yakov a swift nod.

Yakov's hand touched my back – a gesture of comfort or something else? – and left me alone with the killer.

I perched on the edge of the chair, tensing when he propped his elbows on the desk. He linked his stained fingers and tucked them under his chin. Blood, Niall had said. Blood from his victims. "You seem uncomfortable."

"It's been a long day."

"I heard. You've had quite the ordeal. A capture. Interrogation, no doubt." He was assuming. Or testing me.

I allowed a flicker of discomfort.

"I've upset you," he said.

"I'd rather not think about it." A strain slipped through in my voice, and although I mentally kicked myself for it, Niagra's shoulders dropped a touch.

"Of course not," he said. "But you understand I must know what happened."

I'd prepared for this, but my gut still knotted.

Niagra pressed his hands on the desk. "Let's begin with the silence. It was reported you lost communication with Yakov."

"A comms malfunction." No hesitation. Perfect eye contact. I clenched my teeth to avoid smiling. I hadn't got away with anything yet. Not by a long shot.

He raised his eyebrows. "That's not very likely, is it? All our equipment goes through extensive checks."

Unlikely, yes. But not impossible. Besides, he knew I was lying. Because he knew about the blackouts. He had to. I shrugged. "You can't always rely on technology."

"Actually, technology is what we can rely on. People, on the other hand …"

My insides roiled.

"What happened after that?" Niagra said. "After the assignment?"

"I was on my way out. I got attacked."

"You defended yourself?"

"Obviously. I was outnumbered."

"By how many?"

"Two." No hesitation. No shaking voice. He had to believe me. He had to.

He pursed his lips. "Two shouldn't have been an issue for you."

"Two civilians, no." Irritation touched my words. I'd only trained for two months. That hardly made me a black belt. "They were trained. Armed."

"So, they took you," Niagra said.

"I don't know where."

"Foreign soil." He gestured absently. "The SIO have a base in Rio. They questioned you."

I focused on the black flecks in his irises, the greying colour streaked with green. This would work or it wouldn't. I hoped Dakota wasn't watching through some hidden camera. He'd pick up on the lie. He'd know there was more. "They wanted details. Missions. Agents."

He ran a hand over his stubbly chin. "What did you tell them?"

"What could I tell? I don't know anything about Venom."

"They believed that?" His flat tone and neutral expression gave nothing away. But that only made him more dangerous. He was bound to be thinking of Mum – especially since Spencer had got her out. His suspicion radar must've been screaming.

I kept my gaze steady. "Doesn't matter what they believed. It's the truth. I don't even know why you recruited me."

He nodded slowly, eyes narrowed, thinking of the reason, no doubt.

"Why did you recruit me?" I asked. "It still makes no sense." He wouldn't answer. He never did. If anything, every time I asked a question, the listener would change the subject.

"You're exhausted, I'm sure," he said, right on cue. "You should take the day off. A little R&R as it were. It'll perk you right up."

I fought the need to swallow. This wasn't over. I'd never get the NightLock file. Spencer shouldn't have asked me. I walked to the door, longing to run through it, and scanned the place for his computer. There was nothing. Not even a filing cabinet.

"You'll find your room unlocked," Niagra said. "And Sally."

I peered back.

"Get some food, too. You look half-starved." He flashed me the smallest of smiles before dipping back into his drawer.

51

My room looked exactly as I'd left it, down to the open latch on the make-up box. My reflection in the mirror was pale-faced and streaked with blood and dirt. I looked more like the living-dead than a double agent.

A double agent. If someone once told me I'd become this, I'd have laughed in their face.

I stepped in the shower. Steaming water rushed over me, stinging tiny cuts on my arms and scalp. My uncuffed wrists burned, and the marks turned a violent red. I turned the water cold, gasping in the new temperature.

A double agent.

If Venom caught me, they'd kill me. It didn't matter why they'd taken me. They'd never tolerate betrayal. Not that I'd been loyal to begin with. I just wanted freedom. Between working for Lia, being refused my choice of education, and being taken by Venom, I'd gone from one captivity to another. This was my life. I should get to live it my way.

So, I'd do what Spencer asked. I'd find NightLock. I'd deliver it to her, and I'd leave. And no one, not even Yakov, would stop me. I'd shoot him first.

The thought sent a shiver up my face. I'd find a way around that. Yakov was different. At least, some part of him had been kind, even normal in training. In those moments, I almost felt safe.

I dipped my face beneath the water. What a load of rubbish. No one was safe with him.

Which led me to the current problem: NightLock.

I switched off the shower, dried, and dressed in trousers and a black t-shirt. Niagra's villa had no computer. The language villa did, though. Could the file be somewhere in there? Unlikely, but it was a starting point.

I scrubbed the dirt off my boots, tied up my hair and applied a little make-up – Mayra would sniff out my productless face in an instant – then hurried to the foyer where the scent of meat and vegetables filled the air, aching my empty stomach. Voices chattered from the dining hall, marking the onset of evening, and streaks of orange beamed in through the open French doors.

But I couldn't eat yet. If everyone was here, now was the time to begin my search.

I jogged towards the villas, nodded at some women I knew only by face and turned a corner – straight into Nick.

"Woah." He grabbed my arms. "Steady there. This isn't the track, you know."

I stepped away, remembering Stubbles and the way he fell, the way his blood sprayed through the heat. Goosebumps rose on my arms.

Nick ran a hand through dripping hair, sending droplets down his cheeks. "What's your hurry?"

"No hurry," I said. "Trying to jog off some steam."

"Mm." He nodded. "I get that." He waited like he was expecting more. A bottle crumpled in his grip, the clicks grinding in my ears.

"Joe's your partner, right?" I asked.

Nick cast me a sideways glance. "Why?"

"Just asking." A weak excuse. But if Nick worked with Joe, maybe he worked for Spencer, too. Not that I could ask him. It would risk blowing Joe's cover. "Is he here?"

"No, he's out solo today."

Working alone. Nick probably wasn't SIO then. "I didn't realise you did that. Worked alone, I mean."

He shrugged. "Partners aren't useful for everything. Want me to pass on a message?"

"No, I just wanted to thank him – and you – you know, for helping me today." I forced my eyes to meet Nick's. Would he read the lie? Thanking people wasn't very Venomy.

"Don't mention it," Nick said. "We do our jobs. And get paid handsomely for it." He clapped me on the shoulder. "I'll tell Joe you said hello."

"No need." Probably best he didn't know I'd spoke of him. I set off along the path again.

"Not coming to eat?" Nick called.

"In a bit," I said, ignoring the ache in my stomach. "I need to walk some more."

"Suit yourself." He gave a two-fingered salute and sauntered towards the dining hall.

He was so different here. His mannerisms, even his expression changed so completely in the shelter of the island. *And get paid handsomely for it.* An interesting thought. Had Venom paid me for my assignments? Blood money. I shivered.

I pressed on to the villas, shoulders tense. When I tilted my head to stretch my neck, it clicked. How had Joe done it: worked for the SIO and hidden it from Nick? From Dakota? It can't have been easy.

The shadows in the language room held a tinge of coolness that eased away the evening heat. A breeze fluttered my hair from an overhead air vent. I sat down at the nearest computer. The quicker I did this, the better. Of course, the last time I'd been here, I'd blacked out for three hours. I swallowed uneasily, and after a quick glance outside, pulled the drive from my boot and plugged it in.

The screen flashed to life. Code scrolled too fast for me to read, probably searching the database. The question was – how much of Venom's files were accessible here? For all I knew, these computers were filled with training programmes, nothing more.

The scrawling stopped, and a box popped up.

File not found.

Course it wasn't. That would've been too easy. Where'd Spencer get her intelligence from anyway? It made no sense to keep the file here. This was a training base, not a database. I snatched the drive, replaced it in my boot, and trudged to the dining hall.

The room bustled with little over thirty people, all smelling of fresh-cooked food. Chef Marcel stood by the kitchen, handing plates to each person. I glimpsed a salad on one, and the man who took it glowered at Marcel.

I knew that pain only too well.

The chef scowled when I got to him. "Back again."

Not by choice. I accepted the plate he handed me: a meal of chicken, potatoes, carrots, and gravy. A deliberate serving? It was more than he'd ever given me in training, but then maybe he didn't know I'd be here today. I headed to an empty table before he could change his mind, red wrists shining in the dimming light. They ached, too. Clearly the anaesthetic was wearing off.

What were my options? Spencer said someone would find me. I could wait, tell them the file wasn't here. After that she'd have to pull me out. If I could just get another assignment, get off the island again, it'd be easy pickings for her. Theoretically.

Chairs scraped beside me, and Yakov sat down with Nick. The ballet man chuckled. "You were no match."

"I was a hairline behind you."

Nick jabbed his fork at Yakov. "Too slow is too slow." He nudged me. "You weren't long. Feeling better?"

Yakov's suspicion burned into my cheek.

I shoved a forkful of potato in my mouth.

"There's a competition later," Nick said, jabbing his fork at me now. "You should come watch."

"A competition for what?" I asked.

He took a sip of water. "Three students engage in a race to a statue. It's the legendary idol de morte. Venom took it from the tomb decades ago, but archaeologists still search for it." He laughed.

"The idol of death?" I said. "Bit morbid."

"Venom is death," Nick said. "It fits."

It certainly did. I'd seen so many people die in the past few days. So many killed. How was I supposed to move past that?

Yakov kept his eyes on me, maybe trying to catch my eye. I refused to look at him, and dipped a carrot in gravy.

"The winner gets their first assignment," Nick said. "Come? It might take your mind off things."

Not likely, but I couldn't turn him down. They'd think I was struggling and send me to Dakota.

I could not be sent to him.

52

The evening carried a slight chill and gentle breeze over the courtyard where people filtered around me towards the mats, waiting for the competition to start. I hated those mats, the sessions I'd had with Victor. Would he be there? With a fractured knee he could hardly train anyone. Maybe he'd gone away to recover.

I flexed my fingers, struggling to make my legs move. He might've been waiting for me. Ready with a knife. A gun. Anything that would cause pain – and a lot of it. Not that he needed a weapon for that. He'd once spoken of snapping a man's neck with a single movement.

The air grew thick again. Hard to breathe.

"Sally." Yakov took my shoulder, falling into step beside me. His hand smelled like gun powder, and dark smudges marked his fingernails. "What were you doing before dinner?"

Straight to the point, as usual. "I went for a walk."

"A walk?" Scepticism filled his tone, and he gave me one of those looks that said, 'I want to shake you right now'.

"It cleared my head."

His hand tightened. "The real reason."

I pushed him off. His ability to read me was dangerous. If he wasn't so determined to lie for me, I'd be dead already. Or worse. But his secret agenda worried me more. What could he possibly want? "Does it matter?"

"Tell me."

"You've got your secrets. I've got mine."

When I walked away, he followed, keeping close step beside me. "Some truths are best kept hidden."

"Exactly," I said. "So, mind your own business."

He stepped forward then and blocked my path, pausing while three teenagers passed us. He nodded at them and lowered his voice. "I need to know. For your protection."

I almost laughed. A killer with a sense of humour. That was something. I tried to sidestep him, but he grabbed my forearm with a hot hand.

"You will tell me," he said.

"No. I won't." I tugged out of his grip – and he didn't fight it, because others walked past, and he had a secret, too. He couldn't afford to draw attention to us. "You know things," I said. Things that would help me understand why Venom took me. But until he told me— "I'll swap you." Eagerness burst into my tone.

His forehead creased. "Swap me?"

"A secret for a secret."

His eyebrows twitched, and his words seemed to strangle in his throat. He shook his head. "That's not how this works."

"Then, I have nothing to say." I marched past him to the mats. Of course, he'd say no. Deep down, I'd known as much, but it didn't stop the disappointment.

The students gathered around the mats left little room to watch. Nick waved at us from the left and beckoned us over. "All right?" he asked. Russian. I didn't reply, presuming he was talking to Yakov.

Yakov nodded at a teen on the mats. "You think he's ready for this?"

The boy wore all black, his slim stature blending into the shadows. Aside from an excited gleam in his eyes, he wore a relaxed expression – the kind I'd seen on Yakov on assignment. It made my skin crawl.

"As ready as can be," Nick said.

Niagra walked onto the mats, wearing a grey suit with a strange tint of green. He stopped beside a pole – like a lamp post without the lamp. Perched on top was a single statue of a person made of gold and what appeared to be black diamonds. The idol de morte.

Niagra spread out his arms, his red hands crimson in the moonlight. "Welcome to our quadrennial competition. This evening we have three contestants." He gestured to a boy with jet-black hair and a round face, no older than fourteen. "Flint."

A round of applause resounded around the mats. Flint waved.

Niagra gestured to where a girl with twin plaits readied herself, a staff twirling in her hands. "Candace."

The applause came again.

Niagra pointed once more to the teen Yakov had spoken of. "And Dean."

Dean grinned, his focus shifting to the idol.

After scattered applause, silence fell, and Niagra joined the crowd. He surveyed the three. "Begin."

Dean dashed towards the pole. So did Candace. She raised her staff and struck.

Dean blocked and kicked out, catching her in the stomach. She dropped with a whine.

Huh. "I thought she would've lasted longer."

Nick smiled. "Wait for it."

Dean made to run past her, but she twisted, swiping her weapon against the back of his knees. She whirled and hit Flint on the head. A loud crack cut over the crowd.

Flint dropped.

I gripped the wall. "Is he okay?"

Nick shrugged. "He'll recover."

By the opposite wall, the crowd parted, and Dakota stepped into the front line.

My heart burst into a sprint. The lie master. He'd know I was hiding something, even standing over there. But no. He'd have come to see the competition. That's all.

Something I'd believe if he wasn't looking straight at me.

I forced my attention to the contestants, Dakota's gaze burning into me. I'd have run to my room, locked myself inside, but that would only make him suspicious. It'd only bring him to my door.

The crowd cheered, and I clapped along with them, unsure what I'd missed. I had to hide my fear. If Dakota found out I was looking for NightLock, that I was working for the SIO …

Someone scaled up the pole and snatched the idol from its perch.

Applause and cheering erupted amongst the students. Candace stirred on the mats, her hair frizzed. Flint still hadn't moved. A dark patch spread across the back of his head. A man and woman in long white coats rushed to him.

The slim figure of the winner dropped from the pole like a shadow in the gloom.

"Dean won," I said.

Nick nodded. "Thought he might."

Dean raised the idol above his head in triumph, and a sense of dread filled me. He was just a teenager. Younger than me. Now, he'd get his first assignment. Now, he'd become a killer.

The crowd dissolved, leaving Dakota standing, unmoving by the wall. His eyes remained glued to me.

I had to get out of there. I slipped away and jogged down the path, feet crunching on the gravel. Niagra stepped in the way. The shadows on his face distorted his features, painting him like a zombie.

I staggered to a stop, breathing hitching. He suspected me. He knew something was wrong.

"Leaving so soon?" he asked.

If only. "I'm tired."

He glanced at my boots. "You haven't changed since you got back."

I dug my nail into my thumb. He had me. He knew about the drive. "I've changed my clothes."

"But not your boots."

I should've done. I should've hidden the drive in my pocket or changed the shoes after dinner. I balled my fists. "I didn't give it a thought."

"Didn't you?" He surveyed me silently. Just like Dakota used to in our sessions. I hadn't convinced him. I'd cleaned the boots. He'd have noticed that. Obviously, I would've thought about it.

"If there's nothing you need, I'd like to go to bed." I forced my hands to relax before he noticed them. Unless Dakota stood behind me. He'd have noticed. He'd know. But I couldn't look back. I couldn't show fear.

"You're struggling," Niagra said. "Since you got back, you've been more … on edge." He clasped his hands in front of him.

"I'm fine," I said. "I just need to rest."

"Perhaps. Or perhaps you should take some time with Dakota."

Cold gripped me, locking my legs in place. "I don't think that's necessary."

"I do." He cocked his head, as though daring me to argue. "I'll have him contact you tomorrow."

The wrinkles on his neck twitched with his pulse. I counted them. One, two, three. I had to settle my own. Had to breathe slowly. "I really don't think—"

"I insist." He raised his chin. "It really isn't optional."

I let my shoulders drop. Let my tiredness slip into my expression. "It's your choice. Of course." Always their choice. Never mine. This would be my undoing.

53

I pulled my blanket tighter around me while I stood on the balcony and studied the stars. The constellations, although familiar, looked wrong. Wonky. I supposed that's what came from being on the other side of the world. Or close enough. It had been weeks since Blake forced me from the hospital in London.

I'd thought things were bad then. But now, especially since Dakota could see right through me—the blanket shook where my hands did.

Yakov stepped onto the balcony beside mine. He'd changed into a sleeveless vest, white like the moon, and his hair glistened with water. "You disappeared after the competition."

I glared down at the courtyard. Lights embedded in the fountain lit up the tumbling water. "I was tired." Tired of repeating that phrase.

Yakov leaned against the railing. "We need to finish our earlier conversation."

"I thought we established there was nothing to say." Yakov may have saved my life, he may have lied for me, but that didn't mean I could trust him.

He tapped the rail with clean fingers – no signs of the gun powder left – and I caught a scent of shampoo: apple and tea-tree. "Okay," he said.

"Okay what?"

"A secret for a secret," he said. "You can ask me one question – just one – and I will answer it."

I stared at him. He was agreeing? That seemed … too easy. "How do I know you'll be truthful?"

"You have my word."

"What's that worth? Venom lies for a living. You could easily lie to me."

He nodded. "I could. But I won't. It's your choice whether to trust me on that."

Not a light decision. This wasn't like making friends in school. This was life or death. Who knew what he'd do if I told the truth? Lie again, probably.

He rested his chin on his hand. "Go ahead. One question."

Which one? So many exploded in my head, each leading to another and another. "I want an open answer," I said. "Not a cryptic, closed one. No riddles."

"As you wish." His tone gave nothing away. He'd answered so easily. So readily. It had to be a trick.

But this was my chance to get an answer – something I'd never had from Venom. My mind settled on a question. "Why did you lie for me? You took the shot at the bank. You told Backer I did it. Why?"

"I have a vested interest in you."

An open answer. He'd agreed to that much. I waited for more.

He sighed. "I want you safe. If Backer knew you failed, she'd have sent you back here. She'd have killed you if you were anyone else."

"Why am I different?"

"You're not Venom's usual recruit," he said. "An adult with no skills from our world, no desire to join us. They wouldn't go after you without good reason. You even had a family."

"*Have* a family," I said. "They're not gone."

He raised a hand. "As you say."

"Why did Venom take me?" I asked. "What do they want?"

He shook his head. "I said one question. I believe I've answered two."

"You said you want me safe, but if Backer sent me back here, I wouldn't be in danger. Your answer makes no sense."

"You think there'd be no danger? You'd be at Victor's mercy."

I shivered at that. Obviously, I'd be in danger. Not just from Victor. From the language master who struck me, from Mayra's crazy obsession with beauty, from Chef Marcel's all-but starving me. Although that appeared to have settled down. And Niall's nightmare-inducing stories.

Yakov glanced down at a group conversing by the fountain, his brow wrinkling. "You are in danger. More than you know. Venom will stop at nothing to get what they want. You're better going along with them. You'll be protected that way."

"I hardly think protection and Venom go in the same sentence," I said.

His lips twitched. "My turn." He grasped the rail and leaped onto my balcony, stepping in close. After a glance into my room, he said, "Tell me what you were doing before dinner."

I'd hoped he wouldn't ask that, though it wasn't completely unexpected. I could make it work. He only needed half the truth. "I was looking for a file."

"An open answer, if you please."

There would be no going back. If I misplaced my trust, I'd never forgive myself. But he'd lied for me before. Twice. Whatever his agenda, I believed he'd lie for me again. I bit my lip. "NightLock."

At once, every inch of Yakov tensed up until his muscles stood hard under the moon's glow. It took a moment for him to speak again, and when he did, hardness filled his words. "You've mentioned this to others?"

"No. Just you."

"Don't ever say the word again. Forget about it. Understand?"

I retreated a step. The hard face, his cold tone – the killer had surfaced again. Sweat prickled my back. What could possibly be so dangerous about NightLock?

He turned to face my room, hiding his face. Hiding his thoughts?

After a moment's hesitation, I took his arm. His muscles firmed beneath my fingers. "What do you know about it?" I asked. "Why is it so dangerous?"

He whirled back to me, moving in close until shadow covered his eyes. "You're answering *my* question," he growled. "What do you know about the file?"

I swallowed. "You had one question. I've answered it."

He shook his head, and a smug resolve brought out the dimple in his left cheek. "I haven't asked one yet."

"Yes, you did. You said …" *Tell me what you were doing before dinner.* My chest tightened. "The first was a command."

His lips twitched.

He'd tricked me. "That's not allowed."

"We agreed one question," he said. "If you volunteer extra information, that's your prerogative."

Why hadn't I caught that? But I didn't have to answer him. I could refuse. And I'd be no better than Venom.

Yakov tugged my blanket around me more. "The file," he said, his voice softer now. "What do you know?"

Nothing. "Only the name. I heard it mentioned. I got curious."

Everything about his expression, from the tightening of his lips to the tense of his jaw emanated disbelief. "It's risky, going after a file you know nothing about. What if you'd been caught?"

"I wasn't."

"Weren't you?" His hands rested on my shoulders, hot and heavy. "Subtlety isn't your strength. I caught on to you. And with Dakota around …"

My eyes stung. He'd be eager to question me. To see what I was hiding. To watch me squirm. Even when I didn't squirm, he still saw it. Playing with fire. Wasn't that how the saying went? "I'm avoiding Dakota." As much as I could anyway.

I went into my room.

Yakov followed. "Dakota isn't the only danger. There are others capable of reading you, just as dangerous as him."

Like I didn't already know, but I was willing to bet none of them could pick up lies like the master. I stopped beside the bed. "What do you suggest? I hide in here till our next assignment?" Assuming Yakov was with me for that. What if they partnered me with someone else? My palms grew clammy.

"I *suggest* you stop looking," he said.

That, I couldn't do.

He cocked his head. "Why is this so important to you?"

I draped the blanket over the bed, smoothing out the surface. Fluffy beads of thread collected on it, threatening to moult. I plucked them off one at a time, rolling them into a ball between my fingers. "I told you. I was curious."

"Digging will get you killed," Yakov said. "Or someone else."

"But it didn't," I said. "Besides, it made no difference. I didn't find the file."

"Course not. They don't keep things like that on computers. Anyone could access them."

Interesting. I dropped the fluff ball and turned to him. "You know where it is."

His nostrils flared. "Leave it alone. NightLock is dangerous."

"Why? What do you know about it?"

"Stop," he growled. "You have no right to know." He marched to the balcony, his bare feet silent on the tiles, and peered back. "I mean it, Sally. Don't mention it again." He leaped back over the railing and out of sight.

54

Sweat soaked my t-shirt in the early morning heat. Six a.m., and I'd already completed a lap of the four-mile track. Four days ago, Victor had me running laps around here, and now, given the chance to sleep in, here I was still running. Funny how Venom had changed me.

A few clouds scraped the sky like the remnants of flour on a sideboard. I broke the seal on a water bottle and gulped its contents before walking towards the courtyard.

I hadn't been able to sleep. NightLock had filled my dreams, dragging me from rest. So had Dakota. If Mum hadn't been rescued, I might've tried something drastic by now. But she was safe as long as I kept my side of the bargain. The empty bottle crinkled inside my fist. If I failed to find the file, Spencer wouldn't abandon Mum to Venom. Would she? Surely, she had some kind of conscience, which was more than I could say about Venom. All their riddles and secrets brought heat to my face.

But Yakov had shared one. He'd answered one question. What had I learned?

He wanted me safe.

He had a vested interest, though what interest, he hadn't said. I should've asked him to clarify.

And Yakov knew something about NightLock.

I rounded the corner where the villas were and scraped my hand along the wall. Looking for NightLock in there had wasted time. It'd only exposed me to Yakov.

The door to the language villa stood open ahead of me, full of cool air and welcoming shadows. Niagra's voice reached me from inside. Portuguese. Was he training someone? "She sounded legitimate when I questioned her." Or not training. Seemed an odd phrase to teach.

"I trained her well." Dakota.

I jerked to a stop, and a curse bit my tongue. If he caught me out here, he'd grab me at once. I should've never left my room.

"You think she was lying?" Niagra asked.

I'd been lying. Were they talking about me? With trembling muscles, I stepped closer to the door, studying their blurred reflections in an inactive computer monitor. Dakota leaned against a desk, facing Niagra, but I couldn't make out the old man's hands. Probably a good thing. They gave me the creeps.

Dakota folded his arms. "I'll speak with her. Get a second opinion."

"I don't need a second opinion." Niagra's tone fell cold. "I know how to read someone."

Dakota held up a calming hand. "I'm simply reminding you Sally isn't loyal to Venom. She may have been compromised."

Niagra shifted. "She is hiding something. Her mannerism—"

"I noticed."

I knew it. I knew he'd been watching me at the competition. I took a wary step back, aware of the gravel beneath my feet, the crunch under my weight.

"Her blackouts will frighten her," Dakota said. "Sally won't mention them. She's too scared to make a mistake in case we hurt her mother."

"That hardly matters anymore," Niagra said. "The SIO infiltrated the blasted base."

"Sally doesn't know that," Dakota said. "We can still use it against her."

Except they couldn't. By all rights, Venom held no power over me anymore. But my heart still thudded because that wouldn't stop them committing horrors. Even without someone to threaten, Venom were evil enough. They'd stop at nothing to get what they wanted. Whatever that was.

"How are the progressions with NightLock?" Niagra asked.

I froze, half-turned to double back. I should've left already. If they caught me out here—

"As expected," Dakota said. "I left my report on your desk."

Of course! Memories of my first meeting with Niagra exploded in my memory. It was right after Niall's story of the stained hands. Niagra carried a folder at the time. A folder with 'NightLock' scribbled on the top corner.

They don't keep things like that on computers.

Why hadn't I understood before? NightLock wasn't a computer file. It was on paper.

I turned to leave.

"Sally."

My blood grew cold. Slowly, I faced the lie master.

Dakota stood at the door, hand resting on the frame. His eyes grazed the surroundings, like he was looking for someone. "All alone?"

"I've been for a run."

"I see that." His lips pursed. "Well, since you're here, we might as well have our session." He gestured to his office a few doors down. He didn't smile. Didn't show anything, but his suspicion sizzled against my skin.

I pointed over my shoulder with my thumb. "I should shower first."

"Nonsense. A little sweat never hurt anyone." He stepped into the sunshine. Light fell on his olive skin, smoothing it, hiding his pores. It didn't lighten his eyes, though. He waited.

The air thickened in my throat. He'd spoken gently. Kindly. But the threat was there, hidden in the words. He offered me no choice. I followed him and chose my seat by the window.

The cushion sank beneath me, sucking me in. My family were safe. Mum was out. So, why did I feel so trapped? My t-shirt stuck to my back, cold now I sat in shade.

Dakota sat opposite. No clipboard this time. He crossed his leg, bouncing his foot above the floor. The sun spotlighted his dark eyes.

He didn't speak.

Silence stretched on, broken only by the ticking clock. My odour tainted the air. It warmed my cheeks, and made me flex my arms against the itch crawling over my skin.

Dakota knew I'd been eavesdropping. He must have – he'd caught me right outside the door. But he didn't know how much I'd heard. Was he wondering? Debating how to proceed?

His hands rested on his knee. His foot bobbed steadily. He gave nothing away.

I licked my lips.

He blinked.

"What are you waiting for?" I asked.

He cocked his head. "Who said I was?"

Not waiting. Testing me? Putting me on edge? Or just punishing me with sweat and bad odours? Minor things could unsettle someone. He'd said so in one of our sessions. Unsettle someone enough, and you have the advantage.

It was working. I longed to swallow. Longed to sniff, or fidget, or do *something*. I sat still – I wouldn't give him the satisfaction.

He smiled. "You're tense."

"Not at all." *Liar.*

A curve of his eyebrow screamed it. "You were tense last night. At the competition."

There it was. He'd mentioned it to Niagra. Said the blackouts would frighten me. And suddenly, I had my answer. That's what he thought I hid. *Too scared to make a mistake.*

I could make this work.

I let my shoulders hunch. "A little tense."

"Why?" he asked.

Because I was looking for NightLock. Because I was a double agent for the SIO. Because with every move I made against Venom, I risked my life and the lives of everyone I loved. My gaze drifted to the tiles. My pulse throbbed in my chest, but that was okay. The lie master didn't know the truth. If I played to the wrong lie, I could trick him.

I could deceive the deceiver.

He leaned forwards suddenly and placed his hand over mine.

My muscles locked, but I forced my eyes to meet his.

"This is a safe place." His finger ran along my wrist, pausing where he could feel my pulse. "Anything you say here is between us."

Until he told Niagra everything.

I swallowed. "I …" I longed to pull my hand away, to free myself from his grip.

"Yes?" he asked in that sickly gentle voice. Like he was on my side. Like he was coating the thorns in honey. He wouldn't let me go. He wouldn't stop prying. Not until he got a truth. The one he expected.

Play to the wrong lie.

"I lied," I said.

He nodded and withdrew his hand. "About?"

"The comms malfunction." Something Yakov told me to lie about. Why? Venom knew about the blackouts. Why hide the fact? Unless Yakov didn't know that Venom knew. I pressed my fingers against my forehead. The whole idea was a mess.

"There was no malfunction," Dakota said, his tone soft. Almost friendly.

I shook my head.

"What happened?" he asked.

"I've been blacking out," I said. "Losing time. I don't know why. I've tried to figure it out, and I've worked to stay focused, but it keeps happening." The truth spilled off my tongue. "It happened in the language villa first. I lost three hours. And then again two days ago, but it was only for ten minutes. I guided Yakov again afterwards."

Wrinkles framed Dakota's eyes, and he leaned back against his sofa. "There, now. Feel better?"

I let my lips tighten. He'd think I was frightened. That my thoughts were on Mum.

"Keeping secrets from me only hurts you." He pressed a hand to my chest. "Hurts us. You can confide in me. I am here to help you. Please know that."

In another circumstance, I might've laughed. I couldn't trust him if he was the last oxygen particle on earth. It took a moment to nod. "You won't tell Niagra?"

"Not a word." He shifted his hand to his chest. "Now." He leaned on the arm of his sofa. "Your time with the SIO."

My teeth gritted. Why hadn't I seen this? I'd been a fool to think I could trick him. He'd keep prying, keep pushing and prodding until he squeezed every secret out of me. "What about it?" I couldn't help but sound a little breathless.

The door opened, and Nick poked his head in. "Sorry to bother you. He's arrived."

Dakota straightened. "When?"

"Five minutes ago," Nick said.

Dakota cursed and stood up. For a moment, he stood still, like he was torn about what to do. Then, he sighed. "Apologies," he said to me. "I have business. Feel free to shower. We'll finish our session later." After a glare at the clock, he stormed from the room.

55

Heat from the sun seemed to bounce off Nick onto me when we walked beside the villas. Didn't it ever rain here? Every day boiled like the place was trying to melt us.

Dakota had long disappeared ahead of us. I'd been lucky. Another minute with him, and the whole double agent thing might have been exposed. I had to get that file. Get in, get out, get *off* the island. That last part, though – that wouldn't happen before Dakota had his read of me.

I stopped outside Niagra's office and bent to re-tie my shoelace. Nick stopped, too. Great. How was I supposed to get that file? For one thing, there was the closed-circuit camera above his door.

"If you're not busy," Nick said, "why don't you join me in a session? Niagra's got me training the young'uns on security." He stretched his arms behind his head, flexing his muscles. A curling patch of hair clung to his armpit like bleached weeds, wafting a scent of shower gel.

"What kind of security?" I asked.

"All kinds. Understand a place's security and—"

"Half the work is done for you. I remember." I nodded at the villa. "Like the closed-circuit camera, right? Helps to know where it is."

Nick frowned. "Yakov tell you that?"

I frowned, too. Yakov hadn't told me. In fact, no one had. So, how'd I know about it? The blackout? Was it possible languages weren't the only things I'd learned?

Probably best not to mention that to Nick, though. "Should he not have told me?"

"You shouldn't know. Venom are tight about security. And for good reason." He rubbed his chin. Thoughtful. "Keep this to yourself, all right?"

I nodded.

"I'm going to set up," he said. "We start in an hour. Grab some food and join me? You might learn something new." He winked and strolled away, but the crease between his eyebrows stuck. What'd I said that for? Wasn't it bad enough Dakota and Yakov suspected me? Now Nick did, too.

I squinted at the sun. Training would be starting soon. People would be running, shooting, learning to lie. Nick would be teaching. And Niagra? I didn't know.

There was the camera above his office. Two more watching the path. I racked my thoughts, pulling back my weeks of training. I'd seen Niagra patrolling. He watched the students. Visited the nursery. Consulted with Chef Marcel. Which meant his villa should be empty.

Which left the issue of getting the file.

Not an issue. I knew just how to do it.

I jogged back to the courtyard, accepted a sausage sandwich and water bottle from Marcel, and pushed on to my room. A sausage sandwich! Had I wore him down? Or did he not hate me as much as he implied?

After showering and changing, I scooped a watch off the cabinet and fastened it on. Quarter past seven. Forty-five minutes to go.

The balcony provided a good lookout over those flocking in for breakfast. The sausages were amazing. They curbed a craving I didn't know I had.

Soon, students crowded from the hall, splitting off on their way to sessions. Quiet fell over the courtyard.

At five minutes to the hour, I left the room with trembling limbs. A heavy heat settled over the courtyard. Distant gunfire echoed. Nick would be expecting me, but he shouldn't come looking, not mid-session.

I paused near Niagra's villa. My hair tickled my cheeks, so I brushed it behind my ears and studied the closed door through the trees. No sign of Niagra – but that didn't mean he wasn't inside.

I glanced at my watch, timing the seconds. The path lay clear. It was now or never.

The second hand reached the twelve.

I dashed across the path and into the bushes, twisting around the side of the building to Niagra's garden. The scent of jasmine and that sweetness surrounded me, and orange flowers as large as my hand bloomed at the pond's edge. Light rippled on the walls where the back doors stood open, showing Niagra at the desk, a file open in front of him.

My shoulders dropped. I'd have to try again later. Maybe tonight. Even so, I stayed a moment longer, thoughts on NightLock. Was that Dakota's report he read? What could be so important that they'd only keep it on paper?

Niagra slipped the folder in the top drawer, locked it and shuffled to the grandfather clock. He opened the front panel, slipped the key inside, and left the office.

An empty office. A well-hidden key I could access. No cameras inside. What better opportunity was there? Maybe the only opportunity.

Without waiting for fear to rise, I dashed straight for the clock and pulled open the panel. The pendulum swung in time with the seconds. Tick. Tick. At first glance the key was nowhere in sight, but a glint of silver caught my eye, and there it was, tucked away in a tiny shelf behind the pendulum. I plucked it from its perch and rushed to the desk.

My breaths stuttered. If the door opened, I'd be lucky to get beneath the desk, let alone to the garden without being seen.

I fumbled to insert the key and slid open the drawer.

Several brown files lay stacked with handwriting on the top corners: Thriftease, Hardman Key, Instigation – each as inventive and unfamiliar as the last. Tab Ultimatum. Revenant. NightLock!

I tugged the file from the stack. Could I photocopy it? Take photos?

Every surface lay empty. No scanner. No photocopier. Nothing.

I'd have to take the file.

My chest churned at the thought. This was risky. Too risky. How long before Niagra noticed it missing? What sort of search would they do? Could I hide it anywhere? They'd know the place better than me. They'd catch me.

It was the only way.

I glanced at my watch. One minute left of the camera loop. Time to leave.

I turned back to the garden – to the silhouette standing in the doorway – and my muscles locked.

Dakota stepped inside, shadows cloaking his face. His dark hair glistened. The scent of aftershave – sandalwood and sage – mingled with the air. "Well, well. This is a surprise."

"Dakota." My throat constricted. My voice cracked. "I can explain."

"I certainly expect so." His gaze flicked to the file in my hands. "Judging by your demeanour, you're up to no good." He remained perfectly calm, his voice like silk. His hands hung by his sides, relaxed.

"I …" How could I explain without lying? Without revealing my circumstances? Play to the wrong lie. But what lie? I had nothing. "Niagra had this file."

"I'm aware." Dakota stepped closer. "Why do you?"

He was the lie master, the ultimate truth detector. Tricking him was impossible. "I can't tell you."

"Oh?" He raised his eyebrows.

"I've been instructed not to. It's confidential." Not a lie. But it wouldn't make a difference. Even if he bought my story, he'd speak to Niagra.

"My clearance level is higher than yours." He stepped closer again. "Indulge me."

I backed to the desk. "I can't."

"I see." He cocked his head. "Perhaps we should wait for Niagra. Clear this up quickly."

"I don't … think …" I had to get out. Whatever the security, I had to escape *now*. "I'll just come back another time." I dropped the file on the desk and moved to step around him.

He blocked my path, and his voice grew hard. "Who ordered you?"

"It doesn't matter." The air scraped my throat.

"What do you want with the file?"

"It doesn't matter."

His arms flexed. "It matters."

"I was curious."

"Liar." He grasped my forearm, leaning in close. "You're hiding something."

"No." I struggled against his grip. I should never have come back, never should have listened to Spencer. Panic swelled, strangling my breaths.

His free hand grabbed my throat. "What really happened with the SIO?" He shook me. "What did they tell you?"

"Nothing! Please! Let me go."

"Liar!" He drove me back against the desk. The edge pressed into my back, shooting pain through my spine. "What do you know about NightLock?" His fingers tightened on my neck.

I pushed him with a clammy hand and reached behind me, grabbing the first thing I felt. A pen.

I stabbed the tip into his arm.

He cried out, and jerked back enough for me to wriggle around the desk. I raced for the front door. Pain radiated through my spine. It'd bruise. Another mark of Venom's abuse.

He yanked me back with rough hands. They grasped my throat, cutting off my scream. "You will tell me." His breath hissed in my ear. "Who ordered you? What do you know about NightLock?"

I punched his arms. Spots swam before my eyes. My feet found the door, and I kicked hard, driving us backwards.

He jolted. Glass shattered around us, and his grip loosened.

I staggered away from him, tripping over my feet.

Something crunched.

I stared at the unmoving form of the lie master, pinned by what was left of the grandfather clock. Glass and wood fragments covered the floor, and a low clunk, clunk, echoed within the clock. A pool of blood spread out beneath Dakota's head.

He wasn't …

He couldn't be …

I took his wrist. No relief came with the weak throbbing of his pulse. Once Dakota came to, that would be it.

I scrambled away and slipped the file under my top, bending it into shape around my body. The scent of garden flowers sickened me, and my neck turned cold, like my body after stepping out the shower.

A hand to my neck revealed blood.

Dakota's blood.

Nausea washed over me, drawing me to the pond. Cold water ran over my hands and splashed my top when I scrubbed away his blood. Niagra would come back. He'd see Dakota. He'd know.

"Focus," I muttered. "You must focus." Sunlight glinted on my watch. Two minutes until the cameras looped off. Two minutes, and I could cross the path. If I could get back to my room, if I could avoid being seen, they wouldn't know it was me.

Until Dakota woke up.

I heaved and gasped, fighting for control. *Don't show your fear.* I couldn't. Especially not now.

I rounded the building and hovered near the edge of the bushes, watching the path. It was so clear. So quiet. Deceptively so. But the cameras were on. They were watched.

Ten seconds. Three. One.

I ran.

Stones slid beneath me. Air cut at my lungs. Sounds of combat and gunfire from the range reached me on my way back to the accommodation block. I paused twice, forced myself to walk, to blink back my tears, and reached my room unseen.

I slipped the file under the mattress and ran my fingers through my hair. Dakota needed help. If someone didn't find him soon, he'd die.

But I'd get caught. If he never woke, he couldn't tell anyone what happened. He couldn't expose me.

I sucked in a breath. What was the matter with me? Would I let a man die to save myself? My reflection looked white in the mirror, contrasting the streaks of red on my neck and cheek.

His blood. Dakota's blood. On my hands.

My knees met the floor. My tears dotted the tiles like transparent pebbles. I should've been more careful. I should've waited until night time.

Venom wanted killers. They trained killers. What would they do to me for killing one of their own? But Dakota wasn't dead yet. I hoped. Or did I?

I buried my face in my hands. I hated them, the whole murderous lot. In a normal world, I'd help Dakota.

Why not in this one? I wouldn't be one of them. Wouldn't be one of Venom.

But I couldn't help him.

What was I supposed to do?

I had to get off this island – and there was only one person I believed would help me.

56

I didn't know where to look. Yakov didn't exactly train here, what with being a fully-fledged assassin and all. Would he be with Nick? Training another recruit? Or running the track? With four miles of it, finding him wouldn't prove easy.

I'd knocked on his door already. No answer. I ended up in the courtyard, puzzling where to go when the chatter reached me from up ahead. I pushed on to the mats – maybe he'd be there – to scores of people hurrying along the gravel.

Niall walked a short way ahead of me with Meilin, the seven-year-old he'd been training. "What's going on?" she asked.

"Dakota's been attacked," he said.

My airway constricted. Word spread fast, and everyone flocked to the villas. If I was going to blend in, I had to go, too. But If Dakota was awake, I'd be walking right into their hands. And if he wasn't, what then? What if he was dead?

All feeling fled from my face. I forced myself to breathe, to feign peace – a pale face would do nothing for my cause – and fell in with the crowd.

It appeared that everyone had come to Niagra's villa. Students and tutors filled the gravel in front of the stone walls, murmuring to each other while two men carried Dakota on a stretcher, an oxygen mask strapped to his face. His eyes were closed. Unconscious? Had he said anything? Did Niagra know?

I dipped behind two women, letting their height bar me from view.

Niagra stood by the door where the remains of the grandfather clock lay splintered and scatter across the floor. He turned to everyone with cold eyes, and a deathly stillness fell.

"Dakota has been attacked," he said. "Stabbed on the very ground we strive to protect. And a valuable file has been stolen."

At that, a murmur hissed through the students.

"Who would do that?" Meilin whispered and grasped Niall's arm. She was so innocent. So shocked at the violence. Venom would soon change that. Give it a few more years, and she'd be unrecognisable.

My focus settled on Yakov. He stood with Nick a short way away, watching me. Would he help me? He'd lied already, but that didn't make him my ally. Would Dakota's hurt matter to him? No attachments. Wasn't that the rule? I could only hope that whatever the Russian wanted, it'd be important enough that he'd help me out again. Unless Dakota had talked. Unless Niagra knew.

"Dakota lies in a coma," Niagra said, "so he can't tell us who did this."

The truth? Or a lie to throw me off-guard? I stepped further behind the women. What was he waiting for? If he knew it was me, he'd have captured me by now. He had a whole army right here.

"There will be an investigation," he said. "Each and every room will be searched."

My room. The file! I had to get it out. Had to hide it somewhere else. But where?

"And every one of you will be questioned," he said. "Until such time, remain in your rooms until I give you the all-clear."

That could work. I just needed to get back, and with Yakov in the next room, I could talk to him. Appeal for his help.

I glanced over at him, ready to give him a silent look.

But he'd gone.

57

Yakov hadn't been wrong about the danger. I had the file – one point to me – and now guards scattered through the courtyard entered every open door, questioning students and teachers. It was only a matter of time before they reached my room. I had to get rid of the file. And quickly.

When I got to my room, multiple guards ransacked it. One emptied the contents of my dresser. Another searched through my drawers. Makeup clattered on the tiles – Mayra would do her nut – and in the bathroom, someone knocked shampoo bottles into the sink.

Niagra stood by the door, red hands perched on his hips. "Ah, Sally. Come in." He smiled that distorted smile, and it took all I had not to run for the mattress.

"You started with me?" I said.

"Not at all. I have others in adjoining rooms." Niagra cocked his head. "You look worried."

I fought not to swallow and pointed at the guy pulling open the wardrobe. His shaved head only highlighted the point of his chin, like an upside-down, slightly squished egg. "How do you know it wasn't him?"

Egg-head emerged from the wardrobe, dropped hangers on the floor, and grabbed the mattress.

My breath caught. I could do nothing. Couldn't run. Couldn't fight.

He lifted the mattress.

The file was gone.

I balled my fists. That wasn't possible. It must've slipped farther back.

He checked the other side, beneath the sheets, in the pillowcases. "Clear," he said, and the guards filed out.

Niagra frowned. "You're sure?"

"You watched us search," Egg-head said.

Niagra's lips tightened, and he turned to me. "Seems you're not the attacker."

Seems being the key word. I wasn't in any less danger. Where was the file?

Niagra folded his arms. "What happened with the SIO?"

"I told you already." My voice didn't waver. Neither did my eye contact with the bed. It'd been taken. It was the only explanation. No way could Egg-head have missed it.

"There was nothing you missed?" Niagra said. "No details you didn't share?"

"Like what?" I dragged my gaze from the mattress. "I told you everything I know."

Niagra clasped his stained hands together. Convinced? Unconvinced? He wore a pinch between his eyes, shadows in his scowl. Puzzling over me, no doubt. Trying to suss the truth. "Did you see anything unusual this morning?"

"No."

"Anyone you haven't seen before? Anything out of place?"

"No." An easy truth. Hopefully he wouldn't see the difference between that and my lies.

His eyes grazed the bottles in the sink, the sheets and clothes on the tiles. "Well, if you do think of anything—"

"I know where to find you."

58

I lifted the mattress, almost expecting the file to magically appear where I'd stuffed it. Nope. It was definitely gone. Taken. What other explanation was there?

Was Yakov to blame? He knew I was looking for NightLock. Knew I was snooping where I shouldn't have been.

The door opened. Yakov stood in the corridor, hands by his side, mouth set straight. Work-mode. The emerging assassin. "Come with me."

"Where?"

He grabbed my arm and hauled me out, marching me along the corridor. Only when we reached the view of others did he let go. He popped a hand on my back though, and led me across the courtyard with tense muscles.

What I wouldn't give to know his thoughts. Had I gone too far? Was what he wanted important enough to lie for me again? How far could I go before he cracked?

When we got back to Niagra's villa, he went straight inside. Backer leaned against the desk, her shadow distorted over the wrecked clock. Someone had silenced the clacking. Now, the pendulum hung out a little, like bones from a grave.

"Well, what a to-do," she said. "All this carry on over a little file." She paused as though expecting me to confess, but I just gritted my teeth and refused to move. "And poor Dakota," she said. "In a coma of all things. We'll have to see if he wakes to get his account of the incident."

"If he wakes?" I asked, and a shiver flushed down my back.

"His injuries are severe." She nodded at the clock. "Dear grandfather was a heavy soul."

I clamped my hands behind my back to hide their shaking. If Dakota died, it'd be my fault. I'd have killed someone.

"A shame, indeed," Backer said. "Nick mentioned you knew of the camera above the office door."

My insides jolted. So much for our little secret. "We were discussing about security," I said. "He was teaching about it this morning."

Backer nodded. "He said as much. Were you tempted to enter this office?"

A straight question. She'd be watching for my lie, but could she read it? Better to avoid the risk. "No doubt you checked the footage. I'd have been seen."

Backer pursed her lips. "Quite. Well, as it happens, we caught the thieves."

Every hair on my arms stood on end. Had Yakov not taken the file? Had someone else stolen it and been caught trying to leave? They'd blame me. Say they found the file in my room. But they couldn't prove it. There were no cameras in the corridors.

Backer passed a file to Yakov. "Your assignment," she said. "Look at it on the road."

He jerked his head at me and marched outside.

"Oh, Sally?" Backer said when I got to the door. She tapped crimson nails on a pistol at her waist. "Be careful out there. I'd hate for something to happen to you."

59

I half-ran to keep up with Yakov, gravel crunching beneath our feet. I still wore my boots, still carried the hidden drive in the sole. They hadn't found it. Not that it held anything of importance, but the fact I had it would condemn me well enough. "Who have they caught?"

"Quiet."

"But—"

"I said quiet." Yakov padded down to the submarine chamber where armed guards lined the passage. Round lights set into the walls provided a gloomy, almost cold luminance, and the lap of water against the submersible made me thirst.

The Russian stopped by the hatch and gave me a swift nod.

I climbed in without resistance. Was he angry? Did he know what I'd done or only suspected? Niagra never mentioned the NightLock file. Only a file. So, Yakov only had suspicions to go off.

Once down the ladder, Yakov grabbed my arm and marched me to the room with the windows. He shoved me on a chair before taking one opposite, putting a table between us.

"Yakov—"

"I warned you. I told you to leave it alone."

Well, that answered that. "You can't think—"

"Don't." If looks could kill … But he hardly needed the

glare. He had his Beretta. The white handle was visible enough. But he hadn't used it. Nor had he exposed me.

Yet. If I kept pushing, kept angering him, what would he do? What if he really did snap?

I swallowed, already knowing the answer.

The vessel entered deeper water, showing the deep blue of the ocean. Fish rippled past in river of gleaming silver. Sunlight streaked through the sea in rippling rays. The surface pulsed above the top of the window, and we emerged into open air.

"Why have we surfaced?" I asked. We'd always gone to the smaller island, never here. Why now? Why risk being seen by others?

The sea dipped, and through the water streaming down the window, a small fishing boat became visible. Two fishermen stood at the edge, hands behind their heads, eyes glued to the two pointing guns at their heads. One looked directly at us, and they fired.

The fishermen dropped into the sea, staining the water red with their blood.

The scene blurred again. Or maybe it was our descent into the depths. But there was something more. Something that seared its image into my mind. One of the killers held more than a gun. They'd held a file.

The NightLock file. What else could it have been?

Yakov's gaze burned into my cheek.

It wasn't right. Venom was too careful, too clever to make a mistake. "You planted it on them," I said.

"It was our luck they happened to pass by."

"Luck?" He meant they were normal? Simple civilians on a fishing trip? Heat welled in my chest. "You just had innocent people murdered!"

"Lower your voice."

"Why?" I stood up, scraping the chair on the floor. "You know enough to have me killed. Heck, you could kill me yourself. Why on earth would you keep covering for me? What do you want?"

He stood up, too – slowly – and rounded the table until he was close enough to warm my skin with his body heat. He glared down at me, and his breaths came slow and even. "You're right," he said. "I can kill you. So, do yourself a favour, and *stop pushing me.*"

It was then that every part of my core shrivelled up, and the few shreds of confidence I'd built with him shattered. I took a step back.

He was a killer. Not my friend. Not my protector.

A killer.

One with the potential to snap.

60

The clouds through the window of the private jet stretched like cobbled stone, stained pink by the dusk. Yakov sat farther down the cabin, a phone at his ear. He hadn't spoken a word to me after the submarine, no surprise. He'd collected a briefcase and taken me to the jet with the kind of coldness that'd make anyone wary. The file Backer gave him lay closed beneath his window.

He glanced back at me. "Are you sure? She's reckless." His sharp tone drew my shiver. Who was he talking to? He listened silently, and his lips twitched, like whatever the speaker said amused him. His shoulders dropped. "I understand." He hung up.

I picked at a fingernail nervously. There was something surreal about sitting so close to an assassin and knowing he wouldn't hurt me. For now, at least. I wanted to question him, demand answers, but my feet stayed rooted to the floor.

He stood up, earning a nervous glance from the stewardess, and sat across the table from me. "I told you to leave that file alone." He stuck to Russian.

"I don't take orders from you."

He gritted his teeth. "Don't you get it? You're going to get yourself killed."

"Venom recruited me for a reason," I said.

"That doesn't make you safe. You keep going, and you'll ruin everything."

Ruin what? Venom's plans? His? I hardly cared either way. I only wanted freedom, and now I didn't have the file, who knew where I stood? Would Spencer extract me since I'd failed? There was nothing more I could do to get NightLock.

"Why is this so important to you?" Yakov searched my face, leaning across the table. "There's more than curiosity behind this. What did the SIO tell you?"

"I overheard it."

"Don't lie to me." He kept studying me. Reading me. What could he see? He wasn't all-knowing. He was just a man. Like Dakota – and nothing had got past him. "Why that file?" Yakov asked. "Why won't you leave it alone?"

I sat back, lips tight. He couldn't read my mind. He wouldn't know everything. Not if I had anything to say about it.

His jaw clicked, and he slapped a file on the table. The word 'NightLock' was scrawled in the top corner.

I stared from the slightly bent, brown cover to the Russian.

"It's a copy." He stabbed a finger on the file. "You want to know what NightLock is? Read it." He shoved it at me. "But if my word means anything to you, leave it alone. Some truths are better left hidden."

61

I tucked the file in Yakov's case for safekeeping when we landed in Germany. I hadn't read it. Not because I cared about Yakov's opinion. I didn't. Because I didn't care what NightLock was. I wasn't the one who wanted the file. Spencer was. Now I had it, I'd give it to her, get extracted, and finally move on to a life of freedom.

The hotel Yakov brought me to was nothing less than the finest establishment with sun-glistening windows, potted plants, and a crimson overhang sheltering the front door. A uniformed doorman welcomed us inside, his German a welcome change to Yakov's rough Russian. Chairs with marbled cushions dotted the foyer, one of which I sat on while Yakov spoke to the receptionist.

Did I care about NightLock? Whatever it was, it couldn't be good. Not when Venom was involved. It might've been a nuclear bomb. A nighttime abduction. A lockdown of the stock markets.

I huffed. It didn't matter. It wasn't my job to stop Venom. It was my job to escape.

An elderly gent sat cross-legged on a chair, reading a newspaper. Something about the image on the back cover caught my eye. Wasn't that—yes, the road outside Rio where Venom had reclaimed me. Only now a section of the road was damaged – the remains of a car accident. Not the van I'd been in. This was different, involving a Sedan and a people carrier. Below that, half covered by the man's hand, Mum peeked out the page.

"Excuse me," I said, adopting the German language. "Would you mind if I read that back page?"

He handed it to me, and I smoothed it out on my knee. I knew the photo from the previous year. We'd picnicked in the park: Mum, Lia and me. Now, the photo had been cropped to show only Mum. My fingers on her arm looked like cocktail sausages clinging to her jumper.

… explosion on the road. …three fatalities: one Francisco Baros – a stockbroker at the Avila Firm, Beatriz Acosta – a nurse within the unit, and Elizabeth Rivers – a tourist.

My body grew numb.

'Our thoughts go out to the families of the fallen', says Leonor Delgado, Minister of the Firearms Department. Inquiries have been put in place to determine the cause of the fire, but investigations have, as yet, been inconclusive. Police have not ruled out the possibility of a terrorist attack.

The words blurred. Spencer had her. The SIO extracted Mum. She was safe.

Or was she? If she'd been travelling to a safehouse, if Venom found her … They'd killed her.

The sounds around me slipped into nothingness.

I should never have gone back to Venom. I should've gone to meet Mum. If I'd been there, I could've … what? What could I have done? I batted the tickle off my cheek with a shaking hand.

Blood rushed to my face. Spencer promised to protect her. And I'd believed her. I'd put myself in danger again at the whims of a stranger. To get a file I had no business going after.

When Dakota woke, he'd come after me. Everyone would come after me. And this time, it wouldn't be to reclaim me.

No, I was done being the scared little girl on the run. They could come for me all they wanted because this time, I'd be ready. One way or another, Venom and the SIO would pay.

62

There were no balconies on the seventh floor. Even if there were, they'd be too high to jump from. An intentional move on Yakov's part, no doubt. The Russian pulled a tie from his case and fastened it over his shirt. "I need to go out. Give me your word you'll stay here."

I folded my arms. No one's word meant anything anymore. "Would you believe me if I did?"

"I'll find you if you don't." He checked his reflection in a mirror. "Your word."

"Sure, whatever." I'd stay as long as it took to figure out a solid escape.corne

Yakov frowned like he knew there was more to my thoughts and popped his briefcase on the table in front of me. "I won't be long." He left, closing the door behind him.

I sank down on the sofa, the newspaper article running through my mind. Terrorist attack. Explosion. Mum dead. It'd been seventy-six days since Blake snatched me from London. Seventy-six days since I'd last seen Mum. Two-and-a-half very long months. I'd been days away from seeing her again. A couple of weeks at most. But now …

I smudged my tears with my palms. I should've known better. How many times had people told me no one leaves Venom unless they die? Venom had Mum. Now, she was dead.

I'd been naïve to believe she could be rescued.

And what about me? After everything Venom went through to recruit me, to get me back from the SIO, how far would they go to stop me escaping?

The door opened, and Joe bustled in, suited and booted, as Lia would say. A huge difference to his usual tracksuit and bed-hair. "We have little time." He stopped just short of the table.

I brushed the wetness from my cheeks. "What are you doing here?"

"I'm your contact. You got the file?"

He couldn't be serious. After what the SIO had done – or failed to do – did he really think I'd hand it over? Or did he not know? "I want to talk to Spencer."

"I'm your contact."

"I'm not doing contacts. I'm not doing this job! If she wants that file, you tell her to get off her backside and come get it."

He lowered his head, coating his neck in shadow. "You think she'll drop everything 'cause you demand it?"

"After all the fuss she made about the file? Yeah. She'll come." I folded my arms. "And you're not getting it until she does."

He eyed the case on the table. "It's in there, isn't it?"

I balled my fists. Was I so predictable?

"Open it," Joe said.

"No." I wouldn't let him take it. I was done being people's puppet.

He cracked his knuckles. "You can give it to me, or I can take it."

What was I supposed to do? Fight him? I wouldn't stand a chance. The meathead had so much more experience than me. Not just with Venom. With the SIO, too. What good could I do against a spy-killer?

I gritted my teeth, undid the clasps and lifted the lid. My core jolted.

Joe stretched out his hand.

But I was no one's puppet.

I grabbed the black Beretta, cocked it, and aimed at Joe.

He staggered back a step, hand inching towards his jacket.

"I'll shoot before you reach it," I said.

He hesitated, let his hand drop, and his nostrils flared.

I slammed the case closed. "Tell Spencer I want to meet."

"You're making a mistake."

"No." I nodded at the door pointedly. "I don't think I am." After everything I'd been through, every choice I'd made, this was probably the only one I'd finally done right.

"Fine," he said. "I'll relay your message. But you made a deal with Spencer. I wouldn't recommend going back on it." He marched out, leaving the door to swing closed behind him.

Yeah, I'd made a deal. So had she. It was two-way, and she hadn't held her side. I dropped the Beretta onto the table, limbs shaking with adrenaline. This was good. It was my turn to take control. My turn to be the strong one.

The door opened again, and Yakov came in, twisting the lock behind him. His eyes narrowed. "You've been crying."

"I'm fine."

His gaze shifted to the Beretta. "What happened?"

"Doesn't matter." I turned to my tear-streaked image in the window. I thought I'd wiped them away. So much for being the strong one.

Yakov's wary reflection ventured closer. Tears. A gun on the table. He probably thought I'd contemplated suicide. As if I could.

As though in confirmation, he scooped up the gun and tucked it back in the case. "Speak to me."

"There's nothing to say."

"Sally." He placed a warm hand on my shoulder, but I pulled away. No matter how friendly Yakov could be, he was nothing more than the rest of them: a cold-hearted, unfeeling killer.

I went into my bedroom and lay in the dark, silent tears soaking my pillow until moonlight filled the window. All of this over a file. What could be so important that innocent people had to die? That Joe would threaten to go all Venom on me if I refused to hand it over?

I crept to the door and peeked into the living-suite. A little light filtered through the main window, highlighting the furniture. The case still rested on the table. Clicking it open revealed the gun, and beneath it, the scrawled handwriting on the NightLock file. I shivered.

Joe didn't know I'd never killed. He didn't know I'd been bluffing. What if he'd called me out? I'd barely escaped Dakota. His coma was simply bad luck on his part – or good luck on mine. Even with the gun at point blank range, Joe could've disarmed me before I hurt him. And what's to say a bullet in his leg would've stopped him?

I pulled out the file and went back to my room, flicking on the beside lamp.

Whatever this was, it must be important. Innocent people had died. The fishermen. Mum. Who knew who else? Time to find out what all the fuss was about. Only, once I did, I could never go back.

I couldn't anyway. Too much had changed.

I opened the file.

63

"What do you call this?" I slapped the file on the table.

Yakov looked up at me, unfazed. Morning light streamed through the windowpane, brightening his silvery eyes.

"You told me I'd no right to know about NightLock," I said. "It's got my name written all over it. Literally!" I picked it up again and flipped open the cover. "Things are progressing for subject, Sally Rivers, host of the nanites. What does that mean?"

"It means what it states," Yakov said.

I turned back to the page. "After a three-hour time-loss, Sally has absorbed nine languages, and can access these in her speech. Further studies have begun to test the limits of her access. Duplicate records shipped to A.H."

Yakov watched me calmly.

"You're telling me there are nanites inside me?" I asked. "That's the reason I keep losing time?"

"That's what it says."

"Rubbish."

"You doubt it?"

I flapped the file at him. "Nanites. Absorbing information. You can't be serious."

"It's the truth."

"It sounds like someone got mixed up with a science fiction

writer."

Yakov leaned his elbow on the arm of the sofa. "Do you have another explanation? How do you explain your blackouts?"

Alien abduction was more likely. Couldn't he have spun something more realistic? "Where's the real file?"

Yakov cocked his head and waited. Like he was waiting for me to accept the truth. But it wasn't truth. It couldn't be. Sure, I'd lost time. I'd learned languages. I'd mastered knife throwing. But that didn't mean I had technology inside me. It was ridiculous. So what if I knew where the hidden cameras were on the island? So what if it was all detailed in the file? Everything was. All my training. Even the extra parts, like my assault of Victor and the break to his knee. But *nanites*?

"All right, fine," I said, "let's say it is true, and there are nanites inside me. What does that mean?"

The Russian studied me silently.

"What are they *for*?" I asked. "Why are they in me? *How* are they in me? And why me? Why not someone who works for Venom?"

"You work for Venom."

"I'm a prisoner. I never wanted this."

He raised his eyebrows. "Why do you think they took you?"

Your abilities are invaluable.

We brought you here because you have a habit of knowing things you aren't supposed to know.

Lia's office schedule. Mum's room number. The languages and knife throwing and the security room in Brazil. They all had a common likeness. They all involved computers. An iPad. Technology. My stomach twisted. "You don't mean—"

"Venom couldn't use someone else because there was no one else," Yakov said. "The nanites were already in you."

I stepped backwards, catching my heels on the opposite sofa. "That's not possible."

"Venom don't make mistakes."

Back at the office, Blake had stolen my blood. He'd been

244

looking for proof the nanites were in me. But why my blood? I didn't stand out. I'd spent my whole life sheltered. Cut off from the world. Heck, Mum and Lia wouldn't even let me have a social life.

I sank onto the sofa. They never let me have anything. "They knew," I whispered.

Yakov tipped his head, questioningly.

That was why they never let me go to college. Why I'd had to work for Lia. They were hiding me. Hiding the nanites. I'd always felt off. Always felt I was missing something when the two of them would whisper in the kitchen at night, when they'd exchange wary glances when they thought I wasn't looking. But how could they know? How had I got them in me?

"What're they for?" I asked. "The nanites."

"They're a key," Yakov said.

"To what?"

"The world. To world domination."

I stared at him. "Venom plan to rule the world with nanites?"

He shook his head. "Not the nanites. What the nanites absorb." He leaned forwards, resting his elbows on his knees. "Imagine it. The data you could get just by being near a hard drive. The secrets. The *details*. Imagine what Venom could do with that."

Blackmail. Sabotage. Assassinations. They could get wealth and fame, power and glory. Whatever they wanted. With the world's security in their grasp, they could do anything and never have to face the consequences.

Yakov rounded the table and sat beside me. "You must understand, you are the most valuable person to Venom. The most valuable person in the world."

"That's why you haven't killed me," I said. "Because of what you can get from me."

"That's not why I want you safe. But yes, I'll do anything to keep you alive. Including locking you in chains if I must."

I dropped the file and shifted away from him. "This is crazy." If it was true, if nanites really were inside me, any power-hungry maniac would come after me. Even the SIO— Sick realisation hit me. "This is dangerous."

"Exactly," Yakov said. "Now do you understand? Now do you see why you must leave it alone? Why you must listen to me?"

"Listen to you?" At once, the force of reality sliced through my foggy mind.

He reached for my arm, but I batted his hand away.

"*Listen* to you?" I staggered away from him. "If Venom gets that information …" They'd use me to kill. Use me to corrupt and manipulate and destroy everything plain and precious. I rushed to the window and shoved it open, letting cool air rush in. Venom had killed people. They'd stolen things. They'd stolen *me*. "I won't do it," I gasped. "I won't let them have me."

Yakov whirled me around. "You don't have a choice."

I pulled against his hold, but he didn't let go. "If you resist," he said, "if they find out you know, have you any idea what they'll do?"

"Lock me in a box? That won't get them what they want, will it?"

"You still think you have a choice in this." He shook me. "Have you learned nothing? Your stubbornness can't stop Venom."

I tugged against him, but his grip tightened. "They'll keep going," he said. "They'll fill you with data. They'll drain you till there's nothing left of the person you are."

Hot fear prickled my skin.

"Nothing but a braindead puppet strapped down to do their bidding."

"Yakov—"

But there was no stopping him. He drove me against the window, eyes wild with madness, a vein pulsing in his neck. "You'll die," he snarled, "a ghost in an empty room, driven crazy by the load they've stuffed in your head!"

"Let me go!" I struck out.

He blocked instantly and backed away, the madness melting from his features.

I leaned against the window, breaths hitching. He wasn't just a killer. He was a monster. A monster hiding behind a sea of calm.

He stepped towards me, but I held up a hand, stopping him where he stood, and for a moment, I thought I saw regret. When he spoke next, his voice softened. "You must understand, what you've seen of Venom is nothing compared to what they truly are. What they can do."

I swallowed back rising tears.

"But there is a plan," he said. "I can protect you. If you let me."

"Why?" Why would I ever trust him to protect me?

Yakov pressed his lips together, and his shoulders squared.

"After all this," I said, "you still won't tell me."

"I can't."

"Then, how can I trust you?"

Something flickered in his eyes, too fast for me to read, and he turned his back on me. "You just have to."

64

I slept the rest of the morning and some of the afternoon on the sofa, waking to a deep ache at the memory of Mum.

A platter of food lay on the table: meat, cheese, bread, butter, jam and honey. I grabbed a roll and bit into it, only then noticing the case was gone. Light streamed through a crack in the bathroom door. Yakov stood inside, his shirt hanging over the sink. Blood trailed down his waist from a wound in his side. He dabbed at it with a towel and winced.

I wolfed down the bread on my way to him and stopped a few steps from the door. A bottle of whiskey rested on the side of the bath beside the open case. Clean gauze and a roll of tape lay over the files, and a pile of bloody towels filled the basin.

"What happened?" I asked.

"Split a stitch." He dabbed at the blood, coating the towel red.

"A stitch?" He'd already had the wound? "How did—"

"Got shot on the last assignment." He shifted his grip on the towel.

Oh, yeah. Joe shot him. It was easy to forget considering Yakov never showed any pain.

He reached for a piece of gauze.

"Let me." I reached for the whiskey and perched on the edge of the toilet, studying the wound. "It's not that bad. Just a nick in the corner." The blood made it look worse. Its metallic scent filled the air and added taste to my tongue. I wiped his smudged blood gently with the gauze, clearing away the trail where it'd slid down his waist.

Why was I helping him? He'd left people dead in a pool of their own blood.

But I wasn't like that. I didn't have to do the same for him. I plucked a fresh pad from the case and splashed alcohol on it. "This'll hurt."

He took the bottle from me and downed a mouthful.

I pressed the pad to his wound.

He hissed, making my pulse sprint, and his fingers tightened on the sink while I cleaned the cut. A sharp scent of alcohol cut over the blood, wrinkling my nose. I pressed the last strap of tape to his skin and stood up. "That should hold it for now." Temporarily anyway. I was no paramedic.

Yakov panted slightly. The white tiles brightened his skin and reflected in the silver-blue of his eyes. He straightened up, stepping in closer. Sweat beaded on his forehead. The alcohol on his breath reached my nose. His hands slid down my forearms, soft and warm, raising the hairs on my skin.

My breath caught in my throat. My skin tingled beneath his touch.

He hesitated, face inches from mine. His hand slid to the back of my neck, warming my cheeks.

He dropped his hands. "You should change," he said. "There are clothes in your room. We have work to do."

65

Yakov struck a match and dropped it on the file he'd put in the bin. Not the NightLock file. The one Backer had given him. Flames flared like the paper had been doused in alcohol. It probably had. For several moments, he just stood there, watching the file burn.

My cheeks still burned from our closeness in the bathroom. Something about his nearness and the heat of his body on my skin made something leap in my gut. What was all that about? I couldn't stand the man. Couldn't stand the monster I knew lurked beneath. Couldn't stand to be near him without my pulse pounding.

Yakov closed the file. "Time to go."

"Where?"

"Liechtenstein. It's a small country between Austria and Switzerland." He put on his jacket, covering the white handle of his Beretta and headed to the door.

"If Liechtenstein was our destination, why'd we come to Berlin?" I asked.

He grabbed the case. "I'll explain in the car."

An explanation? That was hard to believe. I followed him to the foyer. Memories flashed at the sight of the chair where I'd read about Mum. I drew my arms to my core and kept my head down.

The afternoon air held a sharp chill, a bitter feeling compared to the warmth on the island. Yakov led me to a black Ferrari, and within minutes, we sped along the road, his hands expertly guiding us through the traffic on the wrong side of the road. After a lifetime of travelling in London, the journey felt wrong. Yakov checked his mirror and weaved through the cars, catching my stomach more than once. How could he drive like this without fear? Every turn of the wheel threatened a crash.

I tore my eyes from the road. Out of sight, out of mind. "So, what are we doing?"

"There's a gathering in Liechtenstein, two days from now," Yakov said. "Every four years, representative leaders from major countries gather to renew their agreements of peace."

"Seriously?" I asked. "Why have I never heard of this?"

"It isn't public knowledge."

I could see why. A simple, strategic strike could cause a war. Better to meet in secrecy.

"So, that's the plan?" I asked. "You're going to assassinate them? What will it be? An all-out shooting? How many people arc going to die?"

He changed up a gear and drove us on to a motorway. "No assassinations. Not this time."

"Really?" Well, that was a relief, at least.

"It's a surveillance assignment," he said, and I thought his lips twitched.

"Surveillance? I thought you were an action person. That prep work was boring."

He cast me an amused glance.

"What's it for?" I'd expected Venom to use the nanites, to send me to blackout again and absorb that data that apparently craved. A feeling of dread set my teeth on edge. "It's not a surveillance mission, is it?"

Yakov didn't answer.

"There's something at this meeting, isn't there? Something Venom wants me to absorb." It was so obvious now I knew.

251

That's what the last 'assassination' had been. Yakov had killed people as a decoy for the true reason: my blackout. I'd lost ten minutes in time. The nanites had downloaded something.

Well, it wouldn't make a difference. I wouldn't tell Venom anything. What was in my head would stay in my head. Besides, learning nine languages and knowing where the cameras were hadn't been a conscious effort. The knowledge had just come to me. Who knew how much more lay in my mind? How much I hadn't accessed?

"You don't need to worry," Yakov said. "It'll be a simple job."

"Will I lose time again?"

He weaved around cars. Horns blared, and a Mini cut between two Fiestas and streaked ahead. Three more cars did the same in the next minute. Madness. All of them. Driving in London was crazy, but nothing like this.

"You might as well get comfortable," Yakov said. "There's at least eight hours to go."

"Which takes me to my next question," I said. "Why are we in Berlin? Surely there's an airport in Liechtenstein."

He nodded. "There's something I need to do first."

"What's that?"

He looked at me, and his jaw tightened. "I'm going to kill Dakota."

66

I gaped at Yakov, questions exploding in my mind. "Dakota is in Berlin?"

"He's Venom. He gets the best medical care in the world."

"What if you're wrong?" I asked. "He could be anywhere."

"He's here," Yakov said.

How could he know for sure? Unless he'd been out and actively searching, there was no way he could know. "That's what you were doing," I said. "When you went out last night. And today when you tore your stitches. It wasn't an accident, was it? You were looking for Dakota."

Yakov checked the rear-view mirror.

"Why would you do this?" I asked. "Why kill him?"

"You know if he wakes up—"

"Yes, I know. Why do you care?"

He sighed. "I told you, I have a—"

"Vested interest." I rolled my eyes. "What is that? You said the nanites aren't why you want me safe. What more is there?"

His fingers tightened on the wheel. "That's no concern of yours."

"It's every concern of mine. It's my life on the line." What right did he have to keep it from me?

"Leave it alone," he said.

"No." I twisted to face him in my seatbelt. "I'm so tired of this. So fed up of the riddles and unanswered questions. Just tell me the truth!"

"You're a tool in this," he snapped. "Nothing but the tip of the kremlin. Don't be fooled into thinking you're important. It's the nanites that matter. Not you."

I leaned away from him instinctively, a sudden ache in my throat. I shouldn't have been surprised. Venom cared for no one. Since when had I believed differently with Yakov? I'd seen the monster often enough. I blinked back welling tears and faced forward again.

Sparse trees passed by in a blur, and clouds thickened overhead. Gradually, the cars fell behind, and the road grew quieter.

"That's not exactly what I meant," Yakov said.

"I know what you meant." I was an assignment to him, nothing more. But what assignment? What could he possibly be after? The nanites? Did he want them for himself? One wrong move, and Venom would lock me up. Take me away from him. That would ruin his plans, wouldn't it? That'd stop him from getting data.

"Dakota's in a coma," I said.

"He can still wake up."

"He's unarmed." Vulnerable.

"Would you rather I left him alive?" Yakov asked.

"I'd rather you didn't kill any more innocents."

He sniffed. "Dakota is anything but innocent."

"So are you, but I wouldn't want you killed either."

He looked at me then, his eyes a little wider than usual. It'd been a stupid thing to say. Why on earth would I care about him? "You won't always view the world like that," he said.

"Why? What happened to make you change your mind?" He must've been good and pure at some point. No one is born wicked.

Yakov turned back to the road, and something in his expression hardened. "I saw the world for what it was."

"Did you? Or did you only see it from one side of the

glass?"

"It doesn't matter which side of the glass you're on," he said, "the dirt is visible to both."

"But it's only on one surface," I said. "And it can be washed away."

He huffed. "The dirt, yes. But not the glass. No matter what you do, it'll always be the same: cold and hard."

"Unless it's sunny." Sun warmed glass. Right?

Yakov blinked and pulled off the road into a large car park.

A huge, stone building towered ahead of us, stretching the width of the car park and into the distance. Hundreds of windows reflected the cloudy light, and dirt smeared the walls. Bulbs shone above the entryways where visitors crossed the thresholds.

I could picture Dakota, pale and unmoving, vulnerable in his hospital bed, machines beeping around him. "Don't do this."

Yakov pulled into an empty bay away from other vehicles and switched off the engine. "After all Dakota's put you through, you still want to save him?"

"I don't want anyone else to die." No matter the reason, murder was still murder. It was wrong. I touched his arm, wary, unsure what he'd do.

"Stay in the car." He got out and strolled across the car park, key in hand, and entered the hospital.

A black, unmarked truck with tinted windows pulled up beside me. Spencer watched me through the open window. Her hair curled around her face like a schoolboy's, dirty grey in the gloom.

Without the key, I couldn't lower my own window, so I opened the door a crack.

"You summoned me," she said, her expression every bit as cold as her voice. "I sent Joe because I thought you'd appreciate a familiar face."

Familiar didn't mean friendly. "He threatened me."

"So I heard. Do you have the file?" she asked.

"Do you have my mother?"

She scowled.

"I saw the paper," I said. "I know she's dead." I'd expected my voice to crack. Instead, it turned hard, and heat boiled inside me – heat that made my hand tighten on the door, that swelled an urge to get out and wrap my fingers around her neck. "You promised to protect her. You gave your word she'd be safe."

"That's not—"

"Did you think I wouldn't find out?" I asked. "That I'd still give you the file?"

Spencer leaned closer to the light, putting a bright spot on the edge of her nose. "Your mother is alive."

Goosebumps covered my arms. "What?"

"She's safe, as promised."

"You're lying." They always lied. Venom. Her. They were no different.

"Did you think Venom would leave her?" Spencer asked. "That I would say, 'she's with us now', and they would have mercy?" She shook her head. "We had to fake her death. It was the only way to get her free."

A breeze slipped through the crack in my door, chilling me. "I don't believe you."

"We staged it," Spencer said. "The explosion, the bodies."

No. They couldn't have. Could they? "There were bodies," I said. "People were dead."

She threw me an exasperated look. "We planted the bones, the teeth. *Our* people identified the bodies as your mother and the others in that paper. Sally, your mother and Lia are safe."

67

It made sense. Faking Mum's death to get Venom off her back. But it could be a lie, a way to get the file from me. Spencer had threatened to leave Mum if I didn't do what she wanted. I wouldn't put it past her to lie now. "Prove it."

She sighed and looked down. Holding a phone to her ear, she said, "Put her on," and offered it to me.

After a glance at the hospital, I took the phone and pressed it to my ear.

"Sally?"

"Mum?" The familiarity of her voice transported me home: to our kitchen where she'd make breakfast, the car where she'd hang those awful Christmas trees air fresheners, to the garage where she'd hum while she painted.

"I've been so worried. When they woke me up ..."

"Woke you up?" I asked.

"Venom kept me in a coma. It's been two months." Her voice cracked, and she sniffed.

"I know." I'd been counting.

"I tried to protect you," she said. *"I never wanted it to come to this."*

"You knew, didn't you? You knew about Venom. You knew about—" About the nanites.

Spencer tilted her head, studying me through narrowed eyes.

"I knew about Venom," Mum said.

"Why didn't you tell me? And don't tell me I had no right to know."

"I'd never tell you that. I wanted to tell you. I would have done, one day. I just didn't want—they were hunting you. What kind of life would it be to …" Her voice shook, and the anger in my chest lessened a bit.

"Don't cry," I said, my voice harder than I wanted it. It hadn't been much of a life. I'd been forced to work for Lia, refused the chance to go to college, denied a social life.

Because Mum had been protecting me. "Did Lia know?" I asked. "About Venom." About the nanites.

"She knew. We were trying to protect you," Mum said.

It was like a bad joke. They'd been lying to me, trying to protect me from the very people I'd been trying to protect them from. "Miscommunications," I muttered. "Gotta love them."

The hospital doors slid open, and my heart lurched. A lone woman emerged. We had to leave before Yakov got back. "I've got to go. I'll see you soon." I jabbed the disconnect button and handed the phone to Spencer. "I thought—"

"I know what you thought." She tucked the phone away. "We're not your enemy. We want to help."

"By taking the file?" I asked. Why? She obviously knew about the nanites already. Had she sent me back to Venom just to find out how much they knew?

Her eye twitched. "That was our agreement."

I grabbed the case behind the driver's seat and withdrew the NightLock file. "It's all here."

Spencer frowned at it. "A paper copy?"

"That's all they kept."

She shifted on her seat. "Have you read it?"

She'd expected me not to. She'd thought it was a computer file. She'd thought she could hide the truth about the nanites in that tiny drive in my shoe, that she'd have the advantage over me. Well, I was sick of lies. Tired of being used. No more.

Wariness deepened the wrinkles around her eyes. "You

know."

I tightened my grip on the file. "What do you want with the nanites?"

She retreated into the shadows. "We want to make an antivirus. It'll remove the nanites from your blood."

"Is that possible?" Surely, not. Venom would've made one. They'd have given the nanites to one of their own recruits. Someone loyal. Someone who wouldn't keep resisting them.

"With the right scientists and proper data, anything is possible." She gestured to the file.

An antivirus. A way out of these blackouts. Venom wouldn't need me anymore. They'd leave me alone.

No. They'd kill me. And the SIO would have the nanites. The greatest weapon that ever existed.

Unless this was a lie. A trick to get me to go with her. But Spencer hadn't lied about Mum. She'd freed Mum from Venom. If she faked my death, too, Venom wouldn't know any different. I'd be free.

"Fine." I passed her the file. "Let's go."

Spencer held up a hand. "It's not as simple as that."

I tensed, foot on the concrete. "What do you mean?"

"We need to make a plan," she said. "Get witnesses in place. These things take time."

"You managed with Mum." With less than a day's notice.

"Your Mum isn't the most valuable person to Venom."

What did that matter? We only had to leave. Drive away and never look back. Providing Venom didn't track us to the airport, we'd be long gone before they found us.

But they'd try. Yakov would try, too. He'd kill more people than would be saved. He'd have to be stopped.

"You'll work on it?" I asked.

"Absolutely." She handed me a tiny hair clip with a flat, narrow top. "If you ever need me, plug this into a phone," she said. "It'll give you a direct line to me."

An odd gesture. She'd need twenty-four hours, tops. Why would I need to contact her? I sat back in the car, trying to ignore the gnawing in my gut.

"We'll be in touch soon," she said. "Next time, try not to pull a gun on my agent." Her window rolled up, and the truck pulled away.

I hesitated with my hand on the door handle, and a sinking feeling in my core. Spencer knew the dangers of staying with Venom. Extracting me would be her top priority. Wouldn't it? Why hadn't she already planned for it?

I lifted my hair and secured the clip at the nape of my neck, careful to cover it completely. A couple went into the hospital. The hospital where Yakov was about to murder Dakota.

True, the lie master hadn't helped me. If he woke up, Backer would have people on me in hours. But murder was murder. He didn't deserve that. A lifetime in prison – that he deserved.

A uniformed officer weaved between the parked cars. Polizei marked his jacket.

I straightened. A policeman. Would it be enough? If he acted quickly—I didn't want Yakov killed, but imprisoned? That wouldn't be so bad. He had to be stopped, after all.

Without pausing to doubt, I scrambled from the car, switching my mentality to German. The officer cut between two cars, moving away, but I was fast. I could catch him.

I dashed across the road.

Yakov grabbed my forearm and spun me around. "I told you to stay in the car."

"I wanted—"

"I know what you wanted." He shoved me back in the car before climbing in the driver's seat.

"When will you learn, you can't lie to me?" He drove us onto the road. The policeman strolled along the path. "Do you think it's coincidence I'm your partner?" Yakov asked. "You don't think he anticipated you trying to escape?"

"He? Who's he?" Not Backer. Blake? Niagra? Whoever Yakov had spoken to on the phone before giving me the file?

"You're safer with me," Yakov said.

Oh, yes. The killer from the cradle. "I wasn't trying to

escape."

"Oh, no?" He glanced in his rear-view mirror, and his eyebrows raised. "You were trying to save Dakota." Disbelief coated his words.

Fat lot of good I'd done. "Is he …?"

"He will be, soon enough."

I tucked my trembling hands beneath my legs. "What did you do?"

"Poison in his drip."

"I'm surprised you didn't shoot him and get it over with." It's what I'd expected him to do.

"Too much surveillance. This is Venom we're talking about." Yakov shook his head. "This way looks natural. The poison's untraceable. He'll die in his sleep. Quite painlessly, you'll be pleased to hear."

"And you know that from experience, do you?"

He scowled at me.

"You never know, do you?" Dakota could be in silent agony, and no one would ever know.

68

A barrier of heavily-armed guards surrounded the castle, much to the irritation of the Chinese ambassador. "This is neutral territory," he said to his translator, sloshing his champagne in his glass. "There are too many guns."

Yakov adjusted his cuff. He'd changed that morning into a tailored suit, and given me a dress, diamond bracelet and Russian pin. Our uniforms.

"Bit dressy for a server," I said.

"This is the richest gathering in the world. They expect the best." He'd handed me a miniature smoke grenade, too. "Just in case. Be sure not to breathe in the smoke."

Now nestled inside the castle and balancing a tray of drinks on my palm, I waited while the guests arrived and scanned a card through a scanner. Each delegate wore a pin on their lapel demonstrating from which country they hailed. Servers wearing matching pins had been assigned to each ambassador.

The Chinese ambassador clicked his fingers at me. "More champagne, wench."

"Sir," his translator said, "you can't call them that here."

"Oh, tush, she doesn't understand. She's just a server." He clicked at me again.

My cheeks warmed – the man needed a good thump – and I

took my tray to him.

He swapped his glass wordlessly.

I counted six delegates: Russia, China, North Korea, Germany, the United Kingdom and the United States. Translators stood beside some of them.

A side door opened, and a man strolled out wearing a sash of red and blue with a golden crown at the shoulder.

"That's the general," Yakov said. "He owns the castle. Hosts the meeting."

The general stretched out his arms. "Welcome, friends. I hope you travelled well. Please." He gestured to the double doors beside me. "Let us begin."

The gathering followed him through a long corridor with pedestals, vases and marble busts until we got to a conference room. The delegates took their seats in relative silence. Translators sat with them, but the servers hung back by the wall.

"My servers are on hand," the general said, gesturing to Yakov, me and five others dressed identically. "Should you require anything, please ask."

The Chinese translator relayed his words, and the delegate shifted his gaze to me. I clenched my teeth. What was the horrid man doing here? Someone like him couldn't possibly be interested in peace.

The Russian ambassador twisted in his chair and beckoned to me. "Be a dear and get me a glass of whisky."

I nodded and left their company.

My footsteps resounded in the empty, stone hallway, a far more enjoyable space without all the ambassadors and workers. So, I took my time going to the table of drinks. Wine, champagne, whisky and water covered the surface in crystalised bottles that sparkled under the late-morning light.

Something hissed.

I whirled to the empty corridor, neck prickling.

Muffled voices sounded behind the closed doors, the delegates' figures distorted by frosted glass.

Something hissed again.

What was it? Water running? A gas leak? No, it sounded closer to wind. Whispering wind.

I placed my tray on the table and approached the door on my left. It was ajar. A slight breeze blew through it, carrying a stale scent and that unmistakable sound. Stone steps led down into darkness, and a light set into the brick flickered on and off.

The sound grew.

After a glance at the conference room, I descended the stairs, my heeled shoes clicking on the stone. What was I supposed to do? Ignore it? What if it was a gas leak? They'd have to be warned. Besides, we weren't here to kill anyone. And as far as I knew, I hadn't blacked out yet.

At the bottom, a narrow, stone corridor stretched deeper into the castle, lit by cold, rounded lights in the walls.

"Hello?" My voice echoed. "Is someone down here?" My German sounded strange. Almost warped and swallowed by the hissing. Course it sounded less like wind now and more like a sizzling, clicking noise. I crept along the corridor towards a door and pushed it open.

Rows of machinery filled a huge, underground room. Blue and red lights flashed periodically, and wires criss-crossed beside columns of drawers.

I stepped inside, the hairs raising on my arms.

The sound stopped.

I blinked, eyes stinging, and gasped.

Bodies covered the floor. Blood smeared the machinery where it had, a moment ago, been clean. The hand of a dead guard clung to my ankle, a bullet wound in his head.

I staggered away from him with a strangled yelp and spun towards the exit.

Yakov stood behind me, a guard's neck locked in the crook of his arm. He twisted, a crack cut the air, and the guard collapsed with a thud.

Yakov fixed hard eyes on me. "Are you hurt?"

Something tickled my nose, and when I rubbed it, blood stained my hand. The floor tilted. My knees buckled.

Yakov caught me.

My dizziness, the sudden changes around me ... I'd blacked out again. Absorbed something from this machine. "How long?" I asked.

"Six hours."

Six hours! That couldn't be right. I couldn't have been—A violent shiver ached my legs.

Yakov's brow glistened with sweat, staining the air with its scent. "Come on." He adjusted his grip on me, scooped his gun from the tiles and guided me to the passage.

How could six hours have passed? They'd have found me already. Moved me. It wouldn't have taken long to notice my absence. They'd have searched for me. With all those guards, Yakov couldn't have held them off.

Two guards clattered to the bottom of the steps, rifles raised.

Yakov shot twice, stepped past their corpses and took me upstairs. Weakness flooded me. I grabbed Yakov's jacket, determined to stay standing. Six hours.

"What did I absorb?" I gasped.

A frown creased Yakov's chin. "Everything."

"What?"

He glanced at me before pushing us into the hallway.

"What do you mean everything?" I asked.

The Chinese delegate blocked our way, a swarm of guards behind him. He pointed. "Take her."

Yakov pulled me backwards, shoved me into a corridor, and holstered his Beretta. "Go," he said. "Whatever happens, don't stop." He marched towards the oncoming enemy, crossed his arms and drew out two knives.

What was he doing? He couldn't beat them all. They kill him. They'd kill me. Unless I ran. I staggered away with a tug of guilt, running a steadying hand over the old paint-peeling bricks.

A uniformed figure dashed towards me. He struck out.

I blocked, twisted, and downed him before swinging through an open window into a chilly garden. Ankle-high grass clung to my legs and wet my skin. My heels sank into the soil, and the scent of lingering rain filled the air.

I braced a cold hand against the sill.

The garden sloped down in neatly-trimmed grass and budding flowerbeds, ending at a tall, brick barrier. I guessed twelve feet high. A few trees guarded it, their branches thick.

I took a breath and bolted towards the fence, keeping on my toes. Someone shouted behind me. Dogs barked. I leapt for the closest branch and hoisted myself up. The trunk scraped against my shin, stinging it, but I scrambled up and over and dropped to the outside path. Stones grazed my hands, and a heel snapped. Spots darkened my vision.

No. I wasn't clear yet.

I snapped off the remaining heel and plunged into foliage. Roots and weeds dragged me down, but I got up each time and pushed on with growing weakness and fading vision. The straps of my shoes dug into my feet. My chest seized.

Coughs erupted from me, coating the weeds in red. And a smell surrounded me. Like sweat. And metal. And blood.

69

Crackling. Popping. Heat. Was this what death was like? Weird and comforting and dark?

I opened my eyes. Fire burned in a shallow pit. I lay on a jacket several feet from the flames but close enough to feel the heat burning against my arm. I sat up, rocking in a wave of dizziness.

"Easy." Yakov placed a hand on my shoulder. He'd ditched his jacket and tie, and firelight brightened the dirt on his shirt and face. "You've lost a lot of strength." He handed me an already-opened cereal bar.

"How did you—"

"Find you?" he asked.

"Escape," I said. "You were so outnumbered."

He plucked a piece of grass. "Do you think so little of me?"

I could think of the corpses, the blood on the machinery, the guards ready to attack us in the corridor. "Are they dead?"

"Most of them." Yakov prodded the fire, and sparks shot from the branches. He showed no remorse. He never did.

The wrapper crinkled under my fingers. I took a bite of the bar, and my gut growled, but the dry oats gave me a surge of thirst. Six hours, plus however long I'd been unconscious. Judging by the darkness, it'd been hours more. How long had it been since I last drank?

"You said I absorbed everything," I said. "What did you mean?"

He prodded the fire again, spilling embers over the wood. "When the delegates scanned their cards, it created a link between them and their IDs. Their workplaces."

"So?"

"So, they work for their governments. The Russian government. The Chinese. North Korea, Germany, the U.S., the U.K. The nanites can break past firewalls, link their IDs with their agencies' databases."

My grip tightened, and the bar snapped. The top piece dropped to the dirt. "You're telling me I took in—"

"Everything."

"From *six* government agencies?"

He glared at the fire.

"How is that possible? My head can't hold that much information." My words choked in my throat. I'd collapsed. I'd coughed up blood. All those files, all that data from all those countries … There'd be missions from the past. Missions happening now, and ones for the future. There'd be names of spies, locations of safehouses, dates, details, every employee, secret prisoners. All of that squeezed in my head.

"I can't, can I?" I said. "That's why I passed out. There's too much data to hold." An overload. That's what this was. But when a computer overloaded, it burned up. I wanted to swallow, but the thirst, the fear, it dried my mouth like a desert. "What'll happen to me?"

He stabbed the branches again.

Something inside me sank. "I'm going to die. Aren't I?"

"You don't have to," Yakov said. "We can take the nanites out." He threw the stick in the fire, sparking a wave of heat that burned my cheeks.

I shuffled away. "How?"

"There's an antivirus," he said.

"You mean one can be made."

"No, I mean there is one." He tore up a handful of grass.

"Well, that can't be right," I said. "Spencer told me they'd make an antivirus, not that one exists."

Yakov's focus snapped to me, and I clamped my hand over my mouth. Shadow covered half his face. Light flared on the other half, distorting his features. "What did you say?"

I scrambled to stand. Spencer. I'd told him about Spencer. "I didn't ..."

He stood. The grass poked from his fist like tiny blades. "What did she tell you?"

"Nothing." My voice shook. Like it mattered. Mum was safe. Lia was safe. I just needed—I glanced behind me.

Yakov stepped closer. "I know you plan to run. I won't let you."

"You won't stop me." Venom recruited me for the nanites. They must've known my brain wouldn't cope. They must've known I'd die. But I had help in the SIO. Venom didn't know that. "Where's the antivirus?"

Yakov cocked his head.

"You can tell me or not." I staggered back a step. "But I won't co-operate. I won't give Venom what they want."

A figure moved beyond the flames, feminine in shape, black in shadow. She stepped forwards, letting the flames light her face.

"Backer," I whispered.

"Good evening," Backer said.

The fire crackled on glowing embers, billowing smoke through the black air.

I flexed cold fingers, legs itching to run. "What are you doing here?"

"Checking in," she said. "Your recent assignment was, after all, a significant one." A breeze caught her hair.

"They're killing me," I said, and my chest gave a jolt.

Backer smiled. "A shame, that. You have potential, although your commitment is somewhat lacking."

"I'll never commit to you," I said.

"Not even if you knew the truth?" Her eyes reflected the

fire, like a demon rising from hell. "Can't you imagine what we can do with that data?"

"Oh, I can imagine," I said. "You'd blackmail. You'd kill. You'd do anything to get more power."

"Goodness, no, dear," she said. "Venom can do that anyway. With that information, we can achieve what no one else can. We can stop drug gangs and weed out corrupt politicians. We can lower taxes, end starvation in third world countries, put an end to war. Can't you commit to *that*?"

"If you have to steal and kill to achieve it, it doesn't count," I said.

"Agree to disagree." She shrugged and clapped her hands together. "Enough chit-chat. We've a long journey. We can't extract those files in the middle of Liechtenstein, can we?"

So, they had a way to access them. Well, I wouldn't let them. Something dug into my hand from the pocket of my dress. I slipped my hand inside, and my fingers closed around the grenade.

Backer jerked her head at Yakov. "Unconscious will do. Don't want her making a scene."

Yakov dropped the grass.

I pulled the pin from the grenade. "I won't go."

Yakov stepped closer, his shoulders set. His lips thinned. His eyes hardened.

I threw the weapon in the fire, and fled.

70

The grenade exploded. Sparks and embers rained around me, and pain scorched my forearm, drawing a cry. I struggled through the blackness, spurred on by adrenaline, and burst into a field.

Silence followed. Gone were the cracklings of the fire. The wind even held its breath, watching over the assassins behind me. Unconscious? Pursuing? Hard to tell. But I could lose them in the dark.

I skimmed the field's edge, keeping to the treeline. Knee-length grass rustled and bent under my footsteps, ending at a sudden road.

Now what? I didn't know where I was. I had no clue where Yakov left the car. Was I supposed to flee all night? Follow the road until I found somewhere to stay? Like that'd make a difference when I had no money.

Gravel crunched, and a car rolled into sight, its headlights stretching the branches' shadows over the dirt. It rolled to a stop beside me. "You lost?" The driver watched me through the cracked-open window. Wispy, grey hair peeked below his bowler hat.

"A little," I said, German rolling off my tongue.

"Where you headed?"

"The nearest village."

He nodded. "Hop in if you like. I'll give you a lift."

I climbed in with a word of thanks, Mum's past warning ringing through my mind. *Never get in a car with a stranger.* Normally, I wouldn't, but given the choice between him or Yakov, I'd take him. Besides, I wasn't completely incompetent. Not anymore.

The cut on my arm oozed blood and a sharp scent where the explosion had burned it. Cold air blew through a vent, stinging the wound.

The stranger slipped the car into gear and trundled on.

Something shifted in the wing mirror: a shadowy figure by the roadside. Yakov? I hugged my arms to my chest. He'd keep chasing me. But for now, I was free, and with any luck, I'd stay that way. The killer would never bother me again.

The driver pointed at my arm. "What happened?"

"I slipped."

He raised his eyebrows. "Did you, now?"

I shifted on the seat. Silly. He wasn't suspicious. I was paranoid. "It's just a scratch."

"Smells like a burn."

Smells? How would he know something like that? He turned a corner, passing a high, brick wall. Branches poked over the top. Familiar. Wasn't that the wall I'd escaped over?

"Where are you taking me?" I asked.

He checked his rear-view, turning the wheel with gloved hands.

I studied his face, the high buttons of his coat. A slip of green lay beneath the collar. "I know you," I said.

"I don't think so."

"I've seen you before." Dread made my core cramp. "You're one of the general's guards."

I pulled on the handle. Locked. "Let me go."

He turned us onto a wider road. Stones crunched beneath the wheels.

"No can do, Miss. You're a wanted criminal." And he pulled out a gun, pointing the long barrel at me.

No way. I wasn't getting caught again.

I yanked on the steering wheel, and the car veered. The gun went off, missed my head, but the sound stung and set a whistle in my ears. Branches whipped the windows. Headlights flared on a trunk. The driver cried out. Hit the brakes. Crunching metal tore the air.

I lurched forwards. My seatbelt dug into my chest.

Silence fell.

71

Wisps curled from the bonnet where we'd collided with the tree. The headlights flickered, and an eerie glow settled over the woodland. The driver slumped over the steering wheel, a cut on his forehead. His eyes were closed.

I pressed my fingers to his throat. Still alive. Thank goodness. The engine still rumbled despite the collision. I leaned over and opened his door, undid his belt, and pushed him out. He hit the grass with a thud. Someone would find him soon. He'd be all right.

I peered down at his body. Wouldn't he? The weeds practically covered him. If no one saw him quick enough, it might be too late to save him.

I growled and climbed out. Hooking my hands beneath his arms, I tugged him to the road. There. Now he'd be found.

The road looked empty, but that meant nothing. Yakov wouldn't be far behind.

I rushed to the car, chest thudding, slipped into gear, and reversed back to the road. After one last look at the unmoving guard, I set off, rumbling away with a flickering headlight and miniature cracks over the windscreen.

I couldn't go on like this. I'd stand out easily. If I could get to a village, find a phone box … I slipped my fingers into my hair to feel the slender grip. There was no going back now.

Spencer would have to extract me.

And if she didn't? The nanites were killing me. Sure, Spencer mentioned an antivirus. Yakov confirmed it. If one truly existed, I had to find it. But where to start?

What did I know so far? The NightLock file referred to A.H. *Duplicate records shipped to A.H.* Maybe whoever that was could help me. I'd have to convince him. Or her. And find out where they were. How would I begin to go about that? With Spencer? Would they know anything?

The night passed uneventfully. Plans and ideas buzzed through my head, each as hopeless as the last. A.H. was the closest I came to any kind of answer, short of handing myself to Spencer and trusting her to help. Trust was a hard thing to find nowadays.

The moon arced over the sky as the hours spent. I drove through a couple of villages, seeing no phone boxes. I didn't bother to stop. In the cover of night, it felt wiser to get far away before ditching the car.

By the time orange streaked the sky, my eyes stung, and my body shook with hunger and thirst. The needle on the fuel gage hovered above red. Whatever my plan included, it would have to start with water.

The road into Berlin grew busy with early commuters. Tram lines ran parallel to the road. Twice one passed me, rocking the car, filled with oblivious innocents living normal lives. I passed skyscrapers and businesses, markets and shops. The state of the car earned a few looks from passing pedestrians. The night travel had been a good idea. Day travel wasn't. It attracted too much attention.

I flicked on the indicator and pulled into a side road, drawing to a shuddering stop by the curb. My legs seized when I climbed out, shooting cramps down my muscles, and my arm stung and tightened under the drying, cracked blood. I rubbed my legs roughly and slid into the back streets, following the scent of cooking bacon.

What could I do? The fact that I'd escaped Yakov and

Backer was a miracle, but I needed nourishment, sleep, a change of clothes. And a first aid kit.

The morning air burned my wound, dragging my breaths between my teeth.

Around a corner, marketers set up their stalls for the day, and an idea sprang to mind. I traipsed to where a middle-aged woman busied herself with a rack of scarves. She smoothed each one with chubby fingers, eyes widening when she saw me.

"I had an accident," I said. "I've lost my money and hoped—" I unfastened my bracelet. "Hoped you'd trade for this?"

She took it, running her finger over the stones. "These are diamonds?"

"Yes."

She narrowed her eyes at the jewellery. "Stay here." She bustled over to a jeweller's stall. The man there glanced at me, took the bracelet and studied it through a tiny lens.

Couldn't they hurry up? Venom could be anywhere. No doubt they'd all be on the lookout now. I had to get off the street. The marketers worked on their stalls, chatting to one another. No one looked over. But that didn't mean they weren't watching me.

The woman returned with a smile, the bracelet draped across her palm. "What do you need?"

I hugged my arms around me. "Clothes. Food. Water."

"Help yourself."

I grabbed a blouse, a knitted jumper, and a pair of jeans, scanning the growing crowd.

"There's a toilet in there." She pointed at a cream-bricked building and slipped a euro in my palm. "Try these." She added a pair of boots to my arms and grabbed a scarf. "And this." She crammed a baguette and water bottle on the pile from an adjoining stall, along with a woollen hat. "You need a coat."

"No, this is enough." I backed towards the toilets. "Thank you."

She slid the bracelet in her pocket. "Thank *you*."

It must've been worth a lot. Hardly a surprise considering Venom's taste for luxury. I weaved around the stalls and pushed into the building, catching a blast of heat at the door.

A man dressed in black strolled towards me.

I stiffened. Was he—he was watching me. I twisted sideways, preparing to run. I'd drop the clothes if I had to. I'd throw them in his face. Restrict his vision. I'd—

He turned left into a small shop.

I exhaled, cheek warming. Not Venom. Just a shopper. If the nanites didn't kill me, paranoia might.

72

The toilets carried a scent of cleaning products and gleamed with cleanliness – nothing like the public toilets I'd experienced in England. Those were dirty and littered with muddy footprints and the scent of urine. Here, framed posters advertised October Fest and discounts in local shops. One of the taps dripped – dripping, ticking – like the grandfather clock before it fell. Dakota's face filled my memory – his crushed body on the floor of Niagra's office. I could picture him now, skin white as the sink, lying cold and still on a metal gurney in the morgue.

I tightened the tap with icy hands before ducking into a stall to change. The jeans, boots, and blouse warmed me instantly. The sleeves stopped just above my wound. Leaning over the sink, I used the cold water to wipe away the crusty, brown blood. Blistered, red skin surrounded my burn – not too deep.

A couple of menstrual pads poked out of a vendor. I peeled one open and tucked it into my sleeve, over the wound before pulling on the jumper. The pad rubbed, aggravating the pain, but it was better than nothing. The hat and scarf covered my face a good amount, too, so I returned to the street, somewhat more comforted than before, dropping the empty bottle in the bin.

The baguette had been dry, but fresh, and far from enough

to satiate my appetite. I needed more, but without money or allies—my heart jolted. A phone booth stood in the distance, almost haloed by the rose-dusted sky. I bee-lined towards the booth, keeping my head down. Tiredness weighed my body. My lips stuck together. I shouldn't have used the bracelet for clothes. A room would've been wiser.

I snatched an apple from a fruit stall, and bit into it with a tug of guilt. Sweet juice tingled my taste buds, and I practically inhaled the rest.

The streets bustled with people now: commuters and businessmen, tourists. Children going to school. Life had been so much simpler before Blake dragged me into this. I'd been afraid to speak to Lia then. What'd I been frightened of? Compared to Venom, Lia wasn't scary at all.

I squeezed into the booth and unclipped the phone. The bottom speaker twisted off easily, showing tangled wires and metal prongs. Was that what the nanites looked like? Tiny metal pieces streaming through my blood? The slide caught in my hair when I grabbed it, tugging strands from the roots. I pulled them free and pushed the slide into the receiver.

Now what? Was I supposed to dial something? I wasn't sure I'd chosen the right slot. I might've done it wrong. I held the phone to my ear.

It beeped three times, then clicked.

"State your name."

Huh. It'd done something then. "Sally Rivers."

Silence fell.

I tapped my finger on the phone. "Hello?"

Nothing. Something was wrong. Maybe I'd connected it wrong. Maybe it wasn't supposed to go in that part of the phone. I should've—

"Sally?" Spencer's voice. *"Are you all right?"*

The tightness eased in my chest. I plucked another hair from my jumper and let it float to the ground. "I need help. I escaped."

"You did what?" she snapped. *"I told you to wait."*

"I didn't have a choice. I was compromised." Besides, it'd been over a day. How long did it take to put some plans together?

"They know you're working for us?"

"Not exactly." Someone laughed outside the box, jolting my heart into a sprint. Just a kid. The man with him took his hand and led him across the road. "I need you to come get me."

"Not yet. You need to finish your assignment."

"What assignment?"

"The one with the Russian."

My arm prickled. The assignment in Lichtenstein? Why would she—I leaned against the glass, limb shaking. "You want me to black out. You want me to absorb the data." Why hadn't I realised earlier? Every agency. Every secret. Of course she'd want that. She'd never planned to remove the nanites. She only planned to use me. Just like Venom.

"Sally." Spencer's tone turned wary. *"It's my job to protect our country."*

Excuses. That's all her words were. Excuses and lies and justifications for the horrors she'd commit.

A black, unmarked vehicle pulled up across the road. No one moved inside.

A cold sweat stifled my skin. Venom?

"Let's meet," Spencer said. *"Where are you?"*

The street crawled with people. Cars cluttered the road. I touched my stinging arm. Anyone could be watching me.

A van drew up, two people in the front. They wore black, faces masked.

The glass on the booth steamed over. The air grew hot. I opened the door a crack.

"Sally. Tell me where you are. We'll come and get you."

Two men climbed out of the car, suited in black, hands gloved. A gun hung at one's waist.

I teetered on my toes, ready to run.

Spencer muttered something to someone on her end.

One touched his ear.

No. They couldn't be—I tightened my grip on the phone. "They're not Venom."

"What was that?"

My breath caught. The two by the car, the two in the van—they were SIO.

"Sally? Are you all right?"

"You know where I am," I said. "Don't you?"

Spencer muttered something else.

The van doors opened.

I squeezed the phone until my palm hurt. When would I learn? I should've known by now, I had no allies. No one to trust. "I won't let you have the nanites," I said. "I won't let anyone have them." And I dashed from the booth towards the market. The scent of street food sent pains through my gut. The morning chill nipped my cheeks and fingers and aggravated my burn.

Dark, semi-dried streaks of rain marked the stalls and ground. I barged past a woman, knocking her bag from her hand. She swore at me.

Someone bumped my shoulder. Pain flared in my wound, but I bit back a hiss and pushed on.

A masked man ran into my path. He struck out.

I blocked and twisted around him, knocking over a hat stand. Knitted fabric covered the ground, much to the cries of the owner.

Someone grabbed me from behind. I turned, bowed, and flipped him over my shoulder. His back met a stall. Wood cracked and collapsed beneath him, and the covering tarp billowed over him.

A second man blocked my way. He kicked out, narrowly missed me and flipped over a table.

The first attacker scrambled from the broken stall. Coal-black paint streaked his face.

I grabbed a candlestick and swung it against his head, jabbed his abdomen, elbowed his nose, and ran on, ducking to avoid an attempted snatch from a stall owner.

People blocked my way. They pointed phones, pointed, yelled at me.

Something struck a post beside me, drawing my gasp. A dart.

I bolted down an alley, around a corner, and into a dead end. Nearly a dead end. Two bins blocked the exit, but there was a narrow space between them. Big enough for me?

There was no time to think. I squeezed between them, scraping my back and front against the dirty sides. Bugs scurried through the grease. I tasted rot. A hook snagged my jumper, stopping me with a tug. I grappled with the fabric, snapped threads that clung to the hook.

The coal-streaked attacker banged against the bin. He tried to squeeze through, but his broad shoulders betrayed him. His hand brushed my back.

The jumper snapped free, and I stumbled out into open alleyway.

Hands grabbed me and spun me round, driving my back against the wall. Keeping one hand on my chest, Yakov raised his other and shot twice – once at the half-emerged coal-man, once at the one climbing over the bin.

73

I moved to run, but Yakov pushed his gun to my side, raising a wince. "You shouldn't have run," he growled.

"You won't shoot me."

"Won't I?"

I shook my head. "You want something. You've always wanted—"

"Stop talking." He marched me from the alley, and when I tugged against him, he jabbed the barrel in farther, drawing a gasp of pain.

"I'm not going back," I said.

He led me to the main road. His car sat on the curb, but he headed towards an oncoming tram. "I've just killed two people," he said. "We're getting off the street." The tram pulled up at the stop. "Get in. And stay quiet. You try anything, it won't be you I shoot."

Three passengers shared our car. I watched them silently, willing them to get out. If they'd only look at me, if I could catch their eye, I could warn them. Somehow.

And Yakov would catch on and kill them.

I leaned against a pole weakly. The tram slid away. Yakov moved the gun off my side, and stepped closer, leaning into me each time I rocked.

How could I have been so stupid? All I'd had to do was

think before I spoke. One slip about Spencer, and I'd ruined everything. And I wasn't even allies with Spencer. I was on the run!

After several minutes, the tram drew still. Yakov pushed me out, securing me with a firm hand. His gun was back in its holster. Not that it would stop him killing. An assassin didn't need a gun to finish a job.

He marched me along a side street to a run-down apartment block with peeling paint and weathered brick. A sign with half the letters missing read, 'A DG E'. The E hung from its bracket. He steered me through the door and past an empty reception desk to a narrow set of stairs.

Empty stairs. With no people to shoot.

I struck out at the Russian.

He blocked.

I jabbed again.

He blocked that, too, and twisted my arm into a lock. Pain shot along it, and he forced me to double over and dragged me up two flights, increasing my pain each time I struggled.

I tried to kick him.

He merely knocked my foot aside and shoved me into an apartment at the far end of a gloomy passage.

I staggered away from him, arm aching. No way. I wasn't done fighting yet. I ran for the door.

He pushed me backwards.

But I had what I wanted.

I raised his gun. "I'm not going back." Unless Backer was already here. I glanced nervously around the near-bare room.

Yakov's brow drew down, and he pushed the door shut. "You can't run from this. You must see that."

"I'm not running."

"Yes, you are." He watched me calmly, unphased by the gun pointing at his chest. His hands rested by his side. His feet widened in a ready stance. Unphased, maybe. Ready to attack, definitely. He stepped closer.

"Stay back." I jabbed the gun at him.

"Or what? You couldn't kill the banker." He advanced again. "Can you kill me?"

"I don't have to." I pointed the barrel at his knee.

"You must," he said, "if you want to run again. Because I won't let you leave." He moved closer. "And a bullet in my leg won't stop me holding you."

I lifted the gun to his chest. "Stay away." My voice betrayed a tremor. Stupid. Be strong. The SIO guards were afraid of me. I'd make Yakov scared, too.

"I'll never stop coming for you," he said. "I'll find you every time. Wherever you go."

My tongue stuck to the roof of my mouth. I could shoot his knee. Or his side. But what if I hit something vital? An artery. An organ. He could bleed out. Die on the dusty floorboards. "I'm leaving," I said.

He stepped forwards until the barrel of his gun pressed against his chest. "Even if you do, you can't hide. Not from me." The light from the window reflected in his eyes, highlighting flecks of silver in the blue. "I will never stop coming for you. Never stop hunting you. Unless you kill me." Yakov clasped his hand over mine, sending heat through my skin.

He knew my weakness.

Failing to kill isn't a weakness.

Funny how it felt like one now.

"Don't be afraid," Yakov said. "Trust me."

"I'm not afraid." *Liar.* I could hear Dakota all over again. A voice from the dead, laughing at the shake in my own.

"Not afraid?" he said. "Then, why are you trembling?" He slipped the Beretta from my hand.

74

Yakov sat on a table, holding his gun. He scowled at it, thumb running over the safety catch. Debating? He'd warned me against seeking the file. Lied for me when I failed to kill. Pursued me all night. Maybe he'd had enough. Maybe he thought it'd be easier to kill me now and be done with it.

I shifted uneasily in the sparsely furnished apartment. It only had a table, a sofa and chair, a chest of drawers and mirror. There were no photos. Nothing to show anyone lived here. "What will you do?" I asked.

Yakov stared into nothing, lips pursed, clicking the safety on and off his weapon. "This is a safehouse." He met my gaze with tired eyes. "Venom doesn't know about it. So, you should sleep."

"Yeah, right."

His shoulders dropped. He tapped his gun on his knee. "I know you don't trust me. I know you've no reason to. But you can't go on like this, running blindly, no supplies, no allies. Sooner or later, they'll find you, and I'll be the least of your worries."

"Oh, well in that case, I'll just take nap, shall I? I mean if you insist no one's coming, why wouldn't I feel safe?" I folded my arms. His exhaustion showed in the white of his skin, the rings beneath his eyes. If he fell asleep, escape would be easy.

But his fatigue only made him more dangerous.

He sighed. "No one's coming for you. Not Venom. Not the SIO. No one knows we're here."

I jolted. "The SIO?"

"You rang them."

How could he know that? Had he seen me in the booth? Even then, he couldn't have heard me. Realistically, he shouldn't have found me at all. I'd driven all night, checked behind me a thousand times. I'd lost him. I was sure of it. "How'd you find me?"

"I told you I would."

"That's not an answer." I could've gone anywhere. Driven in any direction. He couldn't possibly have caught up this fast.

"What was it?" Yakov asked. "What did Spencer offer you?" He laid the gun on the table, tapping the side with his forefinger. "You never wanted this life. So, you wouldn't agree to spy for nothing. What does she have that you want? Protection?" His tapping stopped, and he straightened. "Your mother isn't dead, is she? They staged it to get her free from Venom." His jaw tensed. "And you gave them the NightLock file."

And just like that, he knew. My chest tightened. "Yakov—"

He raised a hand. "I get it. You're fighting for your family. He said you would."

"Who's he?"

Yakov picked up the Beretta and walked to the kitchen. "Get some sleep. You're safe here."

My mouth opened with a little pop. "That's it?" No anger? No rage? Not even a flicker of irritation? Where was the ruthless assassin who killed without remorse? Where was the retribution?

Yakov opened a cupboard. "Were you expecting something else?"

"You framed the fishermen. You had them killed because I took the file," I said. "Why aren't you angry with me for handing it over?" Of course, he was angry. He must be brimming with it. Silent anger. The kind that made him most dangerous.

"The file doesn't matter." He stabbed a tin opener in a can of soup. "Neither does Spencer or anyone else."

I shivered. "Then, what does?"

"Food." He emptied soup into a bowl and popped it in a microwave. When it tinged, he stuck a spoon in the bowl and gave it to me.

The scent filled the kitchen and ached my core, so I took a spoonful while he pulled out a second tin. "Venom really don't know we're here?" It sounded more like an excuse to lower my guard, but why bother? I was unarmed. He wouldn't let me leave even if I tried, and we'd already established I couldn't beat him in a fistfight.

"No," he said. "They don't know."

I could see them in my mind, though, creeping down the passage, guns raised. I frowned at the door. "Why not? And don't tell me you have reasons. If you want any kind of trust from me, give me answers."

He tipped his soup in a bowl, stuck it in the microwave, and sighed. "It seems pointless to hide things now. All things considered." When he turned to me, resolve had set in his expression. "All right. I'll tell you what you want to know."

75

My reflection stared back at me, pale and gaunt and worthy of one of Mayra's lectures. The past twenty-four hours had not been kind.

Yakov clattered in the kitchen, cleaning up the bowls, leaving me to clean myself before he'd explain everything. Finally, answers.

Or more lies. How was I supposed to tell the difference? The fact that I stayed here screamed foolishness, but escape wasn't happening. If I'd learned anything, it was that.

I pulled off my jumper, hissing with pain, and studied my burn. It still oozed slightly. The edges had blistered, and the skin shone raw and red.

Yakov came in, laid an open first-aid kit on the bath and sat beside it. "Let me see." He took my arm gently and studied the burn before pulling out a bandage, pack of wipes, padding, and two miniature bottles of alcohol.

What did he want? He'd helped me since we first met on the island. He'd trained me, lied for me, protected me. Why? For the nanites? I wouldn't let him have them. He must know that by now.

Yakov offered a bottle to me.

"I don't drink."

"It'll help."

I stared him down until he shrugged and replaced the whiskey. "Suit yourself."

He cleaned up the surrounding skin before splashing the alcohol on a pad. "Sure you don't want that drink?" He glanced at me, then pressed the pad to the wound.

I yelled like he'd stabbed me with hot needles. Tingles erupted through my muscle and coursed down my arm. I grasped the sink with my free hand, struggling to stay standing.

Yakov pressed harder. "It hurts," he said, "but it helps."

I squeezed my eyes closed, teeth gritted, and focused on breathing while he bandaged the burn. Every movement set pins and needles buzzing through my limb, gradually easing into a throbbing pulse. When I opened my eyes again, he'd almost finished.

"What do you want from me?"

He secured the knot, eyes on his task, and a crease furrowed his brow. "You don't know what you're asking."

"I want the truth." Something I needed if he hoped to gain any trust at all.

Yakov sighed. "You won't understand. You'll fight me."

"I'm fighting you anyway. What difference does it make?"

He stared at the wipes in the sink. What was going through his mind? He'd promised me answers. Was he so reluctant to give them to me, or was this from years of secret-keeping? "I don't work for Venom," he said. "I was planted there as a child."

I should've known. First Joe, now him. It seemed Venom didn't have the perfect loyalty it thought it did.

"You work for the SIO?" I asked.

He huffed a laugh. "No."

"Then who?"

He snapped the lid shut on the kit, his amusement melting into a scowl.

I touched my bandage. The burn still hurt. "You said you'd tell me what you know."

"About my motivation. Not who I work for." He scooped

the soiled wipes into the bin. "I was planted. We'll go from there."

I bit back irritation. Typical. Someone finally agreed to answer me but still wouldn't open up. But some explanations were better than none. "Fine. Why were you planted?"

"To get close to you."

"But if you joined as a child, that can't have been the reason. Venom just recruited me." Seventy-seven days ago, by my count.

He nodded. "Obviously, we didn't know you were the host. It was only a matter of time until we did. But while Venom searched for you, I got trained, established in a mentorship position for when they found you. And then …" He waved a hand and let his words trail off.

And then he got close to me. I sat beside him. Cold from the bath chilled my legs. "How'd I get nanites in me?"

Yakov shrugged. "I don't know all the details. All I know is Venom had you once. You were a few days old, and the nanites were in you then. Someone stole you away, and Venom have hunted you ever since."

"Wait, what?" I stared at him. "Venom had me before? But what—how does …" I shifted where I sat. That's why Mum and Lia knew. Somehow they'd got me back from Venom and had spent their lives hiding me, sacrificing everything I might have wanted for me.

My frustration for them dissipated in a wave of guilt. That's why Lia had disappeared after Blake stole my blood. She'd been … what? Making plans to run? "Blake tested my blood."

"And found traces of nanites," Yakov said. "They leave a mark in your blood."

"And he took me." I stood on weak legs. "The car accident that damaged Mum's kidney, it wasn't an accident. Was it?" Of course, I knew the answer. But I had to hear him say it.

"No. It got her out the way."

Something twisted in my core. "They weren't trying to hurt her, were they? If they'd killed her, they wouldn't have cared."

"It worked better the way it did," Yakov said. "It convinced you to co-operate."

Co-operate? That's what he thought I'd done? I looked into his eyes – the eyes of the man who'd forced me to stay with Venom, who'd known what they'd tried to do – and saw pity. My jaw clenched.

"It was my job," Yakov said. "At first. I was supposed to get close to you. Keep you safe. But then we spent time together, and I got to know you and—"

"What?" I said. "Became *friends*? Give me a break."

His lips tightened.

The whole thing was a bad joke. I shook my head and stormed into the main room. To think I'd ever blushed at being near him. That I'd been attracted to him. A good therapy session wouldn't be amiss right now.

I blinked back the memory of Dakota. Not therapy. Bad example.

"It's different with you." Yakov leaned on the doorframe. "You make me see things from another point of view." The way he stood there with the crease between his eyes, the nervous clasp of his hands – was he *telling the truth*?

I reached up to scratch the back of my neck, and grazed something sharp. What was—I peeled it free, snagging hairs like they were caught in Sellotape. A square, clear piece of tape the size of a five-pence-piece stuck to my forefinger. Not tape. It was thicker, stickier, and wires crossed the middle.

"What is this?" I asked.

The Russian's jaw tensed, and he raised a hand. "You must understand, I had to be sure I could find you if we were separated."

Heat flushed my cheeks. "Is this a *tracker*?"

He widened his stance, dropped his hands to his side. Combat ready. "I had to be sure you were safe."

That's how he'd found me so quickly. He hadn't hunted me. He'd simply followed a tracking signal. "But when did you—"

Back in the bathroom when I'd patched his stitches. He'd

stepped up close, slid his hand around the back of my neck. I'd thought—

My insides deflated. I really was that stupid.

Yakov walked over. "If you only knew—"

"Save it." I backed away. "I've heard enough."

When he stopped, something like pain crossed his features. "I told you, you wouldn't understand."

"No, I understand." I dropped the tracker to the floor and crushed it beneath my foot. "You're all the same. Cold, heartless killers."

76

I lay on a sheetless mattress, staring at the hanging bulb in the ceiling. A head-aching grogginess tempted me back to sleep, but I sat up instead to a pang of pain in my arm. Other than the mattress, the room was bare. Remnants of scraped wallpaper clung to the walls like someone had started to decorate and given up half-way through.

I'd woken once in the night, surrounded by darkness. Now, sunlight streaked through a dirt-smeared window. Judging by the light's angle, I guessed it approached mid-morning. Yakov hadn't disturbed me. Aside from my breathing, I'd heard nothing.

I got up, my steps creaking the floorboards. Splinter fragments jutted out from the wood, unable to penetrate my boots, and sticky sweat covered my feet.

Yakov lay on the sofa in the main room, his booted feet propped up on the arm, eyes closed. A half-empty bottle of vodka stood on the table. If he was so determined to keep me here, drinking himself to sleep hardly seemed wise.

You won't understand. You'll fight me.

I frowned at the memory. He wasn't upset about yesterday?

I was supposed to get close to you. Keep you safe. But then we spent time together, and I got to know you and—

What? Became friends? Give me a break.

I shook my head and went to the kitchen to search the cupboards. One had plates and bowls. Another glasses. A third held tins: mac and cheese, soup, beans. I grabbed the pasta and all-but drank the contents before opening the fridge. A six-pack of eggs and pint of milk lay on the second shelf. I smelled the milk, checked the use by date. Fresh. Either Yakov had stayed here recently, or he'd shopped while I slept.

I drank from the carton until my gut ached and went back to the living room.

Yakov hadn't moved.

I knew the stereotypes. Russians could hold their liquor. But the truth was yet to be seen. Maybe he'd drunk himself out of consciousness. I could search for money. Leave right now.

But I'd never find the antivirus.

Yakov knew where it was – I was sure of that much. If one really existed. Either way, he was going to tell me.

"You could have warmed that up, you know."

I jolted.

Yakov lay with his eyes closed, exactly as he'd been before.

"Haven't you slept?" I asked.

"I have."

I glanced at the vodka. He'd drunk half the bottle. Wasn't he feeling sick?

"Is the first aid kit in the bathroom?" I asked.

"Kitchen cupboard. Second on the left."

I went to get it, glancing back at the Russian. His boot twitched, and I instinctively checked the back of my neck for more trackers. Who knew what he'd done when I slept? And to think he'd tried to pull a fast one.

It's different with you. You make me see things from another point of view.

Sure I did. But maybe I could work it to my advantage. After all, wasn't that the point of Venom? Everyone had their own agenda? I tapped the kit nervously and headed back to Yakov, pausing just short of the sofa. This wouldn't work. "Will you help me?"

His breaths came steadily, and for a moment, I thought he might've fallen asleep. "With what?"

"Finding the antivirus."

His brow twitched, and he huffed out a laugh. "No."

Figures. I knew it wouldn't work, but how could I convince him? Was I supposed to start lying and blackmailing now? I wasn't like him.

"What's your plan?" He'd opened his eyes now, and linked his fingers over his stomach.

"My plan?"

"To find your cure." He swung his feet onto rough carpet and took the kit from me. "You said you had a plan. What'll you do?"

"Less if you told me where to find it," I said. "It'd save my guessing."

He tapped the sofa and waited until I sat down before clicking open the kit. "I couldn't say where it is."

"Can't or won't?" I asked.

He met my gaze with a little smile. "Neither. I don't know where the antivirus is."

Well, that was new. But he didn't deny it was real. Stringing me along? Or did it really exist? "What do you know?"

He untied my bandage. "I know it's hidden. I know no one will tell us where. And I know looking for it will put us in danger."

I balled a fist. "I'm going after it, with or without your help." Doing nothing meant death, so danger or not, it was worth it. "Besides, you want me alive. You know what'll happen if I don't get the antivirus."

He steadied my arm to reclean the wound, leaving silence between us for several moments. Only once he picked a fresh wipe did he speak again. "My employer has interest in you."

"Me or the nanites?" The wipe touched a raw part, bringing a stab of pain. I jerked.

Yakov sighed and laid the wipe down. "Can't I convince you to stay here with me?"

Not a chance. "I will find it. Try to stop me if you like, but I'll never give up." I went to stand, but he grabbed my arm.

"Don't." He didn't look at me. He just stared into the distance, deep in thought. What was going through his mind? Next steps? Options to keep me here? Or debating whether killing me would be easier after all.

I swallowed.

"I'll help you." He let me go. "But I want something in return."

Shocker. "I won't give you the nanites."

He wrinkled his nose. "I don't want them."

"Then, what?"

He straightened and looked me straight in the eyes with the resolve of one who couldn't be dissuaded. The silver flecks in his irises brightened, reflected the dusty wall behind me. "I want your trust."

I blinked. That, I hadn't expected. What was the catch? He'd lead me trusting him back to Venom? To his real employer? He'd asked for something I could never give. Not to mention, agreeing would mean accepting his answers as they were – and not questioning more. It was madness.

But I wouldn't find the antivirus without him. Whatever he knew, I needed it. "Trust has to be earned."

He nodded. "I told you once before, I will not lie to you. If I have something that can help your search, I'll share it."

I could get on board with that. If only I could believe him.

"So, where did you plan to start?" he asked.

Good question. I'd considered it all night. Every option led to a dead end or an impossible complication. But that was without Yakov's help. I tugged a loose thread on the sofa. This partnership was dangerous. One wrong move, and I'd be done for. But honestly, I didn't see another way. "I thought we'd start with A.H. It was in the NightLock file. Duplicate records shipped to A.H."

"And you believe this A.H. will lead you to your cure?"

"Obviously."

Yakov smiled, flashing that dimple in his left cheek. "A.H. stands for Archive Headquarters. It's the most well-defended fort Venom owns. Only three people know its location, and fewer still can survive the journey without consent."

"Great." Here I thought the island was the worst danger. What would it be, a pit of scorpions? Moat of crocodiles? Spears in the walls? Poisonous darts? My nails dug in my palms. Venom was nuts, but if antivirus info was stored at the headquarters, I had to find it.

"You didn't say who you worked for."

Yakov closed the kit. "No."

"Are you going to?"

"No."

I frowned at the door. "You haven't told Venom I'm here."

"No."

"And you don't work for the SIO."

"I don't."

So far so good. Now, for the main question. "Are you after the nanites?"

He hesitated. "Yes. But not in the way you think."

I knew it. I'd worried about it for ages, and now that he'd confirmed it, my gut sank.

"My employer doesn't believe in Venom's ideals," Yakov said. "Nor does he agree the SIO or any organisation should have the nanites. It'd destroy the world."

"So, what? You're saving the world?" It was a desperate excuse. Like I'd believe the ruthless killer was the caring type.

Yakov's shoulders squared. "I was put in Venom. That meant doing immoral things. Committing horrors."

"Murdering innocent people."

He half-shrugged. "No one's innocent. Not really."

"Including your employer," I said.

"Especially my employer." He got up and dropped the kit on the kitchen side, harder than necessary, and he glared at the cupboards. "Sometimes you have to blur the lines to do what's right."

"And you believe right is …?"

He turned to me, jaw set, muscles rigid with some rage rising to the surface. "Destroying the nanites, once and for all."

It was a good answer. Certainly a believable one considering body language, tone, everything I'd learned from Dakota. But that was the point. Dakota trained Yakov, too. The Russian could lie as convincingly as the master himself.

"I've seen the world," I said. "Seen the truth about people. No one does good for the sake of it. They want money. Or power. Destroying the nanites won't give you that, so you can't expect me to lap up—"

"You still don't understand," Yakov said. "I'm not in this for any of that. The reason I got close to you, the reason I haven't told Venom we're here, the reason I've done everything I have – it's not for power." He balled his fists. "It's for revenge."

77

Silence thrummed. I'd been alone for five minutes, give or take, while Yakov 'made a call', and my sweat slicked my skin. This was dangerous. I was putting my faith in him to get us to Venom HQ, but revenge or not, there was no way to know how true his story was.

How long had it been now? Eight minutes? Ten? His voice reached me through the door. Muffled. Impossible to make out. Was he even speaking to his employer? Maybe it was Backer. Maybe Blake.

Nausea welled inside me. I shouldn't have agree to this. I should've left when I had the chance. Should've fought harder.

The room tilted. My head grew light.

I dashed to the window and threw it open, gasping the morning air. This whole deal was a mistake. A naïve, careless error. He wasn't going to help me. He never had before. Not really. My head rested on the glass. Cold washed over me. But the nausea grew stronger, rose inside me until my teeth tingled.

I raced to the bathroom and yanked up the toilet seat. My distorted reflection stared back at me. And a red drop hit the surface. It curled deeper into the water like smoke.

I frowned. Was that—

Another drop joined it. Then another.

I ran my fingers beneath my nose. They came away red.

Splitting pain stabbed through my head. It pulsed with my heartbeat, cut through my skull. I grabbed my head and shrieked, my voice lost under a pitched ringing in my ears. My bathroom dissolved into blackness.

Something shoved me backwards. Said something. Something lost in my cries. Hands clamped my cheeks.

Gradually, the pain stopped, and Yakov's face swam into light.

"Breathe," he said. "In through your nose. Out through your mouth."

I didn't want to. Everything smelled of blood. He pressed tissue into my palm, and I wiped my nose with a shaking hand. Blood streaked my top, filled the creases around my nails, and a strong urge to sleep weighed on my body. Was that my life now? The nanites were overloading, so I was going to bleed from the inside out? My limbs shivered uncontrollably. I had to get that cure. I had to get rid of the nanites before it was too late.

Yakov took my chin. Studied my face. "You're all right."

All right? Was he joking? "I'm dying, Yakov."

"You won't. Not if we get to the antivirus."

Oh, sure. Now, he was eager. Only minutes ago he'd asked me to stay here with him. What changed?

"My employer can get us to the headquarters," he said, "but not without price."

I leaned against the bath. At least I wasn't feeling sick anymore. I hated feeling sick. Hated thinking I was going to—I rested my head on the toilet seat, willing away another rise of nausea. "What's he want?"

"He doesn't know where the fort is. Not exactly. Which means we'll have to take the transport channels. It's safe enough, but we'll have to follow their rules. Any questions, any hesitation or show of doubt, we'll be shot where we stand." He touched my arm. "It'll mean being blindfolded, and it'll mean trusting me – and my employer. Fully."

There was the catch. I had to give him credit, the way he'd

played it. Trust me completely. Don't run. Don't show any doubt. Follow me blindly – literally – and I'll lead you to your death.

If I agreed, I might die.

If I refused, I'd die.

Really, I didn't see another option.

78

Yakov's hidden supply bag held packs of money in different currencies, boxes of ammunition, and explosives: grenades and the little disks he'd shown me at the training grounds. There was a box of darts, a taser, and two more guns. On impulse, I grabbed a handful of disks when Yakov wasn't looking and hid them in my boot where the drive was kept. There were flatpacks of food, water purification tablets, a first aid kit, and a holstered spare Beretta. I counted twelve passports.

Picking up the gun, I opened the magazine – fully loaded. Good – and attached the holster to my trousers. Too much had happened. This time, I'd protect myself.

Yakov's eyes burned into me. Would he take it away?

I huffed. Let him try.

He must've thought the same because he shrugged and scooped a stack of euros and two passports.

I flipped one open and jolted. "This is me." Almost me. My photo. Wrong name.

"Half are yours," Yakov said. "Half are mine. For emergencies."

Clearly, he'd planned ahead. Had he anticipated this happening? I studied the passports: two Russian, two Italian, two English, two Spanish, and two French – and opened the German one. "Emilia Schatzi." Could I pull off Emilia?

Yakov loaded his white Beretta. "I didn't choose the names."

I opened the Russian one. "Anya Novikov. It's pretty."

"My mother's name was Anya," he said, his voice so soft it could've been a whisper.

I gaped at him. "What did you say?"

He kept his eyes on his weapon, running a cloth over the barrel. "If you want to eat, do it now. We leave in the hour."

79

The airport bustled like London at rush hour. Yakov weaved towards the main desk, leaving me as lookout. Not that I'd notice anything in the crowd. If Venom were here, they'd blend in easily. A janitor emptied a bin. Security patrolled the area. A group of children passed, all holding hands. All normal civilians by any judgement.

But that meant nothing. One could pull a gun at any time. One might slip behind me, grab me by the throat, stick a needle in my neck.

I put my back to the wall and scanned the people. What were we doing putting ourselves in public? In Venom's hands. Because that's what the transport channels were: Venom's way to get us to the Archive Headquarters without us knowing its location. Not even those transporting us knew where it was. The whole system was ingenious. And insanely dangerous.

A woman stood across the throng, her eyes—more muddy than brown—fixed on me. Her sleeves had been rolled carelessly over her elbows, revealing slightly tanned skin, and a tree pendant hung over her chest.

Lia.

I rushed to her, shoving people aside much to their frustration. She caught me in a tight hug and pulled me into a wide, draughty corridor, empty of people.

"Lia, what're you doing here?"

She smiled, though it didn't reach her eyes. Her stance stayed wide, shoulders relaxed. Combat-ready.

Silly. All that time with Venom really had made me paranoid.

"I came to find you," she said.

"You shouldn't—" I glanced back at the closing door. "It's dangerous here." Yakov would notice me missing. If he'd looked back, he'd have seen me running. He'd have known I was after something. "You should go. The man I'm with, he's not safe."

"I know. So, come with me. We'll escape." She tried to pull me on, but I jerked away.

"How are you here? You're supposed to be hidden." Protected by the SIO. Had Spencer let her go because I ran from her goons? Surely, she wasn't so heartless. My fists balled. "She sent you to talk me in, didn't she?"

"No, Sally." Lia took my hand. "I came on my own."

"Rubbish, she wouldn't put you in danger." Unless there were agents farther down the passage. "Who else is with you?"

"There's no one with her." Yakov's hard voice cut through the corridor.

He stood by the door, glaring at Lia. He lifted his Beretta, so I leaped between them, limbs tingling in shock. "Yakov. This is—"

"I know who she is. She's SIO."

Every muscle inside me tensed.

Lia huffed. "That's ridiculous."

Was it though? Lia knew about the nanites. She'd worked with Mum to hide me, disappeared after Blake stole my blood to do who knew what?

Venom had me as a baby. I'd been rescued. Taken back to Mum. If the SIO had any part in that, they wouldn't have left us unprotected. They'd have assigned agents to us.

Could Lia have been that agent?

Yakov sidestepped.

I held out a calming hand. "Yakov, this is Lia. My sister." And agent or not, I wouldn't let him shoot her.

"I know one when I see one." His eyes hardened. The muscles in his arm tensed, set in his resolve.

"Please." I stepped closer to him, heart thudding. "Lia's not an agent." She couldn't be. I knew as well as anyone things weren't as they seemed. Lia was family. Exactly that. My sister. A civilian. She was—

Calm. Perfectly calm considering Yakov pointed his gun at her. And it wouldn't be the first time she'd lied to me. Wouldn't be the first time she'd hinted at some secret with her whispered phone calls, her disappearance at the office, her refusal to acknowledge anything I wanted if it differed from her own will. My mouth turned dry. "Lia?"

For a moment she glared at Yakov. Then she sighed, and her voice turned icy. "You had to bring along the Russian." She pointed a gun at me.

Yakov pushed me to the floor, giving Lia time to close the gap. She jabbed Yakov's nose, struck his arm, and his Beretta clattered to the concrete. He grabbed her, twisted, and knocked her over.

She rolled to her feet and rushed him. Punched. Kicked.

He blocked all her attacks with ease, driving her backwards. His elbow struck her chin. She jerked back, and he slipped around behind her, dropping her to her knees. A knife glinted.

"No, don't!" Panic echoed in my scream.

He paused with the blade at her throat. Blood trickled from a cut on her neck. "She's one of them," he said, his voice so low I could barely make it out.

"And you're Venom." Every word shook. "An assassin. That's no better."

"You know why I've done what I have."

"I know." I pressed my hands against the concrete, unsure my legs would hold me if I stood. "But Yakov, she's my sister."

"She's a plant." His knuckles turned white. "She was put with you to hide you, not be your family."

Lia gritted her teeth.

"Is that true?" I asked.

Her nostrils flared, and she tightened her grip on Yakov's wrist.

He twisted the blade a little, and a bead of blood slid down her neck. "Answer her."

"I had a job to do," Lia said. "That doesn't mean I don't care."

Funny how the truth can hurt, even when you know it already. I stood up, pinching my thumb behind my back. I'd had enough of people's games. Enough of wasting time. "Don't kill her. Please."

A vein stuck out on Yakov's head. He looked from me to Lia and back again, rolled his eyes, and slammed the hilt against her temple.

80

Yakov tucked the knife away, retrieved his gun, and marched me back into the crowds, leaving Lia unconscious on the concrete.

I went with him without resistance, numbness in my chest. Lia. My sister. No, not my sister. An agent. In the space of a few months, everything I believed had been torn to shreds. How was I supposed to tell truth from lie? Even Yakov might be trapping me.

"How'd you know Lia is SIO?" I asked.

Yakov tugged his jacket over his belt. "We made it our business to know. Surprises lead to mistakes."

"You never told me."

He bumped into an elderly couple, muttered an apology, and carried on. Weird. He was usually so vigilant. Now he was bumping into people? The conflict with Lia must've shaken him. Had she hurt him? I saw no blood on his shirt.

When the metal detectors appeared, he pressed something small into my palm. I tried to look at it, but he tightened my fist and urged me into the line of passengers before leaning in close. "Walk through. Don't stop. Don't look at your hand. I'll catch up." He sidestepped into the parallel queue.

Cold sweat prickled my neck. We couldn't go yet. We still had guns. We'd be arrested the moment we stepped through the detectors. But the Russian didn't look worried. He walked forward, hand fisted at his side, smiled at the guard and stepped on through.

Nothing happened. No lights went off. No alarms sounded.

Whatever he'd put in my palm dug in like the edge of a penny. I passed through the detector.

Still nothing.

The guard nodded and turned his back on me, leaving me to move deeper into the airport. Cafés filled the space with the scent of coffee and cooking bacon. A speaker beeped, and an announcement called passengers to a gate. Getting in had been too easy. Only being intercepted by Lia was too easy. The nanites were too important to Spencer. If she knew where I was, no way would she let Lia come alone.

So, where were the others?

Yakov took my arm and veered towards a stockroom, picking the lock in seconds. Blue cleaning roll and spray bottles filled a shelf. Collapsed wet floor signs leaned against the wall by upturned mops with hair like braids. Yakov closed the door and took his device from my palm.

"What is it?" I asked.

"A gentle EMT." He slipped it in his pocket. "Disrupts the alarms." He opened the door. "Wait here."

"Where're you going?"

"To get clothes. They've seen us now. We need to move fast. Blend in."

I understood that. "There'll be others. As soon as they find Lia—"

"They don't know where we're going. We have the advantage." He left.

White light filtered in through the closing door until I stood with only mops for company. Cold pinched my nose and fingers, and I blew in my hands to warm them. There'd be cameras here. Agents watching our moves. How were we supposed to board a plane unseen? Even with a change of clothes, they'd spot us eventually. They probably saw us come into the stockroom.

A low squeal rang in my ears, growing louder, shriller. A sudden sting hit my head and stabbed through my neck. I sank to my knees, clutched my hair. Someone screamed. Me? I couldn't tell.

"Sally." Yakov's hands clamped over mine until the pain faded, and something warm ran over my lip.

Yakov gave me a strip of cleaning roll.

I wiped away the blood, too late to stop it dripping on my jumper. Weakness thrummed through me, and when I moved, the toppled mops clattered. A pile of clothes lay beside Yakov. What'd he done, robbed the nearest stand? "How'd you get those so quickly?"

Yakov frowned. "I've been gone ten minutes."

"But that's not—" I slumped against the wall. "I blacked out again." Which meant I'd absorbed something. But there was no computer in here. What could I possibly have—my jaw clenched. "The airport. I absorbed the airport." Which couldn't have been good. If overloaded nanites downloaded more … I'd die quicker. I rubbed my stinging throat.

"You feel all right?" Yakov asked.

"Peachy."

He smiled at that and stood up, stripping out of his shirt in one smooth movement. Muscles protruded over his chest, rippling over his stomach to a rounded belly button. His trousers lay just below his hip bones – lower than his gunshot wound – and a thin, faded scar curved beneath his waistline.

Something flipped in my core, like that feeling you get when you step off a curb. I picked up my bundle, pausing to check the size of the top. My size. I wasn't sure how to feel about that.

"You all right?" Yakov stepped in, resting his hand on my arm. His skin burned – a stark contrast to the cold stockroom.

I clutched my top to my chest. "Turn around."

His lips twitched, but he obeyed, snapping the tag off his polo. His shoulder blades rolled, blending into the curvature of his back.

I tore my eyes from him, and undressed.

Once we'd changed and I'd adjusted my holster, Yakov took the door handle.

"Wait." I grabbed his hand. Outside, slightly to the left … I cocked my head, accessing knowledge I shouldn't have. "There are cameras." I could see them—or sense them—like they were a part of me. Every detail, every position lay there in my mind. I pushed Yakov's sleeve up to show his watch. "They're on a loop," I said. "Just like on the island." We needed to hide. Suddenly, I knew how we could.

The second hand passed forty-five. Fifty. Fifty-four.

"Go." I pulled Yakov from the stockroom, heading straight. A couple giggled when we emerged from the stockroom and whispered together. My face burned, but I pooled my concentration, letting Yakov watch for agents. This was no time to be embarrassed. I had my job. He had his.

Another camera on the right.

We rounded a post, the seconds counting in my head. I glanced at Yakov watch to be sure and pulled him to the right.

"Where're we going?" I asked.

"Gate Seven," he said.

"That means four cameras and two guards on patrol." Easy. In theory.

I led him straight, paused to let a janitor pass, then hurried around a square-shaped pillar and shoved Yakov against it. The camera would twist. It'd catch my back. I pressed closer to the Russian, smelling his sweat, the woody scent of his aftershave.

A guard stood by the window. Behind him, a plane rolled in on the tarmac. A second guard watched the plane from farther down the room. A third strolled past the glass, watching the crowd.

The third.

"Yakov—"

"I see him." Yakov's free hand slid to my back, drawing me nearer and out of view of the agent. I'd seen him at the phone booth. He'd been one of the thugs in the van.

I closed my eyes. Counting.

"Go." I tugged Yakov on, following the signs to Gate Seven. A speaker rang overhead, announcing a final warning for passengers boarding our flight.

A woman slept sprawled across three chairs. Two teenagers sat cross-legged on the carpet, playing a card game. An elderly lady skimmed a newspaper.

I pulled Yakov between them and ducked into a shop – right into the agent. He reached for his gun.

Yakov disarmed him and snapped his neck.

I grabbed a rack, squeezing until my knuckles turned white. No time for grief. No time for shock. We had to go.

I closed my eyes to count, to study the loops. One camera changed. Then another. I bit my lip. There was no blind spot to squeeze through. We'd have to dash and hope no one noticed.

Yakov slid his hand in mine.

"Stop killing people," I whispered.

He leaned in. "If it's us or them, I choose us."

Heat welled. I shook my head – no time for anger – and ran.

Yakov stayed on my tail, weaving around a gathering of golfers and past the gates. When we reached gate seven, I slid into a gap between the wall and a vending machine, and the prickle of watching cameras dissipated. If anyone had seen us, they'd be here soon. If not, at least we were hidden again.

Yakov pressed up beside me, wafting the sharp scent of new clothes. "We need to board."

"Not yet. They'll see us." Tucked up here by the wall, we were safe. But one step into the corridor would put us in full view. When the camera looped off, we'd be okay.

"How long?" Yakov asked.

I lifted his sleeve again, my fingers grazing his skin. Goosebumps rose on his arm. The minute hand reached the six. "Fifteen seconds," I whispered.

The woman at the door spoke into a radio, typed something

on the computer.

"Ten."

She reached for her ID and approached the door.

"Five."

She grasped the handle, pausing to speak to someone inside.

"Go."

Yakov strode towards her. She raised her eyebrows when he handed her two tickets and passports. "Cutting it close, Sir." She scanned the tickets and handed them back. "Have a good flight."

81

The clouds outside the window wisped like thickened smoke. Occasionally, I caught a glimpse of land – fields mostly. Yakov's reflection focused on me, his gaze burning into the back of my head.

"Why didn't you do it?" I turned to face him, keeping my voice low. "Why didn't you kill Lia?"

He leaned back in his seat. "Because you asked me not to."

"Asking never worked before."

"This was different."

"How?"

A stewardess passed us in the aisle. Only once she passed, did he lean closer. "You count her as family."

"What about the banker?" I whispered. "The worker in Rio? What about the general's guards and that agent back there? They'd have had families."

"Their families weren't there when I killed them," Yakov said.

"So, if I hadn't been with Lia—"

"You know the answer."

Something shrivelled inside me. She'd be dead now if he'd found her before me, and I wouldn't even know.

"Why didn't you pull your gun on me?" he asked. "I had my knife at her throat."

I could've done. It would've been easy to shoot him. And pointless. "You'd have killed her before I armed it."

He nodded in confirmation.

"Speaking of which," I said, "I didn't see you pack a knife. You brought more weapons?"

"My Beretta, the knife and EMTs, and this." He tapped his watch.

"Seriously?"

He glanced at the couple sitting across the aisle, drew his hand to his chest and balled his fist. A silver blade punched out the side of the watch, extending about an inch past his knuckles. He flexed his fingers, and the blade retracted.

I shifted on the seat. One punch, and that would be it. Who came up with this stuff? "How'd you get your scar?" I asked. "On your hip. I saw it in the stockroom."

"Oh, that." He shrugged. "Mishap with the watch."

The seatbelt sign tinged on, marking the beginning of our descent, and the plane dipped. "So, what now?" I asked.

"We get picked up."

"By who?"

He shrugged. "We'll know him when we see him." He scratched his chin. "Or her. After that, we obey orders. And we don't speak. At all." He fixed me with a warning scowl. "You understand me right? One wrong move, and we'll be shot."

I dug my nails into my chair. This was madness. I was putting every bit of trust I had on Yakov. On a man who'd murdered again not hours ago.

The first of the Liechtenstein mountains shifted into view like snow-peaked razors. Villages and towns lay spread out between fields and hills, rivers and lakes. The plane tilted, and the airport became visible – a mix of metal and sun-caught glass and runways set out like a giant blueprint. Black specks lined one side of the airport. The sight set my teeth on edge. "Something's wrong."

Yakov leaned over me, and the plane dipped again, plunging my stomach. The closer we flew, the clearer the scene became.

The specks were people: guards or police, all dressed in black. Armour, perhaps.

The wheels hit the runway, bouncing twice before slowing and finally rolling to a stop.

The guards closed in around the aircraft, wearing visored helmets and carrying rifles.

"Yakov—"

"I see them."

I turned to him. "They're here for us."

He nodded once and unclipped his belt.

The speaker system beeped. "Ladies and gentlemen, welcome to Switzerland. I trust you had a pleasant flight. The weather is twelve degrees with a high chance of rain this evening, so have those umbrellas ready."

The passengers leaned to the windows, pointing at the guards.

The pilot spoke again, "Please, don't be alarmed at the sight outside. It's a precaution – a routine check."

"What kind of routine check uses guns?" one woman said.

"Your hosts will open the doors in just a moment," the pilot said. "Please remain calm, and follow their instructions. I assure you there is nothing to worry about. You'll be on your way in no time at all. Welcome to Switzerland, and have a great night."

82

Yakov straightened his jacket at the top of the stairs overlooking the runway and the armed guards, and slipped into Russian. "Stay calm. Don't fight them. They're trained to kill us if we do." He padded down the steps and surrendered himself to a masked woman with a golden pin on her lapel: a snake in the shape of a V. She had to be our contact. Who else would wear such an obvious symbol?

But I froze in the door of the aircraft. What was I doing? If I gave myself to them, I'd be handing the nanites right back to Venom. Sure, Yakov had lied for me. Helped me. Why? As an elaborate plan in case I happened to rebel? Was this how he'd deliver me back to Blake? Or because he really did want revenge?

How was I to make a decision when he'd refused to tell me why he wanted revenge? My past, he'd said, and that was that.

But the way I saw it, I had little choice. Yakov was my only chance of finding the antivirus. I needed to get to A.H., and trusting myself to Yakov was the only way.

I took a shaky breath – this might be my biggest mistake yet – and descended the steps. The woman steered me to a vehicle with tinted glass, round the back of it where the passengers couldn't see us, and took my Beretta.

Every muscle tensed.

A second woman took Yakov gun, his knife, the EMTs, and flung them onto the front seat. She missed his watch, though. She opened the back door. "Get in."

We did. Dry heat blasted through the car, broken by the women climbing in the front. One of them threw something at us. Hessian sacks.

I stared at them. They wanted us blind. Which meant I wouldn't see the danger. I wouldn't see if I needed to fight back.

My mouth grew dry. My body trembled. I shouldn't do this. I couldn't.

I squeezed my eyes closed and pulled the bag over my head.

83

Darkness. That's all there was. Any light that'd filtered through the holes of the burlap sack had long since dissipated in the hours of travelling. I'd been offered no water. No food. My lips stuck together, moisture only by the sweat and breath condensation that dripped to my chin, and my tailbone ached.

Helicopter blades beat and thrummed through my seat. Where were they taking us? Was Yakov still hooded? His arm pressed against mine. At least, I thought it was his. It smelled like him: warm and woody with a sharp hint of new clothes.

I shifted a little.

So, did he. A gesture of comfort? Or a warning to stay quiet?

Likely the latter. Either way, this had to end soon.

84

Someone hauled me into bitter cold and a wind that battered and stung. It whipped my breath away, buckled my knees, and I sank into frozen softness. Icy wetness spread through my trousers. The bag whipped off my head.

Light blinded me. My breath strangled in my throat in a vicious burst of wind, and I shielded myself with whatever heavy thing they dropped on me. A blanket. Heavy and thick and rough like the burlap that'd covered my head for who knew how long?

Snow surrounded me. It fell in misty flurries, almost covering my trousers though it'd only been seconds since I'd fallen. I scrambled with the blanket, pushed it over my head, and turned around. My teeth chattered so hard they hurt.

My Beretta lay on the ground by the grenade, knife and EMTs, fast being buried in the storm.

Blades chopped, and through the whiteness, a shadow lifted, flicking snow and ice in every direction before taking off across a wasteland that stretched as far as the horizon.

Yakov stood blinking a few meters from me, shrugged into his own blanket and trudged to retrieve his weapons. His white Beretta melted out of the snow when he picked it up.

I hugged my arms to my chest and shouted over the gale. "Where are we?"

Yakov squinted and slipped into Russian. "No idea."

Really? Had he been head-sacked the whole time? Or was this part of his game? There was nothing here. No fort, no headquarters, no shelter of any kind. Where were we supposed to go? Or were we not supposed to do anything? Maybe they'd brought us here to die. Revenge for fleeing back in Lichtenstein.

Shivers burned through me, intensified when Yakov popped my Beretta in my holster, letting a burst of cold in my blanket. "So, what now?" I asked.

A rumble cut through the wind, and a jeep crested the ice. A shadow sat behind the wheel, impossible to make out through the tinted windows. The jeep stopped beside us, and the driver cracked open his window. "What're you standing 'round for?" he shouted, his Russian sharp. "Get in before you freeze to death."

I didn't need telling twice – I climbed in the back ahead of Yakov and all-but melted into the warm air. My fingers burned. Everything burned, but that didn't matter. The frost melted around me, leaving my clothes wet and my toes numb. A far side better than they were out there.

The driver aimed a pistol at my head and looked between us, thick eyebrows dipping low. An old scar split his right one in two, while a second scar dented his lip and chin. "What'll it be?"

I stiffened. Was I meant to understand that?

"Six, Three, Two, Alpha, Hotel, Delta," Yakov said.

The driver pointed the barrel at Yakov, studied him for a moment, then tucked the pistol away. "Nice to meet you. Name's Hedge. Gotta say it's been too long since I saw people. 'Cept the others, 'course." He turned back to the wheel, and the car slid on. "You look frozen. Mind you, I remember my own drop off. Nasty business. Morozov was late. I nearly died. Never stopped making him pay for it, either." He chuckled.

We rolled onto a frozen road that creaked beneath the tyres. Hedge slowed right down, and my gut did a flip. This wasn't a road. A lake? If the ice broke, we'd go right through. We'd freeze to death. Hedge caught my eye in the rear-view mirror. "Needn't worry. Ain't nothing out here gonna break. Got hundreds o' years ice on it, see? Bit noisy is all."

Yeah. Because that was comforting.

Some time later, we stopped by a narrow staircase in a sheer cliff. "Here we are." Hedge turned to look at us. "Archive Headquarters. Might as well know you can speak now, but I get your hesitation." He waited a moment. "I was the same when I got here. So used to not trusting. But trust me, we still don't trust you – as ironic as that is." He got out, letting in a blast of snow.

I gritted my teeth and climbed out after Yakov, shrugging into my blanket. Not that it helped much. Would it have killed them to give us a coat? A hat? Snow flurried off the steps, billowed against my face and stung my cheeks. How could anyone live out here? How could anyone stand the cold?

My foot slipped.

Yakov clasped my waist, steadying me, but the wind snatched his blanket and tore it away. The whiteness reflected in his skin. His lips turned purple. The gale flattened his hair to his head.

I grabbed his wrist and opened my blanket. "Get in with me."

He shook his head and pushed me on.

What was he doing? He must know he couldn't survive long out here, especially without the blanket. And who knew how much longer we'd be?

Hedge reached a larger step with an icy panel set into the cliff. He put his hand on it, and a door opened with a rush of heat – right on to the aim of a rifle.

85

The room in the cliff had been carved from the rock, and hard, industrial lights were set in the ceiling between vents that whirred welcoming heat through the enclosure. If it wasn't for the rifle pointing at my head, I'd have all-but fallen through the door.

Hedge stepped inside, stomping snow from his boots. "It's fine, Morozov. They check out."

Morozov flinched at the mention of his name and stepped aside, but he kept his rifle up.

"This way." Hedge gestured and headed deeper into the cliff, leaving the door to slide shut. He hadn't been kidding. They really didn't trust us. And I could see why. Venom had that effect on people. It certainly had on me. What did they think we were doing here? They couldn't have known the real reason. Come to think of it, how'd Yakov manage to get us here? He'd have had to explain the situation to his employer. Wouldn't he? But coming here was a huge step. A dangerous step. Would his employer have agreed to this?

Mental alarms rose the hairs on my arms. This whole situation suddenly felt very wrong.

Hedge took us onto a grated walkway overlooking a maze of shelves in a cavern larger than three football fields. Shelves taller than ten men filled every inch of the space, smothered in ancient books and time-dusted artifacts. Darkness crept though narrow walkways, fading the distance into nothingness, and the ceiling hung so high above that it blended with the shadows, like the night itself had slipped indoors and all the stars had gone out.

It was here: the location of the antivirus. One of these books or scrolls or files out of the hundreds of thousands – even millions – that lay here. It'd take a lifetime to search them all. Ten lifetimes. One hundred lifetimes.

Hedge leaned on the railing. "Impressive, isn't it?"

Morozov shifted. "I'll be glad to get rid of it."

Hedge nodded. "True. You two couldn't have come at a better time. If I'd had to stay here another month, I might've pitched myself down the stairs."

I blinked. That's what had been arranged? We were the replacements? It wasn't a bad deal. I could search the place unhindered, hidden away where no one could find us. I cast Yakov a sideways glance. Had he really come through on this? Me and him, searching for the antivirus together. Not enemies. Allies.

A smile threatened to rise. "So, you have no idea where we are?"

Hedge chuckled. "She speaks. And no, ain't a clue. Best kept secret on the planet, this place."

No surprise there.

"How big is it?" I asked. "The maze."

"Never been in. Ice ain't the only protection 'round here. We guard. We play cards. That's about the gist of it. Here you go." He stopped outside a room marked 'B'.

It was simply furnished with a sofa, table and bed. Along one side lay a counter, sink and cupboards and a side door. Bathroom, most likely.

Hedge pointed. "There's food and drink in the cupboards. Coffee if you want it. Might be here a while. Need confirmation about the switch. I'll come get you when it comes." He turned to leave. "Oh, so you know, Morozov'll be out here. Like I said, trust is a no-go, so don't come out 'less someone's dying, or he'll shoot you." He left.

"Friendly sort," I muttered.

Yakov grabbed a glass and filled it with water.

"So, how're we doing this?" I asked, careful to keep my voice low. There was no telling whether Hedge and Morozov were listening. "Are we actually the new guards?"

Yakov shook his head.

"Right." My shoulders sagged. "Course not. So, we better get looking before they figure that out."

Yakov sat on the sofa, running his thumb around the rim of his glass. The colour had returned to his lips now, and hints of pink coloured his cheeks. "Sit down. Relax for a bit."

"You're kidding."

"It's been a long day. You have time to sleep." He nodded at the bed.

And just like that, that tingling crept up my neck. "We can't sit around." We'd come to find the antivirus, not waste time.

Yakov's thumb paused, mid-circle, and something slipped into his features. Wariness? Determination? Something that shouldn't have been there. Not in the face of an ally.

"You never planned to help me, did you?" I tightened my grip on my blanket. How naïve could I be? To think I'd thought him an ally only moments before.

He leaned forwards. "I just think we should wait a while."

"Why?"

"Trust me."

There it was again. Trust me. Take my word for everything even though I won't give you answers. Even though you might die if you do. I staggered back a step. He was distracting me. Keeping me busy until—I didn't know what. If he'd really come to help me, he wouldn't be sitting around.

I forced a smile. "If you think that's best." Yeah, right. I needed space. A breather. A chance to think. I went into the bathroom – just a toilet and sink – and locked the door. I didn't need Yakov. I could do this on my own. There were two

326

guards and the Russian. Easy.

I buried my head in my hands. Not so easy. I needed into that maze. Yakov wouldn't let me try, and he'd proved more than once he outranked me in a fight. Morozov would shoot me on sight. And Hedge? He seemed friendly enough, but I knew better than to lean on that.

There was a vent above me, too small for any man, but when I stood on the toilet, I could make out the passage outside. Morozov shifted where he leaned on the wall. If I could distract him away from the door, I'd only have to slip by Yakov.

I climbed down and tapped the sink, frowning at the vent. Too small for me. But not too small for …

I opened the pocket where I'd hidden the drive and explosive disks. My feet were white where snow had soaked through. Droplets covered the shiny, silver sides of the disks. Would they still work after being wet?

I picked one up and used my nail to flick a switch on the side. The disk flashed green. This could work. I counted nine disks, three small, six large: like oversized ten-pence-pieces. Since they worked in pairs at minimum, I'd need two to ignite them. Two small ones should do.

I slid a disk into the vent and flicked the switch on a second. There was the green flash. It was now or never. With the others sealed away again, I pressed the middle of the disk twice. It flashed red once, twice, three times.

I popped it on the floor by the wall and hurried back to Yakov. He'd see my anxiety. He'd see the guilt all over my face, in my tight lips, my burning cheeks. He'd know I'd done something.

The wall erupted, showering rubble, rock and dust through the room. The force of it knocked me to the floor, jerking my head back. The back of my neck crunched with the movement. It ached my shoulder. Dust coated my tongue.

I stumbled to stand, feeling blindly for the door. My fingers reached the handle, and I fell through it into the passage.

86

A deep, smoking indentation of rock gaped in the passage where the bathroom had all but disappeared. Water spurted from broken pipes and rained down on flames and rubble.

Morozov slumped against the wall, head lolling, rifle beside him on the floor. I kicked it away and pressed trembling fingers to his throat. His pulse thrummed steadily.

Coughing erupted behind me, kicking my heart into a sprint. I fled through the settling dust before Yakov could stop me. That antivirus would be mine, with or without his help.

It wasn't hard to find the walkway over the maze. The shelves stretched as far as the limited light allowed, curling and flourishing in a masterful piece of art. Deadly art. If I got lost in there, I'd never escape. But escape could wait. I bounded down the steps two at a time.

A bullet pinged off the railing.

I gasped and stumbled, rolling down the last few steps.

Hedge shot again. "This is your only warning. Get up here."

"I can't." I needed that information. An opening stood not far from me. Five meters or so. Hedge said he'd never been in the maze. That there were other things protecting it. Would he come after me? Were those protections worth risking?

Between that or my life? Oh, yeah, they were worth it.

"I've got the shot on you," Hedge said. "Up now."

I could make it.

He stepped towards the stairs.

I ran. Bullets hit shelves inches from my head. The sound hurt my ears, made them ring, but the shadows of the maze swallowed me up, and Hedge's shouts drifted into the distance.

I should've stopped. Should've focused on my path. Determined which way was back. Not that I could go back. I was stuck out here. Destined to die by maze or monster. But if Hedge pursued, his footfalls were silent.

Gradually, I slowed to a walk, breaths heaving in the burst of exertion. I wasn't as fit as I should've been. Not anymore. Thanks to the nanites, no doubt.

Venom's filing system filled every inch of the shelves with books, cabinets and scrolls. Every corner brought something new, tainting the air with the scent of dust, old parchment, and the crisp air of winter. Wind whooshed through the aisles. No, not wind. Water? Naked bulbs swung from chains and cast orange pools over the rock. Chills seeped to my bones, and my soles hurt with every step.

Where should I go? There must've been miles of shelves in here. And maze or not, Yakov wouldn't be far behind. Or would he? He hadn't tracked me this time.

Something caught my eye near the top of a shelf, something bronze and rusted. A letter. C.

I smiled. This wasn't a maze. It was a library. And libraries were alphabetized. I should've known. The place needed a pattern or anyone would get lost.

This pattern started with C.

I retraced my steps, turned two corners, and spotted another C. A little farther on, the path opened in a crossroads. Four letters were nailed on the shelves. C went ahead. B went right. F went left. Weird. No D or E. No doubt they'd be around here somewhere.

What would the antivirus be under? A for antivirus? N for NightLock? Maybe both. Either way, I'd never seen anywhere so complicated. Maybe that's what Hedge meant when he mentioned protections.

I turned left, following F.

G.

I.

When I reached O, I paused. No N. That couldn't be right. I rubbed the chill from my arms. My breath misted. It was getting cold. Too cold. Besides, I'd missed several letters. It might be wise to double back. I retraced my steps until I found L. Three paths split off. L. M. Another M. I chose the latter.

The shadows were darker here. Cabinets lined the aisle on either side – hundreds of them casting elongated patches on the floor. A bulb's light pooled. Dust curled in the beam. And was that—I stepped towards the darkest patch of shadow. Yes, a junction. And there by the highest shelf hung another letter. N.

I squeezed through the gap into an aisle. There were no lights here. Nothing to brighten the way other than the gloomy remnants from the next aisles over. I ran my hand along the grained wood. There were no shelves. No cabinets. Had I taken a wrong turn? Slipped into the space between aisles by accident?

The walkway turned onto a dead end. A single bulb hung low over a single, tiny set of drawers. Jackpot! I tugged one open. Files filled it, each marked with *NightLock* and a date. I flipped one open, dated years before Blake recruited me.

Nanite Creation, Attempt 34.

Subjects Alpha through Delta sustained nose bleeds, jaundice, and internal haemorrhage. Cause of death: aneurism.

Search for true host ongoing.

If I was the true host, what on earth had they been trying to do? Recreate the nanites in my absence? I replaced the file with another.

Sally Rivers. 09:32. Blood taken.

Results: positive.

Plans in place to recruit subject.

I flipped through the pages, through the photographs of

Mum's car, crumpled, destroyed, surrounded by glass. And there I was, third photo in, restrained in the arms of a paramedic.

Burton with host.

Blake on route to intercept.

Burton. The paramedic who'd pulled me from the wreckage. I flipped through the rest, skimming the words through hot tears, and snatched one dated before my birth. It held a single photo: a machine trailing tubes and needles, the kind used for IVs. One word was scrawled beneath the photo: Antivirus.

"Huh." What'd I expected? An injection. Certainly, not a machine. I flipped the photo over.

Location: Egypt.

Classification: Redundant.

Figures Venom would class it that way. A great life-saving machine they never intend to use because the sucker host was collateral. As long as they got their downloads, that's all that mattered, right?

What did I have? A picture dated back two decades. Who knew where the antivirus was now? Assuming Venom hadn't moved it, Egypt wasn't much of a starting point. The country was huge. All I'd done by coming here was expose myself to Hedge. Either one of them – Hedge or Morozov – might have reported us to Venom by now. And that was assuming Yakov wasn't working for them after all.

I turned around, and my muscles locked.

A snowy wolf stood by the turning, its crystal-coloured eyes fixed on me. It bared its teeth, released a guttural growl, and prepared to lunge.

87

My mind leapt into overdrive. A wolf. *That* was their added protection? I scrambled to think. What did I know? Wolves travel in packs.

I cast a glance at the tops of the shelves. Would a pack crest over them?

The creature lifted its tail. A sign of aggression.

What could I do? If I ran, it would attack.

They could smell fear. A drop of sweat curved past my eye.

The wolf widened its stance.

They like an easy catch. They attack the weak.

I *couldn't* be weak.

I raised my arms and shouted at the top of my voice. The sound echoed round the cavern, resounded over the shelves.

The wolf's ears twitched. It lifted its head.

"Bah! Go on! Get away!" I waved my hands at it. My pulse whooshed in my ears. It ached my head. Hedge would find me. Yakov would find me. If the wolf didn't kill me first.

It snarled, hackles raised. But it didn't attack.

What was I missing? Make lots of noise. Keep eye contact. Back away.

Only there was nowhere to back away to.

The wolf crouched. It bluff-darted forwards.

I grabbed a drawer and threw it. Files scattered. Photos and paper showered everywhere. "Get out of it!"

The wolf barked a growl. Saliva stretched between its teeth.

It didn't make sense. I'd seen a documentary on wolves. They were afraid of humans. They avoided them. Why would this one attack? It wasn't mating season, so it wasn't protecting pups.

But they were also among the most territorial species in the world. If this one was showing aggression, I must've been trespassing.

It crouched low. Its shoulders tensed.

I staggered against the drawer. Shock shot through me in a fierce tingle.

The wolf streaked forwards. It roared.

I scrambled for my gun and fired two bullets at the roof.

The wolf yelped. It skidded. Its feet pattered madly, and it fled from the aisle.

I sank against the drawers, breathing deeply. *What* was wrong with Venom? First deadly lanceheads, now wolves. How could anyone thrive off death? It was a wonder they had any agents left when they lived like this. A wonder they had any files in the maze at all.

A trickle of dust coated my shoulder. I brushed it off, looking up at the source. The cavern hissed dust from my bullet holes.

My bullet holes. My gunshots. This may have been a maze, but I'd just shown anyone hunting me exactly where I was.

The shadows deepened on my run out the aisle. Where could I go? I'd never make it out the front door. But maybe I didn't need it. Assuming Venom hadn't trapped the wolf in here, it must've got in somehow.

The crisp scent still hung on the air, and in the distance, the sound of rushing water echoed over the shelves. There was another way out. There had to be. But how was I supposed to find it?

"Sally." Yakov stood by the opening of a junction, his form lit up by a bulb hanging behind him. Dirt coated his clothes, and a fraying rip hung from the arm of his top.

"Are you hurt?" I asked.

He shook his head. The usual brightness in his eyes had gone, replaced by an emotionless coldness – the same coldness he carried on assignment. "You should have waited."

"For what?" I asked. "My time's running out, Yakov. I don't have—"

"Venom want the nanites," he snapped. "They're ready to download the files."

"So?" I wasn't about to let that happen. Hadn't he learned anything from me?

Someone stepped into the light, his bulbous figure enlarged by a chunky, slate-grey coat.

Blake.

He popped a hand on Yakov's shoulder. "Enough of this. I applaud your determination, Sally. You've come quite a way, but it's time to come with me."

I stared between them. "You're working with Blake?"

Yakov swallowed.

"What happened to not working for Venom?" I asked.

Blake shot him a sharp glance. "That's what you told her?"

It was a lie, obviously. Everything he'd said was nothing more than a huge distraction to get me back to Blake.

Yakov shrugged off his hand. "It got her to stay with me."

My breath exhaled in a puff of mist. I should've known better. I had known better. Why on earth had I ignored that? "Well, that doesn't matter now." I lifted my Beretta.

The men stiffened.

"Sally." Yakov ventured a step.

"Stay away from me."

And despite all he knew of my failure to kill, he hesitated. Wise. Maybe something changed in my expression. Maybe he read my resolve. I wasn't going to kill him. But I wouldn't let them take me either. That gun was the only thing between escape and capture, and I wasn't going for the latter.

Yakov's own Beretta peeked at his waist, the holster

unbuttoned. "It's not what you think," he said. "Blake—"

"Stop lying to me!" I flicked off the safety. Blake had ruined everything. He'd been the one to take me, to uproot my pathetic existence, to lead me to finding out the truth. A truth better left hidden.

"Now, don't be foolish." Blake shifted, rustling in his coat. Uneasy. Didn't he know my secret?

Yakov raised a calming hand. "Listen to me."

"No, I'm done listening." It was time to leave, once and for all. If I could just find a way out, follow that wolf. But it was long gone. But maybe I didn't need the wolf.

A poop dropping lay in the shadows. I could practically smell it mingling with that water-rushing fresh scent of winter. That's how I'd find the exit. Not through sight. Through scent and sound.

Yakov drew his weapon, pointing the barrel at me. "You will listen."

"No," I said. "I won't."

Blake shifted again. He inched closer. "We're not Venom. We're independent contractors."

"Yeah," I said. "And I'm a millionaire."

He shook his head and shuffled to Yakov, flashing that look he'd had on the plane. The one he'd worn before Lia's capture. Contempt. Anger. And the skill of endless patience. "Come with us. We have the antivirus. We can save your life."

"You'd have done it from the start."

"Like I told Yakov, the nanites had to be full before removal." His edged nearer to my gun. "Come with us. Let's end this." He lowered his hand towards my gun. "Trust me."

I put two bullets in his shoulder. Blake collapsed with a dull thud, and for a split second, the Russian and I stared at each other, guns raised, with Blake groaning between us.

But I was done trusting. The future was mine now.

I shot Yakov.

88

What had I done? What had I done—what had I—I'd shot him!

The maze twisted, shelves blurred past, and a stitch stabbed my side.

I'd shot him in the torso. Not a lethal shot. He should be fine. But it wasn't long ago that I'd patched his wound in the bathroom. Wasn't long ago that he'd come close to kissing me.

And planted a tracker on me instead. He was the enemy. A lying, deceiving piece of jerk-face. He didn't care.

But he'd helped me. He'd been there when the nanites hurt my head. Lied for me when I'd screwed up.

Except I hadn't screwed up. Failure to kill wasn't a weakness. What was wrong with me?

I staggered to a standstill and leaned, gasping against a shelf. I couldn't think about the Russian. I needed out of here. Scent and sound. That was key. I closed my eyes, inhaling the cold, listening to the rush of water. It resounded through the aisles like white noise, coming from the right.

I followed it, and the library grew colder. What was my plan, exactly? I had no coat. No supplies. Even if I did get out, what then? I'd never survive the snow. Every breath fogged my vision, curled in warning of the danger. But going back would mean death. Was this any better?

I reached a crossroads and stopped to listen. Left.

The temperature continued to drop, so I popped away the gun and pulled my hands in my sleeves. The water sound got louder. The scent grew sharper. I could almost taste it. The taste of Christmas. With something sharper. Something that made my pulse pound and adrenaline buzz through my blood.

The maze ended.

A tunnel delved in the rock, rimmed by stalactites. Poop covered the floor, spiked by fur. This had to be it. The wolf's entrance. And there on the wall, formed of the very fur that walked the library, hung three coats.

I shrugged one on – chilly, but nothing like being without it – and debated drawing my gun. What if more wolves were near? If I entered their cave, no amount of shouting would save me. A bullet would, though.

I drew the weapon, hoisted the coat to my ears, and pressed into the tunnel. Darkness covered me, blocking out the nightmare of the archives. My arm scraped the wall, and I shuffled on, feeling with icy feet for drops or traps or— something crunched underfoot—or skeletons from the wolves' prey.

When light filtered into the tunnel, I rushed through an entrance flooded with moonlight into a glistening wonderland. Waterfalls tumbled into frothing pools. Trees sparkled with icicles. Pine needles littered the ground amongst paw prints, and a few stray flakes drifted to the snow. All signs of the storm had ceased, and now I could see the appeal of living here.

I exhaled, giving off a puff of breath. Here, there were no wolves. No Venom. No killers. Just me and silence.

Which was concerning.

Where were the traps? Weren't the archives the most well-defended place Venom owned? Why would there be an exit completely unguarded? Venom must've known about it. They'd have covered every detail.

Hedge's comment returned to mind. *Ice ain't the only protection 'round here.*

I knew about the wolf. And the maze. What more was there?

What if the woodland was one? What if I was miles from civilisation? What if there wasn't a true escape? In this cold, in the dead of night, without food or drink or warmth, I'd freeze to death if I didn't find someone soon.

But the alternative was going back. Letting Venom have the nanites.

I ventured into the snow. If I knew Yakov, he wouldn't be far behind. In pain, yes. But alive. And likely angry. Blake, on the other hand, deserved so much more than a couple of bullets in the shoulder. I should've broken his knee like Victor's. I should've punched him in his big, stupid face.

Snowfall coated my coat. My stinging feet crunched. The silence unsettled me, like the calm before the storm. Time passed, and the air almost grew warm, like the chill was hidden in softness, slumbering beneath the pines. Shivers flooded my limbs. Even my teeth seemed to absorb the low temperature, pressing on my lips like ice cubes.

The coat stopped working. Or maybe the frost got inside. It stung my legs. Gripped my gut. Cut at my neck.

An ache welled in my head. It got stronger. Sharper. A whistle started in my ears, increasing to a shrill screech. I pressed my fists to either side of my forehead, beating at the pain. "Not now," I begged. "Please."

The pain slammed against my skull like it'd been split with an axe. I screamed and sank to my knees. Heat flared in my face. And I spluttered in a sudden fit of coughing. My lungs strained.

When the pain eased, I gasped the air. Tremors ripped through me, and a metallic taste coated my tongue. I stared at the snow, at the red flecks marking it, and touched my raw throat.

Blood. I was coughing up blood.

How long had I been out here? How long did I have? I

couldn't feel my fingers. Couldn't feel my lips under my tongue. But maybe this was better. Maybe sleeping out here was better than whatever Venom would've done given the chance. Certainly better than giving the nanites to them.

I lay down. The snow was soft. Comfortable. Not so cold anymore.

Yeah. This was better.

A rumbling broke the silence. Like a chugging. Vibrating. No, an engine. Was that—I struggled to sit. Every urge willed me to sleep. But there was light. Something moved in the distance.

A jeep carrying a single driver. Help. I'd found help.

I stumbled onto a frost-covered road behind the jeep, a dull ache in my head. I couldn't give up now. Not when I was this close to rescue.

Tucking my hands beneath my armpits, I shuffled after the jeep. Hedge might be searching. If they learned I'd got out, it'd be their first move: grab a car, go out looking.

My steps felt like needles on my feet. I still had the disks. I could explode a couple. Use them for heat. What I wouldn't give for a bit of warmth.

The road crested at the edge of a treeline. Below me, barely four-hundred meters away, stood a town, its lights twinkling under the stars. I practically skidded down the slope, heart thudding in the hope of warmth, of help, of food. Every breath hurt. I couldn't feel my arms. Or my face.

I reached the first buildings on aching legs. Frost clung to the bricks, glittering in the moonlight. Ahead, the rider climbed off the jeep, his eyes covered in goggles. Not Hedge. Not Morozov, either. His skin carried a darkness to it. A beautiful, rescuing colour, full of promise. He grabbed a bag off the back of the jeep with a chunky mitten, his breath visible before him.

"Help," I croaked.

He turned to me.

"I need help." I took a step towards him, and my knees buckled, collapsing me to the ice.

The rider ran to me, boots banging, and crouched down. My pale reflection stared at me in his goggles, blurring out of focus. The whole road seemed to tilt like it was going to throw me off it.

"You'll be all right." He scooped me in his arms and carried me away, letting me drift into an icy sleep.

89

Falling asleep was easy. Waking up, that was harder. Every part of me hurt. Ached and throbbed like someone had beat me with a sledge hammer.

I opened my eyes. Flames burned in a large fireplace beneath a mounted elk head. The smoky scent of it clung to the heavy, knitted blanket over me. The room was small. Round. Furnished with a wolf-skin rug and wooden chairs. Someone sat on one, barely visible in the shadows, but he leaned forward when I looked at him and let firelight fall over his face.

I jolted. "Niall."

He smirked. "What a story this will be. I've had every agent hunting you, and just when I thought you'd got the better of us, what do you do but walk right up to me."

I slumped back. He'd been the rider. Him, with his dark face and concealing goggles, had been the very man I should've avoided. "I wouldn't have come to you if I'd known."

He chuckled. "It wouldn't have mattered. You came to the archives—a subject we'll get to in a minute—did you really think we'd overlook the back entrance? I presume that's the way you got out."

The thought had crossed my mind. Of course they'd known about the wolf cave.

"We're miles from civilisation," Niall said. "Even those posted here don't know where we are. How did you think you'd escape?"

There were others? I knew about Hedge, Morozov, even Niall. "How many of you are here?"

He raised his eyebrows. "You didn't think the archives were near an actual town?" He gave me a look of sheer unbelief. Like he couldn't quite believe I could be so naïve. "Everyone here is Venom. All guards of the archives."

An ache welled in my throat. I should've known. But how could I? Building a village just to fill it with guards was madness. And genius. Spencer was right about that much. No wonder Yakov agreed to bring me here. I'd had no chance of escape.

Pain stabbed my head, and I coughed violently, splattering blood over my palm.

"Nasty side effect, that," Niall said.

"What do you know?" I snapped. He was just another pawn in Venom's power game.

He shrugged. "I know the nanites are full. And I know you're dying." He smiled at that. "You're in the final stages now."

My coat hung from a rack near the door. His was there, too, fluffy and thick, and no doubt far warmer than mine. A screen covered the wall behind him, black except for a red dot in the bottom corner. "How long do I have?" I asked.

Niall pressed his finger to his chin. "When did the pain happen last?"

"Just before I got to town," I said.

"And before that?"

"Earlier today."

He fell silent. Working it out?

"How long?" I asked.

"Two days. Maybe less." Fire glinted in his eyes. "Which proves a problem if we don't move quickly. I take it your coming here was for a file. What was it? NightLock?"

I glared at him.

"No? The nanites?" He paused, staring me down. "The antivirus?"

I swallowed.

"Ah." He nodded. "The antivirus. I've got to hand it to you, you've done your homework. Did you find the file?"

I dropped my eyes.

He nodded. "Disappointing, isn't it? You come all this way only to find you still can't get it."

I balled my fists. Would it be so bad if I punched him?

He stood up. His pistol sat in its holster, taunting me.

I checked my own. Empty. Well, that figured. He was hardly going to leave me armed.

"Get some sleep," he said. "We'll leave for Egypt shortly, get those files downloaded before they overload that pretty head of yours."

The headache welled again. "If you do, will I live?"

"Oh, no, you'll certainly die. But at least you won't die worthless."

"You can't." There had to be a way out. After everything I'd done, I couldn't lose like this. I grabbed my head. My scream gargled in my ears.

The TV exploded. Glass shattered over the rug. Sparks flared and bounced off my skin, and the whole place flashed.

Slowly, the sting in my head eased. Exposed wires protruded from the TV, sizzling over the fire. Niall lay on the floor, his leg buried under a chunk of rubble that'd fallen from the roof. Scratches marked his hands and face, and blood spread over his trousers.

Was he dead? What happened? No one came in, so the SIO hadn't found us.

Niall moved, and the glass beneath him clinked.

The coats still hung by the door.

Niall locked eyes with me. "Don't."

I grabbed the elk head and swung it at him. He reached for his gun too late. The antler collided with his hand, knocked his weapon away, and I fled, grabbing his coat on the way out.

Someone fired at me.

"Stop, you idiot!" Niall screamed. "We need her!" One more gunshot cut through the night.

I dashed down an alley and onto a bridge that overlooked a railway. Desolated carriages lay dark and abandoned on the track. It would do. I skidded down the hill and skipped over the lines into a new part of town, only stopping when the shadows swallowed me up and no pursuit sounded from behind. Dizziness made the street tilt, and my breaths hurt my chest.

I pulled on the coat, relaxing into the sudden warmth. A fit of coughs erupted, marking my hand with blood.

It was happening quicker.

I covered my face with my hands, and for a moment, gave in. Just a moment. That's all I could have before—before what? There was no way to win. Venom had taken everything. My family. My freedom. My future. I wanted my future. I wanted to live. And if that meant Venom lost, good. I wanted that, too.

Actually, I wanted Venom destroyed. The whole organisation disbanded. Arrested. Their reputation tarnished so severely they'd never recover.

Their losing the nanites would do that. Failing with a barely-trained nobody right under their nose would do it, too. I couldn't take them all down, but if I was going to die, I'd take them right along with me.

I wiped my tears off my palms and trudged a little farther along the shadows. A street lamp flashed on above me. I froze, half-expecting agents to tramp out, but the lane stayed empty. Snow drifted silently, filling the place with a strange and deadly beauty. It wasn't a bad place to die. Was Egypt?

The light flickered and plunged into darkness.

I hurried on.

When I reached the next post, it turned on like the last. Flickered. Crackled. My back touched a door. The bulb beside it shattered, and I coughed, splattering blood on the floor. The streetlamp fizzled out.

What was going on? The exploding TV, the crazy lights – I couldn't be causing that. Could I?

Wiping my mouth with the sleeve of the coat, I jogged to a darkened line of cars. Their alarms went off, filling the street with flashing and wailing sirens. I bumped against a traffic light. It colours flashed like short-circuiting Christmas lights until the red one exploded.

My ears buzzed. My head pounded. I coughed more blood.

It wasn't possible.

But it was. Nothing else could explain it. The nanites could break through firewalls, steal heavily encrypted files, access any hard drive by mere proximity. Now, they were full. Overloading and affecting every bit of technology I touched.

I wasn't a nobody anymore. I was a person with power. And dying or not, that power was mine.

90

My breath steamed where I stood in a new street as abandoned and dark as the rail tracks I'd crossed. Despite all the noise of the alarms, Venom hadn't arrived yet. Not that it mattered. They would soon enough.

Old cars lined the road, and blackness clung to every window, ringed by frost. I hung back, mind racing. How powerful were the nanites? They'd taught me languages in a matter of weeks, shown me cameras, taught me safe routes through a hunt. Now, technology shattered at my touch. With only two days to live, I'd better make it count.

I took a disk from my boot and flicked the switch. It flashed green.

Good. Time to put them to use. I replaced the disk and took a shaky breath. This wasn't the way I thought I'd go, lost in the wild, my only antidote who knew where? There was no escape. No way to survive.

And no way I'd stop fighting.

"Look everywhere." Russian carried over the stillness. "Leave no house unchecked."

I huffed—they needn't disturb the houses—and marched between the cars towards the rails. Alarms howled with my passing. Headlights flashed. Bulbs shattered, spraying glass over the snow.

Guards padded onto the road from the rails. They surrounded me, lifting their rifles with a series of clicks. Hoods and goggles obscured their features, but that didn't matter. I didn't need to see their faces to know they were enemies. Two of them parted to let Niall through. Unlike the others, his face was fully visible and covered with scratches. His stance widened. Combat-ready. And he wore no coat. Wasn't he freezing?

He cocked his head. "You were free. Why expose yourself now?"

"I was never really free."

"No," he said. "I suppose not. But I'm still curious, why the change of heart?"

I flexed my fingers and lifted my foot a little. If the nanites blew up bulbs, could they activate the disks? "I can't keep running."

Niall shivered. "You know what they say. Acceptance is the first step to healing. Or world domination." He chuckled and whipped me around. Something sharp plunged into my neck, forcing a gasp. The scent of sweat and musk filled my nose, and my knees buckled.

91

I opened my eyes to crates covered in plastic netting, a curved, white roof, and tight straps pinning me to a gurney. It vibrated, and the pressure of high altitude ached my ears.

Niall sat near the cockpit, peeling wallpaper off in thin threads.

"Where are we?" I asked.

He looked at me, and his mouth opened with a little pop. "How are you awake?"

I jerked against the restraints, but they held fast.

"I gave you enough anaesthetic to take down an elephant." He pressed his fingers against my wrist. "You can't be awake."

I pulled on the restraints again. "Take these off."

He grabbed a hypodermic syringe and held it to the light, studying its clear contents.

"Where are we?" I asked.

"Egypt." He frowned. "You shouldn't be awake. These side-effects—"

The lights around us flickered.

Niall looked at the bulbs, and the muscles in his neck tensed.

My own heart thudded a bit harder. This was a plane, right? But the streetlamps exploded. The car alarms went off. If I stayed on this aircraft ... "I don't like being tied down."

"You think I care?"

The lights buzzed. They flashed out. In the cockpit, the co-pilot flicked a switch.

I swallowed. If this continued, the plane might stall. My plan, no matter how desperate, would fail before it begun.

Niall scowled. "Go back to sleep."

Like I could if I wanted to. "I'm not tired."

He gritted his teeth. "If we crash—"

Alarms wailed in the cockpit. Niall rushed in, bracing himself on the doorframe. The pilot said something, lost in the whine of the engine. The plane juddered.

Sweat tingled my back. He should never have brought me here. Didn't he realise what the nanites could do?

The plane jolted. Niall staggered back in and strapped himself to a seat. "Better hang on."

Lights flashed on the control board. Needles jerked. The pilot spoke to a radio, pressed buttons, secured his own belt.

The plane dipped, and my gut lurched. I gripped the gurney with slippery fingers. "We'll never make it."

"We'll make it," he said.

"But—"

"We'll make it." Niall clung to his belt. His knuckles paled. Shadows crossed his face, like we were passing huge buildings or trees or—

The plane shook. The engine shut off. So did the lights.

We glided in silence, dipped in altitude. My stomach leapt into my throat.

I exchanged a worried look with Niall.

"Power's out," the pilot said. "Attempting to re-engage." He flicked several switches and pressed a button.

The engine spluttered. The plane juddered. I could imagine flames trailing behind the propellors, streaming smoke through the clouds. Niall braced himself. The pilot and co-pilot shouted to each other.

"Trim the flaps!"

"Radios are out!"

"Deploy the generator!"

The pilot leaned forward. "Lining up now." He pressed another button.

The engine roared to life, and the plane smoothed out.

A voice crackled over the radio.

My ears ached and muffled the engine's grinds until it cut out again, throwing the cabin into silence. My breaths came thick and fast. I didn't want to die. I had to stop Venom. I didn't want to die!

The cabin shuddered.

The pilot leaned forwards. "Brace yourself!"

The gurney lurched, digging the straps painfully into my wrists. Brakes squealed. Wheels whirred. Pressure ground against my ears until we slowed to a forceful and sudden stop.

For a moment, no one moved. Then, Niall exhaled. "See? Best pilot in Venom. Not even nanites can ruin his landings." He unclipped his belt and wobbled into the cockpit, gripping the wall.

I bit my tongue to hide my groan and wriggled my hands in the straps. My wrists hurt. But we'd survived the flight. Had Niall had found the disks in my boot? Any snow had dried up long ago, leaving scuffed and dirt-streaked leather.

"Looks like we're stopping here." Niall pushed open a side door. Sunlight streaked in, along with a rush of heat.

Egypt.

The brightness dimmed as my eyes adjusted. Sand stretched into the distance. On the horizon, mountains rimmed the wasteland, clouded in a foggy haze and that rippling I sometimes saw on the roads in summer.

Niall detached the gurney from the wall.

"It's a bit hot for my jumper," I said.

"Not my problem."

"If I could just—"

He grabbed my wrist, stopping my wriggle. "The sweater stays on. So do the restraints."

I shook him off. "I'll die of heat stroke."

"You're going to die anyway." He wheeled me off the plane.

Sunlight blinded me, forcing my squint. Beyond the plane, a building glittered—the airport, probably—and through the hazy heat, two vans whizzed our way, trailing a cloud of dust. They drew up, the rear doors of one opening before it stopped. Niall and the pilot lifted me into the back, and we set off under the sharp air conditioning blasting from a vent.

"They say flying is safer than driving," Niall said. "But I think we'll make an exception this time." He rubbed his stubbled chin. "You shouldn't be awake."

My feet sweated in my boots. Cold and water hadn't set the disks off. Would heat? Would I? I'd never been able to kill. Could I take lives now to stop Venom?

"You were sedated," Niall said. "I'd just given you more, ten minutes before you woke."

Interesting. Had the nanites burned through the sedative? Pumped me with some electrical version of adrenaline? "Why don't you give me another dose?"

"It'll kill you."

"Aren't you about to do that anyway?"

He smirked.

My nails dug into my palms. The fact had always been there: since Venom found me I'd been doomed to die. Maybe it'd be all right. I'd heard people say it was like falling asleep. That heaven came next. Is that where I'd end up? Or would death be it? What was the point of life if it all stopped at the end? No, I didn't believe it. There was something after life. Something better.

Unless working with Venom ruined my chances. Maybe I'd end up in hell.

I chuckled. No hell could be worse than Venom.

"What's funny?" Niall asked.

"I was thinking about hell."

His brow creased. "That amuses you?"

I shrugged. "A little."

His lips pursed, and he tapped the gurney. "You'd have made a good agent if your heart was in the right place."

"I'd like to think it is."

"Depends where you're standing." He stripped down to a vest-top, releasing dark underarm hair and a whiff of sweat.

I wrinkled my nose. "Where we going?"

Niall crouched beside me. "Have you ever heard of the Lost Labyrinth?"

I shrugged. The last thing I wanted was another of his stories.

"It's a maze," he said, "with thousands of rooms and tunnels and passages so dark you can't get through without a guide. Course, it's been lost to history. Some claimed they found it a few years ago, but their findings were silenced. Government didn't want anyone knowing what lay inside." A hidden maze, kept secret, lost to time and shrouded by mystery. It sounded like the perfect Venom hiding place.

"It's not lost," I said, "is it?" Like the idol de morte Venom used in their competition. Explorers still searched for it. Venom laughed.

"We've had the labyrinth for almost three decades." Niall rested his chin on the gurney. "There are sepulchres down there. Ancient tombs. Mummified bodies. Rooms filled with chests of coins and jewels."

"You and your stories," I said.

He leaned back, seemingly affronted. "You don't believe me?"

"I'll believe it when I see it."

He brushed his fringe from his eyes. "A beautiful privilege. Very few get to lay eyes on the grandeur of the labyrinth."

My throat got tight. "My impending death kind of ruins it."

"That's a privilege, too," he said. "You're sacrificing yourself for the good of the world. For its future." He leaned closer, a mixture of fascination and madness in his eyes. "If you think about it, you're the key to world domination, and that makes you very special, don't you think?" He ran his hand through my hair.

I cringed and pulled away. "I'm not sacrificing myself.

You're sacrificing me."

He shrugged. "However you want to look at it, you're still remarkable."

Let's see if he still thought that when I blew up half the labyrinth.

92

The breeze from the helicopter whipped Niall's hair from his forehead and ears, showing a single, metal stud. The wind scattered sand that scratched my face, stung my eyes, and crunched between my teeth. Not that I could do much but close my eyes and turn my head until my captors lifted me inside and we took off.

Waning sunlight streaked the sky with orange. Dusk-tinted sand stretched to the horizon, dotted with palm trees and patches of brush. A rock like a crumbling pyramid stood on the desert with a flock of birds flying over it.

I couldn't deny Egypt was stunning. If it wasn't for the sick feeling of knowing what would happen, I might've enjoyed seeing it. "Is the antivirus at the labyrinth?"

Niall chuckled. "I wouldn't concern yourself with that. We can only download the files if the nanites are *inside* you." He patted my arm. "Don't worry. It'll be painless."

"Speaking from experience?"

"It can't be worse than coughing up blood all the time. Or maybe it can. I guess we'll see." He flashed a toothy smile.

What I wouldn't pay to give him a good punch. No teeth would suit him better. "Don't you have any remorse?" I asked.

"Not an inkling."

The aircraft flew over rolling dunes, a settlement of houses and blanketed stalls, and a glistening body of water. Nothing beeped from the cockpit. No lights flashed. The blades didn't stop and drop us from the sky. My body ached with tiredness.

"Nanites have settled down," Niall said.

I blinked furiously, fighting the urge to sleep. That nauseous feeling welled – the kind that comes when I stay up too late.

"They're in overdrive," Niall said. "Ready for download. So, they'll be unpredictable, see? Behaving, then not. That's why you're not coughing up blood every moment. Why you have moments of feeling normal."

Like he had a clue what normal was. But then, maybe I didn't either. My life had been anything but. "You know a lot about them," I whispered.

Niall blurred out of focus. "A little."

93

I inhaled suddenly, and the exhaustion lifted like someone had tugged away a weighted blanket. Stars covered the sky, and the moon turned the sand to silver. Niall sat in the co-pilot's seat, a pair of headphones on his head. how long had I been out? Had the sedative kicked in again? Or was this another effect of the nanites? Either way, it didn't matter. If he didn't know I'd woken, I could use that to my advantage.

The helicopter slowed and descended past a sheer cliff-face while I struggled with the restraints. It would've helped if they were looser. I could barely twist, let alone slip free, and reaching the buckle was all-but impossible.

We touched down overlooking a narrow bridge at least thirty feet long that ended at an opening in a sheer cliff face. Armed guards lined the bridge, rifles at the ready. Were they here for me, or was this just part of the security here? It seemed excessive for a long-lost labyrinth.

Niall climbed out the front. The sentry guards faced each other. No one watched me. Why would they? I lay restrained on a gurney with sand in my teeth, sweating in a cheap, dusty jumper. My blood pounded in my ears – I wouldn't have long – and I lifted my foot to my hand, fumbling to open the hidden section.

One, two, three, four explosives tumbled out.

The seventh slid out of reach.

Niall barked an order.

My breath hitched. I strained to reach—got it!—shoved the pocket shut, and hid the disks beneath my leg just as Niall climbed inside.

"Are you ready to make history?"

I glared at him, pressing my leg against the weapons. If he took me off the gurney, I'd get caught, but he wheeled me out instead, jolting the wheels against the floor. Clearly, he was taking no chances. That would be his downfall.

The helipad joined into the bridge like a giant lollipop.

I nodded at the drop. "What's down there?"

"Lower levels." Niall pushed me towards a rough-cut archway.

It was easy to slide out a disk. Easy to flick it on and hide its green flash in my hand. Easy to drop it on to the bridge.

It made no sound.

The guards stayed put.

Even Niall's focus stayed ahead.

I bit my cheek to hold back my smile. This could work.

Niall wheeled me into a tunnel lit by burning, shallow bowls. Egyptian paintings covered the walls of people, hieroglyphs, suns and animals. To an archaeologist, this would be the ultimate find. The treasure of all treasures. The secrets that must be hidden down here, the history in all its richness must be incredible.

But Venom had spoiled it all, because no one would find this with them here.

I activated a second disk and dropped it like the first.

We passed through rooms with carved pillars encrusted with scarabs. Statues of pharaohs and half-naked jackals stood on panels, their stone flawless despite the passage of time. Niall wound me through corridors and down slopes, through rooms painted in gold and emerald, and through a portico covered in ancient symbols.

I dropped the disks one-by-one, spreading them through the

labyrinth.

"Do you know what they say?" I asked after dropping the sixth disk. Adrenaline tingled my limbs. One disk left. Two presses of that, and they'd all explode.

"What?" Niall asked.

"The writing." We crossed a pillar as long as my kitchen, symbols carved into the surface.

"No idea," Niall said. "It's not really my focus of interest."

"Prefer killing, do you?"

He chuckled. "Actually, I prefer this." He wheeled me into another room overflowing with chests of gold and jewels. A necklace made of jade and sapphires lay on a podium. Golden busts of pharaohs stood amongst the chests. Statues nearly touched the ceiling high above us. There were idols of jackals and cats, and golden orbs, small vases, and vases as long as my legs, each painted in skilful strokes.

I gaped. There must've been millions of pounds worth of treasure here. Billions.

"There, see?" he said. "Even you can appreciate the beauty of the labyrinth."

"You have everything here," I said. "Everything you could possibly want." Why would he want more? He could live like a king. Everyone here could.

"Not everything I want," Niall said. "Not yet." And he patted my hand.

I tightened my fist. He was so close to the disk. If he noticed my burning cheeks, if he picked up on my tension, he'd find it.

His focus flitted to my hand.

"What more could you want?" I asked, and used the distraction to tuck the disk under my leg again. "We could run away. You have everything you need to make a life of you own." Wouldn't he want that? Freedom from Venom. The agency to choose his own path.

Niall pushed me into another tunnel. "I don't expect you to understand, but what I'm doing is going to give me exactly what I want. The life I want. Everything. That treasure's great.

But it's not the ultimate goal. And neither, my dear, are you. You're just the beginning."

A stream of industrial light beamed through a doorway we passed, and my heart lurched.

The antivirus machine.

I pulled on my restraints.

Niall patted them. "I don't know what's crueller: seeing salvation before you die or knowing you can never use it."

The passage reached a junction. He turned left, right, left again, and wheeled me into a modernised room. Industrial bulbs beamed from the ceiling – a crude adjustment to the beauty of the labyrinth. The place mimicked a crude version of a hospital with machines, heart monitors and hand sanitisers. It had sideboards, drawers and cupboards, protective gloves and yellow bins.

Yakov flicked switches on a machine and turned to us when we entered. He met my gaze, his expression unreadable, and my headache eased. He showed no pain. No sign of blood where I'd shot him. Course, he'd probably been wearing a vest. Nick, the ballet man, was there, too, dressed in a lab coat, a silver trolley between him and the Russian.

"I'll leave you to it." Niall clamped a hand on my shoulder. "Good luck. You're a hero."

"And you're a jerk," I said.

He left the room chuckling. "Better jerk than a dead man."

94

Nick grabbed the hem of my jumper, all friendliness gone. The ballet man had transformed like Yakov into the serious, unreadable killer. Cold. Unfeeling. Merciless. He held up some scissors. "Ready for this?"

I stiffened. "What do you think?"

He sliced my jumper, grazed the blade along my stomach and chest, and stopped at my neck with the tip touching my throat. Something glinted in his eyes, like he was deliberately holding back. Like he wanted to do more than graze my neck. The killer desperate to get free.

I couldn't swallow – my throat had closed up – but I tightened my fist around the disk.

Yakov had turned to the machine, back to me, head bowed. Was he in pain? Angry? Wishing he had the scissors? He'd lied for me. Lied to me. His 'other agenda' had been nothing but a huge ruse to get me here. But why the elaboration? Why not simply force me here anyway? That's what it'd come down to in the end.

Something didn't add up.

Nick cut down my sleeves, right arm first, then the left. I used my nail to activate the disk. Green flashed against my palm. Two presses, and this would all be over. I'd never have to deal with Venom again.

Nick tugged my jumper open, exposing the top of my chest. Threads snapped like firecrackers. "I'm not your enemy, you know," Nick said, clearing the frayed threads from my skin. His fingers brushed my collarbone.

I cringed, face burning, and strained against the restraints.

"I'm just doing my job," he said.

"Well, why don't you be a good little pawn, and do it silently?" I said. He couldn't be reasoned with, no matter how he tried to justify killing me.

Nick switched places with Yakov and focused instead on the machine while the Russian cleared away the lingering threads. His fingers brushed my elbow, my shoulder, my neck, setting goosebumps on my skin. His eyes met mine, piercingly blue under the hard light. And cold. Colder than I'd ever seen him. Clearly shooting him hadn't earned points. Like it mattered. At least now he didn't have to care about the girl who couldn't kill.

The disk in my hand suddenly felt heavy, and my eyes stung. Stupid. I'd always known who he was, that he never really cared. I didn't care either. Except for the niggling part that ached. That part that wished things had been different. That we could've met at Lia's office. Him and me. Normal. Venom-free.

But that could never have been.

"I won't let you have the nanites." My voice shook. Everything did. I'd run. I'd fought. For what? If it all led to here, what had been the point? "I won't die by your hand." I shifted the disk between my finger and thumb. If I was going to die, I'd do it my way, fighting until my final breath.

Yakov snatched my hand.

I struggled against him and pressed furiously down on the middle.

Once.

Yakov pried it from my fingers and gave a look as if to say *that was your plan?* He put the explosive in a drawer.

Cold dread filled me. I yanked on the restraints, a scream

building in my throat. The leather dug into my wrists, burning, stinging.

"Don't waste your energy." Nick stuck a pad to my temple, trailing its wire past my neck.

"Get off me!" I struggled, trying to shake the thing off, but the wire only flapped against my cheek.

He grabbed my forehead to attach a second. I could do nothing, even when he stuck a third to my shoulder and another to the crook of my elbow.

Tears wet my hair. "Yakov." My voice cracked. He'd played his part well. Too well. It just didn't make sense. I'd never really stood a chance against Venom.

Nick looked between us, and his brow furrowed. "You like him. Oh, that's cold, man." He nudged the Russian, his tone a mix of amusement and pity.

Yakov took Nick's place. "Just finish setting up."

Nick laughed and turned to the machine.

My restraint came loose.

I stared at the clasp, lying undone around my wrist. Yakov turned the strap to hide his handywork, and walked to my other side.

What was he doing? He hadn't actually been telling the truth. Had he? Did he really want me to live?

Yakov undid the last clasp.

The machine beeped. Nick wheeled it to my head and pressed a pad over my heart.

I grabbed the back of his neck, and twisted off the bed, dragging wires with us. He grabbed me. I punched him off and rolled away, kicking his hand when he tried to grab my ankle. Yakov yanked him back and slipped between us, pulling me up by my arm.

Nick stared and slid into Russian. "You're protecting her?"

"I have my orders," Yakov said.

"From whom?"

Yakov lifted his fists.

Nick widened his stance. His expression grew hard. "You're

sure about this?"

"One hundred percent."

Nick sighed and nodded. "Your funeral." He jabbed at Yakov—once—twice—sidestepped, grabbed Yakov's arm and twisted him towards the floor.

Yakov slipped free and countered with strikes of his own.

I punched at Nick.

He ducked. Kicked my arm.

Tingles shot through it. I punched again.

Nick blocked. Dodged. Struck and twisted. His foot collided with my stomach.

I hit the floor.

Yakov grappled him. Glass vials toppled and shattered.

Something spun across the rock.

Yakov's watch.

Nick punched Yakov. Slid behind him. Clamped his arm around Yakov's neck, pinning him down. "You always were the weaker one."

Yakov's face turned red. A vein on his neck stood out, and his eyes rolled back. Yakov jabbed upwards, drove his palm against Nick's nose, and slipped free. He snatched a fistful of Nick's collar.

"Go!" Yakov shouted.

I plucked the watch and fled back along the tunnel. Which way was the antivirus? Left. No, right. Right then left? Hope spurred my pulse faster. It was close. So close. If I could only find it—

I coughed. Tasted blood that splattered the floor.

"You can't run from this." Nick strode into the passage, eyes wild.

I turned to him, struggling to secure Yakov's watch to my wrist. My vision blurred. Cleared. Blurred again. He marched nearer, a fuzzy figure lit up by a nearby flame.

"Where's Yakov?" I rasped.

"Where do you think?"

My chest turned heavy. I should've stayed. I should've

helped him. He'd freed me, and I'd done nothing. I'd run from the only ally I'd ever had.

I swung a punch at Nick.

He countered and pushed me over.

My head throbbed. Stinging tore down my neck.

Nick grabbed the remains of my jumper and curled around behind me. He squeezed my throat, cutting off the air. Spots darkened the tunnel. My limbs shook.

I grappled with his fingers, fought to pry them loose.

He squeezed harder. "If you won't submit awake, I'll take you half-dead."

Not if I could help it. I drove my elbow into his side, spun on the spot, and punched him in the gut.

His breath gargled. His grasp fell away. And my vision cleared with the sharp realisation of what I'd done.

Yakov's blade had found its mark, protruding past my knuckle into Nick's core. The colour drained from his face.

I opened my hand, and the blade retracted into the watch.

Nick collapsed.

95

Nick stared, glassy-eyed at the ceiling. Blood pooled across the floor like a lily pad, filling the air with its metallic scent.

What had I done? I didn't mean to—I didn't think—I fell at his side and pressed my fingers to his throat.

Dead.

He was dead.

My vision blurred again. Pain flared in my head. I clutched it and stumbled on. The antivirus. I needed that cure!

An explosion blasted chunks of rock across my path. Another explosion sounded. And another. And another. The ground shook. Cracks zigzagged up the wall and over the ceiling. Dust trickled from the crevices.

The disks. Yakov must've activated the final one.

My knees buckled, senses dulling like I'd been plunged underwater. The tunnel tilted. No. I tilted. I gasped for breath, clearing my head just enough to stand, and collided with the wall. How much time did I have? An hour? Minutes?

Light streamed from a door ahead. It blinked sporadically, becoming more erratic the closer I got.

I fell through the doorway.

There was the antivirus, just as it looked in the photo: screen, IV needles, a clamp and a small, glass vial.

Blackness welled in my mind, urging me to sleep. My limbs

turned cold.

I crawled to a gurney and heaved myself on. With trembling fingers, I grabbed a needle and tugged off the cap.

My skin fuzzed out of focus. Lights crackled. Sparks rained down, burning my shoulders.

My breaths came in rasps.

A dead weight pulled on my arm. I groaned, flexed cold fingers, and opened my eyes. Except, I hadn't closed them. Had I?

I lay frowning at the ceiling. Chunks had crumbled away to expose wiring, and several craters were steeped in shadow. My wrists were strapped to a gurney once again by rough, leather shackles. Cannulas inserted in the crook of my elbows stung. One connected me to the antivirus machine where my blood flowed into it. The other connected me to Yakov, where his blood flowed into me.

I studied his white face, his dry lips, the patch of blood on his torso where I'd shot him. His unfocused eyes met mine, and they closed.

"What are you doing?" I whispered. The machine was taking my blood. I was taking his. He was getting nothing. If he continued, he'd die. "Yakov." I struggled to get out of the straps.

"I wouldn't bother." Blake leaned against the doorway, arm in a sling.

"He's dying," I said.

Blake nodded.

I tugged against the straps. "Do something."

He cocked his head. "Now you care? Only yesterday you shot him. And me."

"I thought he'd betrayed me." But he hadn't. He'd—what? I knew nothing about him. What was his story?

Blake smiled. "He's certainly a puzzle. Without doubt the best weapon I've created." Blake leaned on the machine, running a finger along the edge of it. Clear liquid trickled into a vial clamped to the side.

Yakov's skin grew paler, almost white.

"Why's he giving me his blood?"

Blake smiled. "He is, first and foremost, my greatest secret. Not that he knew it until today. If he did, he'd have taken my nanites from you weeks ago."

"I don't understand."

"Yakov is the antivirus," Blake said.

I stared at him. "The machine—"

"Is a machine. It collects the nanites but is useless without Yakov's blood. Without the counter-nanites running through it." He ran a finger down the vial. "Did you never notice you felt better around him? Did your pains not cease when he was near?"

"That's—" Exactly right. When I blacked out, when that pain would hit my head, Yakov was the one constant. The one person I woke up to.

Yakov's chest was barely moving now. His hand hung inches above the floor, his fingers slightly purple.

"He'll be a vicious blow to Venom," Blake said. "He was set on it, too. Until he fell for something else."

I twisted in the straps. There had to be a way out. "What?"

Blake fixed me with his coldest glare. "A woman."

My core lurched. It wasn't true. Yakov hadn't fallen for me. He wouldn't.

"I suspected it when he asked that we remove the nanites early. He'd have tried himself if he'd known what he was. Course, he never admitted it, but when one raises a man from a lad, one sees things." He went to stand at Yakov's head, and for a moment, his eyes reflected a gentleness I'd never seen in him, like he was seeing the child he'd raised one more time. He stroked Yakov's hair. "He's got what he wants now." Blake smiled. "He can die for the woman he loves."

When he looked up, the coldness had returned. "I get my nanites. And you get a burial fit for a queen." He plucked the vial from the machine. The screen flashed green, and my blood stopped flowing.

Yakov's didn't.

"It won't work," I said. "You need a living host to download the files."

"Hosts are easy to find." Blake stoppered the vial and raised it. "It's been a pleasure, highness. To your death."

96

The vessels in my hand bulged blue with Yakov's blood. With the antivirus. "Yakov," I said. "Can you hear me?"

His chest rose and fell.

I yanked at my straps. They only tightened. "Come on!" I wanted to break them off the gurney, use super strength, use anything the nanites could give me. But they weren't in me anymore. The inkling of uncontrollable power I'd held no longer applied.

"You're an idiot," I said to Yakov. "What were you thinking? You dying won't save us from Venom." I yanked violently at the restraints. The gurney scraped backwards a little. "What good does it do? You think I believe you care? You think I'll say sorry for shooting you?" A touch of guilt knotted my insides. "I am not letting us die!"

I tugged with all my might, forcing my hand through the strap. The edge of the restraint bit into me. It tore at my skin. Put pressure on my knuckle.

My thumb clicked.

I howled in pain. Bashed my head against the gurney. Screamed curses at the ceiling.

My breaths came thick and fast when I slipped my hand free and risked a glance at the dislocation. My thumb stuck out at a strange angle, bringing with it a wave of faintness, and a deep ache radiated through my palm and wrist.

I released the strap on my right hand, closed the tube valves at my elbows, and swung off the trolley. My knees buckled. If it wasn't for the bar, I'd have fallen. But I was free.

Yakov's skin felt cold beneath my fingers. There was his pulse, weak and fast.

It was simple to pull the cannula from my elbow and connect Yakov to the machine. Easy to ignore the blood running down my arm and focus on the screen. I brought up the menu, set the machine to reverse. My blood flowed from the machine into Yakov. If his blood could save me, mine could save him. I placed my hand on Yakov's clammy head. "That should help." If it wasn't too late.

I tested my energy with a flex of my good hand. No issues there. Yakov replenished my blood as it was taken. My levels weren't low like his. Which meant it was my turn to be the strong one. My turn to win.

I tucked Yakov's Beretta in my waistline but left the watch where it lay on the side. The memory of Nick's corpse flashed to mind. Could I kill again to stop Blake, or would I freeze when it counted most? One way to find out.

"I'll come back for you. I promise." I touched Yakov's arm one more time, then ran from the room.

97

Blood dripped down my arms, barely stemmed by my attempts to block it. It didn't help that my dislocated thumb sucked any strength I had from my left hand, and the drops on the floor left an easy-to-follow trail. If they didn't think I was dead, they'd be on me in moments.

I darted through a tunnel and into the treasure room. Firelight rippled on the walls, no longer contained by the bowls and torches. Smoke billowed and caught my throat, making me cough, and rubble blocked the doorway. Which way could I go? A labyrinth was no mere maze. I'd wander for years before getting out.

Voices shouted from the passage: two agents rushing to the right. An explosion shook the walls. More cracks tore over the rock. They were getting out. That was my way.

I dashed after them and rounded a corner – straight into them.

One raised his gun.

I knocked his arm aside. Disarmed him.

The second stepped in.

I slammed the rifle's butt into his face, floored him with a kick, and aimed at them both. "Drop it." I nodded at his weapon.

It clattered to the rock.

"Kick it here."

He did, and I picked it up, biting back a hiss when I used my thumb.

"Get over there. By the wall."

They did. "We don't want to fight," the first said, his accent thick. I couldn't place it. Why couldn't I place it?

"Where's Blake?" I demanded.

He looked at my blood, my swelling hand, and his eyes narrowed. Judging my weaknesses. He'd aim for the hand, use my pain to take me down. My thumb throbbed, sending waves up my arm.

I cocked the rifle and gritted my teeth. "Where is he?"

"The walkway," he said.

"Take me."

"We have explosion," the second said. "You not survive."

"Take me now," I said.

His shoulders tensed, and they went ahead of me through tunnels and rooms full of statues, paintings and elaborate carvings. Treasures and artifacts lay on pedestals and rocky shelves. Glass and wiring was scattered and broken on the floor. Doorways were blocked beneath rocks, but they pressed on, weaving confidently through the labyrinth.

Every now and then they exchanged calculated looks. Silently planning.

"I will shoot you if you try anything." I'd abandoned the spare rifle in a previous room, and now my hand throbbed with pain. A darkening bruise spread into my wrist and up my arm, partly concealed by blood.

The passage widened. People ran along it: agents, scientists, and everyone in between, all dashing for the exits. I recognised the archway, the bridge no longer lined with guards, the helipad surrounded by cliffs. Helicopters rose from the lower levels, one after the other, all fleeing the destruction. All except the one that brought me here. It still sat across the bridge, waiting for the person who walked towards it.

Blake.

The ground shook, and a section of floor collapsed. The agents with me backed away.

"Go." I jabbed it at them. "Get out of here."

Their resolve showed a second before they acted.

I jerked back as they lunged, narrowly evading the blade of a knife. The second made a grab for me, missed my arm and snatched my hand instead, forcing a strangled cry. But I'd come too far to lose now. I swung the rifle, bashing him square in the face. Something crunched, and he dropped with blood spraying from his nose.

The first slashed again.

I reeled back, caught my foot in a crack, and thudded to the rock. Pain flared through my ankle. My hand stung, but I lifted the rifle, pointing the barrel at his chest.

He came at me anyway. Grabbed the weapon. Kicked at my stomach.

I batted him away, and my wrist clicked, dragging a scream from my throat.

He sliced down with his knife.

The wall exploded. Rock blasted him through the arch, narrowly missing my head. He flopped over the edge of the bridge with a shower of stone and rubble.

Gritting my teeth, I pried my foot free and limped to the walkway, pursuing Blake. Moonlight streaked between the cliffs surrounding us. My skin turned pale. Pale like Yakov. Pale like death. The helicopter's blades began to rotate. I'd never make it. Blake was already on the helipad, climbing aboard the aircraft, the nanite vial in his grasp. Smoke rose around him, clouding the cliffside.

"Blake!" I screamed.

His eyes locked on me.

I shuffled closer, trailing the rifle on the floor. It was all I could do. Every step bit pain deeper into my leg, and blood dripped from my fingers.

Blake stepped back, a smile playing on his lips. "You certainly are persistent."

I stopped short of the helipad. "The nanites. Give them to me."

Wind flattened his hair. "You never learn, do you? You fight and fight. For what?"

I adjusted my grip on the weapon, and tingles stabbed through my fingers. "Give them to me now, or I shoot you."

He pointed at my hand. "You've lost, Sally. Accept that." He stepped onboard.

I aimed at his leg and pulled the trigger.

Nothing happened.

I pressed the trigger again.

Nothing.

Blake laughed. "See? Even the gun knows when to quit."

The walkway shook. Explosions sounded beneath us, bringing a plume of flame and smoke. I staggered. Teetered dangerously close to the edge. A section of cliff burst out in a shower of rock.

Blake saluted me. "This is where I take my leave. Goodbye, Sally."

"No!" I dropped the rifle and whipped out Yakov's gun, aiming at Blake's chest. The people Yakov killed flashed through my mind. The banker. The worker in Rio. The general's guards.

And Nick. I'd killed Nick. My tear-stained cheeks turned cold.

What could I do? Blake was in the aircraft. His escape was set. Even if I shot him, the pilot would take off anyway. They'd get away with the nanites.

Unless there was no pilot. The truth of my situation hit me.

The helicopter hovered above the helipad, gaining altitude.

I had a clear shot. It was this, or give up and let Blake win.

But there'd be no going back. This killing would be deliberate.

The engine hitched. Another moment, they'd be out of reach.

I pulled the trigger.

The bullet struck the window frame.

Weird. That should've been a perfect shot.

I fired again, hitting the rim.

I gritted my teeth.

And shot again.

The pilot jerked and slumped forwards.

The helicopter veered sideways, out of control. The tail scraped the cliff. The propellor tore off and flew towards me.

I dived out of the way.

It struck the bridge, gouged a deep dent in the stone, and careened over the edge.

The helicopter spun down the drop and out of sight, smoke streaming from its tail.

I lay there, gazing at the moon. Everything hurt. But I didn't care. It was over. Blake, the nanites – they were gone. Finally.

Fire crackled around me, mingling with my breaths, the pulse of my heart. It was almost relaxing. A lullaby singing me to sleep.

Except there was something else. Something distinct and human. Grunting.

With some difficulty, I managed to stand and shuffled across the helipad to peer over the edge.

Blake clung to a jagged piece of rock about a foot below, the nanite vial clamped between his fingers. Sweat glistened on his brow, and he stared up at me with wide eyes. No longer unreadable. No longer heartless.

Terrified.

I bent down and took the vial from his hand.

"Help me," he said.

I straightened up, studying the face of my enemy. Yakov's enemy. The world's enemy. He'd been there from the beginning. He'd abducted me, made me a killer.

Blake's fingers slipped.

"You never learn, do you?" I said. "You fight and fight. For what?" It'd taken time, but now I had strength to do what was needed. What I never could before. "You've lost, Blake.

Accept that."

His face twisted in fear, caught in a realisation I'd never thought possible: I wasn't the innocent girl he first met.

He dropped into the abyss.

98

"How are you feeling?" Spencer sat by my hospital bed, wearing a flowery skirt that draped down to her ankles. She'd kicked her shoes beneath her chair.

Yellowed leaves brushed against my window, smearing raindrops across the glass. It'd been three weeks. Three weeks of private care with guards stationed at the door. Three weeks of therapy and multiple antibiotics. Yakov's blood type matched mine, but it hadn't prevented infection.

Spencer nodded at my hand. "Healing well?"

"They just changed the splint." Living with one working hand was difficult, but nothing like losing the nanites. I was less capable now – a side effect I should've foreseen. In the labyrinth, I couldn't place the guard's accent. It took three attempts to shoot the pilot when I should've been a perfect shot.

That was just the beginning. I'd put the television on French, German, Italian – and understood nothing. All my skills were gone.

"I dislocated my shoulder once," Spencer said. "Quite painful."

I sighed. "Why are you here?"

"To check on you." She said it so innocently, like she hadn't abandoned me to the nanites or hunted me across Germany.

"I'm fine," I said. "You can go now."

She crossed her legs. "The doctors say you're recovering. Physically, at least. Shall we talk about what happened?"

"I told you."

"The basics. Not the details."

The splint pressed against my wrist, itching me. Lia said it was good. A sign it was healing. I hadn't seen her in person, but we'd spoken on the phone. Spencer had sent her off somewhere. Something about trails to close up. A part of me was glad. The other part … well, I wasn't sure what to think.

"Talking helps unburden you."

I grimaced. "It won't change the past."

Spencer reached for my hand, but I pulled away. Her wrinkles deepened. "Okay. Perhaps one day."

Rain pattered on the windowpane, and grey coated the sky. "Have you found him?"

"The Russian?"

I frowned at her. "You said you'd look."

"We know where he is."

Yeah, in an Egyptian prison. The military arrived after Blake's death, shooting anyone who moved, taking few prisoners. Since Yakov was unconscious at the time – and coincidentally listed top ten on the most wanted list – they'd captured him, too. Thanks to Spencer and some deal she'd made with the Egyptians, they had a photo of me and specific orders to retrieve, not kill.

"Is Yakov alive?" I asked.

"We believe so," she said. "The Egyptians won't quickly kill him. Especially with this new knowledge of him having the antivirus."

"Not anymore. I told you, it's in me now."

She nodded. "A fascinating development, to be sure. Thankfully, the Egyptians were unaware of this when they saved you, otherwise we might never have got you back."

"Will you get Yakov back?"

Her shoulders squared. "Why would we?"

The television remote lay beside my leg. I hadn't listened to Russian audio. I didn't want to. I'd mostly spoken Russian with Yakov, and if I couldn't understand that anymore, it'd be like a piece of our connection had died. I touched the top of the remote. I'd promised to go back for him. "He saved me."

"That doesn't release him from his many murders." Spencer smoothed down her skirt. "No. He's in good hands."

Liar.

"And the nanites," she said. "You say Blake had them when he fell."

"That's right." Liar. That was one ability I hadn't lost. I'd learned to lie without the nanites' help, which meant I could hide the truth now.

Spencer's forehead creased. "We've had agents in the labyrinth – after the chaos died down, of course." Agents. By which she meant spies. The Egyptians would never have let British intelligence on their land. "There's no sign of the nanites." She leaned in a bit more, as though urging me to confess the truth.

I held eye contact. Kept my expression neutral.

After a few moments, she leaned back. "The bodies in there were ash. It's likely the flames destroyed the nanites, but there's no telling how hot they raged. It would take furnace temperatures."

"That's that, then?" I asked.

"That's that." She held my gaze, and I got the impression her search was far from over.

"When can I go home?"

"Tonight," she said. "But your memories may not align with your previous life."

"Because of Lia?"

"Because of Venom. They've taken a blow, but they're still out there. You'll join your mother in the safehouse for now."

Great. More hiding. "And Lia?" She was due back anytime.

"She's heading out again," Spencer said. "Thought it best to give you time."

Something in my chest dropped. Lies had been told, but she was still my sister. Was that relationship still there?

Spencer slipped on her shoes. "I'll leave you to rest. But Sally, if there's anything you ever need—"

"I'll be fine."

"Be that as it may, keep my offer in mind. Despite what happened, we're not your enemy."

99

Two days later, I strolled in winterwear along a bridge over the River Thames, a crushing loneliness in my chest. Things with Mum were somewhat strained since my return. Hardly a surprise when I wouldn't tell her what happened. I didn't want to. The only person I wanted to speak with was locked away in Egypt.

I paused halfway across the bridge, tasting salt on the wind. Water rushed below me, the sky distorted in its reflection. From my coat I pulled a small, glass vial filled with clear liquid: tiny nanites carrying deadly power. Hiding them from the Egyptians had been difficult. Hiding them from the SIO was insane.

But I'd done it and now, I'd end it.

I removed the stopper and tipped the liquid into the river. Somewhere, a scientist was probably turning in his grave – his life's work gone in an instant.

"No regrets." Despite the threat of the still-free Venom agents, the world was a safer place.

I dropped the vial and stopper into the Thames, pulled my hat over my ears, and wandered back the way I came. Venom thought me the key to world domination, but I'd been the key to their destruction. Or rather the start of it. And that was a role I'd willingly play.

For now, though, I was safe. It would take Venom time to recover and even longer to find me. But they would find me eventually.

And when they did, I'd be ready.

EPILOGUE

Niall lay beside a railing on the rooftop of an abandoned car park, a little west of the Thames bridge. His hand rested on his rifle, finger poised on the trigger. Niall liked rifles. Particularly the McMillan TAC-50, a revolutionary firearm with the stopping power of an AMR and the accuracy of a military-grade sniper rifle.

It could shoot a target over two miles out. There you'd be, minding your own business, then bam, you're dead, and no one would find the shooter because he's lying over two miles away.

Niall smiled. That'd be his story. One of them. He'd be The Legendary Shooter. The Elusive Assassin. The Ghost.

But his greatest story was yet to come.

And it all started with her.

He adjusted the scope of the weapon, bringing the bridge into perfect clarity. There she was, hat pulled low, trudging through the stray snowflakes towards the city. She was a fool being out alone. She knew the danger. Knew she'd be hunted.

Was she frightened? Possibly. But she needn't be. Not today.

Niall ran his finger along the trigger. It'd be so easy. One pull. Barely a pull. The trigger on his rifle was so sensitive, he only needed to will it, and death would be delivered. He was a god. Her life in his hands. Everyone's life in his hands.

Her time would come, but for now, a warning wouldn't go amiss. A message to show he was there.

He exhaled, relaxed into the moment, and tapped the trigger.

Join Sally Rivers
on her next adventure …

DeadLock

Coming Autumn 2025

1

Doctor Roberts studied me over his clipboard. Grey eyebrow hairs strangled the brown like overgrowing weeds, and a particularly long one curled up to his receding hairline.

A year ago, his gaze would've made me uncomfortable.

Not now.

I'd survived therapy sessions with Dakota – the master of deception. He'd spent hours calling me a liar, stating my every fear like a mind-reader. He'd exploited my weaknesses, threatened me, attacked me. After him, no therapist could frighten me again. Especially since Roberts couldn't read me like Dakota had. And Dakota was dead.

I glanced at the clock behind Roberts. Forty minutes to go.

The therapist lowered his clipboard. "What's on your mind?"

"Nothing."

His suspended foot bobbed above the carpet, and he tapped his knee in that way that said 'I don't believe you'. "You haven't spoken for twenty minutes."

I cocked my head. It was the same mannerism Dakota used on me. Tilting his head. Watching me squirm.

But Roberts wasn't squirming.

"I can leave, if you like." I pointed at the door, knowing full well he wouldn't agree.

The wrinkles on his chin deepened. "If you don't want my help, why are you here?"

"Because Spencer insisted." In truth, she'd forced me. I was too valuable to be left alone, she'd said. And since I refused to let her people study me, she'd compromised with mandatory therapy sessions. It would help 'heal my pain'.

For the most part, it wasn't bad. An hour of near silence. Left to my thoughts. Roberts asked the occasional question, but I rarely answered. What was the point? He couldn't help me. No one could.

Besides, therapy was just a front for his true role. I'd fled from Spencer once. She wouldn't let me again. Hence the agent sitting opposite.

Roberts put the clipboard down. "You don't think I can help you."

"No one can help a killer." My tone grew hard. Cold. The way it always did when I spoke of time with Venom, the world's most dangerous organisation. Before them, I'd been normal – or as normal as the lies allowed.

"You killed those people in self-defence," Roberts said. "That's perfectly acceptable."

Memories of Blake flashed to mind: his wide eyes gazing up, his sweating hands clinging to the cliff, my numb hate at the sight of him. I dug my fingers into my leg. "I could have helped Blake. Did you know that? He begged me to. But I did nothing. I let him fall." I swallowed back my guilt. I'd spent too many nights crying over his blood.

"Anyone would have done the same in your position," Roberts said.

I knew that.

Roberts blinked. "How's life at home?"

I shrugged. "Fine."

"Really?" He twiddled his pen between stubby nails. "You are aware that Spencer has you watched."

I knew that, too. I couldn't miss the black sedan constantly parked by the house, the occasional glint of binoculars. Hardly a moment's privacy.

"You sneak out," Roberts said.

"Is exercise a crime?"

"Considering the circumstances." He tapped his pen against his knee. "You're listed top of Venom's enemies. You must realise the dangers of that."

Understatement of the century. It was a wonder Venom hadn't attacked yet. It'd been months since the whole Egypt chaos, but there'd been nothing but silence since then. It made my stomach knot.

"The house is claustrophobic," I said. "Have you any idea how that feels? Just waiting for ..." For someone to kill me while I'm stuck inside with nowhere to run. Shivers prickled me. "Anyway, things with Mum are ... awkward. I can't talk to her. Not really." What happened with Venom, the things I saw and did—I couldn't tell Mum. She'd never understand.

Besides, trust worked both ways. Mum lied to me, kept the truth about the nanites hidden. Even now, she wouldn't open up.

I was supposed to be grateful, Roberts said. She'd spent her life protecting me, sacrificed everything to keep me from Venom. But those lies left me unprepared when Venom attacked. Those lies had made me a killer.

"If you're looking for purpose," Roberts said, "we can give it."

"Spencer's still got you on about that?" My cheeks burned, and I pressed my fists into the sofa.

He raised a calming hand. "Spencer believes—"

"I know what she believes." I carried an antivirus in my blood—technology of sorts, like anti-nanites. They were one-of-a-kind. A true masterpiece of creation. Spencer would give anything to study it.

I wouldn't allow it, though. Nanites in my blood had nearly killed me. It'd been the nanites that let me speak nine languages fluently. The nanites that made me a perfect shot. The nanites that made me the most hunted person in the world. Without them, I was just me. Useless. Talentless. Stuck on English. But if anything remained, the last thing I'd do was give it to Spencer. And since she couldn't take the antivirus without slicing into my brain, I had the advantage. At least, as long as she wanted me alive.

Roberts pressed his fingers against his palm. "The information you hold would contribute greatly to our society."

"I said no." I walked to the floor-to-ceiling window overlooking neatly trimmed lawns budding with blooms and flowers. Ivy encroached on the glass like it was trying to inch a way inside. A weathered, stone wall rimmed the garden, allowing only a glimpse of rooftops on the other side.

My reflection scowled, and the sun glinted off the locket Lia had given me – a consolation gift for all the lies. The jewellery reminded me of life before Venom, back when Lia and I were sisters. Technically, we still were. The adoption papers were as legal as ever. Relationship-wise, I didn't know where we stood. It'd been over six months since I'd seen her.

Six months of Roberts fishing what he could out of me. Testing for signs of remaining nanite data. Naturally, he'd found none. Which meant he'd give the word soon – and Spencer would force my co-operation.

I took a calming breath. Hostility wouldn't hold Roberts off. If anything, he'd give me up faster. I turned to him. "I can't work with Spencer right now. Not after everything. I'm ... struggling."

He nodded slowly.

"I still have nightmares." I slipped a waver in my voice. "Every night." That would do it. His expression would soften. He'd lean back and offer advice to handle the stress.

Instead, he pressed his lips together and, when he spoke, his tone held a touch of coldness. "Our sessions won't last forever, Sally, no matter how difficult you claim life is."

I pinched my fingers behind my back. He was learning. Or Spencer was pushing him. I let the waver slip away. "I won't be an experiment."

"You already are," Roberts said. "You were the moment those nanites were put in you. But if we could study you, make more of them—"

My back met the window, and cold seeped through my blouse. I knew Spencer wanted information, but I never imagined she'd want that. The nanites could've destroyed the world, and she wanted to make them again?

"Don't you get it?" I said. "The nanites ruined everything. Even Yakov—"

"The Russian?" Roberts sat up, new interest in his eyes. "You still think of him?"

I balled my fists. Thoughts of Yakov were my own. Roberts had no right to them. "He doesn't deserve prison."

Roberts tilted his head. "You really believe that?"

Of course not. Yakov was an assassin. A ruthless murderer. He wouldn't hesitate to pull a trigger, to stick a knife in someone's gut. Prison was right for him. But torture? "Yakov helped me."

"One good deed isn't enough to free a man of his crimes," Roberts said.

"It should earn him something." A quiet cell, at least.

Roberts rubbed his chin, contemplating. "He earned our gratitude. That's enough."

Like that counted for anything. "You can tell Spencer I won't co-operate." I collected my coat from a table.

"I suppose then," Roberts said, "our time here is done."

I paused with my arm through the sleeve. There it was again. That same threat. "I just want to be left alone," I whispered, struggling to hide my tremor. "Is that so much to ask?"

Roberts sighed. "Sally, you are unique. You must understand that. The antivirus might carry answers to decades of problems—problems you have no right to keep from the world. Spencer—"

Glass shattered, and he jerked backwards on the sofa, a bullet hole in his forehead.

ACKNOWLEDGEMENTS

I'd like to thank my school librarian, Mrs Yates, for letting me into the best place in school even when it wasn't my turn. You were there when I wrote my earliest draft of NightLock a good twenty years ago! Your polite enthusiasm gave me excitement to carry on. Thanks for that.

Thank you to Barbara Henderson for pushing me for that first, and for going above and beyond to help me find my way. You were my encouragement, the positivity that made me know I could do this. Thanks for giving me reason to hope.

A huge thank you to David Bishop for being the best mentor I could ask for. I wouldn't be half the writer I am without you and still can't believe my luck that I got you.

Evee! I haven't forgotten you. You're the most enthusiastic arc reader I've ever had. The fact that you love NightLock as much as you do already makes me feel successful, and that, I think, is a really good start.

Natalie, you've gone from a beta reader to a really good friend. You've given my writing community a whole new meaning, and I can't thank you enough. Thank you for putting up with me, for letting me think aloud, and for being the competition for my biggest fan.

Yes, Cally, I know that raised an eyebrow or two. But you're on another level. You were there at the start. You read my earliest (and worst) draft. You loved my characters. You had a crush on you-know-who long before I perfected him, and you've read every draft since. Except this last one. Enjoy! I can hardly believe you're not fed up with it yet, but here we are. My biggest thanks is aimed at you.

I want to thank my parents, obviously. They tried. They really did. But here I am with an imagination full of assassins and conspiracies. What can I say? No one is perfect.

I've got to thank my wonderful husband, whose patience is never-ending and who put up with my housework procrastination far longer than he should have. Of course, he's never going to read this book and won't know he's in the acknowledgments unless someone tells him.

And I thank my children, whose enthusiasm and love made completing this book take two years longer.

Lastly, I thank you, dear reader, for giving Sally a chance. I hope you enjoyed her adventure more than she did.

Liked this story? Leave a review!

cb239fbc-29e5-46ec-a1be-9a1f19029a13R01